THE DOG THAT SAVED Christmas

THE DOG THAT SAVED Christmas

NICOLA DAVIES

WITH ILLUSTRATIONS BY
Mike Byrne

Barrington Stoke

First published in 2018 in Great Britain by
Barrington Stoke Ltd
18 Walker Street, Edinburgh, EH3 7LP

www.barringtonstoke.co.uk

A CIP catalogue record for this book is available
from the British Library upon request

ISBN: 978-1-78112-769-8

Printed in China by Leo

To the Family Bookworms
Kit, Nina, Noah, Mummy and Daddy Worm
With love and thanks

Contents

CHAPTER 1

THE INFLATABLE SNOWMAN

Jake hated Christmas. Nothing was normal.
There was no routine. It felt like anything
could happen. Even the food was weird.
And it went on for days. Sometimes, Jake
would go back to bed on the days between
Christmas and New Year, and get up all over
again. He hoped that a second start to the
day would iron out the bumps in it. It never
worked, of course.

Even the run-up to Christmas was horrid. The decorations in the town centre had flashing lights that made Jake's eyes hurt. People did strange things, like standing outside his house in the dark and singing carols. And Jake's parents brought a tree *into the living room!* Fir trees were meant to be outside on mountains, not indoors covered in tinsel and poking Jake in the leg with their spiky needles.

And now Christmas was starting all over again, ruining a perfectly *normal* Sunday afternoon.

Jake was on the sofa with his big brother, Andy, who was almost a grown-up. They were watching Jake's favourite documentary about leopards hunting. Well, Jake was watching. Andy was fiddling with his phone. Mum came staggering out of the cupboard under the stairs with a huge box. She plonked it down in front of the sofa and began pulling out a string of fairy lights.

"Plug these in for me, Andy," Mum said. "There's a love."

Andy reached one of his long arms to the plug in the wall without taking his eyes off his phone. The fairy lights snapped on.

"Ta da!" said Mum. "Hooray. They work! I think that's the official start of Crimbo!"

"You're just a big kid, Mum!" Andy laughed.

The lights were flashing now: on–off, on–off. Jake picked up a cushion and held it to the side of his head to block them out.

"Oops, sorry, Jake," Mum said.

Andy turned off the plug. "There you go, bro!" Andy said. "OK now?"

Jake kept the cushion next to his head and didn't reply. He stared hard at the TV.

This was his favourite bit of his favourite programme. Jake had watched it hundreds of times. The leopard caught the impala, but then the impala got away again. Jake could tell the leopard was cross – it must be very hard to have to catch your food. But the flashing fairy lights still filled Jake's head, burning out the lovely leopard. Christmas had broken in and spoiled everything, like it always did.

Jake threw the cushion on the floor and stomped upstairs without a word, even though he knew Andy and Mum were trying to be nice.

Everything in Jake's bedroom was normal. His model animals were lined up on the top of the chest of drawers – three elephants, two giraffes, a lion, a leopard and five zebras. The numbers on his digital clock glowed green. Best of all, the tree – *his* tree – stood strong and steady outside the window by his bed. Every night, the streetlight cast shadows of its branches on the wall. Jake knew the pattern of the shadows by heart. He sat down on his blue bedcover and let out a long breath. Christmas would never ever get into his room.

The comforting shadows vanished all of a sudden. Jake's bedroom wall glowed white then pink then white. Jake rushed to the window. A massive blow-up snowman stood in the front garden of Mr Elvy's house across the road. The snowman was lit up like a huge light bulb and flashed red, white, then red again. Jake could even hear a faint "ho ho ho" sound coming through the glass of his window.

A big hot wave of panic rushed up from the bottom of Jake's belly. But before it made him start to shriek, something darted out from the hedge beside the snowman. It was a black and white dog with a bushy tail. Its fur coat stood out in a spiky shape against the white of the snowman. The dog's body was tense, and it crouched low. Jake could see that it was very afraid – afraid of the big weird *thing* that had lit up next to its hiding place.

The red and white flashing went on, and the "ho ho ho" began again. The dog jumped at the sound, then it turned round and bit the plastic! The snowman fell like a popped balloon and the lights went out. It was too dark for Jake to see what had happened to the dog, but the hot wave of panic inside him had gone.

The dog had given Jake an idea. This year, he wasn't going to let Christmas just *happen*, he was going to fight back!

CHAPTER 2

TURNING BACK TIME

Jake's alarm woke him up at five o'clock the next morning. Jake got out of bed and turned on his torch. He opened his bedroom door and listened on the landing. Nothing. Not a sound. Not even Dad snoring. He tiptoed down the stairs to the kitchen.

Everything was clean and tidy, just waiting. Three mobile phones were lined up side by side on the worktop next to the fridge. Mum had what she called a house rule: "No mobiles in bedrooms overnight!"

Even Andy's phone spent the night downstairs, charging next to Mum's and Dad's.

Jake knew the access codes to all of the phones. *It would be hard* not *to know them,* Jake thought, after watching his family punching their screens in the same pattern so many times. But Jake had never used this to get into the phones. He'd never needed to, until now.

Jake picked up the first phone and found his way into its settings. There, he changed the date from auto to manual. Now the phone would show the date Jake told it to show. Then he did the same with the other two phones. It had to be a date outside December, and Jake also wanted the date he chose to be a nice one for his family. So he chose their birthdays. Mum's phone now thought it was 9 April, Dad's thought it was 14 July and Andy's showed 27 September.

Jake replaced the phones, then he turned the calendar on the wall back to July and went upstairs. He had changed time and held back Christmas! Yes!

*

On Mondays, Dad took Jake to school because Mum had to start work early. Jake heard her leave the house with Andy, and then Jake went downstairs and slid onto one of the yellow stools at the breakfast bar. He stared at his plate of toast and gave a big yawn. Five o'clock in the morning had been very early.

"You OK, Jake?" Dad asked.

"Toast's not right, Dad!" Jake said. He wasn't cross. It was just a fact.

Dad looked at the toast and said, "I'll eat that, and I'll make you another."

Jake smiled up at him. "Five fingers, Dad, not four!" Jake said. "Ketchup not butter."

"Silly me, of course!" Dad said. He slid a new plate over the counter. "There you go!" Dad said.

Jake inspected the new toast. The five fingers had ketchup on, but they were not all the same size. Only Mum could make perfect toast, but Jake knew he mustn't mind.

So when Dad said, "Eat up, we leave in ten minutes," Jake nodded, and ate all the five fingers. Even the skinny wonky one!

And he remembered to say, "Thank you for my breakfast, Dad!" which made Dad smile in a funny, watery sort of way.

"Time to go, Jake!" Dad said. He scooped up his phone from the kitchen counter and didn't seem to see the date. Or maybe he was just pleased it was his birthday again.

Jake looked at the calendar as he put on his coat. He was pleased to see that it was still on July!

Dad's truck took two goes to start. Jake sat in the front and watched Mr Elvy out of the frosty glass. Mr Elvy was in his front garden scratching his head and looking at his ruined snowman. Jake pressed his lips together so he didn't let out any words about the dog by mistake. He didn't want anyone to know about it. But when the truck growled to life and rattled down the road, Jake spotted the dog! It was in the alley where the people in the flats left their dustbins. It was in the shadows, chewing something. Jake couldn't tell what, but it didn't look nice. He guessed the dog would have to eat anything

it could find. It couldn't be picky. In the
daylight, the dog looked skinny and dirty.

"Don't go near Mr Elvy!" Jake whispered
to the dog, and he raised his hand and waved.

It's you and me, dog, Jake thought,
against Christmas.

CHAPTER 3

CHRISTMAS TREE MELTDOWN

School was great because everything was
always the same. The big yellow sun made
of tiles by the entrance. The dark-green
railings round the playground. The echo
your feet made in the corridors – none of
it ever changed. School days had a pattern
that Jake understood. When things happened
at home that didn't fit the pattern there,
like wrong toast, there was always school.

Registration at 9, assembly at 9.15,
10.30. It was all as regular and nor
glowing numbers on his bedside clo

But when Jake arrived at school, he could
see that Christmas was about to spoil that
too. The green metal gates had a spiky
hat of holly and tinsel, and two teachers
were putting a Christmas tree up inside the
entrance hall. The tree didn't look as if it
wanted to be there – its springy branches
were slapping Mr Hutchins on the back
and tangling Mrs Jones's skinny legs so she
almost fell over. The tree wobbled so much
that Jake couldn't tell what would happen
next. He shut his eyes and flattened himself
to the wall, and kept walking until he was

safe in the corridor. There, everything was still normal.

Still normal for now, anyway. Jake guessed it wouldn't be that way for long.

And he was right.

*

In assembly, Mrs Patel, the head teacher – who was nice but a bit scary – made an announcement.

"Today," Mrs Patel said, "the normal timetable will be suspended."

What does that mean? Jake wondered. *Would it be hanging up somewhere? What was the point of that?* Jake began to feel worried, but everyone else looked fine.

"We are going to start preparing for our Grand Christmas Show!" Mrs Patel said.

Around Jake, children began whispering and giggling.

"All the class teachers are in on the plan," Mrs Patel added. "They'll tell you what you'll be doing when you get back to your classroom."

Jake wanted to yell, "But it's Monday!" After assembly on Monday, it was always Maths. And Maths was his favourite.

*

Miss Sweet, Jake's real teacher, was sick. So today his class had Miss Glover. Miss Glover looked very clean and shiny. She had a squeaky voice that made Jake want to cover his ears. Mr Evans told Jake that covering your ears when someone speaks was not nice. Mr Evans was the classroom assistant and Jake's special helper.

"Today," squeaked Miss Glover, "we will be starting work on our performance for the Grand Christmas Show. Miss Sweet has told me that it's going to be a celebration of the variety of nature." Miss Glover looked down at the instructions that Miss Sweet had left her, and her hand shook a bit as she spoke. "She would like you all to pick an animal to write about and make a mask of its face.

Then you can each wear your mask on stage while you read out what you've written!"

Jake couldn't understand what Miss Glover was talking about. Mr Evans explained to Jake that everyone in the class would dress up as a different animal and write a poem about their chosen creature.

"First," Miss Glover went on, "you need to choose which animal you would like to be in the Nature Celebration!"

Jake was very pleased. He knew lots of animals.

"Put your hand up when you've decided what animal you would like to be," said Miss Glover.

Jake couldn't wait to put his hand up and be chosen, so he just shouted one out.

"Arrow worm!" he said. The children giggled. They knew about Jake and how much he liked animals.

"Don't call out, please!" Miss Glover squeaked. "Now, I don't think that's a real animal, is it, Jake? And besides, worms are not very Christmassy."

Jake was furious. Just because she'd never heard of arrow worms! Miss Sweet would have known they were real. And she would have known that arrow worms were very Christmassy because some of them even glowed in the dark!

Meanwhile, Daniel Williams had said giant anteater. Jake had to admit that was a good choice. He liked giant anteaters. But they weren't any more Christmassy than arrow worms.

"Good, Daniel!" Miss Glover said, and wrote giant anteater on the board. Everyone had their hand up now. Miss Glover chose Tanya to speak next.

"Bear, miss!" Tanya said.

"Lovely!" Miss Glover said, and wrote bear on the board next to giant anteater.

"But bear isn't one kind of animal!" Jake blurted out. "There are eight different kinds of bear – only brown bears are a *kind*."

"Brown is a describing word," said Miss Glover, as if she was speaking to a baby. "It's not a name!"

Jake stood up. He could feel the hot wave coming up from his tummy, and he could feel Mr Evans' arm on his sleeve. But Jake didn't care. Miss Glover was a teacher and she should know that brown bears were grizzly bears. She should know that brown bear *was* a name.

"No, it's not," Jake said. "It's the name of a kind of bear!" Jake knew he was yelling, but he couldn't stop.

"Brown bear, polar bear, spectacled bear," Jake yelled. "And Asian black bear,

American black bear, sloth bear, sun bear, panda bear."

Jake shouted the names over and over again until Mr Evans led him out of the class. He left Jake sitting outside Mrs Patel's office.

Jake knew he was going to be in big trouble for shouting. But it wasn't his fault – it was the fault of stupid, horrible Christmas. He looked at the big tree in the entrance hall. It was now covered in lights that flashed on–off, on–off. They made his brain fizz. The tree didn't want to be here. It didn't want to be standing in a pot covered in tissue paper. Jake rushed to it and pushed it over. It toppled and took the cabinet of football trophies with it. The cabinet smashed into the glass door of the secretary's office.

Take that, Christmas! Jake thought.

CHAPTER 4

RUNAWAY!

Dad picked Jake up from school. Jake couldn't
tell if he was angry. Dad didn't *say* he was
angry. He didn't say anything, not one word,
all the way home. When Jake and Dad got
in, Mum and Andy were waiting. Mum must
have finished work early, picked Andy up
from school and come home. That wasn't
normal.

Jake hung up his coat. There was a bulge in the pocket where he had shoved his sandwiches at lunch time. He'd been too upset to eat. But now he was hungry. Jake just wanted to go upstairs to his bedroom, eat his sandwiches and look at his clock. But Mum told him to come and sit down.

The whole family sat around the kitchen table. No one smiled, no one said anything, then Dad cleared his throat and started.

"Well," Dad said, but he didn't get any further because everyone else began to speak too.

Andy started telling Jake how wrong it was to break into someone's phone and their *personal life*. (Whatever that was.)

Mum started saying that it was a very serious thing Jake had done.

And Dad finally asked Jake if he knew just how much the damage in the school would cost.

It was a big, horrible, loud tangle. Jake couldn't understand any of it. In fact, there wasn't much about today that he did understand, apart from pushing over the Christmas tree and setting the dates on his family's phones to their birthdays.

"I need a wee," said Jake, and everyone stopped talking.

It was true, he did need a wee, but after he'd been, he didn't go back to the kitchen. He walked across the hall, took his coat and went out into the dark.

Jake started to run. He ran down the road and along the alley beside the flats. He ran over the scrappy park with the broken swings and into the graveyard where the path cut between the overgrown graves.

Jake had been here before, lots of times. There was a small dry space between two gravestones that leaned together – a tight gap he could squeeze into and feel safe. Jake

had left a blue plastic whale in there on one
visit, right at the back in the darkest spot.
No one had ever taken it, so he knew no one
had ever found his hide-out. Jake squeezed
in between the two gravestones, wrapped his
arms round his head and shut his eyes.

Snow was falling. Huge white flakes floated down out of the sky.

Jake peered out of his hiding place. Light shone down the path from the streetlamp at the edge of the graveyard. It reflected off the snow, bringing an odd glow to the darkness. Jake scanned the gravestones, brambles and shadows – he knew, somehow, that something was watching him. And there, looking right at Jake, was a face.

Jake saw two dark eyes, one each side of a pale stripe of fur, and dark ears standing up alert. It was the dog. It was looking out of a space between two gravestones, just like Jake's safe place. Jake could only see its head and front paws, but he could tell it was scared. Its body was tense, ready to run off. But Jake wanted to get closer.

"Hello!" Jake said softly. "I know you!"

The dog backed away into the shadows. It had no reason to trust Jake. No reason to trust anyone perhaps. Jake remembered the sandwiches. Slowly, he took them from his pocket, unwrapped them and released their smell of cheese and ketchup. The dog's tongue darted out and flicked over its nose. But it didn't come closer.

"I know it's scary," said Jake. "I know *I* seem scary. But I'm nice really. And I like animals, a lot."

Jake crawled out oh so slowly, more slowly than he'd ever moved. He lay down on his tummy, but he didn't look at the dog. Jake knew that being looked at was sometimes more scary than anything. He sensed the dog hadn't moved. He held the sandwiches out and lay very flat, with his nose on the snowy grass.

Jake kept very still.

Far away, a Christmas tree had been pushed over by a boy, and a family were angry and confused. Far away, traffic grumbled and beeped, and shoes clacked on pavements, eager to be home. But here and now there was only the snow and the warmth of the dog's tongue on Jake's hand as

it licked every last crumb of the sandwiches
from his fingers. Then the dog gently pushed
its nose into Jake's hair.

Jake was face-down in the wet snow,
shaking from cold and away from everything
that was normal. Yet Jake knew that he had
never been happier in all his life.

CHAPTER 5

A DOG CALLED SUSAN

Jake opened his eyes and saw Andy crouching in front of him. He was wrapped up in a padded jacket and a woolly hat, the torch from Dad's truck in his hands.

"You OK, buddy?" Andy said.

Jake nodded. The dog, squashed into the hide-out beside Jake, growled. They were a team now, the two of them, and she was protecting Jake.

"It's OK," Jake told her, "this is my brother, Andy. I love him. You will too."

Andy stared at Jake. "You've never said that before," Andy said.

"No," Jake said, "you knew already. But she doesn't know."

"Well, I guess she does now!" Andy laughed as the dog came to him, wagging her tail. "Has she got a name?"

Jake thought for a moment. The dog had no collar and no tag, but everyone needed a name.

"Susan," Jake said. "She's called Susan."

"How do you know?" Andy asked.

"Because I named her just now," Jake told him.

They walked away from the graves, and Susan stayed very close to Jake's legs, almost bumping into him. Jake felt as if they had been together always.

*

When they got close to the house, Jake could see a police car outside with its blue light blinking. A small group of people were standing under the streetlight. They waved and cheered when they saw Jake and Andy and Susan. Jake stopped still. The horrible blue light made him want to cover his eyes. He couldn't understand why strangers were cheering.

"Are they carol singers?" Jake asked Andy.

"No, they've been looking for you," Andy said. "Everyone's been really worried."

Still, Jake didn't understand. He wanted to turn round and run back to the hide-out in the graveyard. He looked down at Susan and stroked her head. He felt how calm she was. The blue lights and the people didn't scare her.

"I think Susan would like to be indoors," Jake said.

Andy smiled. "Then let's go in," he said. "Ready?"

"Ready!" Jake replied.

They walked past the blue flashing light and the group of people, and Jake talked to Susan the whole way.

"You'll like my bedroom," he told her, explaining things so she wouldn't be worried. "It's cosy and the bedcover is all blue."

*

Jake sat on the kitchen floor with his arms around Susan. He was feeding her the biscuits that Mum had put out for the police officers. The grown-ups, plus Andy, were all talking.

But at last they stopped, and the police went away.

"Can Susan and I go to bed now?" Jake asked.

Mum and Dad swapped a look. Then Mum said, "Yes, of course."

Jake headed for the door, and Susan padded behind him.

"Wait!" said Dad. "That dog is filthy ..."

Mum put a hand on Dad's arm, and he fell silent.

"Go on, son," Mum said.

And then Dad added, "Off you go. You too, Andy. It's very late!"

Mr Elvy had bought a new snowman. Its red–white, red–white flashes filled Jake's room.

"Don't worry," Jake told Susan, "it's just a stupid Christmas decoration. It can't get you in here."

Then Jake closed the curtains. He'd never done that before. Normally he couldn't sleep without the tree shadows on his wall, but tonight he liked the way the curtains made his room feel.

Susan sat with her ears pricked while Jake got ready for bed.

"Lie down, Susan," Jake said.

She lay down, but she still didn't look relaxed.

Jake got into bed and turned off his lamp. Now the only light was the glow from the clock. Jake could see it reflected in Susan's eyes.

"It's OK, Susan," Jake told her. That was what Mum, Dad and Andy were always telling *him*. It was funny to be saying it to someone else.

Jake looked at Susan and thought how it wasn't very comfy on the floor. He patted the space on the bed below his feet.

"Susan, up!" Jake said. She looked at him, her head on one side. He patted the bed again. This time Susan jumped up, turned round twice, flopped down and shut her eyes. She gave the biggest sigh Jake had ever heard. It made him smile and smile.

In the night, Susan wriggled up the bed. Every time Jake woke, thinking about the falling Christmas tree or Miss Glover saying arrow worms weren't real, he reached out and Susan's warm furry body was right there. He patted her and instantly went back to sleep.

CHAPTER 6

FIVE FINGERS ALL ROUND

Susan woke up early. She pushed her nose into Jake's hair and went, "Snnnnffff ..."

So Jake woke up too, giggling. His clock read 05.52. Susan stood by the door, prodding it with her paw.

"You need a wee, don't you?" Jake said.

Dogs didn't use toilets, of course. They just did what they needed to do anywhere outside. So they went downstairs together, and Jake let Susan out into their tiny back garden. He didn't watch. Who wants to be looked at when they're having a wee?

Susan came back in, and Jake gave her some water in a bowl and made them both breakfast. He got the bread out and put two slices in the toaster. He put ketchup on his, but he remembered that most people prefer butter, so he buttered Susan's slice. Then he cut each slice up into five fingers.

Jake was feeding Susan her fingers when Dad walked in.

"What's going on here then?" Dad said.

"I made us breakfast!" Jake said. "Susan likes five fingers too. But not ketchup."

"So I see," Dad said.

Susan wagged her tail at him.

Mum came in too, yawning. Her hair looked just like it'd been in a big fight.

"I didn't know you could make toast!" Mum said to Jake.

"Nor did I," said Jake, "but it's easy."

With Susan around it seemed like many hard things might become easy.

"Ohhhh!" Andy said as he plonked down onto a stool. Susan greeted him like a long-lost friend. "OK, doggie. OK. Good morning. Yes, I'm pleased to see you too." Andy laughed. "Why is everyone up so early?"

"Because I'm making breakfast!" Jake said. "Five fingers all round!"

"But not ketchup!" said Dad, Mum and Andy all together. And everyone laughed. Susan put her head on one side, and Jake told her he'd explain everything later.

Jake's family could eat a lot of toast. A whole loaf of toast. Susan had four slices all to herself.

As Jake cut slice after slice after slice into five neat fingers, he told Mum and Dad and Andy all that had happened the day before.

"You've never talked so much!" Mum told him.

Jake didn't know what to say to that. Was it bad or good? Mum was smiling, so that must mean good.

"Sounds like that Miss Glover is a right muppet!" Andy said.

"Andrew!" Dad growled.

"Well, it does!" Andy said. "Arrow worm was a great idea, Jake. Especially as they glow in the dark. Like living Christmas lights. I think we need to make you an arrow-worm costume, little bro!"

"You don't have to be part of the Nature Celebration if you don't want to be, love," Mum said.

Jake bit into a finger of toast.

"We're going to be Domestic Dog,"
he said. "Susan and me – we'll be *Canis
familiaris*. That's your scientific name," Jake
told Susan.

They all grinned, but Jake was being
serious.

"I don't think they'll let you bring a dog
into school," Dad said.

Jake looked at Dad. He was used to
Mum and Dad being right most of the time,
and knowing things Jake didn't (even if Dad
couldn't cut proper toast fingers). So it was
a shock to hear Dad say something that was

wrong. Susan was a part of Jake now, and if he was going to school, then so was she.

"I don't want to be rude, Dad," Jake said in the most polite way he knew, "but Susan is coming to school with me. Susan and I are going to school together. But," Jake added, "I will give her a bath first."

And that, it seemed, was that.

*

Jake knew that today wouldn't be a normal day. For a start, they didn't go into school at the normal time. Andy stayed at home and helped Jake give Susan a bath, and Jake heard

Mum on the phone to school. But in the afternoon Jake and Susan did go in.

The Christmas tree had been replaced and the glass in the door had been fixed, but it still felt hard to walk in. It was hard for Jake to tell Mrs Patel that he was really very sorry, even though he was. And it was hard to walk down the corridor to his classroom now that Christmas had filled it with paper chains. Jake dreaded the moment when all eyes would turn and look at him.

But Susan was there, warm and steady by Jake's side. When he walked into his classroom, everyone did turn and look, but they all smiled and said hello. Jake was puzzled for a moment, but then he realised that it was because everyone was pleased to see Susan.

Jake felt so happy that when he saw Miss Sweet was back, he did something he'd never done. He went up and gave her a hug. The whole class clapped, and even *that* wasn't weird, because Susan just wagged her tail even more.

CHAPTER 7

THE GRAND CHRISTMAS SHOW

Jake felt like he had begun a whole new life now he had Susan. So many things were different.

He didn't need to stare at the ground as he walked, because if he saw something scary up ahead, he had Susan beside him. And if it was something *really* scary, then Jake had to see it first so he could make it OK for

her. There was much less time for watching
documentaries, because he was busy outside
with Susan. She was brilliant at games of
"fetch", and Andy and Jake took turns to
see how far they could throw her yellow
ball. Sometimes Dad and Mum did too, and

however far the ball went, Susan would always find it and bring it back. And Jake loved taking her to school. The teachers, the kids and even the lollipop man were always so pleased to see the two of them. Everyone talked to Susan, and to Jake too.

Now it felt like even Christmas would be better, because Susan was with Jake, no matter what happened. Susan had become Jake's *normal* – always warm, always waggy and always there.

Jake *did* need to explain to Susan about the Christmas tree in the living room. But she didn't seem to mind the tinsel or the spiky needles that were already dropping on the floor, so Jake didn't either.

*

The end of term was soon here, and with it
the Grand Christmas Show. Jake's class had
rehearsed the Nature Celebration every day.
They had made costumes, and everyone had
a funny poem to say about their animal.

Jake didn't have a costume, because he
had Susan. They would go onto the stage
together after Dan's giant anteater, Tanya
and Stan's bear, and Tilly's jaguar. Jake
had to say the words that Miss Sweet had
written:

My name is Dog, I'm loyal and true.

Through thick and thin, I'll stick by you.

"Why do I have to say my name is Dog when my name is Jake?" Jake had asked Mr Evans.

"Because it's written as if it's a dog speaking, not you."

That still didn't make much sense to Jake, but he learned the poem anyway. He said the words over and over and over – in the car, during breakfast and in bed at night.

Today it was time for the parade. The school hall was full of parents and teachers and children. Jake stood with his class beside the stage, all ready to go on. Jake whispered under his breath:

"*My name is Dog, I'm loyal and true. Through thick and thin, I'll stick by you. My name is Dog, I'm loyal and true. Through thick and thin, I'll stick by you. My name is Dog, I'm loyal and true ...*"

"Shhh, Jake!" Tilly said from behind her jaguar mask. "We're starting."

Jake stopped. He rested his hand on Susan's head, but even the feel of her warm fur didn't make him much calmer. Everything in the hall seemed extra bright and extra loud. A chair scraped the floor, and Jake felt as if it had scratched his brain. Giant anteater, bear and jaguar were already on stage, booming their words.

"On you go, Jake," Mr Evans said.

Jake walked into the middle of the stage. Everything had gone silent. The kind of silent that's like a big wind roaring. Jake knew he must look up, but when he did, he was shocked to see so many faces. So many

eyes on him! He felt panic rise up. Jake knew that in a second he would scream. Then everything would be spoiled. He couldn't let that happen. So he sat down very fast and pressed his face into Susan's fur. She leaned round and licked his ear. He breathed in her warm doggy smell. The panic and the fear sank down, down, down, and vanished.

Jake stood up. The words of the poem had gone from his mind, but it didn't matter. He had other words to say now – words that were true, not made up.

"I'm Jake," he said, "and this is Susan. She helps me to stay calm. Just now, I wanted to scream and scream and scream, but Susan helped me. Now what I want to do is say this:

Happy Christmas to everybody – to all dogs and their humans too."

The cheers of all the mums and dads, teachers and kids were so loud that Jake had to cover his ears to stop them being broken.

*

The car ride home was brilliant. Mum, Dad and Andy sang Christmas songs, and Jake joined in. He knew he couldn't sing, but today it felt like he could. Susan howled along too.

"This is going to be the best Christmas ever!" Mum said.

But it wasn't, because when they got home there was a couple waiting outside in a car. The man got out and came up to Dad as Mum unlocked the front door.

"I think you have our dog!" the man said. "We've come to collect her."

CHAPTER 8

THE BEST CHRISTMAS EVER?

The couple in the car were called Robert and Eleanor. They were very smiley and wrinkly. They told Jake that Susan's real name was Tess and that she was specially trained to be Eleanor's helper dog.

"I'm often ill," Eleanor told Mum and Dad. "And Tess is trained to fetch things for me and to alert Robert if I need help."

"We had a car accident eight weeks ago," Robert said. "It was quite bad – we both passed out and were taken to hospital. Tess must have run off from the car. We've been looking for her ever since."

"Then yesterday, a friend who works for the police phoned us," Eleanor added. "She said she'd heard a collie dog had been found with a missing boy a few weeks back. We knew it had to be Tess."

Jake didn't want to hear any of it. He sat on the floor while the grown-ups talked, and he wrapped his arms round Susan.

At last, Dad said, "I'm sorry, Jake, you have to let her go."

Jake looked up. Eleanor and Robert were standing over him.

"Thank you for taking such good care of Tess," Eleanor said.

Jake couldn't speak. Susan licked his nose. She wagged her tail a tiny bit as Robert put her collar and lead on. Jake could tell she didn't really want to go.

Robert thanked Mum and Dad, and then Robert, Eleanor and Susan headed for the door.

"Wait!" Jake said. Everyone turned round. "Please wait a minute. I want to get something."

Robert looked at his watch, but Eleanor said, "That's fine, Jake, we'll wait."

Jake had made a Christmas card for Susan in school. He still wanted her to have it. He ran up to his room, grabbed it from under the bed and raced back down.

72

"Please give this to her on Christmas Day," Jake said.

"Of course I will," said Eleanor. "Thank you!"

And then they were gone. Susan was gone. Just like that. Jake went up to his room and lay face-down on his bed. He screamed and screamed into his bedcover. He thought he might have to scream forever. There was nothing to stop him now.

*

The last few days before Christmas were horrible. Everything felt worse without Susan. Jake's whole body felt like it was blinking on and off with Mr Elvy's flashing snowman. One morning, Dad cut four toast fingers instead of five, and Jake threw the plate across the kitchen. Nothing made sense. Jake felt that it was too hard to understand words and impossible to speak them.

Jake's family missed Susan too. It seemed nobody wanted Christmas now. Andy was always in his room. On Christmas Eve, Dad dragged the tree out into the garden. Mum put the turkey in the freezer.

"We can have pizza," Mum said. "Jake will eat pizza."

As it got dark on Christmas Eve, Jake sat on the sofa watching the TV. He had cushions propped up on each side of his head, so that all he could see was the hunting leopard. Not Mum on her computer or Dad reading the paper. Not the space beside him on the sofa where Susan had been.

The doorbell rang.

"I hope it isn't carol singers again," Mum sighed.

Jake had screamed for ages when they'd come to the door two nights ago.

Dad got up to answer the door. Jake heard Dad talking. He took no notice. Mum got up to join Dad and whoever it was at the door. Still Jake took no notice.

And then Eleanor was standing in front of him.

Jake turned the TV off.

"Hello, Jake," Eleanor said. Her voice was soft and whispery. "I hope you don't mind, but I gave Susan her Christmas card a bit early. And as she can't read, I read out the card you wrote to her."

What was Eleanor talking about? Of course Susan couldn't read. Jake wanted to turn the TV back on. He looked down, away from Eleanor. But he did let the cushions fall away from the sides of his head. Eleanor sat down on the sofa.

"Do you remember what you said in your Christmas card?" Eleanor asked.

Jake didn't reply.

"Well, I have it here," Eleanor said, and she rummaged in her handbag for her glasses and the card.

Eleanor read out what Jake had written in the card:

Dear Susan,

Thank you for helping me.
    Now you are here, I don't look at the ground when I walk. I look where I am going.

Now you are here, police sirens and bright lights do not make my head hurt so much.

Now you are here, I don't mind when my toast is four fingers and not five.

Now you are here, the children in my class smile at me.

Now you are here, I am not afraid and it is OK to be me.

Your friend,
Jake

Jake remembered what he'd put in the card anyway because it had taken so long to write. Mr Evans had helped him. Jake was pleased with what it said. It was all true. He knew Susan understood without the card, but it had seemed important to write it all down.

By the time Eleanor had finished reading, Mum, Dad and Andy were in the living room too. They were hugging each other. Eleanor's face was all wet.

"It's a very good card, Jake," Eleanor said. "It made me see how much Susan loves you. I know she loves me too, but it's really you she wants to be with. So I brought her back. She's in the car with Robert. Shall I get her?"

Eleanor came back with Susan and Robert. Susan's tail wagged *so* much when she saw Jake.

"I think she's going to wag her tail right off!" said Dad.

"No, Dad!" Jake cried out. "That would be horrible." Jake tried to hold Susan's tail to make sure it didn't come off. She flicked it out of Jake's hand and turned to give him her paw instead.

"It's OK, bro," Andy said. "Dad's just being stupid. Of course her tail won't come off."

Jake sat on the floor and let Susan sniff and snuffle his hair and his jumper. She licked his ears. She was as pleased as Jake was.

Everyone was laughing. Even Eleanor and Robert. He realised they were always smiling. That must be why they were so wrinkly – from smiling a *lot*.

"We should go and leave you to enjoy Christmas," Robert said.

"You've made our Christmas!" Dad said.

"No," Eleanor said, and smiled even harder. "Jake and Susan have made *ours*."

They were saying goodbye when Jake thought of something – Eleanor might feel as bad as he had felt now she was losing her Tess. She would need something to help her feel better. He ran up to Eleanor and pulled at her hand.

"Wait!" he said. "I want to give you something."

Jake ran upstairs to his bedroom and looked at all his things. He didn't think any of the animals would help a grown-up, but the glowing numbers on his digital clock might just do the trick. It was hard to part with it, but Jake would have Susan now, and Eleanor wouldn't.

Jake ran downstairs and gave the clock to her.

"This helps me when I feel like screaming," he explained. "I hope it will help you and that you'll be OK without Tess."

"Thank you, Jake," Eleanor said. "I'll keep this clock by my bed from now on, and I'll be just fine!"

*

After Eleanor and Robert had gone, Mum and Dad put Christmas music on and danced round the living room. Andy dragged the Christmas tree back inside and plugged in the fairy lights. Then they had dinner of beans on toast and peas. The slices of toast were each in five perfect fingers, with the peas in a separate bowl. Dad even tried his toast with ketchup, not butter. All the time, Susan sat at Jake's side. She was warm and waggy against his leg.

Dad tapped his glass and everyone stopped talking.

"I would like to make a toast," Dad said as he held up his glass of squash. "Welcome home, Susan!"

"*Welcome home, Susan!*" they all said.

"Have you got a toast, Jake?" Andy asked.

Jake thought. Yes, he did have a toast. At last he knew what Christmas was *for*. It wasn't for blow-up snowmen or fairy lights or school performances. It was for *this* – *this* feeling, *this* moment, *this* warmth that filled him up.

"My toast is love!" Jake said. "Because that is what Christmas is for!"

Nobody spoke, but they all clinked their glasses.

"And my toast," Andy said, "is turkey for dinner!"

"Oh my goodness!" Mum said. "I'd better get the turkey out of the freezer."

"Yes," Jake told her, "you better had, cos I don't think Susan likes beans and ketchup toast."

Samantha King is a former editor and qualified psychotherapist. Her bestselling debut novel, *The Choice*, was translated into eleven languages and has been critically acclaimed across the world. She lives in west London with her husband and two children. An English graduate and lifelong bookworm, Samantha is always fascinated to hear readers' opinions. You can share yours with her at:

Facebook: @SamanthaKingBooks
Twitter: @SamKingBooks

Praise for *The Sleepover*:

'I was gripped and found it hard to put down . . . Great characters and intrigue, a real page-turning thriller. Samantha King is such a talented writer.' Susan Lewis

'Samantha King takes the worst fears and worries of parenthood and brings the reader to very dark places in this absolute page turner. It's fast-paced, relentlessly tense and terrifying' Claire Allan

'*The Sleepover* taps into every parent's darkest fears and insecurities. Tensely well-crafted and deeply unsettling – I couldn't put it down!' Isabel Ashdown

'Samantha King's intense and twisty thriller is a heartrending tale of broken trust and unimaginable loss in which a single mother is catapulted into the abyss when her only son goes missing; the only way out is the answer to a single question: Where is my boy? I loved this book!' Karen Dionne

'Tautly plotted and thought-provoking . . . I raced through it to the shocking b

Also by Samantha King

The Choice

For Paul, Hani & Rafi.

PROLOGUE

One year before

Sticks and stones may break my bones, but words will never hurt me.
The old nursery rhyme was wrenched from the depths of memory
the second I took the anonymous call. I let it loop repetitively in
my brain, filling my head with noise to drown out unthinkable
questions, unbearable images; I force my feet to pound the icy
pavement in time with the lilting verse, focusing on the rhythm
to block out pain as each hammering footfall jars my gritted teeth.

Fear gives me speed. *A hundred feet to go. Fifty. Ten ...* The
school gates stand wide; a whispering crowd spills out of them. I
charge into it, my terror transmitting a shockwave that instantly
parts a sea of blue blazers. *Where is he?* My legs buckle as I spot
what looks like a pile of abandoned jumble. I rush towards it,
hopscotching through a treasure hunt of scattered pens, badges
and coins to see grey trouser legs bent at an awkward angle, a
bone-white face tattooed with blood.

Stepping closer, I'm still clinging to denial. But in the tip-tilt

1

of his nose, the soft jaw sloping to a chestnut-cleft chin, I see the lingering traces of my baby boy beneath the crumpled contours of a skinny eleven-year-old. *Closer still.* My lungs fill up with pain and panic, choking me as I drop to the frozen ground and reach for his hand; it lies stiff and cold in mine. I stroke back his hair and my probing fingertips sink into a thick, sticky mess.

Rage burns away distress as I stare up at the circle of faces crowding me with ghoulish curiosity … *heartless voyeurism*, I think bitterly. Where were they when my little boy was crying for the bullies to stop? Then I hear a snigger, see a finger point, and suddenly I notice the electronic glow of mobile phones trained like snipers on my son.

'Stop filming him!' I coil myself around Nick, desperate to shield him from the spiteful violation of his pain being videoed for kicks. Pressing our palms together, I weave my fingers through his to warm them. 'Everything's OK, darling. Mummy's here.'

Too late, my conscience screams. I should have been with him. I should never have let him go …

ONE

'Phone me as soon as you're out, love.' I pull Nick against me in a hug, gripping a little harder than I used to, lingering a moment longer than he likes – trying to disguise my reluctance to let go by pretending to bundle him out of the path of jostling teenagers.

'Can't I just meet you at home? Or better still, you could get me a key cut. Everyone else in my class has one.' He takes a step back, rolling his eyes and flicking his fringe.

He's been growing it out lately, ready to dance the lead in his theatre group's production of *Romeo and Juliet* in a couple of weeks' time. His first public performance for a year. The date is ringed in scarlet on our kitchen-wall calendar: a beacon of excitement for him; a red flag of worry for me. After his last starring role, Nick was interviewed by a local paper and dubbed 'the boy with flying feet'; the following Monday, a clipping of the photo was stuck to his classroom door, the word 'sissee' scrawled over it in pink crayon.

The bullies may not have been able to spell, but they knew exactly how to hurt. A week later, they rammed their point home with flying *fists* – just in case Nick hadn't got the message. He had, loud and clear, and so had I: that was the last time I let him leave the house alone, and Nick didn't dance again for six months.

I grit my teeth at the memory, fighting the urge to sweep back a wayward strand of his white-blond hair. Nick hates any public display of affection these days. He only shows his softer side at home now, although lately I've seen little evidence even of that. The cloak of reserve he's learned to wrap around himself at school seems to have become a permanent fixture; sometimes I feel like he wants to disappear inside it completely . . .

It's only on stage that Nick is truly himself, and that is the cruel paradox of life for my shy, whimsical son: dance is his one escape from the harassment that plagued him throughout primary school, yet it's also the bullies' favourite stick to beat him with. 'Secondary school will be easier,' his new head teacher promised: mixing with older kids who had more consciousness of their own foibles and therefore less inclination to tease others about theirs. I wonder if it's true; I wonder if Nick would tell me if it isn't.

'You know the answer to that, sweetheart,' I tell him now, my heart sinking as I see his head drop. 'I don't want you walking home by yourself. It's too cold today, anyway,' I add coaxingly. 'I'll bring the car and wait in the usual snicket, OK?'

'Fine.' *His new favourite word.*

'Just phone me when you're out, yes? Rehearsals have been cancelled this evening. The weekend starts here.' I try to engage him in a smile. 'We can watch a movie, if you like. Your choice. Maybe a takeaway as well.' He continues to stare at his feet, and I kick myself for the careless reminder of happier times: Craig always used to bring home Nick's favourite pizza on Friday evenings.

'It's the sleepover tonight. At Adrian's.' He looks up now, chin jutting and eyes widening with a faltering blend of hope and un-usual defiance.

4

'Oh yes?' I keep my tone mild as I see him bracing himself for yet another tussle on the subject that has dominated every conversation for the last two weeks.

'Don't pretend you've forgotten.'

'I'm not, love. I know it's tonight. And you know my answer to that, too.' I reach out to squeeze his arm, wondering if I dare risk another hug, glancing around to check if there are any groups of smirking Year Sevens loitering nearby. 'No sleepovers. Maybe soon,' I compromise, feeling guilty as I see his head dip once more. 'But not yet.'

'Soon.' He huffs. 'You said that on Fireworks Night. And that was weeks ago.'

'But that was at Jason's house.' I try not to let my wariness of the older boy show. Nick might be a gentle soul, but he's twelve, almost a teenager, and I remember all too well from my own turbulent teens that nothing cements a friendship like being told it's forbidden.

'So?'

'So, um . . . He was going to set rockets off in their back garden, remember?' I tut. 'He obviously takes after his dad.' I know I sound a little churlish, but I can't resist the jibe. I might once have been best friends with Jason's mum, but even then there was no love lost between me and her husband. The only good thing about not seeing Katie any more is that I no longer have to be around Colonel Nathan Baxter.

'He was just messing about, Mum. It's called having *fun*.' Bright blue eyes roll in exasperation again. 'Jase is OK. He just acts tough. He's nothing like . . . the others. Anyway, he's not invited. But Samir's coming. You'd like him.' One soft eyebrow quirks. 'He's an ace at computing. And he's the school chess champion.'

'Is he, indeed? Well, that's good to know. Still—'

'And just because you've fallen out with Jason's mum . . .'

5

Noticing a few glances being directed our way, Nick lowers his voice. 'It's not fair to stop me hanging out with him.'

'Darling, that's not what I'm doing. I don't want to stop you being friends with Jason,' I lie, avoiding his eyes. 'Look, I'm sorry about the sleepover.'

'No you're not.'

'I am. Really,' I tell him, and this time I'm speaking the truth. I'd love nothing more than for Nick to find a nice group of trustworthy friends; I want more than anything for him to enjoy the fun and freedom he should be having at his age.

It goes completely against the grain for me to be this clingy. I've always encouraged Nick to be his own person, right from when he was a little boy, with his golden hair and tiny feet dancing almost before he could walk. I used to call him 'my little sunbeam'; I had no fear when he started school. It never occurred to me that my child was different from anyone else's, or that those differences mattered. His slight other-worldliness was charming; the fact that he hated ball games but loved dance and imaginary play was endearing. He would make friends, and school would be a place of happy adventures . . .

Only it wasn't, and ever since that terrible morning a year ago I've pulled down the shutters – and I know I've forced Nick to do the same. It scares me that he's showing signs of wanting to open them again. I'm not ready to let the world back in.

'So let me go,' he persists.

'Maybe another time, OK? Please try to understand.' I justify the crack in my voice with a cough, then blow my nose for good measure, pretending it's just the wind making my eyes water. The playground is glazed with a hard frost, and the snow-heavy sky hangs low. I hate this weather; each breath reminds me of that desperate flight through the streets, my lungs burning as they dragged in icy air and blew out raw, exhausted sobs.

'Everyone else has sleepovers all the time.' Nick puffs out a sigh. 'It's no big deal.'

'You'll have one too, love. I promise. One day. But right now I'd rather keep you at home where I know you're—'

'Fine,' he cuts in. 'I get it.'

'See you at three thirty!' I call after him as he strides off, shoulders hunched. 'Don't forget to phone me!' He doesn't turn around. '*I love you*,' I add quietly.

Despite his resistance, I will never, ever wave goodbye to Nick again without saying those words. Once he's safely in his classroom, and I'm sitting at my desk at work, I know I'll be fine. Parting is the hard bit, triggering memories of the one day he left home before I had a chance to tell him I loved him – the morning he ran out of the house before I could change my mind about him walking to school alone for the first time.

I was arguing with Craig about it when I heard the front door slam shut, and I still have bad dreams most nights, waking up sweating and convinced I've heard that same bang. Lately, Nick's shadowed eyes at breakfast have made me wonder if he's having nightmares again about that day too, or if there has been trouble at his new school. But he's gone quiet on me, and even though I suspect the silent treatment is emotional blackmail to pressure me into allowing him to go to the sleepover, part of me dreads a more serious reason.

Is it all happening again? He says not, and his form teacher, Mr Newton, assured me he's making friends and settling in well. But I can feel Nick changing – growing away from me. He used to tell me everything; now I suspect he only tells me what he knows I want to hear. Like Samir being the school chess champion. Next he'll be telling me they're only planning to play Scrabble and be in bed by eight o'clock.

'Have a good day!' I call out croakily, needing to say it even though I know he'd rather I didn't. He'd rather I didn't come to the school at all: it draws attention to him, he complains, and he's had enough of that to last a lifetime.

Finally, Nick turns and lifts his arm in a half-wave. I smile and then sigh, shrugging as I catch the eye of another mum on the receiving end of an equally standoffish goodbye from her daughter. She smiles back, but I can see the inquisitiveness in her eyes. This school was supposed to be a fresh start, but gossip is like flood water: it always finds its way. And rumours are like bullies: once they've latched on to you, they are impossible to shake off.

TWO

Two things greet me as I open the front door. The first is an official-looking envelope on the doormat; the second is a broken boiler. I realise the ancient appliance has finally died the second I step into the hall through a cloud of my own breath. The house is so cold that I almost turn around and go straight back to work. But it's my afternoon off; I'm determined to fill it with something entertaining before I go to collect Nick.

'You never know. Maybe this is a party invitation,' I joke to Marzipan, Nick's tortoiseshell cat, who blinks disdainfully at me from her usual perch on the bottom stair. 'My thoughts exactly,' I say, bending to pick up the envelope, knowing full well it's more likely to be a letter from Craig's solicitor.

It's the only way we communicate these days. Even our awkward doorstep chats have ended since Nick asked to put Craig's visits on hold while he adjusted to secondary school. Whenever I mention it, he says he's too busy, and while it's true that dance rehearsals dominate every spare moment, I'm surprised at his reluctance to see his stepdad. They used to be close and, despite my differences with Craig, I'd never stop Nick seeing him.

But I don't want to think about my ex-husband now. I've got a whole two hours to myself; I want to enjoy them. Tucking the letter into my coat pocket, I pull out my mobile instead, trying to decide who I might call on for coffee and a chat. I'm scrolling through my contacts lists when the home phone rings. 'Don't run off. That's probably for you,' I tease Marzipan, as she disappears haughtily into the kitchen.

Hurrying through to the living room, I wince at the torn strips of wallpaper. We were in the middle of redecorating when Craig moved out, and I didn't have the heart – or the money – to continue. We bought this house together, as a project. It's full of Edwardian character but hadn't been touched in decades. Our plan was to transform it into the perfect family home, only we're not a family any more. Every bare, creaking floorboard is a stark reminder of that.

I bat away the depressing thought and reach for the phone. 'Hello? *Hello?*' A faint click is followed by the buzz of the dialling tone and my fingers tremble a little as I dial the number for voicemail. Nick still gets nasty messages every now and then; usually I manage to delete them without him knowing. Steeling myself to hear more childish name-calling, it takes me a moment to recognise the bubbly voice in the recording.

Hi, Izzy. Sorry, I've just realised you're probably at work. I meant to catch you at drop-off. Just to say Samir's still coming for a sleepover tonight. Nick's more than welcome, too. Adrian would love him to be there. Just get him to drop a text if he's up for it. Nick, I mean. Oh, it's Beth, by the way. Sorry, I hate talking to machines. Anyway, bye!

I smile at Beth's rambling message. She seems nice; her son Adrian does too, I ponder, feeling even guiltier about the sleepover. Slinging my parka over the arm of the sofa, I head into the kitchen, deciding to steal some of Nick's favourite hot chocolate in lieu of working radiators. Maybe I'll just stay at home with Marzipan, a binge-fest of sugar and Netflix for company ...

I'm spooning the rich powder into a mug when the phone rings again, the shrill noise startling me so much that cocoa flies up, dusting my cream jumper. I brush irritably at it as I dash once more into the living room, wondering if it's Beth calling back, mentally debating whether I should change my mind and agree to the sleepover after all.

'Surely lightning can't strike twice, hey?' I appeal to Marzipan, who follows at my heels, mewing imperiously for food. 'Like Nick said, everyone has sleepovers. It's really no big deal. I should be more worried that I'm talking to a cat.' I dive for the phone before it can click to voicemail again, frowning now as I picture Nick's downcast face this morning. I miss his smile; I wish I knew what had made it disappear.

'Hello? Beth?' I say breathlessly. 'Sorry I missed—'

'Isobel. It's me.'

'Oh. Hi.' A confusing mixture of resentment and loneliness rolls through me at the familiar voice. Craig hasn't been gone long enough to feel like a stranger; every time we speak I have to mentally readjust once again to our separation.

'Everything OK?'

'Of course. Why wouldn't it be?'

'No reason. Just checking. Nick all right?'

'Yes. Look, Craig, I don't mean to be rude, but did you want something? I, um ... I'm on my way out.'

'Who with? Sorry, I shouldn't ask. None of my business. You're a free woman now,' he quips, attempting a chuckle.

'I always was,' I snip. 'Anyway, I'm going to—'

'Honestly, it's fine. I really don't want to pry,' he cuts in. 'I was only phoning to check you got the letter.'

'Letter?' I glance at my coat on the sofa.

'It should have arrived today. I was wondering what you thought about it. What Nick thinks. Have you had a chance to talk him through my proposal?'

Proposal? Even as my curiosity is piqued, I can feel myself bristling. I suspect Craig isn't really asking if I've talked to Nick; he's telling me I should have.

'Sorry, no idea what you're talking about. The, er, postman hasn't been yet.' Even though he can't see me, I feel myself blush at my second lie of the day. But whatever is inside that envelope, I'll open it when I decide, not my ex-husband.

'Right. The snow must be holding things up. It's probably stuck at the sorting office. Maybe you could get Nick to call me later, then, once you've had a chance to chat. I should be home around eight. If you could ask him to—'

'No.' It's my turn to cut him off, but my voice quivers a little: I can count on one hand the number of times I've contradicted Craig.

It's a bitter irony that on the one occasion I put my foot down, Nick was the one to pay the price. Maybe if I'd asserted myself sooner, stopped allowing Craig to have the final say in parenting decisions . . . maybe if I'd given Nick more chances to tap into his inner strength, taste independence, figure out how to avoid the bullies – or stand up to them. Maybe then he wouldn't have ended up in hospital, and Craig wouldn't have blamed me – *left* me.

I can see now that I was too eager to keep the peace; I so wanted my new husband to feel he had a role in our family that I got into a bad habit of deferring to him. *If only I hadn't chosen that day to finally make a stand.* It broke my heart seeing my little boy sprawled on the pavement in a pool of blood and humiliation; I was crushed when Craig said I was to blame. And when Katie agreed with him, it wasn't just my marriage that ended; it was also my closest friendship.

'Sorry?' His deep voice leaps up an octave; I can tell I've surprised him.

'That's not really your role any more,' I say, surprising myself more.

'I'm still Nick's stepdad, aren't I? That commitment didn't end with our marriage. At least, as far as I'm concerned. Please, Isobel. Don't punish our son for petty differences between us.'

'*My* son, and hardly petty.' I remember Craig calling me an *unfit mother* as he slammed out of the house. 'And I'm not stopping Nick seeing you,' I tell him honestly. 'He just wants to concentrate on settling in to his new school, that's all. His words, not mine.'

'You've turned him against me, you mean. You don't want me in his life any more. That's why he isn't returning my calls, isn't it? Why he's ignoring my texts.'

'No, honestly, it's not. I don't know anything about any texts.' I feel a jolt of surprise. I don't check Nick's phone; I wouldn't dream of reading his messages. I set up every parental control I could when I bought him a laptop for his twelfth birthday, but Nick seems to spend most of his time either doing homework or watching gaming vloggers on YouTube.

'Maybe he's scared to tell you. He probably knows you don't want him to talk to me.'

'I've never said that to him. He's just busy. And I—'

'Be careful, sweetheart. Breathe too hard down kids' necks and you push them into keeping secrets. You know that as well as I do.'

'Nick tells me *everything*.' Immediately I want to bite back my words, cross with myself for feeling the need to defend my relationship with my son. I can hear the hurt in Craig's voice, and I know that's why he's chipping at me. I also get that he's frustrated at losing contact with Nick. But it was his decision to end our marriage, not mine.

'Are you sure about that? Boys of his age don't often confide in their mums.'

'And what would you know about that?' The taunt flies out of

13

my mouth before I can stop it; he's caught my Achilles heel now and it hurts.

'OK, look, I didn't phone you to fight,' he backtracks swiftly.

'Then don't.' I'm not going to let him off the hook that easily, but in all honesty, I don't want to fight, either. This situation is hard enough for both of us: separated yet with a child we each love to distraction – a boy who is my son and his stepson. Craig and I might have gone our different ways, but I don't hate him; I miss him at some point almost every day and I genuinely don't want Nick to lose touch with the only father figure he's ever known. But if Craig wants to stay in Nick's life – in *my* life – it has to be on my terms now.

'Fine. I'm sorry. Really. I didn't mean to upset you. I'll phone you tomorrow, yes? I guess I can always chat things through with Nick myself later.'

'I told you, *no*.' Sensing he's about to put the phone down, I refuse to let the conversation end with Craig thinking he still has a casting vote in what I do. 'He's, uh, going for a sleepover tonight,' I tell him, suddenly making up my mind.

'He . . . what? Seriously? Are you sure that's a good idea? You—'

'Craig, *stop*.' The plea emerges more plaintively than I intended. 'This isn't your decision. And Nick's twelve. Old enough to stay overnight with a friend.'

'Like he was old enough to walk to school by himself.' The sudden smallness of his voice somehow intensifies his anger. 'And look how well *that* turned out.'

This time he hangs up before I can respond, and I take my irritation out on his letter, ripping it open in full expectation of finding a request to discuss divorce proceedings. But it's a proposal for a joint custody arrangement . . . I married Craig because I thought he'd be the perfect stepdad. Obviously, I picked too well: he not only still loves my son; he wants to take him from me.

THREE

'Hi, darling. How was your day?' I've left the heater running in the car and the windows have steamed up. Over the last ten minutes I've used a whole packet of wipes, constantly clearing the windscreen so I wouldn't miss Nick when he appeared at the school gate.

'Fine.' He dumps his bag in the back seat before climbing in the front next to me.

'Forgiven me yet?' I smile and lean over to give him a kiss.

'What for?'

'Oh, you know. Everything.' It hits me how many things I feel guilty about: not just for saying no to the sleepover, but also for not managing to give Nick the life I wanted for him; for his real father no longer being around; for the failure of my marriage . . .

'Yeah. Sure.' He sighs, then rests one hand tentatively on top of mine. 'I'm sorry too, Mum. About earlier. Can we still have a takeaway tonight?'

The simple apology, accompanied by the rare crooked smile and gentle touch I've so missed, almost stops my heart. 'Well, the house is so cold a family of polar bears wants to move in to the spare

15

room,' I joke. 'Stupid boiler's chosen the coldest day of the year to die. The curse of Friday the thirteenth strikes again.'

'Yeah. And I thought it was my lucky day.'

Nick turns to stare out of the window, and I groan silently as it dawns on me that it's exactly a year to the day since he was beaten up. I wonder if he's remembering that too. He never talks about it now; he's stopped telling me about *anything*. Craig's little digs earlier were closer to the truth even than he realised, and I hate that. Maybe the only way to win Nick back is to let him go – just a little. *Just for one night*.

'I think we make our own luck. All that Friday the thirteenth stuff ... Silly superstition. Although I'm prepared to admit our boiler may be inhabited by an evil spirit put on this earth to torment me,' I add, desperate to see Nick smile again.

'Maybe we should go out,' he mumbles. 'The café by the park does cheap pizza.'

He slants me a dubious look and I sigh at his consciousness of the frugality I try to hide from him. While Craig's salary as a director at a City underwriters used to pay the mortgage, my part-time job at a local travel agency mostly subsidised little extras. These days it has to cover everything. The one thing I won't compromise on is Nick's dance tuition; it takes every spare penny, and then some. But even though I can't treat us to a posh restaurant, I know Nick would rather hang out with his new friends anyway. And that's one thing I *can* give him.

'Actually, I was thinking about what you said earlier. Tell me, is your new friend Samir really the best chess player at school?'

'Yeah. Wait ... *what*?' His mouth forms a wobbly 'O' as he turns to look at me.

I lean over again to press my cheek against his. It's cool and smooth, but the roundness is beginning to disappear, and a hint of roughness at his jawline is yet another reminder that he's growing up. I want to keep Nick safe; I don't want to smother him. He needs to get out more, and so do I.

'Do you reckon he'd be up for a Friday-night chess tournament?' I smile, waiting for a sign that my meaning has sunk in.

'I can go? *Really?*' His eyes couldn't get any wider.

'Just don't go setting off any rockets in the back garden.' I feel my stomach flip as his face breaks into a grin; he looks happier than I've seen him in weeks.

'Thanks, Mum. You're the best.'

'Have fun and be good! I'll phone you at ten, OK?' I call out an hour later as Nick disappears inside the neat red-brick terraced house with pretty white window boxes. 'Bye, darling. *I love you,*' I add under my breath.

'Thanks for bringing him over, Izzy.' Beth saunters to the doorstep with a smile, her two-year-old daughter Molly propped on her hip. 'Adrian was buzzing when he got Nick's text. Samir's already upstairs. The Xbox is fully loaded. And no doubt that's the last I'll see of the three of them until they're hungry.' She laughs, jiggling Molly.

'That'll be in about five minutes, then. I'm sure Nick must be having a growth spurt. He seems to have his head permanently stuck in the fridge.'

'Adrian too. I don't know where they put it. They're both string beans.'

I force a smile, but my feet are suddenly rooted to the spot. I stare past Beth, hoping for a last glimpse of Nick. For all the excitement while we packed his overnight things, now that I'm here a hundred worries flood my mind. But I don't want to appear rude: Beth has two children; she doesn't need safety instructions. 'I've put Nick's inhaler in his backpack,' I limit myself to saying. 'He knows what to do, but if there are any problems—'

17

'I'll call you.' Beth rests a gentle hand on my arm. '*Go!* Make the most of the peace. Have a bottle of wine. Watch a movie. I wish I could, but Mike's not here and *this* little madam is teething.' She kisses Molly, who offers a gap-toothed wail on cue. 'Anyway, don't let me keep you. It's freezing.' She hugs Molly tighter. 'See you tomorrow. Eleven-ish?'

'Perfect. Thanks, Beth.' I feel myself blush, noticing her puzzled frown as I still don't turn away. From what Nick says, most of his class have sleepovers nearly every weekend. *Drop and go* is obviously the usual form, and I can tell Beth is surprised by my hesitation. 'I know Adrian and Samir are used to sleepovers. But Nick . . .'

'Honestly, you don't have to explain. I gather Nick had a rough time at his last school. He's buddied up nicely with Adrian and Samir, though. They're all in Mr Newton's book group. Books for Boys, he calls it. It's like bloody *Dead Poets Society* revisited!' Beth chuckles. 'At least it makes a change from Adrian staring at his blasted phone.'

'Nick's the same.' My smile comes easier this time. 'Well, more with his laptop than his phone. He's glued to it. Spends hours in his bedroom doing goodness knows what.'

'I reckon I see more of Adrian on Instagram than I do in the flesh. He's a total gadget geek. At least football lures him outside occasionally.'

'Nick hates sports,' I say quietly. *Prissy dancing boy*, I hear echoing in the back of my head. 'And he doesn't have a smartphone. I just got him a basic one. For emergencies, really. He, um, doesn't walk to school by himself.'

'Sure. I get that.' Beth cocks her head, shifting Molly to the other hip. The glow of the streetlight opposite catches her eyes; they glint with kindness laced with a hint of curiosity. 'Well, I suppose I'd better call those pizza delivery guys. They need to get cracking cooking our boys' dinner.' Dark curls tumble around her pretty face as she laughs.

'Oh, of course.' I reach into my handbag, fumbling for my purse. 'How much should I leave you for—'

'Don't be daft.' She waves away my offer. 'Right, I'd best get on. See if I can shovel some food down her ladyship before bath time.'

'Sorry, yes.' I glance upwards, hoping it won't start snowing before I get home. Although it's still early, not quite six, the sky is already black: a faint scattering of stars peeps blindly through inky drifts of cloud. I shuffle awkwardly, knowing Beth is waiting for me to leave. 'Could you just . . . tell Nick I said goodbye?'

'*Laters*, I think you mean.' She smiles. 'Isn't that what the cool kids say?'

The cool kids. Nick has never been one of those, I reflect, as Beth finally closes the door with another chuckle. Backing slowly down the short path, I look up at the front bedroom window. For a second, I think I see Nick's face behind the glass; then a light goes out, the shadows shift and the fleeting apparition disappears.

Stop imagining things, I tell myself, heading more purposefully along the pavement, forcing myself not to look back. *Nick will be fine.* Adrian seems a sweet boy, and Beth is lovely. I've only recently got to know her, having discovered that parents don't loiter at the secondary school gate in the same way as they did at primary school. I was thrilled when Beth approached me – doubly so when she introduced herself by saying that her son was my son's new best friend. Nick has *never* had a best friend. And I lost mine a year ago . . .

Even chatting to Beth on the doorstep brings home to me how isolated I've let myself become. Work keeps me busy, and ferrying Nick to and from dance classes fills most evenings. But I still haven't got around to picking up the gym classes and book group I gave up when I got married, after Craig insisted we had the best fun as a family, just the three of us. An only child himself, he loved the tightness of *our little gang*, and the peace and quiet of our new home, where we would make our own memories: *us against the world*.

For three years, I was thrilled to be able to immerse myself in the joys of family life, in the novelty of being a *wife*. After Craig left, I retreated behind my own four walls; it's time to break out, start doing my own thing again, and encourage Nick to do the same. Hopefully the sleepover will be the start of new friendships – and the dark days will soon give way to light. But as I drive home, I can't shake the feeling that I've left something important behind.

FOUR

'Hi, honey, I'm home,' I mutter ironically as I let myself back into the house. It's even colder than when I left it, just half an hour ago. Or perhaps it's the dark, bottomless silence in the high-ceilinged hallway that makes it feel as though the temperature has plummeted even further. Briskly, I turn on all the lights and head for the kitchen, switching on the radio and peering half-heartedly into the fridge.

'Excellent. Half a loaf and two wrinkly tomatoes. *Dinner for one, madam?*' Maybe I should follow Beth's lead and let the local pizza company take care of dinner, I think, eyeing the meagre end-of-week supplies. Unpinning a menu from the noticeboard, I remember how Craig always used to like family meals around the kitchen table, whereas Nick and I have become far more informal since it's been just the two of us, eating with our feet up in the living room as we chat about our day.

We haven't even done that lately, I realise: Nick has taken to disappearing to his room, plate in hand and Marzipan at his side, leaving me to enjoy a solitary meal in front of whatever happens to be on TV. I'm not in the mood for banal talent shows or cookery programmes this evening, though. Or a film, as Beth suggested. I feel restless and edgy, and even though I know it's because I'm wondering how Nick's getting on, I project my worry on to the faulty boiler. I need it fixed before Nick comes home; his asthma flares up in the cold.

Returning to the noticeboard, I grab the list of *Very Useful People*, as Nick, in a spiky scrawl, has titled the mini directory I've been compiling since Craig left and I took over sole responsibility for house maintenance. Before we married, I'd been single for eight years and became pretty handy with a screwdriver. But Craig loved DIY, saying it made a nice change from sitting behind a desk. Besides, no one ever devoted the same care and attention to detail as he did, he used to complain. I was happy to leave him to it, mostly spending any free evenings with Katie, either at her house or at mine, or occasionally at the cinema.

The memory draws a sigh. Over the last year, I may have topped up my list of useful household contacts, but my social diary remains empty. I glare at the sheet of numbers in my hand. 'I wonder if Arthur would be up for dinner and a movie,' I tease myself, thinking of the dour, fifty-something plumber as I wander back to the living room.

Keeping my coat on, I curl up on the sofa with my phone, setting the pizza menu down on the coffee table, laughing out loud as my eye is caught by the ecstatic cartoon face Nick has doodled next to his favourite, all-the-toppings extravaganza. 'I like what I like,' he always says when I roll my eyes at the clashing flavours. 'Why choose, when you can have it all?' I remember Craig agreeing with him. And suddenly the cold, empty room fills with the ghosts of a happy family life that died a year ago . . .

*

'How did rehearsals go?' I looked up from my laptop as Nick bounded into the living room. 'Sorry I couldn't be there tonight, love. Laura asked me to do the late shift. She's driving up to her parents in Shropshire with Bessie for the weekend.'

'Doesn't matter. We just practised the same bit you saw yesterday.'

'Ah, the death scene.' I felt a little shiver; Nick was far too convincing in the role of a tortured lover flinging himself tragically over the edge of a cliff. 'Everything go OK?'

'Yeah. Except I whacked my cheek on Imogen's shoulder when I landed.'

'Oh dear.' I smiled at his indignant frown. 'Was she all right?'

'She laughed her head off, Mum! Said I'm supposed to act like a swan, not a dead duck. I only fell funny cos she refused to hold my hand,' Nick protested.

'Really? That doesn't sound like Immy.' She was older than Nick, and a kind girl.

Nick shrugged, then grinned. 'I had cheese and onion crisps in the break. She said they smelled rank. Worse than my trainers.'

I laughed. 'Well, that'll teach you to snack before dinner. Which I see you two pizza junkies have taken care of. Very healthy after a two-hour dance class. *Not*.' I raised my eyebrows at the greasy takeaway box in Craig's hands as he entered the room, still dressed in his suit having left work early to collect Nick and take him to his dance class.

'It's Friday,' he said. 'It's traditional.' He gave me one of those long, direct looks that I was never quite sure was serious or teasing, until he smiled.

'I'm starving,' Nick declared. 'Can we eat now?' He didn't wait for a response, grabbing the box from Craig and carrying it triumphantly aloft into the kitchen. 'I put my kit in the washing machine, Mum!' he called out over his shoulder.

'By that he means it's screwed up in a pile on the utility-room floor,' Craig huffed, but he was still smiling as he came to sit next to me on the sofa.

'Naturally.' I smiled back. 'How was your day?'

'Ended better than it began. I love watching Nick dance. I should do it more often.'

'I'm sure he'd like that. And it would give me a chance to pick up with my book club again,' I suggested eagerly, only realising how much I'd missed it as I saw a glimmer of possibility to rejoin the group of mainly single parents I'd known since Nick was in nursery. It had been a wrench when I'd had to give up our get-togethers, albeit for a good reason: the extra dance tuition Craig set up for Nick after we were married. The daily lifts to and from his classes mostly fell to me, as Craig worked longer hours and had to commute into the City.

'Retail therapy with Katie not quite as stimulating, hey?' he deadpanned.

'I love hanging out with her. But, yes, she's not a reader.' I laughed, thinking of my energetic friend, who was never happier than when blitzing an antiques fair or shopping mall.

'You don't seem to be getting very far with that.' Craig nodded at the report I'd been typing, which still hadn't progressed much beyond the first paragraph. 'Need any help?'

I sighed. 'Thanks, but it can wait till Monday. I'm too tired to think straight now.' I yawned and then stretched as Craig closed the laptop, gently taking it from me and setting it on the coffee table. 'Thank God it's the weekend.' I rested my head on his shoulder as he sat back against the cushions, hooking his arm comfortably around me.

'You need more time out, love. In fact, I was going to suggest – how about I take over taxi duties for a while? Kill two birds with one stone. Give you a break and me more time with Nick. I could switch things round at work so I can leave a bit earlier.'

'Really?' I looked at him in surprise. Craig was rigorously dedicated to his career – he was conscientious about everything he did, but especially his work.

'Yes, I . . . I think I've finally had a breakthrough with Nick. I want to build on it.'

'A breakthrough?' I watched Craig take off his glasses and reach into his pocket for a handkerchief. After two years of marriage, I was getting used to his quiet, understated ways. He didn't like to show his emotions, but I could see plenty flitting across his face now.

'Yes. He called me Dad for the first time tonight. Instead of Craig, I mean.' His hands covered his face as he put his glasses back on, but not before I noticed the glint in his eyes.

'He . . . what? Wow.' I'd never insisted Nick call Craig by anything other than his first name, hoping that gradually, in his own time, he would feel comfortable thinking of his stepfather as *Dad*. Likewise, I knew he alternated between our two surnames, sticking with Blake at school, but sometimes using Craig's name: Brookes. We'd talked about changing it officially, but Nick said he *wouldn't feel like himself* if he did that.

'I know. It knocked me for six, too.'

'I bet.' I smiled, deliberately hiding a sudden pang of something that was not quite jealousy, but almost. I was happy for Craig – for Nick, too. It was a good thing that the initially tentative bond between them was growing stronger. But at some deep, primeval level I also wondered if each step Nick took closer to his stepdad carried him a tiny bit further away from me. 'That's great. Honestly. I couldn't be happier,' I said, pulling myself together.

'Me too. I closed the Arkwright deal yesterday. The buzz didn't even come close.'

'And he said it just like that? Out of the blue?' It was Craig's moment; instinctively I felt I shouldn't pry. But I couldn't help myself; I was eager to hear details, wishing I'd been there to witness what felt like a huge turning point in our little family.

'Yeah. While we were waiting for the pizza. He came over and gave me this big hug and said, "Thanks, Dad."'

'Ah, right.' Pre-Craig, money had been tight, and Nick still got ridiculously excited about treats like takeaways. Perhaps that explained his affectionate impulse.

'Awesome, hey?' Craig said, then laughed as he caught my eye, both of us recognising how comical Nick's favourite word sounded on adult lips – especially Craig's.

'It's wonderful,' I said sincerely. 'And so are you.'

I leaned over to kiss his smooth cheek, feeling butterflies in my stomach as he turned to kiss me back with surprising passion. Bonding with Nick had obviously put him in a good mood, and I loved that he cared about him so much. I loved *Craig*. Life was good. I was confident it was only going to get better.

'Hi, darling. How's it going?' I can hear the breathlessness in my own voice. I've been staring at the phone for the last ten minutes, waiting to call Nick, feeling rather flat after spending the evening alone with my memories. Thinking about the past completely erased my appetite, too; in the end, I made do with toast rather than ordering pizza, zoning out in front of a box set after arranging for Arthur to come and fix the boiler tomorrow afternoon.

'Fine,' he says. *That word again*.

'Good. That's great, darling. I, um, just wanted to say goodnight, really.' Suddenly I feel like I need to give a reason for calling him. 'Are you having fun?'

'Yeah.'

'Sure? Everything's OK?' He sounds different – not unhappy, but . . . subdued. Or is it just that I'm not used to speaking to him on the phone? The intensity of only being able to hear and not see him makes me acutely aware of every tiny inflection in his voice.

'Totally. Sorry, Mum. Gotta go.'

'Hang on, love.' I start to panic, wondering if there's something he's not telling me – if something has happened to upset him. 'What have you boys been up to, then? Have you—'

The call disconnects. I press redial but it goes straight to voicemail. Hesitating for a moment, I decide to text Beth, apologising for disturbing her but *just wanting to check in*. Her reassuring reply comes through immediately. *Too quickly?*

I'm being paranoid, I tell myself. She's probably been waiting for me to contact her, knowing I was a little anxious about leaving Nick. And he obviously doesn't want to chat with his mum in front of his friends. It's all completely normal. I send Nick a text: *Sweet dreams, love you*. He doesn't reply, and I sink back against the pillows, waiting for sleep to anaesthetise worry.

FIVE

'Izzy! You're early.' Beth tightens the belt of her dressing gown, hugging herself against the cold. Her curly hair is dishevelled, her cheeks are flushed; she looks tired and flustered.

'Sorry, I can come back.' I half turn away, feeling embarrassed.

'No, I'm sorry.' She pushes back her hair and smiles. 'Come on in. Please. Ignore the mess, though. I haven't had a chance to tidy up yet.' Opening the door wider, she steps forward and pokes her head out, glancing quickly all around the quiet cul-de-sac.

'Everything OK?' I say, watching her.

'Of course.' She smiles, moving aside to let me squeeze past her into the hall.

After hooking my coat over a pile of other jackets on an old-fashioned wooden stand, I tuck my ankle boots next to a sprawling shoe mountain by the front door. 'Ah, your husband's back. Mike, isn't it?' I say, spotting muddy Timberlands.

'Sorry? Oh. No, I put those there myself. Just a little hint. Mike's big enough and ugly enough to clean his own boots. Once he's fixed this wonky latch.' She tuts as she closes the front door. 'And

28

the leaky shower. In fact, I've got a whole list of jobs for the useless sod. When he finally deigns to show his face.' Beth smiles again, but her laugh sounds a little forced as she leads the way into the living room.

'He doesn't know anything about boilers, does he?' I say, tactfully ignoring the hint of marital strife. 'I've got a plumber coming later who wants an arm and a leg to fix mine.'

'Don't they all? I'll ask Mike. If I manage to get hold of him, that is. He's actually working away, and I'm not sure when . . .' She seems to hesitate, then sighs as she surveys the living room. 'God, would you look at the mess.'

'You have a lovely home,' I tell her, glancing around at the piles of books and framed family photos competing for space on every surface. The room is cosily cluttered, with a scattering of antique furniture, squashy sofas and jewel-coloured walls. It's vibrant and welcoming, just like Beth, even if she does seem unusually edgy this morning. If her husband wasn't away, I'd guess I've inadvertently walked into the aftermath of a blazing row she's politely trying to pretend hasn't happened.

'When it's tidy. Sorry, I'm not usually this grumpy. Tough night. Not with the boys,' she adds quickly. 'Teething tantrums.' She nods at Molly, asleep under a fleece on the sofa. 'Or maybe it's her way of hogging the spotlight. Even *bad* attention is attention, right?'

I offer a sympathetic wince, wondering whether Nick managed to sleep through the noise. 'Shall I make you a coffee? And I *am* sorry for being early. I know we said eleven.' I don't need to look at my watch to know it's closer to ten.

'Don't be silly. You're welcome any time. Coffee would be great, though. But I'll make it. You're a guest.' Beth pats an armchair invitingly. 'Come on. Make yourself comfy.'

It occurs to me that I should maybe have brought something

as a thank-you. Katie and I were friends for so long that we never stood on ceremony: we didn't keep a tally of who bought coffee last; we each knew where the other kept their spare keys. But I'm conscious of being out of the loop in terms of sleepover etiquette. I don't want to lose Nick brownie points for having a rude mum, not when he's finally found a couple of genuine friends.

'Thanks again for including Nick,' I say, settling into the armchair.

'My pleasure.' She looks thoughtful for a moment. 'He's incredibly like you, isn't he? Same slim build, blue eyes. That blond hair. Those cheekbones. Lucky boy. Lucky *you*.' She smiles. 'He obviously takes more after his mum than his dad, bless him.'

'Craig is his stepdad,' I tell her, obligingly picking up on the leading comments.

'Ah. That explains . . .' Her head tilts. 'Sorry, I just thought I heard Nick say . . .'

'Say what?' Nick has said next to nothing about Craig moving out; I'm eager to hear even second-hand information about what he's thinking.

'Nothing, really. The two of them get along OK, then?'

'Yes. They're pretty close. Or at least they were. Before we separated.' I pause for a moment, thinking of Craig's letter. 'Nick doesn't see so much of his stepdad these days.'

Beth doesn't look surprised, and I wonder if she knew that already. I feel a pang of awkwardness at her knowing more about me than I do about her. I know she gave up teaching to be a full-time mum, and that her husband Mike is some kind of sales rep. But I don't know them as a family – as *people*. Beth doesn't strike me as gossipy or judgemental. Then again, I never thought Katie would turn her back on me as she did.

'Well, anyway. It's great to see the boys getting on so well. They must have had fun – they're still out cold. Which means we get to drink our coffee in peace. Hallelujah!' She yawns widely before finally disappearing into the adjoining kitchen. 'How do you like it?'

'Milk and no sugar. Thanks.' I check my watch. 'Nick's usually up by now. I hope he didn't disturb anyone, by the way. He sleepwalks occasionally, and in a strange house . . .'

'Really?' Beth reappears, coffee in hand. 'Well, don't worry, Adrian sleeps like a log. And it would have taken a jumbo jet to wake me. I know I fell asleep at some point. The night is just a blur. As are most days, to be honest. I'd forgotten how exhausting toddlers are.'

'I remember not knowing what year it was some days when Nick was little. And *teething*. Oh, my God. The fifth circle of hell.' I groan. 'But I'm glad the boys had fun.'

'They really did. They overdosed on pizza. Watched spooky movies. Nothing too scary,' she adds quickly. 'Then once Jason arrived they—'

'*Jason?*'

'Jason Baxter? Year Nine? He's in the book group too. They all seem to be *huge* fans of Mr Newton. Which is fine by me. Anyone who can convince Ade to put down his phone and pick up a book gets my vote. And Jason is—'

'Yes. I know who he is.' I dry swallow. 'I just didn't know he was coming.'

'Nor did I, to tell you the truth.' Beth props a hand on one hip, frowning. 'It was a last-minute thing. He said his mum had a late meeting or something. Is that a problem?'

'Nick's had a few issues with Jason, that's all.' I downplay it so as not to worry her, but I can feel a familiar tension stiffen my shoulders.

'He has? Oh God. *Sorry*, Izzy.' Beth's forehead creases. 'I had no idea.'

'It's not your fault,' I say, not feeling cross so much as anxious. And strictly speaking, Nick isn't the one who has a problem with Jason: *I am*. He's always been a little bossy with Nick, but towards the end of their friendship I'm sure he started picking on him; I recognised the signs, even if Nick tried to hide them.

'I'll go wake the boys.' Thankfully, Beth picks up on my anxiety, setting down the coffee jar and sweeping through the living room, silky dressing gown swishing.

'Shall I come?' I'm already following her.

'Sure. Oh, actually, would you mind keeping an eye on Molly? I'll be quick.' She pauses, turning to look at me. 'Honestly, there wasn't any trouble. But I do feel dreadful.'

'You weren't to know. And like you say, I'm sure it was fine.' I hold my smile, even as I remember Nick's stilted manner on the phone last night, wondering if Jason's arrival explains it.

As Beth hurries off, I sink down on to the sofa next to Molly, taking care not to disturb her. She seems completely out of it, though, and I'm about to head into the kitchen to stick the kettle on when I hear Beth yelling. Thinking she might need moral support, I cross the living room and step into the hall.

'Nick? *Nick?*' Beth's voice is shrill as she dashes across the landing.

'Everything OK? Can I help?' I call up, trying to decide whether it would look rude if I go up the stairs uninvited. Before I can make up my mind, Beth comes flying down them.

'Did Nick come down?' Her face is chalk-white, her mouth a pinched line.

'Sorry?'

'He's not in any of the bedrooms. Or the bathroom.'

'What?' My pulse roars in my ears; my voice sounds like it's coming from far away.

'The boys haven't a clue where he is, either. I don't understand. It's like he's vanished into thin air.'

'He can't have. He must be hiding somewhere. Maybe the boys had a fight.' I scrabble in the back pocket of my jeans for my phone, my fingers trembling as I search for Nick's number. The ringing tone repeats endlessly and I can feel my palms sweating as I wait for the call to click in, for the electronic drone to be replaced by the sound of Nick's voice. Any second now . . . now . . . *now. Please, please answer, Nick.*

Holding the phone away from my ear, I strain to hear his ringtone, but the house is silent. I push past Beth to hurry up the stairs, my mind sprinting ahead to visualise Nick sitting on his bed, shrugging as if to say, *What's all the fuss about?* I keep focusing on that image as I crash into the bedroom, panic blinding me so that I've whirled around the room touching each bed once, twice, three times before acceptance filters through disbelief.

Nick really isn't there, only Adrian, huddled at the top of his bed, and Samir, a mirror image on a twin bed opposite. Backs hunched, eyes wide; the two boys are both twelve, but their round, shocked faces make them look much younger.

'He's not here, Mrs Brookes.' Adrian points to the end of the bed, where Nick's pyjamas are bundled on a pillow, then towards a Batman backpack I'd recognise anywhere propped against the wall. 'Is he, Sammy?'

'No.' Samir shakes his head, long black fringe flying.

'Maybe he got homesick.'

Jason. Turning in the direction of the low drawl, I'm surprised to see how much my former best friend's son has grown since I last saw him. He has his dad's height and broad shoulders, while his red hair and lightly freckled face are instant reminders of Katie.

'Did something happen? Did you fall out?' I stare at him, his heavy-jawed face blurring as my mind tries to assimilate the jarring images of Nick's pyjamas on the bed and his backpack on the floor. *He got dressed and left, but didn't take his stuff?*

Jason folds his arms, and I turn back to Adrian and Samir, but their frozen expressions confirm that they're either too shocked or too scared to tell me anything. Ignoring any regard for their privacy, I drop to my knees and look under each bed, sweeping with both hands. But all I find are trainers, a stack of magazines and the unidentifiable shapes of abandoned toys.

Nick isn't there. Nor is he hiding in the built-in wardrobe, the airing cupboard on the landing or in the other two bedrooms. There's nowhere left to look up here, and I'm certain I would have heard his footsteps on the wooden stairs if he'd crept down while I was chatting to Beth. He hasn't just sneaked out: wherever he is, he was already there before I arrived.

SIX

Stepping out of Adrian's room on to the landing, I force myself to breathe through the panic – to try to get inside the mind of a twelve-year-old boy who changed his mind about wanting a sleepover. *Or was made to feel unwelcome*. The thought pulls my attention back to Jason, and I turn to find him watching me from the bedroom doorway. His eyes flick upwards for a second; I look up too, gasping as I see that the entrance to the loft is open a crack.

'I've just checked around the garden.' Beth is breathing heavily as she appears at the top of the stairs. 'And the shed. Nothing. No sign of him.'

'What's up there?' I nod at the small, square hatch in the ceiling.

'Junk. Mike's old stuff. Rubbish, I don't know.' She fiddles with her dressing-gown belt. 'Nothing really. There's no ladder, anyway. Nick couldn't have got up there.'

My eyes assess the ceiling height, then Jason's. *If Nick stood on his shoulders, he could reach the hatch.* 'Did he go up there? Were you messing about? Did you help him climb up to have a look?'

35

'Negative.' Jason folds his arms again. 'We played Xbox, down-loaded some new apps. But Nick wasn't really up for games. He said he was tired.'

'He was reading in bed,' Adrian chips in from the bedroom. 'I was at the top. Nick went at the bottom.'

I brush past Jason to step back into the room, picking up Nick's pyjamas from the bed and yanking back the duvet. 'He's left his inhaler.' The room seems to spin as I reach for it. I always remind Nick to carry it with him at all times; in truth, he never forgets. 'Where's his book? You said he was reading.'

Adrian shrugs. 'Search me.'

'And he was definitely there when you went to sleep?' I glance between him and Samir, who immediately nods. 'You weren't playing a game. Not . . . I guess you're too old for hide-and-seek.' I rack my brains to think of what they could have been doing that Nick would feel the need to hide; nothing good springs to mind. 'There weren't any arguments?' I press again, unable to stop myself glaring at Jason. 'Nothing to upset him?'

'Nope.' Jason holds my gaze.

'We just chatted,' Adrian says. 'Well, Nick didn't say much. He was into his book. Then we went to sleep.' He stares around the room, as if he too is expecting Nick to burst out of a cupboard door at any moment, yelling, *Surprise!* 'Then Mum came up and—'

'I looked in on them when I came to bed,' Beth interjects breathily, bundling her hair into a high ponytail as she reappears in the doorway.

I didn't see her leave the bedroom, I didn't hear her return, and I notice that she's changed out of her dressing gown into the same black jeans and plum-coloured jumper she was wearing yesterday. I know it's reasonable for her to get dressed, but I feel irritated that she can think of something so ordinary at a time like this. 'When was that?' I snap.

'Midnight. No, a bit before. They were sound asleep, though.' Beth comes to sit next to Adrian. 'You didn't go down for a drink in the night, any of you? Nick didn't . . . ?' She looks up at me. 'You said he sleepwalks sometimes. Maybe . . . Oh God, the front-door latch.'

She blushes, and as I watch her squeeze Adrian's hand I know what she's really thinking: *Thank God it isn't my son.* But I left her in charge of my boy. Her responsibility was to take care of him; at the very least to make sure he was physically safe.

'So someone could have got in?' I glare at her, anger firing up beneath the panic as I remember Beth joking about her *list of jobs* for Mike. I wonder again if she was rowing with him on the phone. It would certainly explain her twitchy mood – and perhaps her lack of attention to the boys last night.

'I was thinking more that Nick might have gone out,' she offers meekly. 'Perhaps Jason's right. Maybe he felt homesick. Or needed some fresh air, or maybe he wanted to play in the snow and went—'

'Went *where*? Where on earth would he have gone in the middle of the night?'

'Home?' Her voice is barely a squeak.

'He would have called me to come and get him.' *Wouldn't he?* Unless he didn't want to drag me out in the cold, and thought he'd make his own way home instead . . .

It seems so unlikely that Nick would have gone anywhere in the dark, but if he didn't, what other possibility is there? He isn't a toddler like Molly who could be silently snatched. If there was no disturbance in the house that woke the other boys, there has to be a simple explanation for why he isn't here.

I close my eyes, picturing him disappearing into the house the day before; I imagine him chasing up the stairs after Adrian, dumping his backpack before flopping on to the bed with his book.

Pizza, Xbox, movies . . . Jason arriving. *A fight?* Nick waiting until everyone's asleep to creep out of the house . . .

My mind rattles between places he could have gone. He wasn't hanging around our home; I've just come from there. His dance school? The park? Local shops? My heart leaps at the thought that he might have sought refuge with his stepdad. But even though there is clearly unfinished business between me and my ex-husband, I have no doubt Craig would have called me if Nick had turned up at his flat in the middle of the night.

'I'm so sorry, Izzy.' Beth's voice is plaintive. 'He was right there in bed. I checked they'd all brushed their teeth and phoned home. I turned off the lights myself.'

I hurry down the stairs, with Beth following close behind, desperately hoping she's right: that even now Nick is outside her house, waiting to be let back in having innocently wandered off to gather bits and bobs to decorate a snowman. As we reach the hall, Molly wakes from her nap, wailing loudly. Tutting, Beth marches past me into the living room, her exasperation reminding me of her complaints about exhaustion.

'But like you said, Molly was screaming last night,' I call after her. 'And you were tired. You crashed out. Maybe the boys had a spat later on that you didn't hear.'

'They seemed fine when they were watching TV,' Beth says, reappearing with Molly nuzzling into her neck. 'And you heard them just now. Not a word about any fights. Adrian doesn't lie,' she insists, sounding a little defensive now.

I give her a straight look. 'All children lie when they think they're in trouble.'

'You're angry with me. I deserve it. I would be too.' Another blush creeps in patchy blotches up her neck. 'I'm so, so sorry, Izzy. I can't think what—'

'You checked the back garden, right? I'll check out the front.

Maybe you're right. Maybe Nick got up early to mess about in the snow. He does love it. He was gutted we didn't have a white Christmas.' I fight back images of him pressing his face against his bedroom window, staring eagerly at the stubbornly grey sky.

'Exactly! He could be secretly stockpiling snowballs as we speak.'

I grab my cream parka from the stand, turning back to Beth in a daze as I see Nick's matching khaki one still hooked underneath. 'Oh. His jacket's still here.' I scan the hall floor. 'I can't see his trainers, though. It's freezing out there. Why would he put on his shoes but not his coat?' I search the sprawling pile again as I pull on my boots. 'They're definitely gone. So are Mike's Timberlands.' I glance curiously at Beth. 'Is he back, then?'

She shakes her head. 'I put them out in the shed just now. They were leaving mud everywhere. And, well, look at this mess. Nick's trainers wouldn't be the first to go missing in this house. Adrian's already lost two pairs.' She frowns. 'And I can't see his new Nikes, either. Typical. Brand new they are, too.'

'You put Mike's boots in the shed.' My eyes linger for a moment on her pretty, flushed face, then I look away, feeling awkward at the direction of my thoughts. 'He definitely didn't come home, then. You don't think there's a chance he could have come back sooner than you expected. Maybe decided to show up unannounced?'

'Of course not.' Beth cocks her head, giving me a quizzical look. 'Why would he?'

'Sorry. I guess I'm just wondering if he might have taken Nick out. To look at the moon, or go star-gazing, or something,' I finish awkwardly.

'Well, he's not here. He didn't take his house keys, for one thing. Never does on work trips. Always loses them.' She sighs. 'It obviously runs in the family. Keys. Shoes.'

'Right. Sure. OK, I'll just . . .' I open the front door, tutting as the loose latch waggles up and down. It would have been easy for someone to get out – *or in* – without anyone noticing, I realise. But if Mike Atkins didn't come home, that at least scuppers one fear: that Beth's husband secretly returned and, for some inexplicable reason, stole my son. The idea is ridiculous, I tell myself. And even if someone, *anyone*, managed to sneak into the house without anyone hearing, one of the boys would surely have cried out.

'Any sign?' Beth hovers behind me in the doorway, jiggling Molly on her hip.

'None.' I stare at the trail of my own footprints in disappointment before stepping outside, looking all around as I stumble towards the gate. There isn't a snowman in sight. I gaze slowly along the rows of houses, most of which still have their curtains closed. Nothing catches my eye, and after one last scan, I turn and make my way back into the hallway.

Beth holds out her phone. 'Do you think you should call—'

'Craig,' I say, even while I know she means the police. The thought is pulsing in my mind, but I still can't bring myself to accept that this is an emergency – that Nick isn't safe somewhere, having bolted after an argument. I call him again, biting my lip when voicemail kicks in. I leave a message, then pull up Craig's number.

The possibility of another lecture on parental responsibility fills me with dread, but I can't shake the thought that Nick might have gone to his stepdad's flat rather than come home. Perhaps because it's a couple of streets closer to Beth's house; perhaps because he had some kind of exchange with him last night. Craig did mention that he's been texting Nick . . .

I'm about to press 'dial' when I notice a low door further along the hall. 'Is this a cupboard?' I crouch down and tug at the handle, and as it opens with the graze of wood-on-wood, a damp chill hits my face, followed by a pungent, earthy smell that makes me cough.

'No. That leads down to the cellar,' Beth says. 'But we don't use it. It's full of—'

'Junk,' I finish for her, exasperated to find yet another hiding place: first the loft hatch, now this. I could hardly have insisted on her giving me a thorough tour of the house before I let Nick stay here; now I wish I'd been less polite, more inquisitive.

'We're bursting at the seams.' Beth's hand flutters anxiously around her neck. 'What with all Mike's sales catalogues and my books. The kids' old toys. There's nowhere to—'

'Nick? Are you down there?' I ignore her nervous, guilty rambling, kneeling down to peer into the darkness. 'Nick, it's Mum – can you hear me?'

My voice is sucked into the void; goose bumps chase across my skin. Nick is terrified of confined spaces: if he's down there, he might be too scared to answer. I feel around for a light switch; I'm going to have to go and look for him.

SEVEN

The air is too cold to breathe; I lean against the garden wall, bent double, coughing until my throat hurts. My lungs feel bruised as they reject the icy gulps of wind I swallowed in desperation to clear the rancid-chemical fumes of a cellar used not for junk, as Beth intimated, but for what appeared to be someone's stuffed wildlife collection: a squirrel, some kind of bird, a rabbit and an enormous rat, all posed in a decaying imitation of life.

Road kill, I thought, gagging on the smell. There were bottles and jars, tins and boxes, all crammed on to the makeshift shelves lining the walls of the small cellar. The chalky stone floor was swept clean, with nothing to suggest Nick had been down there. I made a swift retreat, clambering my way back to daylight and staggering out of the house.

'He's not there.' I press a hand to my mouth, almost retching on a combination of fear and the acrid stench I can't swallow, can't breathe out. 'What *is* all that stuff?' I ask Beth as she appears at my side. 'Is it Mike's hobby? Does he—'

'I've called the police, Izzy.' She pulls at my arm. 'Come back inside.'

'I can't. I've got to go home. He might be there.' I don't waste time explaining that I don't mean my current house. Thinking about Craig has reminded me of the very first thing Nick said when his stepdad left: *Are we going home now?* He meant to the place we lived before I got married, when it was just Nick and me in the tiny flat I've always told him I shared with the first and, in truth, perhaps the biggest love of my life ... His dad. Alex.

'But the police ...' Beth's girlish tone begs me not to hate her – to let her make up for what has happened.

'I'll be really quick. I can't just sit here, Beth.' I take hold of her hands, giving them a quick squeeze. 'I have to look for him. And if he's there, we won't even *need* the police.'

Please be there, I think as I turn and hurry off, trying not to picture the state I found Nick in the last time I had to go looking for him. Exactly twelve months ago ...

The coincidence of the timing nags at me as I jog out of the cul-de-sac and along the main road, my eyes darting all around until I reach the college sports field. My boots sink into the snowy grass as I sprint across it, and then at last I'm standing in front of the familiar Victorian townhouse. Four down from the railway track; the one with an apple tree half-heartedly waving its spindly arms.

Once, that tree was the centrepiece of a beautiful garden Alex created especially for us: two teenage desperadoes the council finally took pity on, after I found out I was pregnant at seventeen and both sets of parents threw us out. Now the pretty borders are strangled by weeds and the tree seems to hang its head in despair. The treehouse is still there, though: the secret den Alex built for the son he swore he couldn't wait to play with.

It still hurts unbearably that he didn't stick around to see how it became our little boy's favourite refuge when the playground taunts got too much to bear. Nick always used to barricade himself in there with toys and teddies, and he's wistfully begged to revisit his old hideout dozens of times since we left this flat. If he's hiding anywhere, I'm certain it would be here. I hop over the low wall and approach the tree.

'Nick? Nick, are you there?' I'm about to climb up when a train thunders past, the deafening clatter and strident horn echoing beneath the railway bridge instantly transporting me back thirteen years: to Alex leading me towards this very tree, with the same gentle, crooked smile as the son he never met. *Look, Izzy! Come and see what I built for our boy . . .*

But as I finally haul myself up to peer inside, I discover only rotten, mossy timbers that crumble beneath my fingers. It's no one's secret sanctuary any more, and Nick isn't here.

'Oh, Beth. You were right.' I fall into her open arms, still breathing heavily from jogging back to her house. 'I checked the bus stops. Newsagent . . .' I pull away, casting a yearning glance up the stairs, hoping against hope that Nick will appear at the top of them. 'It's like he's vanished into thin air.'

Beth hugs me again, rubbing her hands up and down my arms. 'I've been going over and over everything. Every conversation last night. What the boys talked about. They've hardly said a word. I think they're in shock. And the police said they can't formally interview them without their parents present. They've called Katie Baxter and Ayesha Matlock, but—'

'The police.' *Nick is really gone.*

'They're here, Izzy.' Beth reaches for my hand. 'So is—'

'Craig,' I say, stumbling past her into the living room to see him sitting on the sofa, with Jason, Adrian and Samir, now all dressed in almost identical jeans and hoodies, lined up alongside him.

'Isobel.'

'What are *you* doing here?' Fear emerges as antagonism. I

wonder who phoned him; I was so certain Nick would be at our old flat that I didn't make that call.

'Are you OK, sweetheart?' He doesn't rise to my hostility but stands up and walks slowly towards me, arms outstretched as though ready to pull me into a hug.

'Nick isn't with you?' I take a step back, looking up at his face, the flint-grey eyes as hard to read as ever. 'He didn't come to your flat, or phone you?' I take out my own phone, checking for the hundredth time that Nick hasn't called me.

'I've been trying his number too.' Craig shakes his head. 'No reply.'

'So how did you know—'

'Izzy,' Beth interrupts, 'this is DCI Maxwell.' She gestures to a tanned, dark-haired man in a navy overcoat standing in front of the fireplace. 'And DS Clarke.'

'That's me.' A tall woman in a black trouser suit smiles and holds up her ID. 'And you're Mrs Brookes? Mrs Isobel Brookes? Your son is Nicholas Brookes, aged twelve? Sorry about the formality. We just need to confirm everyone's identities for the record.' She writes something in her notebook; I notice in surprise that she's already filled two pages.

'I understand young Nick's gone walkabout, Mrs Brookes. Izzy, isn't it?' The senior detective steps forward with a smile; he looks as though he's about to try to sell me insurance.

'Yes. Nick's my son. But his surname's Blake. I didn't change it when I married his stepdad.' I nod at Craig, watching him settle himself back on the sofa. 'We're separated.'

DS Clarke checks her notes. 'Right. I see. It's just that Mrs Atkins called him Nick Brookes when she reported him missing.'

'Oh, right. Well, Nick's always tended to use both names. He worries that people might think it's odd we have different surnames, you see. He still introduces himself as Nick Brookes sometimes.' I glance at Beth, who nods, confirming my guess. 'It's a little confusing, I know.' *For him too, probably.* 'Anyway, I just thought it might help you to have all the facts.' I watch DS Clarke jot down another note, wondering if she thinks I'm scoring points against my ex rather than offering any information that might help them find my son.

'And you were right.' DCI Maxwell smiles again. 'It *is* helpful. My very first question was going to be who has parental authority for Nick.'

'I do. I have sole custody. He's my son.' I can't resist a sideways glance at Craig. 'But he was here last night. When he . . .'

'He was here for a sleepover, yes? Is that a regular thing?' The detective's smile is encouraging, intended to put me at ease.

'No. It was his first, actually. I thought he might have got . . . upset. I wondered if he'd run back to our old flat. We used to live somewhere else, you see. Before I married. That's where I've just been. Nick was very attached to his old treehouse. I thought that's where he might have gone. But it wasn't.' I bite the inside of my lip, fighting tears.

DCI Maxwell nods understandingly. 'Sorry to ask the obvious, but I take it you've rung him and he's not picking up?'

I stare at my phone again, willing Nick to call. 'It goes straight to voicemail now.'

'Any medical concerns we should know about?' DS Clarke looks up, pen poised. 'Any history of anxiety or depression. Self-harm.'

'*What?* No. I mean, things haven't been great for Nick at school. But nothing like that. He does have asthma, though.' I reach into my bag. 'And he left his inhaler behind.'

'I see.' DCI Maxwell's smile fades. 'That is a worry. Given Nick's age, we wouldn't generally class him as officially missing until after twenty-four hours. His asthma, though . . . That does leapfrog him into the high-risk category.'

Tears blur my eyes now. Not *officially missing*. Nick couldn't *be* more missing. 'He left without telling me. He's never done that before.'

'Apart from when he ran off to school by himself,' Craig points out. 'Sorry. Just making sure they have all the facts,' he adds, when I swivel round to glare at him.

'Every detail helps.' The detective nods at Craig before turning back to me. 'We'll need to carry out a thorough risk assessment. DS Clarke here will take care of that. If you could talk her through everything, Izzy: what's been going on for Nick – at home, school, any problems he's been having. That sort of thing. In the meantime, we'll liaise with the Missing Persons Bureau. We'll need a recent photo of Nick, of course.'

'Try not to panic, Mrs Brookes,' his colleague says gently. 'We're here to help.'

I stare blankly at her delicate-boned face, neat ponytail and earnest brown eyes. She looks so young that, fleetingly, I worry if she's experienced enough to be left in charge, as her boss seems to be suggesting she will be. 'Thank you,' I say automatically.

'You're in good hands with Sarah,' DCI Maxwell says, as though reading my mind. 'She'll walk you through what happens next. As I say, the first step is to build up a picture of Nick's life. Daily routine, friends, worries. Whatever springs to mind. Anything that might, for instance, have caused him to run away.'

'Run away? Surely he's been *taken*?' I blurt out, unable to contain the fear any longer. 'Why else hasn't he called me? What if he's trapped or hurt? What if he left the house and someone saw him, *snatched* him? You need to get out there and start looking for him!'

'And we will,' DCI Maxwell says calmly. 'Starting with every likely place you can think of. Anywhere Nick likes to hang out. Places he might be hiding.'

I've already looked, and he wasn't there. 'He doesn't go out much.

47

School. Dance class. Like I said, this was his first sleepover.' I try not to catch Craig's eye, but I sense that he's bursting to say how much he disapproved of it all along.

DS Clarke lifts her pen to get my attention. 'Did he say anything odd last night? You phoned him around ten, yes?' She checks her notes. 'Notice anything different about him?'

'Yes. No. I'm not sure. He . . . I . . .' I stare at the window, watching sleet pelt against the glass like tiny bullets. I imagine Nick's face stinging with cold; I try not to picture him lying dead in a ditch, eyes wide and staring, blood seeping around his body after some dreadful attack. Or holed up with a kidnapper: blindfolded, terrified, *tortured* . . .

EIGHT

'Take your time, Izzy.'

DCI Maxwell's mellow voice pulls me back from the dark place I can feel myself sinking into. I try to return his sympathetic smile, and I'm just managing to get a grip on my emotions when I notice Craig frowning at me. I can guess what he's thinking: *I've let Nick down again*. I can't bear his disapproval. If he hasn't come here to help, I want him to go. It also occurs to me that he might not have any right to be here, given that we're separated.

I'm about to ask if that's the case when I notice DCI Maxwell watching Craig too, while DS Clarke's serious brown eyes are still fixed on me. Suddenly it dawns on me that we'll *all* be under scrutiny. A child has disappeared overnight; the detectives' sympathy will no doubt be tempered by suspicion. *A risk assessment*, DCI Maxwell said. That means investigating if someone close to Nick has hurt him, I think nervously.

'Nick was a bit quiet – last night on the phone,' I say, wishing I'd pressed him harder to say if something was wrong.

'Quiet as in tired? Or grumpy?' DCI Maxwell smiles kindly.

'Kids can do that, hey? My two have definitely perfected the art of the cold shoulder when it suits them.'

'We're very close,' I say firmly. 'Nick's been a bit thoughtful lately. But then he's just started a new school and, well, he got badly picked on at his last one. Maybe last night ...' My eyes automatically flick to Jason. 'Maybe something was said that drove him out.'

'Mr Brookes told us what happened last year. It must have been tough for you, too.'

'Yes. Yes, it was. Very.' I glance at Craig again, remembering the part he played in that. He doesn't take his eyes off the detectives. I turn to look at Beth, but she busies herself gathering cups. They had coffee before I arrived, I realise: *coffee and a chat about how I mollycoddle Nick?* I lingered too long when I dropped him off; I arrived too early to collect him. A *clingy, over-protective mum.*

I suddenly realise why DCI Maxwell has only turned up to introduce himself, before handing the investigation over to his more junior colleague. This isn't a crime scene, as far as he is concerned; he doesn't believe any offence has been committed other than a slightly neurotic mother smothering her son so much that he had to get away. Anger bubbles up as I turn to him. 'You think Nick has run away from *me*, don't you?'

'Puberty's a tough time.' DCI Maxwell shrugs off his coat before coming to sit next to me at Beth's kitchen table. 'Body changes. Family relationships. Friends. Homework and exams. These days you can throw social media into the mix. That adds up to any number of reasons Nick might have decided to take off. I'm not saying that's what happened.' He holds up his hands, as if anticipating my objections. 'We just have to consider all the possibilities.'

'Not without telling me. He would have *told* me,' I say again, even as a voice in my head reminds me how little Nick has told me lately, about anything. 'Unless he can't. I've phoned and phoned him. Someone might be stopping him picking up.'

'I'm absolutely not dismissing that possibility.'

'Honestly?' I appreciate his discretion in suggesting we *have a quiet chat in the kitchen*, but I still feel impatient with the detective's phlegmatic calm.

'I give you my word on it. But there are no signs of a break-in. Nothing to suggest an abduction. Our FSIs – forensic scene investigators,' he clarifies, 'will confirm that, of course. I'm just saying we need to keep an open mind at this stage. Teenagers can and do go missing for perfectly innocent reasons sometimes. Take last month. Sixteen-year-old girl in Teddington told her mum she was going shopping. Didn't come home all night. Parents called the police. Twelve hours later, daughter turns up saying she'd gone clubbing instead.'

'Nick's not a teenager.' I dig my fingernails into my palms. 'He doesn't go shopping. Or clubbing. He's not on Facebook. He's only twelve, for God's sake.'

'Yes. And it's a tricky age. Look, I promise I'm not ruling *anything* out. But family issues do tend to be the best starting point.'

'Nick was fine when I dropped him off. Excited about the sleepover. Happy to see his new friends. I can't believe they have nothing – absolutely *nothing* – to say about last night.'

'Maybe not to us. But we've got specialist officers trained to interview children. I know you want to grill them, Izzy. I can't let you do that. We have strict protocol with youngsters. I'm sure you appreciate that. But *I* appreciate how frustrating it is that they're saying so little. Given the right questioning, though . . . hopefully they'll open up.'

'They better had,' I snip, thinking of Jason's cagey glances.

'Sleepovers can be fun. In my experience, they can also turn sour. Parents relaxing the rules a bit. High spirits can get out of hand. I'm not saying that's what's happened. I just want to reassure you we don't believe abduction is high up the list of probabilities. I know it's your worst fear. But there's nothing at this point to suggest Nick has been taken.'

'You're sure?' I wish I felt more convinced. 'I mean, so someone might not have broken in. They could have been hanging around outside. And if Nick did go out . . .'

'We'll check everyone local who's previously come across our radar. I'm not discounting the possibility of an opportunist crime. I'm just saying that in these cases we often find there's either a push or a pull. That has to be our starting point. Has Nick run *to* someone or did something, or someone, drive him away?'

'Which brings us back to last night. The sleepover. I promise I won't grill them, but I'm simply not going to be able to go home without those boys telling me *something*.'

'I've got football in half an hour, Mum.' Adrian's is the first voice I hear as we return to the living room. 'Coach said I'll be off the team if I'm late for training again.'

'I'm not sure you'll make it today, sweetheart.' Beth flashes me an apologetic look, and I know her blush is for the awkwardness of mentioning everyday clubs when there is no chance of Nick attending his own. 'Let me give him a call.'

'How about we chat some more, hey, guys?' DCI Maxwell suggests as Beth leaves the room. 'Just while we wait for your parents.' He smiles as three heads nod in unison. 'Nothing heavy. The officers at the station will take official statements from you. But I bet you're all very worried about your friend. I'm sure you can imagine how upset his mum is.'

His head jerks in my direction, and the boys' faces swivel towards me: a line-up of fear, nervousness and the instinctively guilty expressions I know all children have when their behaviour comes under scrutiny. It's impossible to know how much of their reticence is due to the shock of what's happened and how much to remorse – or a guilty conscience.

'You were the only ones there when Nick disappeared.' I try not to sound accusing.

'I slept in the spare room,' Jason points out.

'What time do you reckon you called it a night, son?' DCI Maxwell asks.

'I'm not your son.' The look Jason gives him could start fires.

'Point taken.' The detective holds up his hands. 'But you're Nick's friend. And I know you want to help.'

'Please. Anything you can tell me. *All* of you,' I add, looking at Jason, Samir and Adrian in turn. 'If Nick said anything. Or if one of you had a fight with him.'

'He's my best friend.' Adrian's chin wobbles. 'I told you everything. Honest.'

'Don't worry. You're doing great.' DCI Maxwell gives Adrian a quick thumbs-up, before turning back to Jason, the oldest and clearly the least intimidated by the situation.

'I left this lot to it about half eleven,' he says, speaking to the detective rather than me. 'I had my earphones in so I didn't hear much. I've got no idea how long they stayed up. They were messing about. Just kids' stuff, like,' he scoffs, as if he's above that sort of thing.

'Nick was reading,' Samir offers, dark eyes widening as he speaks for the first time.

'I told them that already, dude.' Adrian punches his arm.

'Thank you, Samir.' I smile at him, recalling Nick referring to him as a quiet boy who 'prefers computers to people'. I can tell he's the least confident talking in front of adults.

'Do you need to take our fingerprints?' Adrian's knees bounce up and down.

'Yes, we will indeed.' DS Clarke jots yet another note on her list. 'If that's OK with you guys? We'll need to identify all the prints found in your mum's house.'

'Let's concentrate on last night for now, OK?' DCI Maxwell crouches down in front of the boys. 'Don't worry about what *we're* doing. Think about what *you* know. The last thing Nick said to you. Anything going on at school. Unfamiliar names he's mentioned.'

'Something must have happened.' I try really hard not to yell.

'Think of it like a puzzle.' The DCI shoots me a discreet warning glance. 'Nick's sleepover. And we need you guys to fill in the pieces.'

'Adrian's sleepover.' Adrian waves a hand. 'It was my sleepover. At my house.'

I almost smile at his eagerness, in contrast to Jason's scowl as he slumps deeper into the sofa cushions. Samir still looks terrified, watching me with tear-filled eyes.

'I hope he's OK, Mrs Brookes,' he says. 'He told me he's got a show soon. He was teaching me a few dance moves. We watched some last night on YouTube.'

'Good on you,' DCI Maxwell approves. 'I'm impressed. Two left feet, I've got,' he adds, rolling his eyes with comic self-deprecation. 'Nick do anything else online?' he asks casually. 'Visit any chat rooms, log into group video apps? FaceTime or WhatsApp anyone?'

'He hasn't got a smartphone.' Jason swipes the screen of his own iPhone. 'Ade refused to lend him his.'

'I got it for my birthday,' Adrian protests, pouting.

'Yeah. And don't we know it.'

'OK, boys, let's keep our eyes on the ball.' The detective claps his hands together, extinguishing the spat before it flares into a fight. 'You're all tired. I suggest we take a break.' He straightens up. 'But I want you to put your thinking caps on, right? Your parents are on their way.' He turns to DS Clarke.

'Should be here any moment,' she confirms, checking her watch.

'So, this is the plan. When they arrive, I'll go with you guys down to the station. I'll introduce you to our specialist officers. They'll talk to you in more detail. In the meantime, Sarah – DS Clarke – will head over to your house with you, Izzy. OK?'

'I'd like your husband to join us too.' DS Clarke finally tucks away her notebook.

'Ex-husband,' I say under my breath.

'Of course. No problem.' Craig comes to stand next to me. 'I know the first few hours are crucial after a child goes missing. Anything and everything we can do to help, we will.' He rests his arm across my shoulders. 'Nick's our boy. We just want him back.'

NINE

'We need to let the police do their job, Isobel. Chasing round the streets is going to help no one. Least of all Nick.' Craig draws me into the living room, guiding me towards the sofa, at the same time unhooking the car keys from my hand and putting them on the coffee table.

'I have to do *something*.' Reluctantly, I sit down on the red leather chesterfield that, along with two matching armchairs, was the first piece of furniture Craig bought for our new home, I remember incongruously. 'You heard what the detective was saying. I'm sure he thinks Nick's run off in a sulk. Either that or I've driven him away.'

'No one thinks that.' Craig sits next to me, looping his arm around me.

'I wish I had your confidence,' I say, edging away from him.

'Look, please don't get the hump with me. I know we've had our differences, but we need to pull together now. For Nick's sake. The DCI's pretty laidback, sure. But he's taking this seriously. He has to. Don't forget he'll have been in this situation before. We haven't.'

'You mean he's seen it, done it, and now he's just going through the motions.' I'm still too wound up to let go of my impatience with DCI Maxwell. 'Thank God for DS Clarke. At least she seems determined to find answers.'

'She was certainly very thorough in her questioning,' Craig says drily.

I can tell he's still raw too, even though he hides it far better than I do. The younger detective's quiet manner belied the probing intensity of her questioning after she returned home with us. While officers searched the house from top to bottom, DS Clarke sat with us in the kitchen, firing off questions and taking yet more notes until I know both Craig and I started to feel uncomfortably like we were the ones under investigation.

While I was happy to spill out anything and everything that might help, I could see Craig's feathers were ruffled at being grilled about his relationship with Nick, our separation – and his movements last night. Eventually, he plonked the keys to his flat on the table, swept them towards DS Clarke and said it might be quicker and easier if she simply searched it.

'I just hope we've convinced her that the answers don't lie *here*. The truth is out *there*. Somewhere.' I stare longingly again at my car keys.

'I know it's frustrating,' Craig acknowledges, following my gaze. 'But I still think the police are right. It makes far more sense for you to stay here. In case Nick does come back. And I'm sure he will, once he's had time to think.'

'So you keep saying. But what if he's had an accident? Nick always has his head in the clouds. He *never* looks before he crosses the road. What if he's been kidnapped?' I stand up and stride to the window, feeling frustrated and more terrified with each passing minute.

'Try not to torment yourself, Isobel. I know it's easier said than done, but it won't help. We need to stay positive. The detective said they've phoned all the local hospitals, remember?'

'But what if he just hasn't been found yet?' I watch Craig wander over to the fireplace, propping an elbow on the mahogany mantelpiece as he picks up a framed photo of Nick. I feel baffled and irritated that he can remain so calm.

'I love this shot of him,' he muses, looking over his shoulder at me. 'Which photo did you give the police, out of interest?'

'DS Clarke chose it, actually. A snap I took of him at Christmas.'

'Oh. I see.' He frowns. Photography is Craig's hobby, and I sense he's a little peeved that one of his own pictures wasn't selected.

'It was the most recent one,' I explain, not wanting to get into petty point-scoring. 'And Nick was wearing his green hoodie in it. The same one he had on last night.'

'Ah, right. Good thinking.' He dusts the frame and puts it back.

'I got him it for Christmas.' Immediately I picture Nick's grin as he unwrapped the orange Nikes he'd coveted for months. 'And the trainers he had on. The parka he left behind.'

'It is odd he didn't take his coat, I'll give you that. If he *has* just gone off in a huff, I mean. It's freezing out there.' He tugs at the shirt collar beneath his grey cashmere sweater. 'Actually, it's not much warmer in here. Is that boiler playing up again?'

'I think it's finally packed in.' Remembering that I'd booked Arthur to come over, I glance at the carriage clock on the sideboard. It's past lunchtime; *Nick will be starving.*

I wonder if he has any money on him to buy food. I didn't give him any, and he doesn't have a bank card yet. He has pocket money, though, and DS Clarke said they'll be checking local cafés, along with CCTV at garages, supermarkets – anywhere he might have been caught on camera. The train station? My heart races at the thought of Nick on the Tube. He's claustrophobic. What if he has a panic attack? Where would he even be *going*?

'I'll take a look.' Craig pushes his glasses up his nose in a familiar gesture as he strides towards the living-room door. 'Give me something to do while we wait.'

'It's OK. I've got a plumber coming. In fact, there's really no need for you to hang around, Craig. I'll call you if there's any news. You may as well—'

'Pressure gauge probably just needs resetting. I can do that, if you like. Save you some cash too. Yes?'

'Right.' He has a point: paying Arthur's call-out charge will mean I won't be able to treat Nick at half-term. *If he's home by then.* 'OK. Thanks,' I say absently, distracted by the thought that Nick might *never* come home; that the photo I gave the police might join the legion of forgotten faces staring out from 'missing' posters across cities everywhere.

I remember Nick asking about them at the airport three years ago. We were on our first family holiday, and Craig was in a buoyant mood. Rather flippantly he quipped that they'd probably all decided to start a new life and found it too hard to say goodbye to their loved ones. I was cross because Nick had never known his own father and I didn't want him thinking Alex hadn't wanted to say goodbye to *him*. Just as Craig didn't when he left . . .

DS Clarke asked me who I thought Nick blamed for the break-up. I couldn't answer, and I can't stop thinking about it. He woke up one morning to find his stepdad gone, and while I can understand him being angry with Craig about that, it happened a year ago. Maybe it *is* me he's angry with, after all: not for smothering him but for disrupting our family home and, as far as he was concerned, driving Craig away. Perhaps he wants to teach me how it feels to be abandoned in the middle of the night . . .

As I finally showed the detectives out, DS Clarke asked me to give it some thought. In the meantime, she would speak to Nick's teachers, tell them what's happened and solicit any insights they might be able to offer. I felt dreadful that I could only remember the name of one of them: Nick's form tutor, Mr Newton. It brought home to me again how much I've lost touch with my son. I've sensed something preoccupying Nick, but I wanted to give him space to work it through himself. The irony is horrific; the guilt is beyond bearing.

'Why don't you give me the number?' Craig says quietly, watching me. 'I'll call and cancel. Save you the hassle.'

'Sorry?'

'The plumber, Isobel.' He reaches into his back pocket and takes out his phone.

'Oh. No, it's fine. I can do it.'

'It's a shame Nick doesn't have a smartphone. We could have traced him in seconds.'

'What? Oh God, you're right.' That must be why DS Clarke wrote down the brand of Nick's phone as well as his number, I think, watching Craig tap the passcode into his Blackberry. 'I just got him a basic one. For emergencies.' *Like this. Except he hasn't called me.* 'Damn. I thought anything fancy would make him a target. And I was worried about more bullying. Group-chat cliques. That kind of thing. Can't the police still track it?'

'Not easily. Not if it's turned off. But what I meant is a tracker app. See?' He holds up his phone to show me the screen.

'What's that wiggly line?' I cross the room quickly, curious to get a closer look.

'That's you, Isobel. This morning. That's the route you took.'

My eyes follow his finger across the map, tracing the line zigzagging between my road and Beth's, then my old flat, then back to Beth's, and suddenly I remember my surprise at seeing Craig in her living room, before I had even phoned to tell him Nick was missing.

'*Chasing round the streets.* That's what you meant, isn't it? Not me driving around looking for Nick. You meant earlier. This morning. That's how you knew where I was, isn't it? You were *following* me.'

His eyebrows arch. 'You're not serious.' His dark brows crinkle into a frown when I don't reply. 'You are, aren't you? *No*, Isobel. I wasn't following you.'

'Then why have you got this ... this *stalker* app?' I glare at his phone.

'Because it's a standard function on most smartphones. You've got it on yours.'

'What?'

'Check it and see.'

'Oh. Right.' I bite my lip as I take out my phone and see a similar icon on the screen, slightly different from the one Craig has on his, but nevertheless recognisable as some kind of tracking facility. I wish I'd known about it; I wish I'd had the foresight to ensure Nick had a phone with the same feature. 'Sorry.' I feel deflated and a little stupid. 'I had no idea.'

'It's fine,' he says with a small sigh. 'Look, I know you don't bother much with all that tech stuff. I don't usually. I'd forgotten I'd even set it up to track your phone. In case you lost it,' he explains quickly. 'I haven't looked at it in months. It only caught my eye this morning because it kept pinging. You were all over the place. I was concerned.'

'So you decided to show up at a complete stranger's house and ask if your ex-wife was in trouble?' I'm too rattled to drop the point entirely.

Craig shakes his head. 'No,' he says patiently. 'That's not how it was. I was worried about Nick, that's all. I mean, of course I was concerned about you too. But you'd mentioned Nick having a sleepover at a mate's house. I thought ...'

'You thought *what*? That you'd check out where I let him spend the night? Make sure it was a suitable home, with the right kind of people? When are you going to stop questioning every decision I make about Nick?' I draw myself up to my full height, still a foot shorter than Craig. 'When are you going to accept that he's not your son?'

61

TEN

'I'm sorry. That wasn't fair.' I lean my elbows on the kitchen table, gripping my hands together to stop them shaking. 'I'm just so worried.'

'Sure. I know.' Craig doesn't look up, concentrating on pouring milk into two mugs.

It was his suggestion that we move into the kitchen, to calm things down with a hot drink. Still bristling, I try not to feel irritated by how he's making himself at home. Grudgingly, I admit that he's right: we need to pull together. It won't help Nick if I'm at loggerheads with his stepdad. The trouble is, in taking our fractured relationship out of the box again, the sharp edges are slicing twice as deep.

'I know how much you care about Nick,' I force myself to admit.

'I'm not going to lie. I wasn't happy about the sleepover.'

'No kidding,' I huff before I can stop myself.

'I just wanted to make sure Nick was OK. Believe it or not, that's all I've *ever* wanted. To take care of him. And you.' Craig sets a mug of coffee in front of me, hovering at my side as though waiting for me to invite him to sit down.

'Craig, don't. Please. Now really isn't the right time.'

'On the contrary, I think it's *exactly* the right time. I shouldn't have left.'

I give him a knowing look. 'Why, because if you hadn't Nick might still be here?'

'No, that's not what I meant. It's just ... what happened last year ... I tried so hard to look after Nick. I felt I'd let him down, and I couldn't deal with it. So I blamed you instead. It was unforgivable. I'm not proud of it. I'm not proud of how I handled *anything* back then. Or the fact that I've been too stubborn to tell you this until now. I've got no excuse. I'm sorry.'

His eyes flick around the kitchen, but I sense he's looking beyond the heavy pine furniture, dated seventies Formica cabinets and garish floral tiles we never got around to updating, and I know we're both remembering that morning. Ironically, Craig and I were in exactly the same positions as now, only we were both dressed for work: I was sitting at the table transcribing Nick's new-year dance timetable from my phone to the kitchen calendar, while Craig was sipping coffee before heading out to a meeting ...

'I won't take the short cut, Mum. I'll stick to the main roads.'

Nick leaned on my shoulder as he reached over to grab a piece of toast from my plate. I caught the scent of citric muskiness and smiled as I remembered Craig promising to show him how to shave when he was older. He must have been trying on his stepdad's aftershave, I thought, feeling a pang at how fast he was growing up.

'I'm not sure, darling,' I said slowly.

'You said you wanted me to get used to doing it before secondary school. That's only, like, in September.'

'True. And I'm glad you want to try.' I chuckled as I spotted jam at one corner of his mouth, toothpaste at the other. I could never get over the contrast between Nick's mesmerising poise on stage and his dreamy absentmindedness off it.

His chin was definitely up this morning, though. He looked determined, *defiant* almost, and I felt happy that the reviews of his show we'd spent the weekend sticking into a scrapbook must have given him a boost. I was so proud of him, and I really wanted to encourage that budding self-confidence. But when we'd talked about him walking to school alone, I'd had the summer term in mind, not a bleak, frozen day in January.

'So? Can I?' Nick wheedled, sashaying towards the kitchen door.

He lives in his head, and it's full of dance, I thought, worrying again about him being picked on if he walked to school alone. 'It's actually your dad's turn today, love,' I reminded him. 'You always enjoy your chats with him, don't you?'

'I guess.' Nick's head dipped as he looked away.

'You guess?' I raised my eyebrows. 'But—'

'I've got an early meeting. You'll have to walk him,' Craig cut in, setting his coffee down on the worktop and unhooking his coat from the back of the kitchen door.

'I can, of course,' I said, still watching Nick, trying to read what was going on in his head. 'I'm just wondering, though . . . ' I hesitated, knowing Craig probably wasn't going to like my suggestion. His solution for avoiding the bullies was simply to keep Nick apart from other kids. Only I knew Nick was being teased about that too: *Loner! Weirdo!* He couldn't spend his life running away, and I couldn't hold his hand for ever.

'Wondering . . . ?' Craig checked his Rolex. 'Sweetheart, I need to get the early train.'

'I could walk a few paces behind Nick. That's all I was thinking. He could go on ahead, but I could be there. Keeping an eye out.'

'I don't want him walking alone. He's not up to it.'

'He's not helpless,' I said, taken aback by his dismissiveness.

I wondered if something had happened. Usually, Craig loved hanging out with Nick, and Nick *did* always say how it helped to talk things over with his stepdad. I felt the same. While I tended to be driven by emotion, Craig operated purely on logic, so much so that I'd often wondered if, as a step-parent, he was able to view problems without the cloudy filter of paternal emotion. Generally, I saw that as a good thing. Occasionally, though, he came across as dogmatic. This was one of those times.

'Look, I've got to go,' he said, checking his watch again. 'I'll be late for my meeting. Just walk him, would you?'

'I have a say in this too.' I glanced between Craig and Nick, sure I must be missing something. 'It's only a few streets away. Other kids come from miles—'

'I said *no*, Isobel.'

'You don't get the final say in every decision, you know.' I didn't necessarily disagree with what he was saying, and I certainly hadn't made up my mind to let Nick walk alone, but I was shocked by Craig's uncharacteristic sharpness.

It was also the first time Nick had made a big deal about walking to school by himself. I wanted to understand *why*; I didn't want to stamp on his burgeoning confidence. Only when I looked up, he'd gone. A second later, I heard the front door slam shut.

I don't need Craig to remind me that I should have stopped him, but I can't change that now. All that concerns me is what happened at the sleepover, and what might have made Nick sneak out in the middle of the night without saying a word to anyone.

I shiver, reaching for my coat on the back of the chair and pulling it on. But as I thrust my hands into the pockets, I catch the sharp corner of the envelope I'd forgotten about, and the hairs on the back of my neck start to prickle. Yesterday, I received Craig's letter asking to discuss joint custody arrangements. Today, Nick

65

has vanished. The timing suddenly strikes me as more than a coincidence.

'This app. It helped you track me to Beth's house. Then what?' I have to force myself to remain in my seat – not to leap across the kitchen, grab hold of Craig and try to shake the truth out of him.

'I told you, that's not quite how it was.' He finishes his coffee and carries the mug to the sink, meticulously washing it then setting it on the drainer to dry. 'Sure, I tracked you to Beth's house. But I only realised there was a problem when Jason texted me.'

'*Jason* texted you?' I stare at him in astonishment. 'Why would he do that?'

'Why not? Our families may have drifted apart, but we always got on. He was worried about Nick. He's got my number. It was good of him to let me know, I think.'

'He didn't seem that bothered to me. And he never mentioned that he'd sent you a text.'

'He's a teenager, Isobel. Kids his age don't say much at the best of times.'

'Fine.' He's probably right, I concede. In fact, it's the most frustrating thing about this whole situation: persuading the three boys to talk. 'So you introduced yourself. And the police invited you in. Questioned you. Is *that* how it was?'

'Pretty much.'

'And by the time I got there, you'd told them everything. About Nick. Me. Us.' I recall DS Clarke's copious notes, understanding now why she'd written so many before I had even arrived. Even if I accept Craig's explanation about the tracker app, and that he wasn't deliberately following me, there's no doubt in my mind that he seized the opportunity to speak to the police before me ... *To lay the foundations of justification for what he'd done?*

My head swims as a terrible suspicion takes hold: that Nick hasn't disappeared; he's been taken. By Craig. To get back at me for keeping Nick from him, and to pave the way for his joint-custody claim: by proving I'm not a diligent enough parent.

He accused me of it a year ago, and he made it abundantly clear that he disapproved of the sleepover. Did he put the phone down after our fractious call and come up with a rash plan to prove his point? Nick's mood was so odd when I spoke to him last night. I can't help wondering if Craig contacted him, blamed me for keeping them apart, and persuaded Nick to come to him . . . And if so, what the hell has he done with my son?

'I'm not sure I get where you're going with this,' Craig says, frowning as he crosses the kitchen and pulls out a chair, sitting down next to me at the table. 'Yes, I spoke to the police. I talked to them about last year. The incident at the school gate. Our separation.' He raises his eyebrows. 'So?'

'You make it sound like it was a mutual decision.' I glare at him. 'You left me, Craig. You left Nick. You made a judgement about my parenting and you walked out.'

'And like I said, I'm sorry. Extremely.' He leans his elbows on the table, rubbing his hands wearily over his face. 'Please, don't let that muddy the waters now. We both just want what's best for Nick, don't we? We might have our different methods, but—'

'And your methods are always right, aren't they?'

'Sorry?'

'No you're not.' I feel a lump in my throat as I remember Nick saying the same thing to me yesterday morning. 'You're not sorry at all. Nick is out there, *somewhere*, and you don't seem stressed at all. In fact, you seem . . .'

'What? Like I'm remaining calm? Rational?' He shakes his head. 'That's because not a single disaster I've ever dealt with in my career has been solved by panicking.'

'This isn't business, Craig. It's personal. It's about *my son*.'

'And mine. My *special*-son,' he insists, using the term he's always preferred to stepson. 'I care about him too, Isobel. And I like to think I know what's best for him.'

'You'd love to prove that, wouldn't you?' My heart is hammering, but the sight of Nick's school backpack in its usual place against the kitchen dresser gives me strength. If Craig is hiding my little boy, I won't rest until I've found him.

'Look, I know you're upset,' he pacifies. 'We both are. But it's going to achieve precisely nothing taking our stress out on each other. I'm really sorry about my letter. In hindsight, it was ill-judged.' His mouth twists. 'I was just trying to get your attention, I suppose.'

'By demanding custody of my son.'

'Proposing a discussion for *joint* custody.' He links his hands together, as if to illustrate the point. 'I miss our family. I want us to be together again. All three of us.'

'I think you're missing the point. There aren't three of us right now. There's just *us*. And I want you to stop playing games and tell me the truth. Is this some kind of set-up?'

'What?'

'Nick disappearing. Is it some sort of horrible ruse to prove I'm a bad mother? Oh, I know you had nothing to do with the sleepover. But you did know about it. And you didn't approve. As you didn't approve a year ago. You're the parenting expert, aren't you – the one who knows what's best for Nick. Getting him away from *me*, in other words.'

'I have absolutely no idea what you're talking about.'

'Are you sure, Craig?' I give him a direct stare, trying to read his thoughts, trying to let him know that I won't be fobbed off. 'Because it's not too late to own up. I won't press charges. I'll tell the police we just had an argument that got out of hand. Please, if you've got Nick . . . Please, we can talk. Just give him back to me.'

'I can't believe you'd even think that.' He leans forward, taking

68

hold of my hands and gripping them tightly. 'I'd *never* hurt Nick. He's my son. Fine. *Step*son. But I love him like he's my own flesh and blood. Why do you have to keep pushing me away?'

'I don't. I . . .' Jerking my hands away, I stare at Craig's handsome face, the tell-tale twitch of a muscle in his cheek. He looks devastated, and I wonder if I've just made the most horrendous misjudgement.

'You said it yourself to the police. You didn't change Nick's name when we got married. Why not, Isobel? Was I such a terrible father to him? Sweetheart, we're on the same side,' he continues before I can answer. 'I hate that something like this has brought us together again. But that's exactly where we belong. *Together*. I was wrong to leave. I'm not too proud to admit my mistakes. I want to put them right.'

ELEVEN

I need space to think. Thankfully, Craig agrees and doesn't make a fuss when I quickly show him out, promising to call him later. As soon as he's gone, I dash upstairs to Nick's bedroom, throwing myself on to his bed and pressing my face into the pillow that still smells of him.

For a fleeting moment, I feel furious with him for not being here. 'Where *are* you, Nick?' I pummel the soft bedclothes with my fists, needing some release, finding no relief. Deciding to phone DS Clarke for an update, I fumble in my pocket for the card she left me. Startled when she answers on the first ring, I blurt out a rather garbled explanation of the angry exchange I've just had with Craig.

Magically, the detective manages to calm me down, reassuring me that they've already searched his flat – as he himself suggested they do. His next-door neighbour in the apartment block also confirmed that he saw Craig shortly after midnight last night, when he asked him to move his car so that he had space to park his own. He remembered it particularly because he'd admired Craig's new Mercedes, and they'd had a chat about it.

'His alibi checks out, Izzy.'

'God, I'll be suspecting the plumber next. I'm such an idiot.'

'No, you're a *mum*,' DS Clarke reassures me briskly. 'You wouldn't be human if you weren't questioning everyone around you. Who'd be the first person I'd suspect if my son went missing? My ex-husband. Not that I have one. Or a son. But you take my point.'

'I do.' I smile tearfully, glad I phoned her. The young detective's manner is a little intense, but I realise I'm going to need her straight talking to keep me grounded over the coming hours ... *days*? I think fearfully. Craig always used to caution me about the pitfalls of being led by my heart, not my head; I suspect I've just proved his point. *Again*.

'You believed your son was safe,' DS Clarke continues. 'Your trust was broken. It makes you wary. Suspicious. I get that. And if Craig is any sort of husband, ex or otherwise, I'm sure he will too. OK?'

'OK,' I echo uncertainly. I'm not so sure, but I will phone Craig later, I decide. I'm shocked he could even talk about us being a family again, but perhaps that's his way of coping with the stress of the situation. We've both made mistakes, and as he said: we need to put our differences aside and work together to find Nick. 'Yes, you're right,' I say quietly to the detective. 'I'm just feeling a bit ...'

'I know. It's tough. Don't beat yourself up too much. Emotions are bound to be running high. For you *and* Craig. Let's chat more when I come over, OK? I'll be with you in about half an hour. A suggestion came up at our team brief. I need to talk it over with you.'

'What is it?' I'll do anything – go anywhere; sitting at home waiting while the police carry out their searches is driving me mad.

'The boss thinks going public might help. I know you said you'd rather keep Nick's name out of the news, but—'

'Go on TV, you mean?' I grip the phone tighter.

'It can help. Press releases have gone out now. Alerts across social media. Bulletins with Nick's photo, descriptions of what he was wearing, when and where he disappeared. A dedicated phone line has been set up. But I think DCI Maxwell is right. We need to do more to get Nick on the public's radar. I spoke to Nick's doctor. We're all worried about his asthma. Time is of the essence here. A media appeal could be life— could be crucial.'

She was about to say life-saving. 'I see.' I try to swallow, but my mouth is too dry.

'Don't worry, I'll be right there with you. I know how hard this is. We all want to bring your boy home, Izzy. To do that we need as many eyes as possible looking for him.'

I stand up and drift to the bedroom window, looking out at gardens stretching into the distance. I've lived in this area all my life; it's as familiar to me as the back of my hand – *or my son's face.* But the world suddenly feels bigger, full of hidden corners and dangerous possibilities.

'OK. Yes, I can see that.' I bite my lip to fight off yet more tears. I haven't cried so much since this time last year. I felt sure, then, that I must have used up all my bad luck. I was wrong: lightning can strike twice.

'There's still some time today. We'll have to draw a line for the night at some point, of course. But the guys are out there knocking on doors. We've got an alert out at bus and train stations. We found Nick's passport in his room, so we're not targeting airports as yet. For now, we're focusing on the local angle. Talking to Beth's neighbours, local residents. Anyone and everyone Nick knows, and who might know him.'

'And if no one has seen anything?' I grip the phone even tighter.

'We keep looking. Then we look again. Tomorrow afternoon we'll have divers trawl the Thames from Richmond to

Twickenham. Just to rule it out,' the detective adds, when I gasp in shock. 'You mentioned during our initial interview that Nick calls the river one of his "happy" places. Accidents can happen.' She pauses. 'I won't leave any stone unturned, Izzy. I promise.'

'Thank you,' I manage to say, feeling overwhelmed by the thought of my little boy at the centre of such a vast operation. It makes him seem so small. So very lost. *As am I.*

Nick's bedroom, in stark contrast, suddenly feels huge – and strangely empty, even though only one thing is missing: his laptop. I hadn't realised how large its presence loomed; how accustomed I am to seeing Nick always behind it. Shock rippled through me earlier when DS Clarke said the officers searching our house needed to take it away: to examine Nick's internet activity and liaise with child protection agencies. I immediately knew what she meant: specialists in tracking down predators who use the internet to groom children . . .

Feeling myself starting to slip into another pit of horrific imaginings, I jump when the doorbell rings. It can't be DS Clarke already; I've only just got off the phone with her. Maybe it's Craig returning to pick up where we left off . . . Heart racing, I hurry downstairs, steeling myself to apologise to him for letting my imagination run away with me.

It's Arthur. I'd forgotten all about cancelling his appointment. Thankful for once that the taciturn plumber doesn't do small talk, I leave him to fix the boiler and hurry back to Nick's room, eager to hunt through his things and search for any clues the police might possibly have missed. I half hope I might even find a note . . .

There's nothing. All I unearth as I root through the jumbled assortment of one-armed superheroes and Lego figures is the ghost of Nick's childhood. Tiny bubbles of memory float up along with each translucent dust mote, engulfing me with the unique perfume of the past. I breathe it in, gripped by painful nostalgia as I lie down on the bed once more, turning to stare at the wall where Nick has doodled his favourite cartoon characters.

Closing my eyes, I remember the low murmur of his imaginary play, realising that it's always been so present in my consciousness, I can't recall exactly when it fell silent. Nick's invented characters were as real to me as they were to him. They *were* him, each voice reflecting part of who he was, his hopes and worries projected on to little plastic figures. Now those toys have been packed away, abandoned in favour of the more powerful lure of the internet; a big part of my connection with Nick is buried along with them, I reflect sadly.

'Dammit. I should have just bought him a diary,' I mutter, and I'm about to start searching his desk again when the doorbell rings for the second time.

TWELVE

'Honestly, please say if I'm intruding, Mrs Brookes.' Nick's usually laidback young form tutor is tense and solemn-faced, his blue eyes clouded with concern. 'I wasn't sure if now was the right time. It's just that I was out for a walk, and passing near here, so I thought . . .'

'Mr Newton. No, I'm glad you're here. I was expecting the police, but . . . Please. Come in.' I push back my tangled hair and tug half-heartedly at the bottom of my jumper, pulling it down over my jeans. I'm sure I must look a state; I can't bring myself to care. 'And it's Izzy.'

'Thanks, Izzy. Likewise, please call me Sean.' Stepping into the porch, he offers a gentle handshake. 'OK to leave this here?' His eyes widen anxiously as he props a skateboard against the wall, before kicking off muddy trainers and lining them up neatly on the doormat.

'Of course.' I smile, touched by his youthful politeness.

As I close the front door behind him, I notice bumper-to-bumper cars on the road. DS Clarke said on the phone that she'd be here in half an hour. She must be stuck in traffic, I realise. Or perhaps still caught up phoning round Nick's teachers . . . It's kind of Mr Newton – Sean – to come straight here after speaking to her. I know he's Nick's favourite teacher, though, and his prompt visit shows how much he cares about Nick in return.

'I won't stay long,' he says, following me into the living room.

'Please, it's fine.' Any company is better than being alone with my fears. 'Can I get you a coffee?'

'No, don't worry. But thanks. I just wanted to check you're OK. Apart from *not* being OK, obviously. Sorry. That sounded idiotic.' He screws up his face as he perches on the leather armchair nearest the fireplace. *Craig's chair*, I try not to think. 'You must be so worried.'

'Going out of my mind,' I tell him honestly, curling my legs up on the chesterfield. 'The police told me to stay here in case Nick comes back. I know they're right, but I want to be out there looking too. And questioning the boys. Not that they're saying much.'

'About the sleepover, you mean? *Something* must have gone on, right? I mean, Nick simply isn't the kind of kid who wanders off for no reason. What have the other boys said? Have they given you *any* idea what happened last night?'

'Barely anything.'

'I'm not surprised about Adrian or Sammy, to be fair. They wouldn't say boo to a goose. As for Jason, well, he doesn't display quite the same reticence,' he says tactfully.

'That's one way of putting it.' I recall Jason making Nick watch him play games on the Xbox for two hours straight without letting him take a single turn.

'I've tried to channel his energy into drama. I won't repeat where he told me to go.' Sean pulls a grimace, then glances up at Nick's photos on the mantelpiece. 'I guess Nick's the performer. He's got a show coming up, hasn't he?' He turns back to me with an expectant look. 'You don't think he might have been feeling the pressure, do you?'

'The police asked me that too. But Nick lives for his dance. Almost every day he says he can't wait to get back on stage. Unless he's just been putting on an act.' I frown, remembering Craig saying that boys of Nick's age don't usually confide in their mums. 'I was hoping he might have let something slip to his new friends. But they've said nothing.'

'Nothing at all? Wow. I'm not surprised you're going out of your mind. The police will keep trying, though?'

'I'm not sure. I guess there're only so many times they can listen to the same answer. All three just keep saying the same thing: there was no fight, nothing unusual. Nick was there. Then he was gone.'

'Do you believe them?'

'No.' It's only as I speak the denial aloud that I realise the stark truth of it. 'I just get the feeling they're hiding something, you know? I can't believe they didn't hear Nick go. Or have any idea why he left. Even if they don't know where he went. It's like they've made some kind of *pact*, or something.'

'A pact of silence, you mean? I suppose it's possible. Kids sometimes have strange codes of honour. Perhaps they think they're protecting Nick by keeping quiet.'

'More like protecting themselves.' I take a deep breath. 'Sorry. That probably sounds harsh. I don't mean to be. It's just that Nick hasn't had much luck with friendships. I thought these boys were different. I really did. But now . . .'

'Totally understood.' Sean nods vigorously. 'Especially after what happened last year. Nick getting beaten up, and everything.'

'A year ago yesterday.' I look at him in surprise, trying to recall when I'd told him about that. 'I think it might have been playing on his mind, too. He looked pretty thoughtful right before I dropped him off for the sleepover.'

'He chatted to me about it as well. Little horrors. It's no wonder Nick's still having nightmares about it.'

'He told you that?' *I wish he'd told me.*

'Only in passing. He hung around for a bit after our book group yesterday. I did tell the police officer all this on the phone,' he says anxiously, as though I might think he's withheld information. 'DS Clarke, I think her name was.'

'Yes. She's leading the investigation.' I feel a stab of hurt that Nick has opened up to this young man about feelings he no longer shares with me, then remind myself that it's good he's at least found someone he trusts to talk to. 'You say he mentioned the bullies yesterday. Was he *worrying* about them? Or other stuff? Did he say anything else?'

Sean sits back in the armchair, looking thoughtful for a moment. 'You know, looking back, I think he might have wanted to. But no, he didn't. Nothing major, anyway. He said something about people being like sheep. Doing what everyone else does. Never thinking for themselves. I'm afraid I assumed he was still talking about the bullies.'

'It does sound like it.'

'That's the horrible thing about bullying. Even when it stops, it never leaves you.'

'Exactly. And if Nick was picked on last night, it could have brought it all back. Even a bit of teasing from one of the boys might have tipped him over the edge. Don't you think?'

'One of them. Let's be straight. We're talking about Jason, right?'

Sean flicks back his hair, and the floppy blond fringe suddenly reminds me of Nick. I think of the funky trainers and psychedelic skateboard in the porch, and reflect that it's little surprise Mr Newton gets on so well with his pupils. He's trendy and easy-going, and he can't be much older than some of them. Jason may have told him *where to go*, but he clearly likes him enough to stay in the book club. Maybe Sean feels like a big brother to him; I know how much he's always wanted one . . .

Katie and I first met at a school fundraiser, but what really bonded us was discovering we'd both been teenage mums. Her baby had tragically died, and I used to feel sorry for Jason when he pretended his big brother was away in the army with his dad. I thought spending time with Nick would soften his hard edges, and that Nick might absorb some of Jason's confidence. Only Jason was clearly far more influenced by his father: Nathan is bossy and controlling, and so is his son.

'There's definitely history between Jason and Nick,' I say, without going into detail. 'If he teased Nick, goaded him into running off . . . The other boys are clearly in awe of him. Maybe they're too frightened to tell tales.'

'It takes a brave kid to speak out,' Sean agrees, then suddenly sits forward, frowning. 'Damn. Perhaps that's what Nick meant to do yesterday. Maybe something had happened, and he wanted to tell me about it. I'm so sorry. I should have picked up on it.' He jerks out of the armchair and paces towards the window, hands hooked anxiously behind his head.

'It's not your fault. Really.' There's plenty I'm realising I should have picked up on.

'I do feel bad, though. Nick deliberately stayed on after book group, but I was too busy prepping my next lesson to talk for long.' He crosses the room to sit next to me, his youthful face creased in apology. 'It probably took a lot of guts, too. Nick's a quiet lad, but he's actually braver than he knows. *Dance to your own tune.* That's what I tell all my boys. And it's exactly what Nick does. Quite literally.'

'Thank you. It means a lot to me to hear that.' I rest a tentative hand on his arm, sensing him beating himself up. I know how that feels, and Sean is only young – he can't have been teaching that many years. I also feel a little overwhelmed at the affirmation

I've so rarely heard about Nick. It's exactly how I see him, but I've never heard anyone else speak of him in those terms. 'Thank you for caring about him.'

'I do. Really. You know, teachers meet a lot of kids. Some just pass straight through your classroom. In one door and out the other, as it were. Zero impact on either side. Some you feel a real connection with. Nick's one of those kids. Maybe because I teach drama and he ... God, this is awful.' He rubs his hands over his face. 'If I feel like this, I can only imagine how you ...'

He leans closer, giving me a quick hug, and as I catch a waft of his aftershave it unleashes a memory of Nick a year ago, trying on his stepdad's cologne to feel more grown-up before running off to school – straight into the arms of bullies. I'm hit by a wave of need to hold my son; it's so powerful that for a moment I find myself clinging on to his teacher. 'Sorry,' I say, feeling awkward as I finally manage to pull back.

'No need to apologise. Or thank me. I'm only speaking the truth. You've raised a good kid. I know you're doing it alone, too. Nick always talks very fondly of you.'

'He does? Did he mention me yesterday?' I root inside my jumper for a tissue, using the sleeve itself when I don't find one. Briskly wiping my eyes, I try to pull myself together. 'I'm guessing not. He was probably far too preoccupied with the sleepover.'

'Well, he—'

'No, wait. What am I thinking? I didn't tell him he could go until after school.' Feeling flustered, I think through what DS Clarke told me. I know she's been phoning Nick's teachers to tell them he's missing; I'm not sure if she will have mentioned the exact context, or if the sleepover – the involvement of the other boys – is even a confidential part of the investigation. 'You mentioned the sleepover.' I look anxiously at Sean, hoping I haven't just been carelessly indiscreet. 'The police told you about that, right?'

'Actually, no.' He rolls his eyes. 'Kids and their apps. Every lecture about privacy settings seems to go in one ear and out the other.'

'What? Are you saying someone posted about the sleepover *online*? On—'

'Facebook. The sleepover's pretty much all over it.' He gives me a curious look. 'Not just *someone*, though. Nick posted the pictures himself.'

THIRTEEN

The room seems to tilt. 'You're not serious? You've actually seen photos of last night?' I feel even dizzier as Sean nods. '*Show* me. *Please.*'

'I'm really sorry.' He dips his head, hiding behind his fringe, looking more like a mortified teenager than a teacher as he pulls out a rose-gold iPhone and swipes at the screen. 'I guess I just assumed everyone's on Facebook.'

'No. Not me. I had no idea Nick was, either. I can't believe I didn't *know*.'

'Don't be too hard on yourself,' he says, looking up from his phone. 'Most parents haven't a clue about half the stuff their kids get up to online.'

'But I've set up so many restrictions. For apps, internet sites.' I shake my head, picturing Nick at his desk, on his laptop; I wish I'd never left him alone with it for a second.

'I'm sure you have.' He sighs. 'Kids usually find a way around them, though. Setting rules is like throwing down a gauntlet for most of the pupils I teach.'

'Nick's not a rebel. He's *sensible*. He's—'

'A bright boy. But at his age, all kids are trying to figure out who they are. Or, more importantly, decide who they want to be. Social media lets them do that, you know? Create their own myth. Reinvent themselves. Put out the image they want the world to see. It's page one of the school survival handbook: blag your way into being one of the cool kids.'

The cool kids. That's how Beth referred to the boys. I assumed she was being ironic; I'm so used to people regarding my son as the odd one out. But maybe she wasn't; maybe that's how Nick has presented himself to her – the image he's been trying to cultivate.

I glance surreptitiously at Sean as he looks down at his phone again. I thought Nick was growing his fringe out for his next dance role; now it seems more likely that he was modelling himself on this young, trendy teacher – *reinventing himself* in order to fit in at secondary school. It would only have taken a scathing response from Jason last night – or teasing comments from other kids online – to drive him out again.

'And you're quite sure it was *Nick* who posted the photos?' I say, watching him scroll through a seemingly endless succession of selfies.

'Not just photos. There were a couple of videos, too.'

'*Videos?*' I'm used to Nick being on stage, but a sleepover with friends is private. Filming it feels so invasive; sharing it publicly is the complete opposite of everything I would expect of Nick. 'Isn't he too young to sign up for all these websites, anyway?'

'Probably.' Sean rolls his eyes again. 'But since when did legal age limits ever stop a kid doing something they really want to do? Especially if everyone else is doing it.'

'Peer pressure, you mean. Yes, Nick's had plenty of that. I never thought he'd put himself up for more. Social media. God. It's just another vehicle for bullying, isn't it? One-upmanship. Sorry, I'm not a fan.' Over the years, I've tried my best to shield Nick from other people's comments, rather than inviting them. And I've never felt the need to live my life in a goldfish bowl. Craig felt the same. *Our family, our memories*, he always used to say.

'Me neither. But we have to know the world our kids live in. Know it and adapt to it,' Sean adds, sounding more like a teacher again. 'It's been my book club theme of the month, actually. To reimagine a classic novel to reflect the digital age. Just a ruse to get them reading, really. They'd pick up *War and Peace* if I told them we could relate it to *Fortnite*.'

'I've banned that too,' I say faintly, wondering if being so strict about Nick's online activity has pushed him to secretly rebel after all. I only wanted to protect him; maybe I've put him in a box he's felt compelled to break out of.

'The photos were pretty innocent. Honestly. Just four boys hanging out. Pulling faces at the camera, eating pizza, playing Xbox. Generally clowning around, you know? A typical sleepover, I guess. A bit crazy, but nothing out of the ordinary.'

'They weren't doing anything stupid, were they?' I rack my brains to think what that might be as I watch his fingers continue to swipe across the screen, frustrated now that I can't spot Nick amidst the sea of grinning faces.

'No. Really. If I'd spotted anything worrying, I'd have called their parents. I'm sure they upload worse stuff, of course. Thankfully, I don't get to see it. I only looked at public posts. I'm not friends with any of them. Not in Facebook terms, anyway.' He looks up with a wry smile. 'It's only because of this month's book group theme that I was looking at all. I just did a quick check of the boys' online activity to feed it into our next discussion.'

'And this was on Friday night?' I remember lying in bed wondering how Nick was getting on; it never occurred to me that I could simply log on to my computer and check.

'No, this morning. Ten-ish, I think. I'd just had breakfast, anyway. I did mention the photos to DS Clarke. As soon as she told me Nick was missing. She hadn't seen them.' He continues swiping. 'Which right now doesn't surprise me. I can't seem to find *anything*.'

'Really? That's so frustrating.' I wonder if the boys have changed their settings to private after all. But if the sleepover photos were public long enough for Nick's teacher to see them, who else was looking? Strangers who get a kick out of ogling children? Or maybe the bullies who attacked Nick last year ... And if they were on Facebook last night too, they'd have known *exactly* where to find him. I reach for my phone. 'I need to speak to the police.'

'Of course.' Thankfully, Sean takes the hint and immediately stands up from the sofa, moving swiftly to the living-room door. 'God, I'm so sorry. I came here to help. Instead, I feel like I've dropped a bomb on you. Internet safety is such a minefield.' He sighs. 'And don't get me started on secret apps.'

'Secret apps?' I stare at him in horror as we head into the hall.

'Dummy profiles. A calculator that's really a chat room. That sort of thing. Yeah, scary. I'm forever warning kids about the dangers. Plenty get sucked in, though. Especially if they're feeling lonely or misunderstood, which is pretty much every teenager I've ever met. The internet gives them a form of escape, I guess. A way of pretending to be someone else.'

That sounds exactly like Nick, I think, looking up at dozens of framed photos on the hall walls – shots Craig has taken of Nick on stage. I stop in front of one, staring into his eyes. As always when he's dancing, Nick appears so lost in the part he's playing that he barely looks like himself; he lives and breathes every role until it's like he *becomes* them.

'This book you asked the boys to read,' I say, a thought taking hold as I recall the boys saying that Nick was reading last night.

'They each picked their own, actually.' Sean zips up his hoodie and pulls a beanie hat out of his pocket. 'I get the boys to read their books, post comments on our website. Then we all sit around in the book group and try to guess each title. Nick's posted a few thoughts on his. I haven't figured out yet what he's been reading. Why, what are you thinking?'

'I'm not sure. Just that ... maybe Nick was so engrossed in a character – a story – that he decided to act it out?' I watch Sean's face, trying to gauge from his reaction whether he thinks it's a silly idea. 'The boys said Nick was reading last night. I didn't find a book anywhere. It seems odd that he'd take it with him and not his backpack. Don't you think? Unless he was trying to follow in some character's footsteps.'

'Could be.' Sean wrinkles his nose as he pulls on his beanie, completing the skater-dude look I now see Nick has been emulating. 'Sorry.' He sighs. 'I've been no help at all.'

'No, really, you have,' I tell him honestly. 'It's been good to talk. Thank you.' I shiver as I open the front door. Snow twirls in sparkling drifts from the black sky, and the freezing air steals my breath. I try not to think of Nick out there, struggling to breathe too.

'If it's any help ...'

'Yes?' I stare at the young teacher as he bends to put on his trainers, willing him to produce a rabbit out of a hat.

'I've read some of the stuff Nick's written for this month's book club,' he says, straightening up. 'It might not be the book he was reading last night, of course. But if you were to ask me to guess ...'

'Please.' Any clue might be helpful.

'Well, my sense is that it's a story about a little boy who lost his dad.'

FOURTEEN

'The tech guys are already on it, Izzy. That's why I was late getting over here. I've just been talking to them about the photos. If it's digitally possible to retrieve them, they will.'

DS Clarke slides a mug of tea towards me across the kitchen table, positioning it deliberately next to the plate of toast she made for me after finally arriving, an hour after Sean left. I haven't touched it; I don't have any appetite at all. The emptiness inside me can't be filled by any amount of food.

'I hope so. I know they won't hold all the answers, but I just want … I really need to see them for myself.' I can't stop tormenting myself that those images might be the last I ever see of my son.

'Absolutely. And I'm hopeful we'll retrieve something. Whatever we do online leaves a digital footprint. It rarely disappears completely. Even though some might wish it would.' She pulls a face. 'Plenty of people get caught out by their online history.'

The detective reaches into her suit jacket for her phone, and as she flicks through a bewildering array of social media sites, I catch a glimpse of the Instagram logo. It reminds me of Beth saying that's how she keeps tabs on Adrian. I wonder if she was aware that the sleepover was being broadcast for all the world to see, and how she feels about that. I realise I have no idea, and fresh guilt washes through me that I left my son with a virtual stranger.

I lean closer as DS Clarke loads her own Facebook – photos of her with friends, dressed up in party clothes with cocktails lining the bar behind them, arms around each other and big smiles on their faces. The images are the polar opposite of the smartly dressed young woman sitting next to me, hair neatly scraped back in a ponytail, eyes dark with concern.

Photos only tell part of the story, I think, wondering if Nick's pictures were deliberately staged to show the world he's finally fitting in. Maybe he has, or maybe it was all an act to cover up what was really going on between the boys. I'm convinced I'll be able to read the truth in his eyes – if I can just see those photos . . . But it's more than that.

'It's not just that I want to see the pictures,' I say quietly, 'to see what the boys were getting up to. It's the fact that they've *disappeared*. And not just the photos. Nick's entire profile has gone. Sean – Mr Newton – couldn't find it again. And I've checked too.'

'I couldn't find it either,' DS Clarke admits.

'Doesn't that seem strange to you?'

'Perhaps.' She frowns. 'Although my niece and nephew are forever posting then deleting stuff. Loading and unloading apps. Joining websites then changing their minds and unsubscribing. Kids are easily bored, aren't they? But I'll check again with the boys.'

'Have they said anything else?'

'Nothing from Jason or Samir since we interviewed them this morning. Not that their statements told us much.' She gives me an apologetic smile, as though it's her fault.

'Right. Still sticking to their story, then.' I don't bother to hide my cynicism.

'Maybe because it's the truth? Several different officers have talked to them now. They're not deviating from what they first told DCI Maxwell.'

I fold my arms. 'So they've got their script straight.'

'I think they're trying, Izzy.' DS Clarke rests a hand on my arm. 'They're shocked. Sometimes it can take a while for things to filter through. We have to have a little patience.'

'For how long, though?' I stare at the kitchen window. It's pitch black outside; all I can see is the reflection of my own anguish.

'Adrian did tell his mum something this afternoon. Apparently, Nick mentioned having "stuff on his mind" last night. That's not much. But maybe it's something? Any ideas?'

I gaze around the kitchen, trawling for clues, remembering other Saturday evenings here, with Craig pouring wine, Nick and me playing cards at the table. 'Stuff on his mind.' I've sensed it myself, but I can kick myself a thousand times for not asking Nick what was worrying him, it's no use now. 'Could mean anything. It still doesn't necessarily mean he ran away,' I add quickly, anxious about the police downgrading their investigation if they think no foul play has occurred; I'm convinced it has.

'You're right. It doesn't. And we're keeping an open mind. It's a process, Izzy.' DS Clarke takes out her notebook. 'Pulling everything apart. Putting it back together. We've looked at Nick's home life. School. Friends. Next we'll focus on the local community.'

'And online. Who was watching those videos? Who might have figured out where Nick was last night? Even if he did run off, for whatever reason, someone could have been waiting for him – *snatched* him.'

'I know it's your worst fear. Look at it this way, though. Nick's

Facebook was live this morning. Mr Newton saw it. I did a routine social media check after I'd spoken to you and Craig here. I didn't find anything. And that was early this afternoon. At some point between those times, Nick's account was deactivated. Given that he disappeared at some point after midnight yesterday, that's potentially more than twelve hours after he left Beth's house.'

'So?' I frown, struggling to see how this is good news.

'So if Nick was able to deactivate his Facebook account late this morning – well, to put it bluntly, that's the strongest indication we've had yet that he's alive. Yes? Hold on to that. Nick's missing. But he's not *gone*.'

'Not gone. But not necessarily safe.'

'We're not giving up, Izzy. I promise. But I appreciate it's going to be a long night. Try to get some sleep. Or at least rest. And don't forget to eat something.' The detective smiles as she stands up from the table, carrying my untouched toast over to the worktop. 'I'll see you in the morning. Call me at any time, though. You're not in this alone, OK?'

'Thank you,' I say, even though that's exactly how I feel.

DS Clarke was right: there is no way I can sleep, not while Nick is still out there, and I feel another flash of anger as I think of the other three boys tucked up safely in their beds. Walking slowly upstairs after I've seen the detective out, my feet carry me almost of their own volition towards Nick's room.

The silence hurts, even though Nick never makes much noise. He listens to music on his laptop through headphones, and watches Netflix the same way, the old portable television I gave him collecting dust on a shelf. *TV is old school, Mum.*

He has a radio, though. It used to be Alex's, and as I turn it on I get butterflies hearing his favourite classical music pour out of the speaker. Feeling unaccountably disloyal to Craig, I wish

Alex was here now, giving me one of the crooked smiles so like his son's, telling me *everything will be OK, babe*, as he always did. Only it wasn't, it *isn't*, and if Nick doesn't come home, it never will be again.

'Come on, Izzy. Stay positive,' I mutter, finally forcing myself to move. I leave the door open on my way out, wanting Nick's presence, so strong in his room, to unfurl through the house. 'I'll leave the light on for you, darling,' I say softly, flicking the switch.

The only reply is the sound of an engine revving violently. 'What the heck?' Hurrying to my study at the front of the house, I stare anxiously out of the window. It's just a car doing a U-turn, but fearful and on edge as I am, any sudden sound startles me, and I remain transfixed, watching the tail lights of the Range Rover until they're a red blur in the distance.

I promised DS Clarke I would try to relax, but I can't – and I can't stand the thought of lying in my bed alone all night. Sitting down at my desk, I fold my arms and let my head sink down on to them. Maybe I could just rest here for a while . . .

Loneliness steals around me. I wonder if Nick has been lonely too, and if that explains why he searched online for something, *someone*, to fill a void I didn't even know he felt. He's had so few friends in real life, it's hardly surprising if he struggled to recognise the threat from virtual ones . . . if by innocently reaching out to someone, he fell smack bang into their trap.

FIFTEEN

Despite my restlessness, I must have nodded off, because when my phone rings I almost fall off the chair scrabbling for it. 'Nick?'

The call disconnects. I check the number; it's withheld. I listen for any messages, hope lodged breathlessly in my chest. There aren't any, and frustration crashes through me, even as I tell myself I'm grasping at straws, kidding myself it might have been Nick – that he might indeed have simply run away and now feels too scared to come home, worrying that he'll get told off. I have no way of knowing if that's the case, or if the Facebook photos hold the clue to a far darker scenario.

Irritably, I log on to my computer, wondering if the other boys have remained active on social media. I run a search on Samir's name first, finding nothing. Next I try Adrian, but he appears to have heeded his teacher's advice after all: I'm clearly not on the authorised list of 'friends' able to view his content. Beth must be, but when I type in her name, too many 'Beth Atkins' profiles appear for me to know at a glance which is hers.

On impulse, I type in 'Katie Baxter'. She hasn't phoned to see how I am, which both saddens and angers me. I pick out her profile immediately: Craig took the photo at a barbecue in our back garden two summers ago. Cuddled up to Nathan, Katie is playfully ruffling her husband's spiky blond hair. She's pouting; he's smiling. 'A picture paints a thousand lies,' I mumble, remembering sparks flying between them that afternoon.

I click on more photos, and the more I look, the more I realise that Sean was right about people reinventing themselves on social media, deceiving not just others but perhaps themselves too. The loved-up images of my former best friend and her husband bear no resemblance at all to my memories of the last time I saw them together . . .

'Merlot. My favourite. Thanks, Mr B.' Katie stood on tiptoes to kiss Craig's cheek, then hooked her arm through his, drawing him along the panelled hallway into her kitchen.

'Shall I do the honours?'

'Please. Help yourself. You know where everything is.'

Katie reached into a cupboard for wine glasses, while Craig rifled in a drawer for the bottle opener. Nathan stood watching them for a moment, before turning to hold out a hand to me. I glanced around the hall in confusion, until I realised he was offering to take my coat.

'Oh. Thanks.' I handed it over, watching him hang it on one of the antique silver hooks Katie had salvaged from a junk yard and restored.

Her home was full of such beautiful touches; as with her clothes, everything was designed to make a statement. It would have been easy to feel dowdy in comparison to my more glamorous friend, but my usual choice of jeans and jumper was a practical one: I was too busy rushing Nick between dance classes to bother with anything fussier, and I was nowhere near as bothered about appearances as Katie. *Elegant*, I called her; *vain*, she always acknowledged with her wicked laugh.

'Shall I sit here?' I hovered at the end of the beautifully set dinner table, after trailing behind Nathan through the neutral drawing room into a more formal dining area beyond. Usually I would make myself at home, but Nathan's prickly presence made me feel awkward. It always did, and I was pretty sure he only tolerated me for Katie's sake. He certainly never made any secret of his dislike of Craig.

'Help yourself. You know where everything is,' he parroted drily.

The awkwardness continued throughout dinner. I escaped upstairs a few times to look in on Nick and Jason, playing Xbox in the den. Partly I wanted to make sure Jason wasn't bossing Nick around again: I could hear loud yells at regular intervals, but every time I went up there, the two boys were sitting quietly, as though nothing untoward was going on.

I wasn't entirely convinced by Jason's butter-wouldn't-melt expression. Each time I checked, Nick was the one sitting on the floor, while Jason sprawled across a giant leather beanbag, hogging the remote control. Nick insisted he was fine, but still I felt the need to pop upstairs a couple more times – admittedly as much because it gave me a breather from the tense atmosphere around the dinner table.

'Craig's offered to show Jason round his office over half-term,' Katie announced as I returned downstairs for the last time to see her carrying in the dessert: a spectacular *croquembouche*. She plucked a profiterole from the glossy tower, offering it to Craig. 'You get first dibs, Mr B. For bringing the wine.'

Nathan's hooded gaze scythed between them. 'Jase isn't interested in being a pen pusher. He's got a bit more spirit about him than that.'

'Still, it's a day out for him. And it would help me,' Katie said. 'You'll be away. *As usual.* I've got to work. It's really kind of you, Craig.'

For a moment, she rested a hand lightly on his arm. Craig patted it, and Nathan's thick fingers pinched the stem of his wine glass so hard I found myself waiting for it to snap.

No one would be able to guess any of this from the photos I can't stop myself scrolling through – just as I'm sure that whatever pictures Nick posted online won't tell the whole story about the sleepover. The trouble is, with the boys still saying nothing, and the police investigation so far yielding no leads, only Nick knows the real truth about last night.

Sighing, I do what he always does when he has a homework query I can't answer: I google it. *Where is my son? Has he run away or has someone taken him? Has he been bullied? Or groomed? Was he unhappy? Is it my fault?* My head is bursting with questions; frantically, I purge them all into the search engine. I know I'm being ridiculous, but I just need to put everything *out there*.

Almost of their own accord, my fingers type Nick's name – then, on impulse, I type in all the boys' names, my hands freezing on the keyboard as 'Jason Baxter' leaps out at me, appearing over and over next to a website that makes me feel queasy with shock.

'*Dare or Die*. What on earth?' I feel sicker still as I read the copy urging followers to *conquer their fears by acting them out*. I check the number of 'likes': hundreds. I skim the comments: Nick's name isn't among them, but then most are clearly made-up avatars.

Clicking on a link attached by *Deathstar*, I'm taken to a video which buffers and loads. My mouth drops open as I watch a boy about the same age as Nick hanging over a railway bridge, clinging on by his white-knuckled fingers as a train approaches. Before he vanishes into clouds of smoke, I stare into his wide, dark eyes. He looks terrified, yet almost *jubilant*. Fear but undeniable excitement, even bravado, is etched on his round-cheeked face.

I can't bear to see what happens next, and I close the clip – only the next one I load is no better. My heart is in my mouth as I watch a slightly older girl, dressed in school uniform, clambering over a balcony a dozen storeys up on a tower block. Holding on with one hand, her phone is clutched in the other as she leans backwards to wave exuberantly at a group of teenagers jumping up and down countless metres below.

'Death isn't cool,' I tell her pointlessly. 'It's for *ever*.'

I shake my head in disbelief as I keep scrolling through dozens of other shocking stunts and extreme selfies; I hunt again for Nick's name, desperately hoping I won't find it. Gradually, it begins to register that the most recent posts all have a horror theme: kids dressed as vampires, leaping between rooftops; zombie-costumed teens dodging traffic. Always with a phone capturing their starring moment – a heartbeat away from it being their dying one.

A tingle runs down my arms. *Yesterday was Friday the thirteenth.* Did Jason, inspired by the spooky occasion, challenge Nick to do something crazy to post on this website? Did Nick feel pressured into agreeing, only it went wrong and the boys are too scared to say? Beth said they never left the house – but Nick clearly did. If she didn't hear him, what else did she miss? The boys seem bound to a silence not even trained police officers have managed to crack. But maybe I can persuade them to break it. I at least have to try . . .

Reaching for my tote bag, I check inside for my car keys, almost dropping them as I hear a loud scraping noise outside, followed by a clatter. *Footsteps?* Hurrying to the window, I peer down at the road for the second time. It's still empty, and there are no houses opposite – only Osterley Park beyond a high wall. Its gates are locked at night, and the vast estate is a black void, but my skin crawls with a sudden sensation of being watched.

Ducking down, I tell myself I'm just getting freaked out by the voyeurism of snooping through other people's photos. 'Come on, Izzy. Pull yourself together.' I grab my coat and head downstairs, allowing myself only a quick check around as I leave the house.

I do a double-take when I notice a broken plant plot under the living-room window, as if someone has cracked the brittle terracotta by standing on it – to look into my house?

Peering suspiciously at the bushes dividing my garden from Mr Thompson's next door, a scream fills my throat when a shadow springs out from them. 'Oh, *Marzipan*. You scared me. Are you hungry, sweetheart?'

I quickly re-open the front door and wait impatiently for her to slink through the gap, before turning back to survey the frozen street. The wind picks up a drift of voices and I strain to listen, my heart beating faster as I remember the anonymous phone call just half an hour ago, wondering again if it was Nick – if the noises I heard might even have been him . . .

'*Nick?* Nick, if you're there, it's OK! Please, just come inside.' I skid down the short drive to the street, looking frantically up and down the pavements. The shadows yield no sign of him, and my hopes plummet as a couple of older teenage boys saunter past, laughing, on the other side of the road. I stand and watch them, feeling powerless and angry.

What if the police don't find Nick? *What if he doesn't want to be found?* The cloak of invisibility he seems to have been drawing around himself for weeks has finally worked. I should have noticed his withdrawal sooner, questioned him harder – just as DCI Maxwell should have the boys. He stopped me questioning them, too, I think bitterly.

But he's not here now . . . Neither is Alex. Or Craig. I remember my mum's tipsy parting words of advice: *Look after yourself, Isobel Blake, because no one else will do it for you.* She was wrong about so many things, but maybe she was right about that. I can't sit back and wait for others to solve my problems; I have to be the one to do it. Fired up with determination now to find out the truth for myself, I climb into my car, reverse out on to the road, and set off for Katie's house.

SIXTEEN

'Jase told the police everything he knows. Today's been stressful enough for him. He's barely left his room. He needs sleep,' Katie whispers, ushering me into her darkened kitchen.

All the house lights were off when I arrived. I had to ring the bell twice and knock five times before she opened the door, and her hissed urgency for me to keep my voice down made me want to shout in her face: *Where is your son, and what the hell did he do to mine?*

'Stressful for *Jason*? You've got to be kidding me.' I stare at her back in disbelief as she strides ahead of me. 'My son's missing, but yours is the one who's upset. He—'

'Shh. He'll hear you.' Katie quickly shuts the kitchen door, then opens it a crack, listening. 'I don't expect you to believe me,' she adds quietly, 'but he's gutted.'

'Well, no one likes having to justify their actions.' I can't bite back the dig about how she judged me for mine a year ago. She ignores it, pushing past me to get to the fridge, and I glance curiously around the vast kitchen-diner, lit only by an enormous tropical fish tank and the glow of garden lights through bi-fold doors. I haven't been here for so long, but everything looks the same – except a lot messier than it used to be, I'm surprised to notice.

'Jason hasn't done anything wrong. I'm sick of everyone getting the wrong idea about him. Sure, he's boisterous. But Nathan fills his head with too many tough-guy army stories. You know that. Jase wants to impress him, that's all.' She yanks the fridge open; the contents on the door rattle precariously. 'All boys show off to their dads.'

I'm hurt by her tactlessness, but I've come here for answers, not a fight. It's awkward enough seeing her again after all this time, so I don't point out that Nick never had the chance to impress *his* dad. I shouldn't have to say it, anyway, not to Katie; she knows my history with Alex. But as she takes out an almost empty bottle of white wine, draining the dregs into a glass, I suspect it's not her first of the evening, and whether that explains her insensitivity.

'Something really bad happened last night at the sleepover, Katie. Are you *sure* Jason doesn't know more than he's telling the police?' I wish she wouldn't keep turning away. I want her to look me in the eye; I'm convinced then I'll be able to tell if she's genuinely blind to her son's faults or lying to cover them up. But she keeps her back resolutely turned on me.

'I said this to them, and I'll say it to you. Nick was there when Jason went to sleep, and gone by the time he woke up. That's it.' She pours herself more wine, red this time.

'That's *it*? But didn't Jason tell you—' I break off as Katie finally turns around. Even though it's after ten, she's still dressed in her work clothes. Her fitted taupe suit is as elegant as ever, but not even the over-heavy make-up smothering her fair, lightly freckled skin can conceal its sallowness, or the purple shadows under her eyes.

'*What?*' she snaps, pulling out a high-backed cream leather chair

99

and slumping down at the kitchen table. Red wine sloshes on to the glossy white floor tiles.

'Nothing. You just look a bit . . . tired, that's all.' I know Katie would hate me to notice that she isn't looking her best, and despite our fallout, I'm upset to see it. *A guilty conscience can be very draining*, I reflect acidly, reminding myself too that while Katie is worried about Jason, she hasn't shown the slightest concern about Nick.

'Gee, thanks.' She waves her glass; a trickle of wine spills over the rim, staining the cuff peeping out from the sleeve of her jacket. A silver charm bracelet jangles on her wrist.

It looks exactly like the one Craig gave me for our third and last wedding anniversary, I notice. Katie always admired it, as she admired Craig. So much so that when push came to shove, she happily switched her loyalty to him. Coming here was a mistake, I realise.

'I'll leave you to rest,' I say quietly. 'Maybe Jason could call me when he wakes up?'

'He's got work in the morning.'

'*Work?* I mean, he's fourteen. What kind of work?'

'Oh, just a casual, part-time thing. He helps out at a friend's boat yard down at Eel Pie Island. Nathan thought it would be good for him. Toughen him up. You know.'

'Right. Well, I've got to do a press conference in the morning, anyway. The police think a media appeal could help find Nick,' I say deliberately, hoping to prick her conscience. 'Maybe I could grab Jason after that.'

'Maybe. Look, I know Jason feels awful about Nick. He'd never hurt him.'

'I never said he did.' I raise my eyebrows at her, suspecting that might be a revealing slip on her part. 'But maybe Nick thought he might?'

'Nonsense. Jase has really looked out for Nick since he started secondary school. Who do you think got him into the book group thingy?'

'Adrian,' I say, even as my heart sinks at the news that Nick needed watching over.

'I don't think so. Adrian's sweet, and everything. But he's very young for his age. Jase has actually got quite a paternal streak. He always looks out for younger kids.'

I stare crossly at her; I can't think of anyone less paternal than Jason. 'Is that why he gatecrashed a sleepover with three twelve-year-olds?'

'He didn't. I asked him to go. Nathan and I . . . needed to talk.' Katie flicks a glance at the kitchen door then gives me a wry look. 'Oh, don't worry. He's not here. I know how you feel about him. Lucky for you, he flew back out to the Gulf late last night.'

'Are you sure about that?' It suddenly strikes me that her jittery manner might have less to do with guilt about Nick and more about Craig – and a relationship between them that her husband is beginning to suspect. I eye the charm bracelet again, wondering if I've hit on the explanation for its similarity to mine: because Craig bought Katie the exact same one. And maybe Nathan knows it.

'Of course I'm sure. He left about midnight. I went in to work as usual this morning. Then the police phoned and I came home. I've spent all afternoon answering their questions. Jase, too. He really is devastated about Nick, you know.' Her voice softens, her touch gentle as she leans towards me and takes hold of my hand. 'For what it's worth, Iz, so am I.'

I feel a rush of tears. Once, Katie and I were as close as sisters. Then she sided with Craig, and I couldn't forgive her for it. I always knew she had a soft spot for my husband. I honestly never felt threatened by her: she was my best friend. And, until the day he left, I had absolute faith in Craig. In hindsight, I wonder if I was blinded both by the optimism of a new marriage and by the complacency of an old friendship. At the very least, I should have guessed Katie would take Craig's side over mine. After all, she did more or less pick him for me . . .

'Him. He's the one.'

'Mr Suited and Booted? I don't think so. He writes beautifully, though. I'll give him that.' I studied the letter clipped to the photo of a handsome thirty-something man with dark hair and intense grey eyes. 'See, that's the point about dating ads in actual newspapers. I get to analyse their handwriting. How much can you tell about a person from text speak?'

'Sure. Because serial killers all have bad grammar. Come on, Iz. Don't be such an old fuddy-duddy. Everyone meets online these days. You've been off the market too long.'

'Huh. I know you're an estate agent, Katie, but I'm not one of your property listings.' I stood up and reached for a takeaway menu on the kitchen noticeboard. We'd spent the whole evening sifting responses to my ad, and I was tired, hungry and beginning to regret placing it in the first place. The prospect of dating again after being single for eight years terrified me; Katie seemed more excited by the idea than I was.

'Sorry. I just want you to be happy, hon. You *and* Nick.'

'You're not getting any commission out of this, you know,' I teased her.

'Shame. I'd do a much better sales job on you.'

'Charming.'

She grabbed the local paper and prodded my ad. 'See, this doesn't exactly shout *hot property*. More *slightly run-down semi with good potential but in need of some updating*.'

'Cheers! I take it you won't be wanting me to get you a discount on your next holiday. Anyway, semi-detached? What the heck?'

'Alex,' she said bluntly. 'You've never got over him.'

'He was Nick's father. What do you expect?' I turned away to study the pizza menu – Nick's favourite. The reminder that I was doing this partly for him weighed heavily on me. I was tired of sitting through school parents' evenings alone, being fobbed off by teachers who sympathised a lot but seemed to do little. Maybe Katie was right; maybe having a man around would be good for both Nick *and* me.

'Well, *I* say this guy has *perfect stepdad* written all over him. Look at that chiselled jaw. Those piercing eyes.'

'All the better to find fault with me. Sundried tomato and olives, or shall we blow the diet and go for a cheese feast?' I deliberately waggled the menu.

'Rubbish. There's something a bit Cary Grant about him, don't you think?' She sighed. 'Whereas Nathan seems to be morphing into Bruce fucking Willis.'

'He works in banking, Katie. I was hoping for a little more . . . Oh, I don't know. Passion? "Craig Brookes, City underwriter",' I read out loud. 'Could he sound more dull?'

'He might have hidden depths. You know what they say. *Still waters run deep*. Besides, dull – I mean serious, *responsible* – might be just what you need right now. Nick, too. You've had to cope with so much. Do you good to have someone to share the load. And think of the dinner parties we can have,' she added, grinning to lighten the mood. 'He can keep Nathan in check.'

'Poor guy.' I gave up resisting and sat down at the kitchen table again, taking the photo from her. 'You've got him washing the car and carving the Sunday roast before I've even met him.'

'But you're going to, right?' Katie topped up my wine glass, chinking her own against it. 'Here's to meeting the man of my dreams. I mean *yours*,' she said with a laugh.

SEVENTEEN

For three years, that's exactly what Craig was, I reflect: an affectionate partner for me and a rock for Nick. Where I ranted and raged about the seemingly never-ending bullying, Craig calmly removed Nick from situations where it might occur – and made it clear to the head teacher that he'd 'take immediate action' if they didn't address it. He never needed to raise his voice; he just had this quiet way of enforcing his position by making others doubt their own.

And he made me feel safe; I felt confident *Nick* was safe. It seemed like we finally had the perfect family … until a year ago when, in the space of one nightmarish day, Craig bafflingly turned from mild-mannered husband to a critical stranger who accused me of being a bad mum. I know he tried to apologise, and to explain, this afternoon, but it feels like too little, too late. The damage has been done; it can't be undone.

I wonder if the same applies to my friendship with Katie; I wonder if there is a correlation I've never recognised between Craig leaving and Katie turning her back on me – if Nick running away that morning gave them both an excuse to shun me and be together. Only things haven't panned out as they hoped: Nathan refuses to let Katie go, and I won't let Craig share custody of Nick. Especially if he only requested it with a view to making another perfect family: with Katie and Jason. A second son to replace the one she lost ...

If I wasn't so frantic with worry about Nick, I would challenge them both about it. As it is, all I feel when I think about them having an affair is that they're welcome to each other. But they will never get their hands on my son. *If I ever get him back.*

'Do you ever wish you could turn back time?' I ask Katie softly, sitting next to her at the kitchen table, as I have so many hundreds of times before. 'Do things differently. Ask different questions.'

'Sorry?' She turns towards me but doesn't quite meet my eyes.

'We think we know someone, but actually we only know what they tell us. And when they tell us nothing, we fill in the blanks for ourselves. With whatever we want to believe. About our husbands. Friends. Our children. And then something really bad happens, and we discover we got it all wrong. They're not who we thought they were at all. But by then it's too late to fix it, to turn back time and do it all again – only this time knowing the truth.'

'Izzy, you're not making any sense.'

I take out my mobile phone and load up the internet. 'Maybe this will help. There's something I want to show you. A website.'

Even though I barely touched the wine Katie kept trying to foist on me, no doubt to make herself feel better about drinking alone, I drive home at a snail's pace an hour later, not so much worried about the trace of alcohol in my bloodstream as the tears running down my face, making the already poor visibility on the snowy roads a hundred times worse.

The website had vanished. First the Facebook photos, now this. It feels as though the universe is gradually erasing every last atom of my son. And I don't get it. How could I have been watching videos of kids performing crazy stunts one minute, and the next everything has gone? I'd hoped to show Katie she was being gullible about her son's true character. Instead, *I* was the one who appeared deluded.

Without being able to show her Jason's website, I knew it looked like I was making it up simply to put all the blame for Nick's disappearance on him. And when I begged her to let him explain for himself, she threatened to call Craig. It felt like a deliberate slap to the face; it also reinforced my suspicion about them having an affair. In the end, I had to leave – before we got into a battle I simply didn't have the energy to fight.

I had intended to go and see Beth and Ayesha as well, but by the time I left Katie's house it was way too late. In any case, if I couldn't even get Jason to talk to me, there didn't seem much point trying to speak to Adrian or Samir. Their silence is driving me crazy, though. It's one thing having their friends' backs when it comes to cheating on a test or playing hooky from school for a morning. But Nick isn't just cutting lessons; he's dropped off the face of the earth.

I'm back to square one, I reflect, banging my hands on the steering wheel in frustration as I turn into my road. All I can do is wait for morning and pray that DS Clarke is right: that the TV appeal will either lure Nick out from wherever he's hiding or prompt whoever is holding him to come clean.

Steering the Mini on to my drive, I stamp on the brake as the headlights illuminate a trail of rubbish across the front garden. 'Oh, great. Not *again*.' I sit staring at the mess for a moment, then slam out of the car. My son is missing; my former best friend is probably in love with my ex-husband. I don't know who to trust or where to turn. A fox scavenging through my recycling for the second time in two weeks is the last thing I should care about.

Picking my way through cereal boxes, juice cartons and old newspapers, I cast a wary eye around to see if the fox is still here. Sensing something moving at the side of the house, I follow the shuffling noise. 'Mr Thompson? Is that you?'

A quick glance next door confirms that all the windows are dark. It must be after eleven, and my neighbour is in his seventies. He's probably in bed by now, not putting out his rubbish – or cleaning up mess left by foxes. I notice his recycling bin hasn't been touched, in any case. 'Just mine, then. Fabulous.'

I hear the same shuffling again and head cautiously towards the pathway between our houses, treading carefully so as not to spook the animal but determined to see it off. As I reach the side gate, I hear a noise on the other side. *Crunching*. A scraping noise, somehow familiar. I heard it earlier, from upstairs in my study, I realise – and it doesn't sound like anything on four legs. It sounds like footsteps . . . boots treading along the icy path?

'Nick? *Nick?*' I call out hopefully. I wait a few seconds, but there's no reply, and when the shuffling noise comes again, fear courses through me.

Glancing around for something to defend myself with, I grab a loose brick from the garden wall. 'I'm calling the police!' I dig into my bag with my other hand, rooting for my phone, straining to make out whether the noises are moving closer or further away.

A loud crash makes me jump, my body's momentum carrying me towards the tall wooden gate. In a panic, I turn the handle and push. The gate won't budge: there must be a build-up of snow on the other side, I realise. I push harder, and as it finally gives way, I tumble into the dark alley.

'Stop!' I call out, even though the thought of a physical confrontation terrifies me. But ever since Nick disappeared, normal rules don't seem to apply. I would never normally chase after an intruder, yet without a second thought I leap over a broken window box, scrabbling as I become tangled in overhanging branches of winter-brittle wisteria. By the time I've torn my way through it, there's no sign of anyone. The back garden is empty.

'*Damn*.' It's pointless trying to attempt further pursuit, I realise. Stupid and probably dangerous. I wait a few moments more, imagining shapes in the darkness, then hurry to check the downstairs windows, looking for any sign of a forced entry. Nothing has been disturbed, only the broken window box – which suddenly reminds me of the cracked flower pot outside the living room . . .

Shrinking against the side of the house, my heart thumps as I allow the fear I realise I've been suppressing for hours to surface: *Is someone watching me?*

EIGHTEEN

My legs are shaky as I finally force myself to push away from the wall and dash round to the front of the house, fumbling with my keys as I fly across the litter-strewn garden. I all but throw myself into the hallway, double-locking the front door behind me.

Spotting Marzipan's orange eyes in the dark, I leave the lights off and follow her into the kitchen, hiding in the darkness as I peer out through the kitchen window. There's still no sign of anyone, but I catch a faint sound of laughter; a chorus of raucous young voices.

'God. Here I go again. Letting myself get carried away. I need to knock this paranoia on the head,' I tell Marzipan. 'I bet it was just teenagers messing about. Playing Knock Down Ginger.' That must be it, I tell myself firmly, feeling a lot calmer now I'm safely inside the house. It's Saturday night, after all; some kids will be out late.

Not Nick, though; I never let him go out alone in the evenings. 'Was it you, darling?' I close my eyes and wish again for the impossible: the sound of my son's voice answering me, telling me: *Everything's cool, Mum.*

Feeling a little tearful, I set down food for Marzipan and drift through to the living room, deciding to call DS Clarke anyway. She said I could at any time, and I want to tell her about Jason's website, as well as mentioning a possible intruder – and also ask if she thinks I'm being ridiculous imagining it might be Nick loitering out there . . .

Before I can take out my mobile, the landline rings. 'Hello?' I pour all my hope into the handset, waiting for the magic word to bubble to the surface: *Mum*. A crackle on the line teases me; I plummet heart-first into the long pause. 'Is that you, Nick? *Nick?*'

'Sorry, did I wake you?'

'Oh! Mr Newton. Sean.' I immediately recognise his melodic voice. 'No, it's fine. I wasn't asleep. I . . . what time is it?' I hurry to the window and peel open a chink in the heavy velvet curtains. A black sky glowers back at me; it must be close to midnight. I slide down on to the sofa, sinking tiredly into the cushions.

'Damn. Sorry, I didn't realise it was so late. I guess I lost track of time. I hope you don't mind me calling. I've just been sitting here worrying about Nick. And you. How are you doing? Have the boys said any more about last night?'

'Nothing,' I say bitterly. 'They've still said *nothing*.'

'That's a shame.' He pauses so long, I wonder if the line has cut out.

'Hello?' I prompt.

'Sorry. I was just thinking. I wonder if the boys would open up to me. As their form tutor, I mean. I spend a lot of time with them in the book group, too. We chat about all kinds of stuff. I could try?'

'Really?' I chew on a thumb nail, gripped by the possibility that Mr Newton is right – that the boys might open up to him – before remembering DCI Maxwell's reluctance to let me speak to the boys. 'The police do have pretty strict procedures, though. I'm not sure—'

'Oh God. Yes. You're right. Sorry, scrub that thought. I was just trying to figure out if I can be of more help. But of course. Interfering with a police investigation isn't—'

'It's not a bad idea, though.' I sit up straighter, suddenly feeling energised. 'I know how much the boys like you. They'd probably trust you more than the detectives, too. They're nice people, but they're still the police. They might be intimidating the boys. Only if you're sure, though. I know it's asking you to go above and beyond duty.'

'You didn't ask. I offered.' His sigh echoes down the line. 'I know Nick wasn't at school when he disappeared. Even so, I feel a duty of care. All teachers do. That's why we do the job. Because we like kids and want the best for them. Anyone at the school would do the same thing, but I'm these boys' form tutor. Not Jason's, but—'

'Oh, I doubt you'll get anything out of him anyway,' I cut in. 'I've just tried, and his mum wouldn't even let me speak to him. But Beth and Ayesha have been really kind. And they know you. I'm sure they won't object to letting you chat with Adrian and Samir.'

'Really? You think so? OK. Leave it with me, then. I'll call them in the morning.'

'Thanks, Sean. Nick's right. You're the best teacher he's ever had.'

I know I'm feeling fractious and over-emotional at the possibility of uncovering new information, but I mean it: it's extremely kind of Sean to put himself out like this to help. I just wish Nick hadn't had to wait until secondary school to find a teacher like him; I wish I could turn back time and swap him for the teacher who unintentionally first planted the thought in my mind that maybe parenting might be a lot easier with a partner at my side . . .

*

'I'm sorry we have to meet again in these circumstances, Miss Blake.' Mrs Jenkins put down her pen and gestured for me to take a seat. 'It is Miss, isn't it? Or do you prefer Ms?'

'Miss is fine.' I sat down in the low chair opposite her desk, pulling Nick against my side. 'But what do you mean?' I thought our meeting was a regular parents' evening chat; I'd been given no indication that there was anything out of the ordinary about our appointment.

Mrs Jenkins' mouth pursed. 'There's been another little incident, I'm afraid.'

'Another . . .' *Little incident* seemed such an inadequate phrase to describe what Nick had endured on almost a daily basis since starting school. 'Can you be more specific?'

'Do you want to show your mum, Nick? She won't be cross.'

'Of course I won't be cross.' I gave the teacher a sharp look, annoyed at the suggestion, then turned to look at Nick. His eyes were so wide, I could see the entire blue of his irises. 'What's happened, love?' I said gently. He'd seemed a little happier lately; I had even begun to hope things might have improved after my last meeting with the school.

'He's torn his shirt.' Mrs Jenkins nodded. 'Lift up your jumper, Nick.'

I turned him around to give him some privacy, lifting his shirt myself. 'Oh my God. Who *did* this?' My fingers shook as I pressed them gently against four long, bloody scratches, clearly fingernail marks, all down his back.

'He was climbing the tree again,' the teacher answered for him.

'Really. *Was* he?' I wondered if she was being deliberately obtuse, or if she genuinely had no idea about what seemed obvious to me must have happened. 'Were you?' I said more softly to Nick.

He shook his head again, blond hair flying up, but no words came out of his mouth.

'That tree is out of bounds,' Mrs Jenkins said. 'You know that, don't you, Nick?'

'He knows it. So do the bullies,' I pointed out sternly.

'Sorry?'

'Look, everyone knows Nick loves climbing.' After dancing, it was his favourite thing to do: hiding out in the little treehouse his dad had built for him. 'It's easy enough to make scratches look like he's slipped on the branches. Don't you think?'

'Are you suggesting those marks were inflicted by another child? That's a serious allegation, Miss Blake. As you know, we take bullying extremely seriously, and—'

'Do you?' I fought to keep hold of my temper; antagonising her would solve nothing. She already seemed to have Nick labelled as a 'problem child'; after so many meetings, I suspected I was becoming known as a 'problem mum'. 'So you think this is Nick's fault?'

'It isn't the first time he's been caught playing where he shouldn't.'

'Or that he's tried to hide somewhere he thought he'd be safe, perhaps?' I countered.

'Is that what happened, Nick?' Mrs Jenkins leaned over her desk. 'Were you hiding?'

Nick shuffled his feet and turned to look up at me. 'Mummy, can we go now?'

'Yes, darling. We can go.' I squeezed his hand as I stood up.

'I'm happy to talk this through some more,' Mrs Jenkins said, looking a little flustered as I ignored her proffered handshake. 'If you'd like to make another appointment.'

'Oh, I'll be sure to do that.' I picked Nick up and carried him, even though he was seven years old and would no doubt protest later that he was perfectly capable of walking by himself. 'Only next time it will be with the head teacher. To make an official complaint.'

*

I only discover that I've fallen asleep clutching the phone when its shrill ring hurts my ear.

'Izzy? It's me. DS Clarke. I'm at your front door.'

'Sorry, what?' Groggily, I check my watch. *Eight in the morning.* I must have crashed out, emotionally exhausted. I had meant to call DS Clarke after speaking to Sean, I recall in a rush, feeling down and disoriented as I realise that, just for a moment, I'd forgotten why the detective is even here ... that Nick is gone.

'Izzy? Are you there?' The detective's voice cuts through my sleep-muzzy thoughts.

'Yes. I'm ... ' My fingers curl tighter around the phone. 'Has something ... is there any news?'

'I think you'd better let me in.' There's an uncharacteristic edge to her usually soft, low tone. 'Bit of a crowd gathering out here.'

'A crowd?' I haul myself upright, every cramped muscle protesting at my accidental, uncomfortable night on the sofa. Hearing voices, I peep through the curtains, puzzled to see a group of people congregated outside my front gate. Several have camera cases slung over their shoulders. *Reporters.* 'No. *No.*'

Disconnecting the call and throwing down the handset, I dash to the door. Then hesitate. I know DS Clarke said going public could help, and I'm happy to brace myself for the necessity of a press conference. I'm *not* happy for journalists to snoop around my home.

It occurs to me, too, that it was most likely one of them hanging around last night, hoping for a snap of a distraught mother to sell to the tabloids. The timing of their appearance seems way too much of a coincidence.

I have to count to ten before, finally, I can summon up the courage to open the front door. Cameras flash; the clamour of voices grows louder.

'Izzy – over here!'

'Can we talk, Mrs Brookes? Anything you'd like to say about Nick?'

'What do you think drove your son away? Did you have a fight with him?'

'Is it true your husband left you because he thought you were a bad parent?'

'Nick was at a sleepover when he vanished. Do you feel guilty about leaving him?'

'Are *you* guilty, Mrs Brookes? Have you done something to hurt your son?'

NINETEEN

'OK, people. That's enough. Press conference is this afternoon. Save your questions for then, please.' DS Clarke pushes her way through the small crowd. Stepping into the hallway, she closes the front door firmly behind her. 'Sorry about that.'

'They're like ... *vultures*. Is that normal?' I yank the curtains closed over the hall window, wishing I could blot out the grating sound of the reporters' voices as easily.

'Don't take it personally. It's just how news agencies work. They'll have picked up the story from the bulletins. Cases involving children always provoke lots of interest. Those guys will have been hounded by their bosses to get the first scoop.'

'Fine. But that's why we're doing the press conference, isn't it?' I don't care what their bosses want; I feel shaken and upset at the reporters' hostile questions. 'I can't believe they have the insensitivity to turn up at my house. How did they even know where I live?'

DS Clarke sighs. 'Two clicks on Google and you can find anyone these days.'

'Except a missing child,' I snip, feeling shakier still as the chatter outside grows even louder now the reporters have caught a glimpse of me.

'Sorry, Izzy. I should have warned you this might happen. They were quicker off the mark than I expected. Try to ignore them. They'll give up soon if we stay put for a while. How are you, anyway? Did you get any sleep?'

'A bit.' I run my hands over my face. 'Here. Let me take that.' I turn to hang up her coat, stiffening as I spot Nick's old parka looped over a peg. I've been meaning to take it to the charity shop; now I'm glad I didn't. Just for a moment I allow my fingers to rest on the sleeve, letting it slide between my fingertips, imagining his hand peeping out of it.

'You OK?'

'Yes, I just … Do you mind if we talk upstairs? I can't hear myself think with that racket out there.' Without waiting for her to reply, I head for the stairs.

'Sure.' DS Clarke follows me. 'You do look exhausted,' she says as we reach the top and make our way along the landing. 'I mean that kindly. I'm worried about you. Have you had a hot drink this morning? Eaten anything?'

'I'm fine.' I force a smile and keep walking. She's right, though: I am exhausted. And overwrought. But if she's kind to me now, I know I'll break down completely.

'OK.' Thankfully, she lets it drop. 'In that case, why don't we run through the format for the press conference? These things can be a little intimidating. I want you to feel as comfortable as possible. Would you like someone to come along with you? A friend?'

I sigh, thinking of Katie. 'No. There's no one.'

'Craig?'

I shake my head. 'I don't think that's a good idea, either.'

'The boss seems keen for him to be there,' DS Clarke says carefully. 'To present a united family front, as it were.'

United. I ponder the word, wondering if we ever were. I've clearly missed whatever has been going on for Nick; it's a small step to believing I didn't spot a relationship between Katie and Craig happening right under my nose. 'We're not together any more,' I point out.

'True. And for what it's worth, I'm not sure I agree with the DCI anyway.'

'Oh?' I slant her a surprised look as we reach Nick's bedroom. I had intended to go into my study, but every time I come upstairs my feet seem to automatically carry me here, the place I feel closest to him.

'You mentioned a row about custody. Is it possible that Nick was worrying about that? I know you said he and Craig always got on, but, well, he's had a year without his stepdad, hasn't he? Maybe he was feeling odd about him coming back into his life.'

I shake my head, crossing the room to sit down on Nick's bed, picking up Sleepy Bear and hugging the soft threadbare toy against me. 'I never told him that's what Craig wanted. I only found out myself on Friday. You're right, though. Nick does seem to have avoided seeing his stepdad lately.'

'Does that surprise you?' DS Clarke perches on the desk chair, her eyes still on me.

'A bit. But Nick's a kind boy. Maybe he thought he was pleasing me by refusing to see Craig. Showing loyalty.'

'Sure.' She gazes around at the posters covering the pale-green walls, most bought at West End productions Craig has taken Nick to see. 'He's been to a lot of shows, hey?'

'Nick lives for his dance. He used to love going to The Royal Opera House with his stepdad. It was kind of their thing. I haven't been able to afford it for a while,' I admit, feeling guilty. 'Nick's never complained. He must miss it, though.' I pause. 'Sometimes I wonder . . . maybe he was happier when Craig was around.' I can't swallow the painful thought any longer. 'All those luxuries I can't afford to give him.'

'I doubt that. From everything you've said, I get the impression Nick's closer to you.'

'Not lately, though. He's been so quiet. Maybe that's why. Maybe he and Craig even talked about it. Nick could have let slip that he was missing him.' I think back to the shock of Craig's letter. 'I thought his custody request came out of the blue. Perhaps it didn't.'

'That's a lot of what-ifs and maybes,' DS Clarke says gently.

'I know. You're right.' I sigh, impatient with my own insecurity. 'I'm probably way off beam. It's just so hard when kids don't tell you what's in their heads.'

'My sister says the same thing. Only hers are a bit older. *A law unto themselves*, Rach calls them. She wouldn't dare ask what they're thinking. Too scared of the answer.'

I sit quietly, asking myself if I'm guilty of exactly that: not asking Nick what was on his mind, because I was afraid of hearing the truth. That he wanted to live with his stepdad rather than with me. And, realising how much it would hurt me to hear that, he decided to simply avoid making any decision at all – and ran away instead.

I cup my hands around the mug of tea DS Clarke brings me ten minutes later, sinking back against Nick's pillow, wondering how many nights he stared up at this ceiling, plotting his escape. I've spent the last twenty-four hours convinced he would never just run away; it hurts to admit I could be wrong. Something bad still might have happened en route to wherever he was going, but DS Clarke said there has been no ransom note, no other children reported missing locally. And as Craig pointed out, Nick hasn't turned up in any hospital. *No body has been found . . .*

'I know I asked you this in our very first interview,' DS Clarke says, perching on the end of the bed, 'but Nick didn't keep a diary, did he?'

'Not that I've found. And believe me I've looked.'

'The guys did too. They went through all his stuff yesterday. Didn't find one.'

Her gaze works around the room; helplessly I follow it. I might not agree with DCI Maxwell about everything, but he was right about one thing: the complexities of puberty. I see the evidence of Nick's transition from boy to young adult everywhere. Pokémon cards stacked under cans of deodorant; colouring pencils in a pot with the razor Craig gave him *in preparation*; comics stuffed between school textbooks. My little boy is changing so fast, I haven't been able to keep up with him.

'I just feel like I'm *missing* something.' I frown thoughtfully as DS Clarke stands up and starts pacing the room. The floorboards creak; a memory stirs. 'There is one place . . .'

'Oh?' She stops pacing and turns to look at me.

I leap off the bed and pull back a corner of the shaggy green rug, kneeling down and running my hands over the bare boards beneath. 'We had mice when we first moved in here. Craig had to pull up the floor and put down poison. It got rid of the mice, and Nick . . .' I manage to slip my fingers into a gap between the wooden planks, gaining enough purchase to waggle free a small cutaway section. 'He loved the idea of a secret hideaway for his treasures. I'd forgotten all about it, but . . .'

'Wow. Now that *is* interesting.' It's DS Clarke's turn to frown as she watches me pull out a glossy adult magazine from the small hiding place.

'I can't believe it.' I sit back on my heels, flicking through it. 'I can't believe he'd want to *look* at this stuff.' I understand natural curiosity, but Nick isn't a prurient boy; he still makes gagging

120

noises at kissing scenes in movies. His body consciousness has only recently kicked in, too; it's not that long since he'd happily wander round the house in his underwear. I try to remember when that changed. Probably about a year ago, around the time Craig left. But *everything* changed then.

'Has he talked about his sexuality? Any worries about puberty?' DS Clarke sits back down on the bed. 'We spoke about that yesterday. Does this prompt any more thoughts?'

I trawl my memory, trying to recall Nick ever seeming anxious about the changes his body has begun to go through – the *emotional* changes that I have noticed: a little more moodiness; a greater insistence on privacy. I've respected that and, in doing so, I realise I've allowed distance to creep in between us. I have no idea if Nick's recent change of mood has been due purely to hormones or to real-life problems bothering him.

'He likes a few girls at his theatre school,' I say uncertainly, picturing Imogen. 'But I think he just sees them as dance partners. And he thought the idea of shaving was funny. Not that he needs to do it. It was just, you know, a sort of father-son ritual Craig wanted to do with him.'

'And Craig did "The Chat"?' DS Clarke mimes speech marks.

'No. Actually, I did.' *Leave it out, Mum. We learn all that at school.* 'To be honest, I thought I might have timed it a bit early. He didn't seem at all interested.'

'Masking something, maybe? It can be overwhelming for kids when they start to be aware of physical feelings. Confusing. Scary. Do you think it's possible he had questions he was too embarrassed to ask? Hence looking at …?' She nods at the magazine in my hands.

'Maybe. But how would he even have got hold of this?' Nick is twelve, but he looks much younger.

'Could have been passed around at school. Let me give our tech team a call.' The detective stands up and moves to the door. 'I want Nick's laptop checked one more time, just to be absolutely sure we haven't missed anything.'

'You mean contact with someone who encouraged Nick to look at *this*.' I stand up too, flapping the magazine. 'Someone pretending to be a friend, who was actually . . . ?' I'm too upset to say more as I think of the chat rooms hidden inside *secret apps* that Sean mentioned. My legs suddenly feel weak; I sit down abruptly on the bed.

'Let's not panic. There could be a perfectly innocent explanation. Honestly, we found nothing like this in Nick's internet history.' DS Clarke steps forward and takes the magazine from me, flicking through it one more time before setting it down on the desk. 'That would be the most likely place to find porn searches.'

'Sure,' I say faintly, horrified at the possibilities of what my twelve-year-old son might have seen online – at the ease with which it's possible to bypass any restrictions.

'And we're still investigating everyone local on the sex offenders' register,' DS Clarke adds quietly.

'The sex . . . ?' My throat dries as the implication sinks in.

'Don't worry, Izzy. If Nick's been in touch with an inappropriate stranger, we'll find them.'

'What if it's not a stranger, though?' I can barely force the words out. 'What if it's someone he already knows?'

TWENTY

'Craig, it's me. When you get this, can you call me, please? It's important,' I add, as if every conversation we've had since Nick went missing hasn't been.

After DS Clarke steps out to make her call, I remain on Nick's bed, trying not to stare at the magazine on his desk. I keep my eyes focused instead on my phone, willing Craig to call back. He was the one who said that boys don't always confide in their mums, and I can understand if sexuality was something Nick felt awkward talking to me about. While it pains me to admit it, Craig might be able to shed more light on any such concerns Nick was having.

I try not to feel piqued at the idea of him knowing more about Nick's inner turmoil than I do; I tell myself I don't care if Craig is planning to be with Katie, or if Nick wants to live with the pair of them. *I just want him safely home first.*

My mobile rings. 'Craig?' I say breathlessly.

'Izzy? Are you OK?'

'Oh, *Laura*. Hi. Yes, sorry, what?' I was so expecting it to be my ex-husband that for a moment I'm completely disoriented.

'I've just heard about Nick. I can't believe it.'

'You've just heard . . . ?' It's one thing reporters following the story; I have no idea how my boss can have found out. So far, the police investigation has been focused but low-key. The press conference will change all that, but I'm not due there for two hours.

'I've got the breakfast news on. Bessie, stop that. Please. Finish your toast. No, darling, you had waffles *yesterday*.'

A second later, Laura is drowned out by the sound of the TV, and I realise her four-year-old daughter must be playing with the control. Voices boom down the phone line: *Missing since Friday night . . . Urgent appeal for information.* I leap up and scrabble around Nick's desk, looking for his portable TV remote.

Finally unearthing it in a drawer, I frantically hop through channels until Nick's blue eyes stare out at me. *Thanks, Mum, you're the best.* Only I'm not. I'm the worst mum in the world, and I'd give anything to have him here right now, subjecting me to more of the silent treatment I should have realised was about far more than wanting to go on a stupid sleepover.

'Take all the time off you need,' Laura says. 'And if there's anything I can do . . .'

'Right. I've spoken to the guys, and—' DS Clarke pulls up short as she returns. 'Sorry. I didn't realise you were on the phone.'

'It's fine. It was just my boss.' I flick off the television and sink back on to the bed, feeling a bit wobbly as I realise Nick's name and photo are now public property. I know that's the whole point of the media appeal, but the reality feels far more invasive than I'd imagined it would.

'She's heard the news, I'm guessing. Nick's making all the headlines now.' DS Clarke leans against the doorjamb, giving me a kind look. 'This is good, Izzy. I know it doesn't feel like it. But like I said, we need the public's eyes and ears. A two-pronged strategy.

That's what we need. Unravelling clues close to home. Chasing up leads out *there*.'

'A push or a pull,' I say, thinking of *her* boss now.

'I've kept DCI Maxwell fully updated.' She picks up on the reference. 'He'll be at the press conference.'

'Oh, right. And you'll make sure he knows not to invite Craig?'

'If *you're* sure, Izzy.'

'Completely. I don't want to confuse Nick. If he's watching. I do want to speak to Craig, though. I want to know if he and Nick ever discussed custody arrangements.'

'Our tech guys didn't find anything like that in Nick's emails. I just spoke to them.'

'What about texts? You can access those remotely, can't you?' I dredge my limited knowledge of technology.

'Through the server, yes. We didn't find anything significant. A few texts from Craig suggesting theatre trips. Nothing about moving in with him. Same for his voicemails. Just a couple of messages asking Nick to be in touch. There are a few from you, too, of course.'

'Yes, I left him … some.' *Dozens, constantly pleading for him to call me.*

'I understand. Sorry, Izzy. I had to listen to them. No one else had picked them up, though. They were all highlighted as new messages. Oh, but the guys did manage to reactivate Nick's Facebook account. Apparently, it was only set up a couple of weeks ago.'

'A couple of weeks ago? *Really?* That's when Nick went into full-on pester mode about the sleepover.' I study DS Clarke's face, waiting to see if a light bulb sparks in her head as it just has in mine. 'That can't be a coincidence, can it?'

'You know, I don't think it is,' she says slowly. 'There are no actual status updates on Nick's timeline. No posts about what he

125

was doing or thinking. He hadn't shared any of the usual circular jokes or memes. The only photos were of Friday night. Look. I'll show you.'

She takes out her mobile, and I watch eagerly as she loads the website. My hands shake as I take the phone from her; my eyes eat up the screen, desperately trying to look beyond the silliness of the photos to find something more – anything at odds with the boys' fun antics ... I can't find anything. Sean was right: the photos are completely innocent, just the boys larking around, being playful with each other – exactly as I'd hoped for Nick when I agreed to the sleepover. His shy smile tugs at my heart but it tells me nothing.

I keep scrolling, clicking on photo after photo, then I look up at DS Clarke, feeling more puzzled than ever. 'You're right. All that's on there is—'

'The sleepover. Yes.' She frowns, looking pensive. 'It's almost like Nick's profile was created specifically with that in mind. And once it was done, once Nick had disappeared, he got rid of it.' She hesitates. 'Or someone else did.'

'Someone else?' My mind does a three-sixty-degree flip.

'Nick doesn't have a smartphone, does he?' she says, coming to sit next to me on the bed. 'And we've checked local internet cafés. The library. Everywhere with public computer access. No one has seen Nick.' She chews the end of her ponytail thoughtfully. 'So how did he delete his account?'

I stare at her, feeling sick as I realise she's right. It has been my worst fear, but to have it seemingly confirmed is devastating. 'But who? *Why?* These photos' – I take one last look, then hand back her phone – 'they're hardly incriminating evidence. Of *anything.*'

'No, but any messages might be.'

'Messages? I didn't see any.' I watch her fingers flick expertly across the screen again, wishing I knew more about the digital world Nick seems to have tumbled into.

'That's because Nick's account wasn't just deactivated,' she says, turning to me with a serious look. 'It was permanently deleted. Whoever closed it wanted it gone for good. Luckily, data is still stored online for a while. That's how our guys managed to retrieve the photos. But no messages or instant chat reappeared. If Nick has been chatting to anyone, Izzy, those conversations have been wiped.'

I lean back against the headboard, piecing together what she's saying, hating the picture that begins to form in my mind. Maybe the sleepover wasn't a casual event that went wrong. Maybe what happened on Friday night was far more deliberate, with Nick setting up a Facebook account specifically to communicate with someone: using the sleepover as a decoy, posting those photos purely to convince everyone he was having a good time, before quietly slipping away to meet whoever it was he'd secretly been in contact with.

That person *could* be a friend I don't know about. But if so, and Nick's disappearance is simply a pre-teen statement of independence, why hasn't he been in touch? Unless he was messaging someone who had bad intentions ... someone who manipulated Nick into trusting them, persuading him to sneak out from the sleepover to meet them, forcing him to delete his Facebook profile to cover their tracks – before hurting, abusing ... *killing* him?

TWENTY-ONE

I check my rear-view mirror constantly as I drive, unable to shake off a sense that I'm being followed – although, in theory, I'm the one doing the following. After running through a quick rehearsal for the press conference, DS Clarke kindly offered me a lift, but I wanted some time to myself, to gather my thoughts before facing the media. I'm regretting it now.

I'm so preoccupied trying to decide if the black Range Rover I've seen in my mirror the whole journey really is tailing me that I'm finding it hard to keep the detective's nondescript blue car in my sights. Soon I realise I've lost her, and when my mobile rings I have to admit defeat and swing over to the side of the road, hoping it's DS Clarke phoning to check where I am and give me directions. If not, I'll have to manage with my ancient satnav.

'Izzy? It's Mr Newton. Sean. Can you talk?'

'Oh, Sean, hi. Yes, of course.' I don't take my eyes off the Range Rover as it drives past, slows down, and then speeds around a corner. As soon as it disappears, I rest my head on the steering wheel, puffing out relief, lecturing myself to *stop with the paranoia already*.

'Are you sure? You sound like you're in Piccadilly Circus.'

'Sorry, traffic's bad. I'm driving. Well, parked at the moment. Did you speak to the boys?' I ask, although I'm beginning to suspect they really are as much in the dark as me. If Nick has been targeted by someone on the internet, he clearly hasn't told his friends. Insisting on secrecy, instilling shame ... I know it's the modus operandi of online predators.

'Only briefly, I'm afraid.'

'Jason?' I say doubtfully.

'Unfortunately not. He'd already set off for his Sunday job. But you were right: Mrs Baxter was somewhat ... resistant to the idea of me speaking to him. Adrian and Samir's mums were fine about it, though. They both met me for a quick chat with their boys. Samir's dad Richard Matlock joined us too.'

'And? What did they say?'

'I'm really sorry, Izzy. I couldn't get much out of them after all.'

'Right.' I bite my lip. 'That's OK. You tried. I'm grateful for that.'

'I honestly thought they might have opened up to me. I'm sorry if I gave you false hope.'

'No. It's OK.' I struggle to keep the disappointment out of my voice.

'There was one thing,' he says hesitantly. 'It might be nothing, though.'

'What is it?' I can tell he just wants to give me *something*, just as he did when he told me about the book Nick was reading. I don't care; I'll take any scrap of information I can get.

'Apparently, Nick's started hanging out a lot with someone new. At break times, lunch. Whenever they're out of lessons. Adrian was a bit worried about telling the police. I think he was scared it might sound like he was being a bit, you know, jealous of his best mate buddying up with someone else.'

'Oh, right. I see. Wow.' I feel a buzz of hope as I think about

Nick's Facebook account, set up a fortnight ago. Maybe the simple explanation is that he's found a new best friend. He hasn't mentioned one – but that no longer surprises me. 'Has he noticed it more recently? Over the last two weeks?'

'He didn't say, I'm afraid. Do you think it's worth the police checking it out? The name's Cass Parker, by the way. In Year Eight.'

'Cass . . . Gosh, yes. That could be very helpful indeed.' The buzz intensifies, butterflies dancing in my stomach now. 'Thanks, Sean. I can't thank you enough.'

I end the call, fizzing with thoughts. *Does Nick have a girlfriend?* Not only could that explain why he joined Facebook in the first place – to chat privately with this girl – it might even be the reason he pestered me so much about the sleepover. There's no denying it would have provided the perfect cover for the pair to sneak off together, if that *is* what's happened.

It feels unlike Nick to be so thoughtless, but my conversation with DS Clarke reminded me how fast he's growing up. Perhaps even now he and this Cass are enjoying their big adventure too much to think of how worried their parents will be. I can't decide whether the possibility makes me feel hopeful – that Nick isn't in danger; he's off having illicit fun – or terrified. Two young children on the streets; the risks are enormous.

I turn on the ignition, punch the TV studio's address into my satnav, and drive. Frustratingly it's another half-hour before I arrive at the studio, and not just because of the heavy traffic. Every time I see a blond head passing by, or two almost-teenagers walking along arm in arm, I stop, turn and stare, hopes soaring – only to be crushed yet again.

'Mrs Brookes? My name's Lexie. I'll be looking after you today.'

I turn to stare at the dark-haired young production assistant at my side. 'Sorry?'

'Are you ready for us to start? Two minutes?'

My eyes follow the direction of her hand as she gestures towards the table set at the head of the room on a platform. The TV studio is small but chaotic, overrun with cameras and cables. Technicians mingle with journalists, and despite the production assistant's friendly smile, the whole place feels bewildering and slightly hostile.

I look around anxiously for DS Clarke. She was waiting for me outside the studio, and as soon as I'd parked the car, I relayed everything Sean had told me on the phone. She immediately agreed it presented a potentially useful lead and strode off briskly to investigate, promising to return before the press conference got underway. She's still not back.

'Mrs Brookes?' The production assistant repeats. 'Are you OK?'

'Yes. Sorry, thank you. I'm fine. I was just waiting for—'

'Izzy! Sorry. Calls took longer than I thought.' DS Clarke hurries towards me, tucking her phone in her jacket pocket. 'How are you doing?'

'Better now you're here,' I say, eager to know what she's found out. 'Did you find the girl? Have you spoken to her parents? Do they know—'

'I'm so sorry.' DS Clarke shakes her head. 'I was hoping for a lucky break too. But I managed to get hold of someone from Nick's school. There's no girl called Cass Parker in Year Eight. Could you have misheard?' She reaches into her pocket for her notebook.

'Oh, what? No ... no, that was definitely it.' I stare at her in disappointment, realising I've spent the last hour unconsciously painting an entire scenario in my head: Nick secretly messaging his first girlfriend before sneaking out to meet up, the pair of them crashing on another's friend's sofa ...

I should have realised I was simply projecting experiences from my own teenage years on to Nick; I should have known it was wishful thinking. After all, no other parent has come forward to say their daughter is missing.

'There *is* a boy called Cassidy Parker,' DS Clarke continues. 'He's in Year Twelve, though. Did Nick's teacher specifically say it was a girl – and that she's at Nick's school?'

'A boy.' *I'm such an idiot.* 'No. He didn't. I just assumed. On both counts.'

'Well, you may still be right on at least one of them. Don't worry, I'll look into it some more when we're finished here. Maybe Mr Newton got his names mixed up.'

'I don't think so. He was quite clear about what Adrian said. I'm sorry if I was wrong to ask him to speak to the boys,' I say, feeling deflated. 'I've probably confused things.'

'No, not at all. It was a good thought, actually. They obviously trust their teacher.'

'They do. To be honest, that's why I thought he might be helpful.'

'And he has been, don't worry. He's answered loads of questions about school, playground cliques. All that stuff.' DS Clarke glances over her shoulder as murmurs from the studio floor grow louder. 'Let's hope the media appeal does the trick. I know this is all a bit overwhelming, Izzy. It'll be worth it, though, if seeing you nudges someone's memory.'

'Or conscience,' I say bitterly, still grappling with disappointment.

'Quite. The sight of a mother's distress . . . You'd have to have a heart of stone to resist it.' She gives me a hug. 'Just be yourself. And don't worry about that lot.' She nods at the assembled journalists. 'We kept the guest list select. They're all on your side.'

'I hope you're right.' I remember the parting shot of the reporter outside my house: *Have you done something to hurt your son?* I think of press conferences I've watched on TV myself, the suspicion – the *judgement* – that often lands on the parents of missing children.

'Ten minutes and it will all be over. No questions from the floor. A simple appeal for witnesses or information. Exactly as we rehearsed. Just speak to the camera as though you're talking to Nick, OK?' She rests a gentle hand against my back. 'Looks like DCI Maxwell is about to get things started. Shall we go?'

I nod mutely and follow her to the table, my legs trembling as I step on to the platform and take my seat. Avoiding what feels like a thousand eyes boring into me, I take out my notes and stare down at them, skimming them repeatedly, trying to fix them in my mind. It feels like the most important job interview of my life, and my mouth is dry, my hands clammy. I rub them on my jeans, looking up as DCI Maxwell starts to address the room. Moments later, the production assistant gives me a thumbs-up.

Taking a deep breath, I focus on the camera in front of me, exactly as DS Clarke advised, and lean into the microphone. 'If you're listening, Nick, I'm not cross. I'm just worried. I miss you. Every second of every day. Whatever has happened, whatever is worrying you, there is nothing we can't sort out. Nothing at all. I promise you. Please, just come home, darling. I love you. So, so much.'

I keep my eyes fixed on my notes. I haven't stuck to them; I can't even see them clearly enough to read. Every time I look up, the studio lights blind me and camera shutters whirr, their flashes making coloured circles swim in front of my eyes. Forcing myself to stare once more down the dark tunnel of the TV camera, I wish I could reach through it, grab hold of Nick and haul him back to me.

It's only as DS Clarke touches my arm that I remember I need to appeal for any witnesses. Thankfully, she takes over, and I sit with my head down, barely hearing her recite the phone number of the information line, before DCI Maxwell steps forward to fend off a scattering of questions, wrapping up the whole surreal event with a closing statement.

Then it's over. Camera flashes once again flare across the room like an electric storm; more nightmare images flash across my mind . . . Nick crying as he watches me on TV, calling out to me for help, rough hands silencing his screams.

Hold on, darling. Don't give up. I'll find you. I promise.

TWENTY-TWO

'How did the press conference go?'

'Like I was in a dream. Make that a nightmare.' I take a gulp of much-needed coffee, smiling my thanks as Beth sets a cafetière down on her kitchen table in front of me.

It was actually DCI Maxwell's idea that I go to see a friend, to decompress after the stress and intensity of the last hour. They'd be busy following up any leads that arose as a result of the televised appeal, he said, and DS Clarke would keep me posted on anything more she managed to find out about the mysterious Cass – or Cassidy – Parker.

'Have you eaten?' Beth pauses as she clears lunch plates, even though it's almost three o'clock. 'Sorry about the mess. I should tidy while Molly naps. I'm just so *tired*.' She yawns as she sits down opposite me. 'Adrian's worse than useless. He says he'll help, then I turn around and he's vanished. Oh, God. Sorry.' Her face turns pink. 'Me and my big mouth.'

'I'm not hungry. But thanks.' I don't take offence; I'm used to her scattiness now, and I have far bigger things to worry about. I check my phone, desperate to know if the agony of being thrust into the media spotlight will be worth it.

'More coffee, then.' She tops me up.

'Thanks, Beth. I mean it. It's good to see a friendly face. I feel like I'm falling apart.'

It's strange because yesterday I didn't think I'd ever be able to bring myself to talk to Beth again. *She lost my son.* Only now she feels like my strongest point of connection to him. She was the last person to say goodnight to Nick – to touch him, show him kindness, see him smile. Being here with her, in the house where he spent the final hours before he vanished, somehow conjures up his presence, bonding me to Beth. She was his substitute mum for that one night, and I can even feel sorry for her that this nightmare began under her roof.

'You're not falling apart.' She gives me a hug. 'I can't believe how strong you are.'

'It's just so hard finding out things about Nick that I never knew. I know he's gone *physically*. But I feel like I lost him in *here*' – I press both hands to my chest – 'even before he disappeared. How did I not know what was going on in his head? Sorry. I didn't come here for a pity fest. How's Adrian?'

'Adrian's Adrian.' She rolls her eyes. 'Never sits still for a minute.'

I smile. 'Is he at football? No, it's Sunday. Rugby today, is it? He'll be back soon, wanting his tea, I imagine. I should go.' I can't believe how much it hurts to picture Beth's son dropping his boots in the hall, asking what there is to eat.

All at once it feels like torture being surrounded by the mess Beth keeps apologising for, but which I yearn to have back: Nick's dirty laundry on the bathroom floor, cereal bowl left on the kitchen table for me to clear away. I'd give anything to be able to nag him about it all again. I have to get out of here. I stand up, reaching for my coat.

136

'Yes. Football on Saturdays. Rugby on Sundays. Anything to burn off his energy. He's a good boy, though.' She smiles then looks awkward. 'I'm sorry if the thing about the girlfriend was his mistake. He's desperate to help. So am I. I feel so guilty that . . .'

'It's not your fault, Beth. Truly. This could have happened anywhere, at any time.'

'Thank you for saying that.' She stands up too and gives me a quick hug. 'I just wish I could turn back time. Press reboot on my life, like Ade does on his bloody computer. So many things I'd change.' She blows her nose, then laughs as Molly starts crying, waking from her nap. 'That girl has *no* sense of timing.'

'She needs her mummy.' I can see Beth battling her emotions, but the press conference has drained every ounce of mine. I feel strangely numb. 'I'll leave you to it.'

Pulling on my coat, I drift into the hall, forcing myself not to look up the stairs – to imagine Nick scampering up them. It's been almost forty-eight hours now. I've never gone a day without seeing him; not an hour without knowing where he is. I look away as Beth follows, not wanting my distress to cause her more guilt, but she looks straight past me, green eyes wide and fixed on the coat stand.

'Did the police find any evidence on Nick's coat?' she asks. 'Fibres, DNA. Whatever it is they look for? You see this stuff on TV. You never think it's going to happen to . . .'

'I know. I keep thinking Nick's going to bound through the door at any moment. Oh, before I forget, DS Clarke mentioned something else Adrian said. Something about Nick having *stuff on his mind*. Has he said anything more about that?'

Beth's brow creases. 'It was to do with his dad, I think. Not his stepdad. His—'

'Alex?' I had no idea Nick ever thought about him.

'Was that your first husband's name? Gosh, you don't think . . . ?' Beth's eyes widen even further. 'I know how messy break-ups can get. Kids can get caught in the middle.' Her cheeks flush pinker. 'You don't think Alex was feeling bitter about the divorce, and—'

'We didn't get divorced. Alex and I never married.' I close my eyes and picture the apple tree, the little treehouse that was supposed to be a secret den for father and son. 'His dad left us before Nick was even born.'

Although I arrived at Beth's house thinking about Craig, wondering if I've offended him even more by excluding him from the press conference, it's Alex that preoccupies me as I climb back into my car. I think of the book Sean told me Nick was reading: *about a little boy who lost his dad.* When he first mentioned it, I automatically thought of Craig. Now I wonder if Nick was in fact thinking about Alex . . . He frequently asks to drive past our old home; it's why my first impulse was to check there. I thought it was pure nostalgia, but maybe Nick has been so unhappy that he's started fantasising about the father he never met.

Deciding to check in with DS Clarke, I pick up my phone, staring at it in surprise as a text from Katie flashes up. It's a short message, just two words: *I'm sorry.* Thankful for the apology, and curious about what prompted Katie to offer it, I decide to drive over and speak to her in person. Her house is only a couple of minutes away, and before I can change my mind I find myself striding towards the white Georgian townhouse that I'm surprised to see looks a lot shabbier than I remember. In my agitation yesterday, I didn't notice.

As last night, I press the doorbell repeatedly, with no answer. Realising Katie might have been out when she texted, I call her mobile, bending down to the letterbox as I hear her familiar ringtone. Spotting her iPhone on the hall table, I disconnect the call and bang on the door before stepping across to the living-room window to peer inside. The house is filled with shadows and an air of neglect: a vase of dead flowers on the table; a coat thrown on the sofa, as though discarded in a hurry.

I'm about to turn and leave, when a muted scream draws me quickly back to the front door. Heart pounding, I press my face against the stained glass. This time I make out figures jostling, then the muffled sound of footsteps disappearing up the stairs. I bend down again, calling Katie's name through the letterbox. Still no answer comes, and I mentally replay the tangle of arms and legs I saw. I can't be completely sure it was her: the coloured glass distorted everything beyond an impression of movement, a sense of coercion . . . *violence?*

I bang on the door. 'Katie! Are you in there? Are you OK? *Katie?*'

Turning to scan the street, I wonder whether it would be quicker to call the police or run to a neighbour, before remembering the olive tree where Katie always used to keep her spare key: tucked inside a glazed pot, concealed within a fake stone. Squatting down, I let my hand glide over the pebbles until I find the right one. I gasp in shock as it springs open. There is no key, but something else is concealed inside the artificial stone: Nick's phone.

'What the . . . ?' *No wonder he hasn't been answering my calls.* But he definitely had his phone at the sleepover: I spoke to him before he supposedly went to bed . . .

I lurch to my feet and hammer on the front door again; still there is no answer, no sound at all other than the engine of a BMW slowing down on the street behind me: Katie's neighbour. He gives me a frosty stare, and it dawns on me how odd my behaviour must look. Making a split-second decision, I grab Nick's phone and hurry back to my own car, sliding down in the driver's seat and waiting for the stern-eyed man to go into his house.

I can't stop shaking as I take out my mobile and dial DS Clarke's number, groaning in frustration when it clicks into voicemail. About to try her boss instead, I turn on Nick's phone, desperate to know what secrets it holds. DS Clarke reassured me they didn't find anything suspicious in his texts, but, like the photos, I want to see everything for myself. There might be messages that meant nothing to the police but which I might be able to decipher. Bullying dressed up as banter, perhaps. Or coded plans for Friday night.

I hold down the power button; nothing happens. The battery is dead. 'Dammit.' I reach for my phone again, pressing DCI Maxwell's number.

'Maxwell.' His voice is unusually curt as he picks up on the first ring.

'Hi. It's Izzy Brookes. Can we talk?'

'Izzy.' His intake of breath crackles down the line. 'DS Clarke was just calling you. We came to your house to see you in person, but there was no answer. Sarah's headed over to Mrs Atkins' house. She thought you might still be there. We need to—'

'I was phoning *her*.' I tut in exasperation. 'But why has she gone to Beth's? What's happened?' I don't wait for him to answer. 'I've found Nick's phone. At Katie's house. I had a text from her, but there's no answer. I've knocked and knocked. I heard someone scream. And I found Nick's phone outside,' I repeat, rubbing the small silver Nokia like a talisman.

'You found Nick's phone?'

'*Yes*,' I say impatiently. 'What does it mean? Why is it here? Something is going on inside that house. No one will answer the door. I think Katie might be in trouble. In *danger*. I can't leave. Not till I know Nick's not in there too. You need to send someone over here. Now. *Please*.' I can feel myself growing hysterical. DCI Maxwell has to say my name three times before it registers that he's trying to tell me something.

'Izzy, please, take a breath and listen to me. The person you saw in Mrs Baxter's house is most likely Matt Haynes, one of our

140

family liaison officers. He went to see her because … Look, I'm still here outside your house. You need to come home. There's something I have to tell you. I'd rather not say it over the phone. If you could—'

'No, please, what is it? Is it about Nick? Have you found him?'

'No.' The detective hesitates. 'It's about Jason.'

'He's done something, hasn't he? And hidden Nick's phone to cover it up. He—'

'Izzy.' The detective cuts across my spiralling panic. 'I'm sorry to put this bluntly. I know DS Clarke told you that police divers were searching the river. I'm afraid they've recovered a body. Down by Eel Pie Island. I'm very sorry to say that it's Jason's.'

TWENTY-THREE

DCI Maxwell cups a hand under my elbow, steering me into my living room where I half sit, half drop down on to the sofa. 'I just can't believe it. Poor Jason. *Poor Katie.*' I'm numb with shock, yet all I can think about is how devastated my former friend must be.

No, not former: we may not have been in touch over the last year, but I've never stopped caring about her. I'm in bits at the thought of what she will be going through. I think back to the figures I saw in her hallway. In my heightened state of fear after finding Nick's phone, I imagined violence. But it was Katie's cry of distress I must have heard; it was the family liaison officer trying to comfort her, not someone attacking her.

'It's a tragedy.' DCI Maxwell perches on the coffee table opposite me. 'And the worst part of any police officer's job. Delivering news like that.' He leans over, resting a hand on my arm as if to acknowledge that I may yet receive similar news about my own son.

'And Katie was alone when she found out?' I'm finding it hard to fight back tears.

'Matt will have broken the news as carefully as possible. But yes. We're still trying to contact her husband.'

I draw in a sharp breath. 'You mean Nathan doesn't know . . .'

'About his son drowning. No. Not yet.'

Drowning. The word is so shocking, I hardly dare ask: 'How did it happen?'

'That's precisely what we need to find out.' He pauses. 'I'm afraid there was a sense amongst the officers attending the scene that Jason might have taken his own life.'

'He *what*?' I sink back into the cushions, recoiling from the horror of what the detective is telling me, however gently. 'How do you . . . ? Did he leave a note?'

He shakes his head. 'No. As far as Mrs Baxter was concerned, Jason had gone off to his Sunday job at the boat yard as usual. A dog walker found his house keys on a bench. Along with his coat. His phone, too, which suggests it wasn't a mugging. There was no evidence of a struggle. No marks on his body. The post-mortem will tell us more, of course. But at this stage, very sadly, we have to at least consider the possibility that it was suicide.'

'Suicide,' I echo faintly.

'I know it's hard to hear. I wouldn't normally reveal so much to someone who isn't family. I'm telling you not because you're Mrs Baxter's friend. I just want to prepare you. We've managed the press pretty well so far. We won't be able to keep *this* out of the papers.'

My eyes are drawn to a pile next to him on the coffee table, reminding me of the hostile comments thrown by reporters outside my door. I wonder whether it will be Nick's photo or Jason's they plaster under salacious headlines tomorrow morning. *Or both.*

'You mean—'

'Jason and Nick were at the same sleepover. There's bound to be speculation about how his death relates to Nick's disappearance.'

143

'Yes. Of course. I can see that.' Pressure builds behind my eyes; my skin hurts. I feel like someone is sticking a thousand pins into me.

'Can I get you anything?' DCI Maxwell asks, watching me.

'My son. That's all I want.'

'You and me both.' He rubs a hand back and forth across his jaw. 'We'll coordinate the two inquiries, of course: the inquest into Jason's death alongside the search for Nick.'

'Jason's body was found very fast. If Nick—'

'The police divers didn't find anything else, Izzy. We've also followed up on a couple of sightings reported after the media appeal. Nothing doing there as yet. Oh, and DS Clarke has managed to get hold of Cassidy Parker, the boy in Year Twelve.'

'And?' I hold my breath in hope.

'Never heard of Nick, I'm afraid. Only joined the school a week ago. It was a long shot,' he adds when I groan. 'Sarah will look at other schools. If that yields nothing, we'll have to discount it as a meaningful lead. There is one positive development, though. None of the feelers we put out online has found anything connected to Nick. We've got undercover officers infiltrating known paedophile rings,' he explains. 'Nothing to report there.'

'Thank God.' I realise I've never prayed so much as I have over the last two days. 'Everything comes back to the sleepover, doesn't it? Whatever has happened to Nick is down to something that went on in Beth's house. Between those four walls. Those four boys.'

The detective frowns. 'I wish we could be certain of that. All we can do is keep piecing together the evidence.' He holds out his hand. 'Can I see Nick's phone?'

'His . . . Oh, yes, sorry.' I dig into my pocket and hold out the small Nokia, trying not to feel as though I'm handing over the last remaining part of my son.

DCI Maxwell reaches into his own pocket and takes out a

handkerchief. 'I'll need to keep hold of this, if I may. Our forensic guys might be able to recover prints from it.'

'Prints. I'm so sorry. I didn't think.'

'You're not a detective, Izzy.' His mouth twists, as though wryly acknowledging my need over the last two days to become an amateur one.

'The battery's dead. You'll need a charger.' I stand up and cross the room to the sideboard in the corner. The top drawer is full of odds and ends, and it takes me a few moments to untangle the correct USB cable. 'Sorry. I hope this is the right one.'

'Let's see.' DCI Maxwell takes the cable, plugging it into a wall socket by the sofa and carefully connecting it to the phone. 'Bingo.' Perching on the bulky arm of the chesterfield, he studies the screen as he waits for the Nokia to power-up. 'Any passcode?'

I shake my head. 'I asked Nick not to put one on his phone. Not that I ever checked it,' I add, not wanting to sound like a snooping parent. 'But I wanted the option. Just in case.'

'You did the right thing. We've already looked into Nick's text history via the server. Didn't find anything of interest. But . . . Ah. This message is new. Hasn't even been read, by the looks of it.' He tuts. 'Which explains why it didn't show up on our searches.'

'What is it?' I stand next to him, craning my neck to get a look. 'Who's it from?'

'"True friends don't tell,"' the detective reads aloud. 'Sent shortly after midnight on Friday.' He looks up at me with a frown. 'From Jason.'

'What?'

'Yep.' He stares at the text again, saying almost to himself: 'So he sent this *after* Nick went missing.'

'Was there any reply?' My heart is pounding; my head is spinning.

'No,' he says, without looking up. 'Like I say, it doesn't appear that Nick read it. Damn. We must have missed this when we checked Jason's texts on the server.' He frowns at the phone, then pulls out an evidence bag from his jacket pocket and slips it inside.

'What does it mean?' I watch as he starts pacing the room, desperate to know what he's thinking. 'Is it a threat? Jason warning Nick to keep quiet about something?'

'Perhaps,' he says noncommittally, still pacing.

'Or some kind of pact. "True friends don't tell." Maybe the boys made a pledge to do something crazy.' I look at DCI Maxwell in horror.

He stops pacing and stands in the middle of the living room, his expression taut with concentration. 'Neither Adrian nor Samir have mentioned any pact.'

'Well, they haven't said much about *anything*, have they?' I slump down on the sofa, disappointed that what feels like it should give us answers only seems to be adding to the confusion. I feel like I'm trying to run towards Nick on quicksand, and with every passing minute I sink deeper and he disappears further out of reach.

'True. They haven't,' the detective agrees.

'Maybe this text explains why? Maybe Jason pressured them into silence.'

'Well, there were no texts like this in *their* message history, either. If the boys did make some kind of pledge . . . ' He pauses. 'They're young. Scared. My hunch is that if there *was* a pact between the boys, Jason's death would almost certainly prompt them to break it.'

'Unless it was just between Jason and Nick. And Adrian and Samir weren't in on it?'

'Again, possible. But let's not jump to any conclusions. We could interpret Jason's text in any number of ways. A vow as part of some kind of pact. A threat. Even a suicide note. It's all speculation, though. He could simply have been having a joke with the boys.'

'A *joke*?' I shake my head.

'It was Friday the thirteenth. The boys were having a sleepover. Messing around. Sending scary messages, perhaps? Yes, the timing appears to suggest a connection with Nick's disappearance, but that's purely circumstantial. Possibly even coincidental.'

'Oh. Right.' My hopes of finding answers dip even further.

'Kids send thousands of texts, Izzy. There's no particular reason to believe this meant more or less than any other.'

'But Nick's phone was hidden outside Jason's house. That has to mean *something*,' I appeal in desperation. Jason was the first one I suspected of knowing something about Nick's disappearance, not only because of their past relationship but also because of his evasive manner yesterday morning. However cautious the detective is being, the discovery of Nick's phone at Jason's home rings loud, clanging alarm bells for me.

'Nick could have put it there himself,' DCI Maxwell points out logically.

'But when? *Why?* I'm not sure he even knew about that hiding place, either.'

The detective sighs, holding his hands up. 'Look, I'm slightly playing devil's advocate here. The point is, we can't just join up all the dots and make the picture we think fits. We're still almost completely in the dark about what happened on Friday night.'

The word 'dark' pulls my eyes to the window. It's early evening now, and almost pitch black outside. I glance at the clock on the sideboard. Nick has been gone since Friday night, and it's now Sunday evening. If we don't find answers soon ...

Where are you, Nick? I close my eyes, remembering TV news interviews with parents of missing children convinced they'd *feel it* if their child were dead. I trace Nick's face with my mind's eye, searching for any sense of him. All I see is darkness; all I feel is blank terror.

'So what's next?' I say, pinning all my faith on the detective now.

DCI Maxwell doesn't reply. Instead he takes out his phone, swiping the screen before pressing it to his ear. 'Sarah? Yes, I'm with her now. The boys are with you at the station? Good. Yes, I thought that too.' He ends the call abruptly, without signing off.

I take in the tension around his mouth, the sharp expression in his eyes. 'You think Adrian and Samir are in danger now too, don't you?'

'All I know is that four boys were at that sleepover. One is missing. One is dead. That leaves two.' He buttons up his coat, heading to the door. 'It's like a bloody ring of roses.'

And they all fall down, I think, sending up yet another prayer: that Nick isn't next.

TWENTY-FOUR

The police station feels like a maze of corridors. I check my voicemail as I follow DCI Maxwell, wondering where Craig is and why he's still not picking up his phone. It's beginning to feel as though he's dropped off the face of the earth too. After insisting to DCI Maxwell that I accompany him to talk to the boys and their parents, I phoned Craig, leaving yet another message, this time asking him to meet me at the police station. He hasn't replied.

Now I think of it, he hasn't been in touch since he left my house yesterday afternoon. I know I upset him with my impulsive accusations; I guess I offended him further by excluding him from the press conference. I made the decision with the best of intentions – so as not to confuse Nick, if he was watching – but I suppose it's understandable if Craig feels hurt.

I hope he isn't sulking: aside from wanting to ask him if Nick ever talked about going to live with him, I want to break the news about Jason in person. I look around, hoping to see him as we emerge into the main reception area. The first person I see is DS

Clarke, talking in a low voice to a dark-haired woman I recognise immediately. 'Beth. *Beth!*'

She doesn't hear me; all her attention is focused on Adrian as she turns and hurries him towards the exit. DS Clarke must have told her about Jason, I realise. That will have been shocking enough, and I'm sure she and Ayesha are both acutely worried about their own boys' safety now. *Two boys down; two to go.* I can't stop myself imagining the headlines.

'Where are they going?' I ask DCI Maxwell. 'They can't have interviewed Adrian already.' I was hoping to speak to him myself. Samir too.

The detective rests a hand on my shoulder. 'Let me find out.'

I try to overhear his hushed conversation with DS Clarke, but I'm distracted when Adrian lets go of his mum's hand to turn and wave at me. Touched by his brave smile, and concerned to know how he's really taking the news about Jason, I start walking towards him. DCI Maxwell blocks my path.

'Samir Matlock has made a statement,' he says immediately.

'A statement?' So his hunch was spot on: Jason's shocking death has driven Samir to talk after all. 'Does he know where Nick is? Has he told you what's happened?'

'Let's find a seat somewhere quiet, Izzy.' He takes hold of my arm, leading me back up the same corridor we walked down moments ago.

'Oh. Sure.' I look over my shoulder for Beth and Adrian. They've gone now, and I feel a jolt of frustration that Beth has heard Samir's statement before me. I hate the feeling that I'm always the last to know; I'm suddenly terrified about what the detective needs to usher me into a private room to tell me.

Drifting through the door he holds open, I look around blankly as we enter the small room. With radiators blasting out heat against the winter freeze, it's oppressively airless. I can hardly breathe, and my chest tightens even more as DS Clarke follows us in, closing the door behind her.

They have bad news; I can read it in her eyes. She doesn't greet me as she usually does, either; she doesn't offer condolences for Jason's death. Instead, she takes hold of my hand. I want to yank it away; I don't want to hear what I think she's about to tell me.

'Izzy, we think we know where Nick might be,' she says gently. 'Samir told us everything.'

'Is he . . . ?' *Alive? Dead?* The room seems to spin and I grab the chair DCI Maxwell pulls towards me just in time: the quicksand is tugging harder; it's about to swallow me up.

'I'm afraid all we can confirm at this point is that he was in Osterley Park. On Friday night, at least.'

DCI Maxwell strides back to the door. 'Izzy, I'm going to leave you here with Sarah, OK? I need to organise a search party. If you could bear with—'

'No. *No.* I'm coming with you.' I lurch to my feet, crossing the room in two strides to grab hold of his arm, hanging on for dear life – for my son's life.

It feels like the car journey will never end. Even while I'm dizzy with relief, fear crowds in, more stifling than ever. To be so close to finding Nick, yet not knowing if he's all right, if he is even alive . . . He's been in the woods for two nights, and this late in the day the temperature must be close to zero.

'It was some kind of dare, by the sound of it.' DCI Maxwell sits in the front passenger seat of the police car, eyes fixed on the road ahead. 'Samir described it as an "initiation trial" – a stunt the boys cooked up before Nick was allowed to join their gang.'

'Their gang. A *stunt*,' I repeat in disgust, closing my eyes and resting my head against the back seat. The glare of street lights flashes across my eyelids; my stomach churns with motion sickness and dread.

'We'll be there soon,' DS Clarke says at my side. 'Samir gave us clear directions.'

'Can I read what he said?' I nod at the file on her lap.

'Sorry, Izzy. Witness statements are confidential.'

'Oh.' I feel surrounded by walls of silence at every turn: blocked from seeing, stopped from hearing. Left to flounder in a vacuum of not knowing.

'But I can give you the gist of it,' she offers, picking up on my frustration. 'Basically, as the boss said, the boys set Nick a dare. A "terror test" they called it. Nick was the last to join their little gang. The others wanted him to prove himself worthy of being a member.'

'Prove himself worthy? What kind of . . . ? I thought they were his friends.' I clench my fists, furious that Nick has been let down again – this time by kids he thought he could trust.

'It was supposed to be just for a laugh, apparently. Yes, I know. Not funny to us. But they saw it as a harmless prank.'

'A sort of elaborate game of Chicken,' DCI Maxwell chips in. 'You know, testing how long you can hold your nerve. The loser gives in first.'

'Yes, but . . .' I turn back to DS Clarke, frowning. 'What did Nick have to do to *win*?'

'Hide out in the woods until his disappearance became breaking news,' she explains with a slight shake of her head. 'That was the agreed goal.'

'What? They *wanted* Nick's name to be splashed across the headlines?'

'Apparently so. At that point he was supposed to come home, confess it was all a dare, high-five his mates and be fully accepted into the gang. Only he didn't come home. The boys got scared, realised they'd messed up, panicked and—'

'Clammed up. They kept their mouths shut to protect

themselves, in other words. Great. Just great.' *All children lie when they think they're in trouble.* That's what I said to Beth, and I was right. 'So why own up now?'

'As I guessed, Jason's death has hit the boys hard,' DCI Maxwell says with a sigh.

'Oh, right. But they weren't so bothered about the state Nick might be in.' I can't hide my anger. I feel awful about Jason, but it strikes me as horribly typical that his life seems to have been deemed more important than Nick's.

'I know it doesn't help you, Izzy, but the boys have been terrified.' DS Clarke rests a hand on my arm. 'They haven't got a clue why Nick didn't come home. They've sort of *frozen*. Jason's death was the bombshell that shocked them out of it. Samir was in bits giving his statement.'

'He's a gentle boy,' I acknowledge, digging deep to find sympathy.

'He did ask me to pass on how sorry he is,' DS Clarke adds.

'And Adrian?'

'Showing all the symptoms of shock, I'd say. Not saying much. Acting like none of this is really happening. Samir was the one who finally talked.'

'I guess they're only twelve.' I picture their pale, shocked faces as they sat on the sofa in Beth's house yesterday morning. 'They must be feeling completely overwhelmed. Out of their depth,' I acknowledge. 'What a stupid, stupid thing to do.'

I sit back as DCI Maxwell directs the driver to take a left turn, bracing my hands against the black leather passenger seat in front of me to counteract the motion of the car as it swings around a corner. We're almost at the park now. I recognise the houses flashing past and try to make out the faces pressed to windows, their interest caught by the flashing lights. There are no sirens, just a convoy of police cars, a trail of electric blue streaking through the darkness.

'Thanks for filling me in, anyway,' I say to DS Clarke.

'Of course. I get that the hardest thing is not knowing.'

'Did Samir mention Nick's phone? If Jason hid it?' That's still bothering me.

'No. He knew nothing about Jason's text, either.' She opens the file and double-checks, frowning as she closes it again. Leaning forward, she rests a hand on DCI Maxwell's shoulder. He turns around in his seat to look at her, eyes narrowed.

'Nick didn't have his phone with him,' he says quietly before DS Clarke can speak. 'When he went into the woods. And it isn't a smartphone, in any case.'

'Dammit.' DS Clarke screws up her nose. 'It's just like his Facebook account. No phone. No internet connection. There's no way he could have deleted his profile. Likewise, how was he supposed to know when he'd completed this *terror test*?'

'Exactly,' her boss agrees. 'And if this was just a dare – an *initiation trial* – as Samir suggests . . . Why did none of them go back to tell Nick he'd passed?'

I'm about to interrupt their low, urgent conversation and demand to know what they're thinking, when the car suddenly jolts. Looking out of the window, I see we're entering the grand gateway into Osterley Park. All four of us fall silent, cocooned in our own thoughts as we speed along the drive and around the lake towards the stately home that sits at the centre of the vast, rambling estate.

Seeing a police cordon ahead, the driver slows down and cuts across rough parkland, finally pulling up behind a line-up of police vans. I stare out at them, pressing my fingers against the rear side window, tracing the skeletal outline of trees silhouetted against a purple sky. The detectives talk quietly between themselves again, but all my questions evaporate, my mind filling with only one thought: *My son is in those woods*.

TWENTY-FIVE

The line of torches is incongruously pretty as it hovers like fat fireflies in the dark. I know this park, I've walked here hundreds of times, and I can already imagine the heavy stamp of the officers' boots, the swish of their canes as they cut through the trees.

I know the police looked here once before, in their initial searches after Nick went missing, but that was on the other side of the park, in the formal gardens where I told DS Clarke that Nick liked to play when he was younger. This time uniformed officers are preparing to go deeper into the woods at the other, wilder, less cultivated side. They have Samir's statement and, whatever inconsistencies it holds, the detectives seem confident his directions will lead them to Nick. An ambulance is on standby; multiple officers emerged from the police vans. DCI Maxwell assured me they will search all night if they have to.

I want to get out there and hunt for Nick too, but DS Clarke pacified me by saying it would be faster and more effective if I left it to the experts. *She wanted to be sure Nick was alive first.* I knew that was the truth behind her gentle diplomacy, and my heart pumps furiously as I stare out into the darkness. It almost beats out of my chest as a fist raps sharply on the window.

'Craig! Where the hell have you *been*?'

Let me in, he mimes back, pointing at the door.

Before I can reach for the handle, he disappears from view, and I shuffle around, trying to see where he's gone.

'Beat you to it,' he says, sliding in next to me a second later.

'Dammit, Craig. You made me jump.' Icy air rushes in behind him, stinging my face.

'Sorry. Here. Let me warm you up.' He wraps an arm around my shoulders; I pull away, even though I'm shivering almost uncontrollably.

'Where *were* you? I've been calling and calling you. I left messages.'

'Sorry. I've had a few things to sort out. I was going to phone you back. Then I thought I might as well head straight to the police station and talk to you in person. You'd already left, though. The duty officer filled me in. I got here as fast as I could.'

'Did he tell you about the dare? The *terror test*?'

'Yeah.' His lips purse. 'What the hell were those boys thinking?'

'Did they tell you about Jason too?'

'Jason?'

'He's dead, Craig.' I don't have the energy to soften the blow.

'*What?*' He pulls back, his eyes narrowing in shock.

'The police divers found him in the river this afternoon. They were looking for Nick. They found Jason instead.'

'In the river.' Craig's rich baritone voice turns even huskier, his dark brows furrowing so deep that his eyes almost disappear. 'Was there some kind of *accident*?'

'I don't know. The police are still investigating.' I draw in a breath, wanting to tell Craig everything, but dreading saying the words aloud. I dig my fingernails into my palms. 'DCI Maxwell did say they can't rule out the possibility that Jason took his own life.'

'Christ, no.' Craig leans forward, covering his face with his hands. 'I can't believe it. Why would he *do* that?'

'I don't know,' I repeat, biting my lip as the shock of Jason's death ripples through me once more. 'But the detectives are worried about a connection with Nick. They seem to be having some doubts about Samir's statement now, too.'

'What? Four boys mucking around at a sleepover. Getting the new kid to prove himself. What's not to believe?'

'I'm not sure.' I bite my nails, thinking through what DCI Maxwell and DS Clarke were saying about Nick not having his phone with him, trying to figure out how that changes their understanding of what happened on Friday night. 'But I have a bad feeling too.'

'That's probably exhaustion. Anxious overthinking. Totally understandable. It's been a nightmare few days. Let's hope it's over soon.'

We both glance outside, watching the search party stretch out into a long line, and I feel my body stiffen with a fear I can't express. 'What if he's . . . ?'

'Don't even think it.'

'I can't not, Craig. He didn't have his phone with him. It was hidden outside Katie's house. Nick would have been alone in those woods. No way of calling for help. What must he have been going through?'

'Nick's phone was at Katie's house?' Craig's voice lilts in surprise.

'Yes. Jason must have hidden it there.' I still can't think of any other explanation.

'That would be an odd thing for him to do. Mind you, Katie said he's been all over the place lately. Not his usual self at all.'

'Did she? You still see her, then.' I don't really care; I just don't want either of them to think they have to lie to me, or conceal any relationship that's developed between them.

'Occasionally.' He waves a dismissive hand. 'Nathan's never there. I've helped her and Jason out a few times.' He turns to give me a direct look. 'There's nothing going on between us. In case you were wondering.'

'No, of course not. Anyway, I don't—'

'You were, weren't you?' He lets out a sigh. 'Sorry, that's my fault. We should have had this conversation months ago. I promise you, Isobel: there has never been anything between me and Katie. Never has been. Never will.'

He reaches hesitantly for my hand; this time, too tired and anxious to argue, I don't pull away. 'It's fine. You really don't need to explain yourself. You're a free man,' I quip, echoing his own comment to me on Friday.

'Sure.'

He looks disappointed, as though he's expecting something else from me, but before I can gather my thoughts to say any more, lights flash across the car and I see the chain of torches heading towards the trees. 'They're going in.' I turn to look at Craig, feeling my mouth dry. 'They're taking their time, though,' I add, turning back to watch the group of officers milling around, frustrated that they aren't already plunging into the woods.

'They have to be systematic,' Craig says quietly. 'Plan their route so they don't miss anything. They'll be trawling for evidence as well as trying to find Nick.'

'Right. If indeed he's even there.' Unaccountably I'm gripped by the sudden thought that Samir lied – that, for some reason, he's sent us on a wild-goose chase.

'We'll know soon enough.' Craig sits back, hands thrust deep in his coat pockets as though settling in for the wait.

I reach for the door. 'Well, I don't know about you, but I can't just sit here.'

'Isobel.'

'He's my son, Craig.' I make no pretence of sparing his feelings now; I refuse to waste time quibbling over who cares most about Nick. *I do*. He is my priority. First, last, always. 'No matter what state he's in, I have to be there when they find him.'

'Right. You're right.' Craig hesitates a moment longer then opens the car door and steps outside, buttoning up his coat and blowing on his hands as the cold bites. Then he holds one out to me. 'Come on. Let's go find our boy.'

'Keep up, Izzy. The police are way ahead. We need to keep moving.'

It's the first time Craig has ever called me 'Izzy', I register, staring at his back as he snaps a slender branch to help cut his way through the dense undergrowth, powdery snow flying up at every swipe. Underfoot, I can feel the velvet carpet of snow melting into a peaty mulch. Here in the woods, the thaw is happening faster.

'There they are! What's happening? *Craig?*' Spotting a group of officers in yellow high-vis jackets huddled together a few metres ahead, I speed up, twisting my ankle as I hurry towards them. Wincing against the pain, I limp as fast as I can towards DS Clarke, who I can now see holding up what looks like a bundle of clothes. Craig has got there before me, and my heart pounds sickeningly as I see him cover his mouth with one hand.

'Izzy, you shouldn't be here.' DS Clarke looks startled as I half sprint, half tumble towards her.

'Have you found him?' Glancing frantically around, I have to shield my eyes against the glare of torch beams combing the trees. I jump when DCI Maxwell appears at my side.

'Sarah's right. You'd do best to wait in the car. Both of you.' His

159

breath puffs out in an icy cloud as he turns towards Craig, patting his shoulder with a reassuring but firm hand.

Craig brushes it off. 'Are those Nick's?' He coughs to clear the huskiness in his voice. 'Have you found him?'

'I'm afraid not.' DCI Maxwell shows no reaction to Craig's brusqueness. 'We've just retrieved a yellow T-shirt and green hoodie from outside that shed.' He nods at a rickety-looking shack, almost entirely hidden by thorny scrub. 'It matches the description Izzy gave us of what Nick was wearing on Friday night. And one of his trainers was over there.' He points towards the river a few feet away. 'It has his name in it. But there's no sign of Nick himself. Yet. We'll keep looking. Please, you should both go back to the—'

'He'll be frozen. Two nights outside. In this weather.' I stare at the officers carefully stowing Nick's clothes into evidence bags then towards the icy river, before my eyes are drawn in horror back to the shed. 'What *is* this place?' I watch in a daze of disbelief as another officer cordons off the area surrounding it with blue-and-white police tape.

'Abandoned wood shed,' DCI Maxwell says, staring at it too.

'Nick's hoodie is torn,' DS Clarke tells me, clearly accepting now that I'm not going anywhere. 'It's dotted with splinters. Looks like he ripped it trying to get out of the shed.'

'But his T-shirt. Why would he take that off?' I pull up the collar of my parka, shivering more in fear than cold. I can barely feel the icy chill now; adrenalin pulses hot and urgent through my veins.

'Shock and exhaustion . . . dehydration. They all play tricks on the mind,' DCI Maxwell explains. 'If Nick's been out here for two nights, it's possible delusions have set in. Hallucinations, perhaps. I've seen it happen before. Nick might have mistaken cold for heat.'

'Is there . . . did you see any blood on his clothes?' I look between the two detectives, scrutinising their expressions for any clue that they're hiding something from me.

'We need to conduct a forensic examination to be absolutely certain. But at first glance – no,' DS Clarke reassures me.

'But that's for later,' her boss adds curtly. 'Right now, we need to keep looking.'

'We're coming with you,' Craig says, striding off before anyone can stop him.

TWENTY-SIX

'It doesn't make any sense. I can't believe he'd willingly go *in* there,' I say, more to myself. Craig has already forged way ahead of me. Still ignoring the jarring ache in my ankle, I try to follow as fast as I can, but as I pick my way across slippery rocks and the gnarled roots of ancient trees, I can't stop thinking about the wood shed ... and the horror Nick has always had of confined spaces.

I remember the day he cried all the way home, having been locked in the changing cubicle after school swimming lessons. He had nightmares for days, and he's been claustrophobic ever since; it seems incredible that he'd accept any kind of dare that involved hiding in a shed. In the woods. In the dark ...

'Craig! Wait!' I call after him, eager to share my doubts, pulling up short as I notice him veer suddenly off the main path, away from the police search party. He seems to be moving faster and faster, and despite urging myself onwards, I can't keep up.

Glancing anxiously at the line of police torches disappearing in the opposite direction, I hover uncertainly, wondering which way to go, what to do. Desperation surges inside me. If I can't find Nick, maybe he will find me . . .

'Nick! NICK!' I summon up all my breath to scream, listening to the eerie echo rebounding through the woods. A sharp breeze stirs pine needles, lifting the incongruous scent of Christmas from gently swaying spruce.

The smell instantly reminds me of Nick's excitement each year as he rushes to discover his presents under the tree. The happy image is immediately followed by one of him sobbing after he took his favourite new book into school for Show and Tell, only for the other kids to toss it around the classroom, teasing him because it was about ballet.

Even when it stops, it never leaves you, I remember Sean Newton saying about bullying, and my knees almost give way as I wonder if Samir *was* telling the truth: that as far as the others were concerned, this was all a dare, a challenge – but for Nick it went further, deeper . . .

What if he set out to *conquer his fears by acting them out*, as Jason's website urged, only the bitter, claustrophobic darkness defeated him, and the thought of being sneered at – *Wimp! Loser!* – as he has been so many times before, tipped him over the edge?

'No! *No!*' I try to pull back from the devastating thought, but it won't let go of me. I think of the book Sean said Nick was reading: about a little boy who lost his dad. Missing Craig, had Nick started thinking more and more about his father? Terror rushes through me as I wonder if he found out the truth about Alex – and what impact that had on him . . . Had it led him to believe that when life never seems to get any better, there is one final way to end the pain?

Looking up at the spidery treetops in despair, I see the shadow of my worst nightmare: the day that has haunted me for twelve years . . .

*

'Alex? Where are you?'

I looked around eagerly as I let myself in through the back door, heading straight for our tiny kitchen, the long hike back from the doctor's having worked up a burning thirst. Alex always told me to get the bus, but walking saved the fare and we were going to need every penny he made from his paintings once *Nicholas Alexander Blake*, as I'd finally made up my mind to call him, arrived in a month's time.

'Ouch. Your son and heir is really making his presence felt!' I yelled, hoping to guilt-trip Alex out from wherever he was hiding – no doubt with headphones on while he painted. He loved music as much as art, and he'd vowed to fill our boy's world with both, painting the flat every colour of the rainbow and planting borders to match in the small front garden.

Guessing that's where he was right now – tucking yet more bulbs into the soft earth beneath the apple tree, where he'd built our son *the perfect hidey hole* – I headed out through the front door. The sun was dazzling; the apple tree cast a dappled shadow on the bright green grass. Noticing it was oddly shaped, I looked closer. Then I stared up at the lush, fruit-laden tree to see the love of my life hanging from its branches.

I never thought I would let any man close to me again, or trust someone else with the most precious thing in my life: *my child*. It was Katie who convinced me to try – and it was Craig who finally persuaded me that he would be the perfect husband and stepdad. I've spent the last year blaming him for leaving me, but the truth is undoubtedly far more complicated. Being a step-parent isn't easy, and at least he finally seems to be admitting his mistakes. Maybe at some point we'll even be able to talk them through like sensible adults.

I never had that chance with Alex. I'll never know if our

relationship was just a schoolboy crush for him and it burned out. Alex left nothing for me but questions; he left nothing for the son he promised he couldn't wait to meet but an old radio and the set of paintbrushes I've tucked away. Perhaps, in the end, it was all too overwhelming. He was only nineteen, after all. Just seven years older than Nick is now . . .

'NICK! *WHERE ARE YOU?*'

I stumble in the direction Craig went, eager to know where he was walking with such purpose. The wind picks up; the trees seem to be whispering about me: *You drive away everyone you love.* I shut my ears and keep my eyes on the ground, concentrating on putting one foot in front of the other. Claustrophobia squeezes tighter as I fight my way deeper into the woods, panicking as I glimpse Craig's long grey coat, half-camouflaged by shadows.

'You know this place. It's fine. *Nick's* fine. You know this place. It's fine. *Nick's* fine.' I repeat the mantra over and over, ignoring the thorns that grab at my coat sleeves, as if to pull me back. I have to go on. *I have to find my boy.*

I spent hours in this park with Nick when he was little, ever since he was weeks old and I brought my books here to revise for retakes of the exams I missed, first while pregnant then coping with the horrible juxtaposition of Alex's suicide and Nick's birth. He would lie on his blanket, kicking his feet and smiling at the sky, and I would happily give in and put my work aside to make up names for the fat, curious ducks that came to scavenge for crumbs.

Nick took his first steps here, and the wide, open spaces became a place he could run free, safe from playground taunts. If I close my eyes, I know I'll see him pirouetting through golden leaves, a carefree seven-year-old boy in pink wellington boots, spot-lit by autumn sunshine. *'Are you sure you want pink?'* *'But it's my favourite colour, Mummy!'*

Over the years, we've come here far less often, but when Craig and I got married, I was determined to keep those memories close, and I chose our house because of its view: of the woods, fields and wild ponies Nick loved to talk to when he was a little boy, giggling when their velvety noses tickled his palms. Only those sunlit memories will never be the same. And now, as I stare into the black abyss of the park, I tell myself Nick can't be here. *Not here*, lost in the place we have both loved.

I look around, searching for any familiar landmark; this part of the estate is unfamiliar to me. I look up at the smudged-charcoal sky to find the moon, hiding her face in despair behind a wraith-like drift of clouds. 'Where is my son?' I ask her, before peering ahead to see a small copse, an outcrop of rocks. I smell the river. I hear voices. No, one voice: Craig's.

'I've got him. Izzy, I've found him. *Come quick.*'

TWENTY-SEVEN

Only his face is visible: the gentle slope of his jaw, the chestnut-cleft chin I would recognise anywhere. His white-blond hair is so dirty, his skin so pale, that if I blink I would surely mistake his head for a log or a stone. I claw my way closer, ripping through the thorny curtain that shrouds the small clearing. Stepping into a bowl-shaped gulley ten feet wide, my eyes sweep the violent hollow, a mist-filled amphitheatre where my son lies, cruelly centre stage.

Closer still. His body is swaddled by a drift of leaves, as though careless hands tucked him up for the night. A circle of snow-laced rocks crouches around him, their jagged edges explaining the tar-black gouge on Nick's forehead: one wrong foot in the darkness, and he would have gone flying. Arms stretched wide, he looks as though he was reaching for someone as he fell. My heart throbs with guilt that I wasn't here to catch him.

'It's OK, darling. Mummy's here now.' I half stumble, half fling myself towards him, dropping to my knees at his side. Stroking the blood-matted spikes of his fringe with one hand, I slide the other beneath the dank leaves to find his arm; it's ice cold. I trail my hand upwards to feel his chest; his bare skin is smooth white marble, with no rise and fall.

'Please God, *no*!' Acid nausea burns my throat as I howl my pain. My scream hangs in a frosty pall over Nick's face, but not a whisper of his breath clouds the air. I feel for his heartbeat, my mind filling with memories of bending over him exactly so, a dozen times a night, when he was a baby – frightened and alone, missing Alex, devastated that I wasn't enough to make him want to live, terrified I didn't know how to keep our son alive, either.

It seemed like a miracle that he survived, grew up, became the light of my life. I would lie down on the frozen earth right now and beg the universe to take *my* life, if it would mean Nick keeping his. Praying like I've never prayed before, I coil myself around him, desperately trying to infuse my body heat into his. He doesn't move; his eyelids are sealed with frost, his lashes encrusted with ice.

'Nick? Nick, can you hear me?'

'I couldn't tell either. If he's . . . ' Craig steps out of the darkness.

'Call the police. He needs that ambulance. *Call* them,' I yell, as he stands as rigid as the watching trees, staring blankly down at me. '*Now*,' I scream.

He jerks into action, taking out his phone, swearing when he can't get any reception. 'Where are they? Where is that fucking detective?'

Two firsts in one day, I think hysterically. First Craig calling me Izzy, now forgetting his usual decorum and using bad language. Maybe it takes a tragedy to crack the smooth, polished veneer he shows to the world: something so completely beyond his control that he is forced to behave just like everyone else. Flawed, fallible. Frightened.

'Nick? Darling, can you hear me? Please. Please wake up. Please, come back to me. I promise I'll never let you go again.'

*

White walls. White bed sheets. The bright, stark minimalism of the hospital room bizarrely reminds me of Katie's house. I wonder how she will bear to live there now, surrounded by ghostly reminders: Jason's school bag by the door; his rugby kit still in the washing machine; conversations, hopes and plans left to hang awkwardly in the air for a while, before fading away into the distance of time, leaving only the shadow of memory, the ache of loss.

I lean over and take hold of Nick's hands, torturing myself by imagining them lying forever still. I cannot imagine never hearing his voice again; I tremble for the silence that will greet Katie each time she returns home. She's already lost one child; now another has left her. She gave Jason life, but he didn't want it any more.

My heart splinters into a million pieces. *What happened between these boys?* How can a fun Friday-night sleepover have ended with such tragedies?

'Izzy, can I have a word?' DCI Maxwell knocks gently then hovers at the door.

'Oh. Yes. Please.' I'm desperate to talk to him, and this will be my first chance since the shock and commotion of finding Nick, the yellow swarm of high-vis jackets in the woods, the surreal blur of the ambulance journey. 'Here?' I look down at Nick's bandaged forehead, the tubes and wires criss-crossing his body, the ventilator breathing for him.

I can't leave him. I'm terrified I might miss the first glimmer of life; the tiniest sign that Nick knows I'm here. The doctors told me it's possible he can sense my presence. They've induced a coma to allow the swelling on his brain to subside; they've used phrases like *severe hypothermia, contusion, blunt-force head trauma.*

They just haven't been able to give me a concrete prognosis – nothing beyond a sense that Nick's recovery is as much down to luck as to medical science. He may live, he may not; he may walk out of here with his brain function fully intact, or he may never walk again. *My beautiful dancing boy*.

'Here's fine. Mr Brookes, you stay too.' DCI Maxwell nods at Craig, who sits quietly in the corner, lost in his own thoughts. 'I've asked our family liaison officer to join us as well. Jo Peters. She should be here any second.'

'She?' I have a flashback to a tall figure in Katie's hallway, arms comforting a distraught mother. I'm sure DS Clarke mentioned a man's name. I try to remember it, but details slip through my exhausted brain. 'Not the same one as . . .'

'Matt Haynes is still with Mrs Baxter. Jo will check in with him, though. Once we have a clearer idea of the connection between Jason's death and Nick's injuries. We're still waiting on the pathologist's report. And things have escalated pretty fast over the last few hours.'

'Escalated?' I look expectantly towards the door. 'Where's DS Clarke?'

'Back at the station. She'll still be assisting me, though.'

'Assisting you?' I frown. 'I thought she's been doing a great job.'

'She has. A terrific one. We just need a bit more experience behind the wheel now.'

'Oh. Right. I see.' *I don't see*, and I feel a stab of irritation on DS Clarke's behalf that she has been superseded.

'So, I'll come straight to the point, Izzy.' DCI Maxwell pulls up two low, leather-padded chairs, gesturing for me to take one of them, before sitting down himself. He waits for me to settle before continuing. 'There have been a couple of developments since we brought Nick in last night.'

'Developments.' It should be a positive word; he makes it sound the opposite.

'I've had a long chat with Nick's consultant, and we're both agreed. The bruising on his body wasn't only caused by climbing

170

out of the wood shed. Yes, it looks like he panicked and fought his way out. His torn clothes, the splinters under his skin, scratches on his midriff. They all fit with that. But he shouldn't have needed to fight his way out at all. Not if he was hiding there voluntarily. For a dare, as Samir said.'

'I knew something felt wrong.' I flick a glance at Craig, remembering his insistence that I was just *overthinking* things, but his eyes are fixed on the detective. I turn back to him. 'Are you saying Nick was *forced* into that shed?'

'I'm afraid so,' DCI Maxwell confirms. 'Nick may well have gone into the woods of his own accord. But he wasn't alone.'

'*What?* How do you know? Are you sure?' I'm desperate for the detective to be wrong, even though I've witnessed his caution for myself: he never *joins the dots* until he's double-checked each and every one first.

'Yes, I'm sure. Because whoever was with Nick locked that shed from the outside.'

'No. Oh, no.' I want to weep at the pain and terror Nick must have suffered.

'Ah, Jo. Come on in.' DCI Maxwell raises a hand in greeting as a middle-aged woman in a blue trouser suit enters the room, wafting sweet, heavy perfume that makes me feel light-headed. 'Izzy, this is Jo Peters, the family liaison officer I mentioned.'

'I'm so sorry to meet you in these circumstances,' Jo says formally.

'Thank you.' Automatically, I accept her handshake, but my attention returns immediately to DCI Maxwell as questions pile up in my head, clamouring to be answered. 'You mentioned developments?'

'Yes. And there's no easy way to put this, Izzy. Mr Brookes.' DCI Maxwell nods at Craig, who moves closer now, taking his glasses off, his eyes black holes of shock.

'It wasn't just a prank, was it?' I jump in. 'That's what you're going to tell me.' I shake my head. 'I knew it. I've been thinking and thinking. What Samir said . . .'

'You're right. This went way beyond a game of Chicken,' DCI Maxwell says meaningfully. 'As I said, I've had a long chat with Dr Lynch. In addition to the bruising around Nick's wrists and ankles, she found grazes. Chafing. Rope burns, in point of fact.'

'Rope burns?' The sick feeling in my stomach gets worse. 'You mean . . .'

'In Dr Lynch's opinion, Nick's injuries are conducive with his having been tied up. I'm sorry, Izzy, there's more. The FSIs have now carried out a fingertip search around the shed. They've recovered a knife. I'm afraid this is now an attempted murder investigation.'

TWENTY-EIGHT

'Murder . . .' The word is so stark, so shocking, I can't believe it has anything to do with my son. Staring at Nick's bandaged forehead, I remember the rocks; I try to replace the image I've had in my head of Nick slipping on them in the dark with a picture of him being struck by one. 'He didn't just fall and hit his head, did he?'

'I've asked Dr Lynch to consider that possibility.'

If I wasn't sitting down, my legs would give way. 'He was assaulted. Tied up. Then locked in that shed and left to die. And a knife . . . But he doesn't have any knife wounds?' I mentally catalogue Nick's injuries, my imagination tumbling back to the woods once again – only this time visualising Nick running not towards an adventure, but away from danger.

'Correct. Thankfully, Nick wasn't stabbed,' DCI Maxwell confirms. 'We think the knife was used purely as a threat. To coerce him into the shed. You don't need to inflict actual injury with it for a knife to be considered an offensive weapon. Curiously, though, the only prints found on it were his.'

'Oh. But . . . how can that be? Did the other boys mention

Nick having a knife?' I picture Adrian's bedroom, Nick's back-pack against the wall. Had he hidden it in there? But why? Where would he even have got it? 'Was it a penknife?' Nick doesn't have anything like that.

'No. It has a very unusual blade, as a matter of fact. DS Clarke is investigating potential sources. Samir and Adrian know nothing about it. They've both gone in to school this morning – their parents thought it best to maintain normality – but I had an officer pull them out of their first lesson, to ask about the knife and clarify Samir's statement one more time.' He pauses. 'I'm really sorry to give you all this information at once, Izzy. I know it's a lot to take in. Are you OK? Can I get you anything? Some water?'

'I'll get it.'

Craig has been so quiet, I jump at the sound of his deep voice. He doesn't wait for me to reply before hurrying out, and I wonder if it's not water he's going in search of but a place to hide his tears. I can't stop mine; they flood out of me, along with a tirade of anger.

'Of course the boys know nothing about any knife. Because this was all *Jason's* idea, wasn't it? That's why he killed himself. Out of guilt. Fear. Whatever.' Fury overrides rationality; desperation to find answers overtakes my distress at Jason's death. '"True friends don't tell." He did his best to make sure of that, didn't he?'

'There's nothing forensic to place Jason Baxter at the scene,' Jo interjects gently.

'Jo's right,' DCI Maxwell says, nodding at her. 'As I say, the only prints on the knife were Nick's. We're working on the assumption that his assailant was most likely wearing gloves. But we can't dismiss the possibility that Nick brought the knife with him into the woods. That he was secretly carrying it. Pretending to be a spy, or a soldier, perhaps.'

'Play-acting. That does sound like Nick,' I admit. 'But a *knife*?

Where would he even get one? And Nick's never been into war games. He's terrified of violence.'

'Most people are.' DCI Maxwell's eyebrows arch. 'It's one thing zapping baddies in video games. Quite another when faced with a living person. Whoever hurt Nick and forced him into that shed clearly has the stomach for cruelty, but maybe not for bloodshed. Rather than simply stabbing him, they played a game of mental cruelty. But the intent was equally deadly. Nick wasn't supposed to get out of there alive. Whoever did this—'

'Whoever ... You're saying it *wasn't* Jason? But what about Nick's phone? Jason must have been the one who hid it. Did you check it for fingerprints? Were his on it?'

'Yes. They were,' he confirms. 'So were yours, of course.'

'Oh. Right. Sorry.' I kick myself again for my carelessness.

'Not just yours. All the boys' prints were on it. That's not unexpected, though, given they were at a sleepover together. Kids pass their phones around, don't they?'

'Yes, but ... So the phone isn't proof of anything? And only Nick's fingerprints were on the knife.' Thoughts hurtle around my brain; understanding still hangs frustratingly out of reach. I return to the only theory that makes any sense to me. 'But what makes you so sure Jason *didn't* do this?'

It's not that I want him to be guilty; the absolute last thing I want to believe of my friend's son is that he tried to kill Nick. It's just that, in a bizarre sort of way, I find it less terrifying to imagine Nick being assaulted by a friend than a complete stranger. The idea of him having been targeted, pursued through the woods and held captive by some random *monster* is so appalling, I simply can't deal with it.

'As Jo said, there's nothing forensic to place Jason Baxter at the scene at all. Or *any* of the boys, in fact,' DCI Maxwell emphasises. 'We can't completely rule it out, of course. But we did a thorough search of the Atkins' house. None of the kids' shoes were muddy.'

I follow the direction of his eyes as he looks pointedly at my boots, which are still filthy, as are the hems of my jeans. I came straight to the hospital in the ambulance with Nick last night; changing my clothes was the last thing on my mind. 'I guess they would have been,' I concede, 'if the boys had been in the woods.'

'I would certainly suggest so. It's possible Nick slipped out of the house without Beth Atkins hearing. It's extremely doubtful that three boys – or even one, for that matter – could have cleaned their shoes in the middle of the night without her noticing.'

'Yes, you're right. Of course. *Who*, then? Who did this? What kind of *animal* would try to kill a twelve-year-old child?' I stare tearfully at Nick.

'Sarah's working on a psychological profile right now.' DCI Maxwell takes out his phone, checking for messages. 'We'll set that against information we find from other angles of the investigation. I wasn't planning to go into it all in detail right now, but . . .'

'I'm not sure Izzy can take much more waiting,' Jo says, giving me a rueful smile.

'Yes. Please. Tell me now,' I say, desperate to know.

'Right.' The detective sits back in his chair. 'Perhaps the simplest thing is if I walk you through our projected scenario for Friday night. Yes?'

'Yes.' I've imagined it endlessly myself; I want to hear his version.

'OK. So, first off, Nick goes into the woods for the dare. As per Samir's statement.'

'You're sure about that?' I frown, still struggling to believe that Nick would have overcome his fear of the dark and small spaces to accept such a challenge.

DCI Maxwell nods. 'As I said, we've spoken to Samir again this morning. Adrian, too. Both together and separately. Their stories are consistent. The evening started with a dare they all decided on.'

'Trained officers interviewed those boys, Izzy,' Jo chips in. 'There's no indication they're lying. The initiation trial seems to have been real. Tragically, the boys had no idea what would happen once Nick entered those woods.'

'Without his phone,' I point out.

'Yes. And that may indeed suggest a degree of spite on Jason's part,' DCI Maxwell says. 'Possibly to ramp up the fear factor. Unfortunately, we can't question him about that.'

'No. Of course not.' I feel a wave of guilt before remembering the videos I watched online – the 'dares' Jason had seemingly encouraged other kids to attempt. 'I found this website. *Dare or Die*. Jason set it up.' I should have mentioned it before, I realise. I'd meant to several times, but on each occasion I got distracted by bigger things: the press conference; the news about Jason's death . . . 'It's probably not important now.' Even if Jason was the instigator for the 'terror test', a far worse crime was committed that night.

DCI Maxwell takes out his phone, loading the internet. '*Dare or Die*, you say?'

'Yes. But it disappeared. At least, I couldn't find it again. It was full of stunts like this, though. YouTube videos of kids doing crazy dares.'

'I'll get the guys to look into it. It may be relevant; it may not. We certainly didn't see it when we retrieved Nick's internet search history. Nor any of the darker websites or social media kids sometimes get hooked into. *Dare or Die*.' He pauses, thinking. 'It sounds like it might at least add weight to the idea of Nick going voluntarily into those woods – for a challenge or play-acting some kind of mission. Whatever. The key point is that he appears to have left Beth Atkins' house alone. None of the boys, including Jason, was with him.'

'Fine. So Nick wanted to go into the woods, to prove himself worthy of joining their little gang, or whatever.' It's hard to speak around the lump in my throat. 'Tell me this, then: how does a simple, stupid kids' dare turn into attempted murder?' My voice cracks. I stand up from the chair and stride to Nick's side, wanting to lie down next to him and sob out all the heartache I feel that it's always *him* who is singled out for the amusement of others.

DCI Maxwell shoots a questioning glance at Jo.

'I know this is stressful, Izzy,' she says. 'Perhaps we should leave it here for now. Talk later once you've had a chance to—'

'*No.* Please. I have to know. *Everything.*'

'OK.' DCI Maxwell pauses a second longer, then begins again. 'So, Nick is sitting in the wood shed, thinking he just has to tough it out. But someone else comes along. Let's call them Suspect A. Nick comes out to see who it is – perhaps expecting it to be one of his friends. It isn't. It's someone who, for whatever reason – and we're still working on a motive – wants to do him harm.'

I want to scream in frustration. '*Who*, though? I need a name. I need—'

'To answer that question, we need to break it down into smaller ones. Such as: did Suspect A *know* Nick was going to be in the woods? Or did he or she just happen upon him?'

'While out for a midnight stroll, you mean.' Craig huffs as he walks back into the room – tellingly, without any water. His eyes are bloodshot, though, as if he's been crying.

'Precisely.' DCI Maxwell doesn't flinch at the sarcasm. 'Which leads us to the likelihood that Suspect A had found out about the dare, most likely from one of the boys. Adrian and Samir insist they told no one. Perhaps Nick did, whether intentionally or not.'

'You searched his texts. And emails. DS Clarke said you found nothing suspicious.'

'Correct. But the internet is vast. Chat rooms, the dark web. Less dramatically, Nick might simply have chatted to someone online, through instant messages, which—'

'Disappeared along with his Facebook account,' I finish for him, wanting to stamp my feet in frustration.

'Exactly. DS Clarke had a word with the boys about that, by the way. They said they felt it wasn't right to leave the photos up. With Nick being missing. Adrian helped Nick set up the account. He took it down for him.'

'But before then ... on Friday night,' Craig chips in. 'Izzy told me the boys posted about the sleepover. Anyone could have seen what they were up to.'

'No one posted specifically about the "terror test", though,' DCI Maxwell counters. 'We've checked. And you both saw how hard it was to find Nick. Someone had to have had precise info on his whereabouts. Only the boys knew about the dare. Ergo Suspect A *must* be known to one of them. Unfortunately, that makes for quite a list. But we're on it.'

'That could take weeks.' I sigh. I'm still no closer to knowing the truth. 'Maybe Nick will wake up before then.' I stare at his white face, the machines keeping him alive; I pray silently for a miracle. 'He's the only one who really knows, isn't he?'

'Whoever did this won't get away with it, Izzy,' Jo says firmly.

'No, they won't,' DCI Maxwell concurs. 'Our FSIs are examining the rope we believe was used to tie Nick up, as per Dr Lynch's suggestion. Ditto the padlock on the shed. We might be able to retrieve DNA from both. DS Clarke will also be visiting local hardware stores today. Maybe someone bought them recently. I've got officers checking CCTV around the park. There's no sign of forced entry through the gates. Our Suspect A found a different way in. We need to find it too.'

'And all the while this monster is still out there.' I continue to stare helplessly at Nick. He's in a critical condition medically, but I thought he was at least in a place of safety.

'We have a plain-clothes officer outside as a precaution,' Jo says.

'And I'll be around. I'm here to look after you, Izzy, as well as keeping you in touch with the investigation.'

'On which note, I've got to head back.' DCI Maxwell checks his watch and stands up.

'Thank you, Detective.' Craig holds out his hand. 'I'm sorry if I was a bit sharp. It's just the shock, you see.'

'I understand, Mr Brookes. No apology needed. We're all praying for your son. The whole team is committed to finding whoever did this. Before they do it again.'

My eyes drift fearfully to the door. 'Or come back to finish what they started.'

TWENTY-NINE

I weigh Nick's laptop in my hands. It's basic and clunky, and I make a silent promise to him that I'll treat him to a brand-new one when he comes home. He *will* come home, I tell myself for the thousandth time, staring at his poker-stiff body, willing there to be some sign of movement. At least his vital signs are beginning to stabilise, Dr Lynch assured me. For now, I'm trapped in a waiting game: waiting to find out if Nick will pull through; waiting for the police to find whoever did this to him.

In the meantime, I need something to keep my mind occupied: to brace the door shut against the hovering shadow of terror. I look back at the laptop Jo has just returned to me; they found nothing of any significance on it, and Jo thought I might like to have it here with me. There was one thing that caught their eye, she added quietly: a video diary.

'Seriously? Nick has a diary?' I thought of how many times I'd searched his room, hoping to find one. 'On his *computer*?' That had never even occurred to me, and I lifted the laptop lid, thinking of my own dog-eared notebooks of teenage scribblings, hidden under my bed along with novels I'd pinched from my mum's bookshelf. I stared at the black screen, admiring its power, hating its secrecy; its hold over my son.

'It's really not extensive. Just the beginnings of a vlog,' Jo said quickly, as if to reassure me that the police haven't been prying into my son's private thoughts. 'They were short clips – recent, but nothing that casts any light on the investigation,' she added, correctly anticipating my next question.

'Right.' I wasn't sure if that was a good thing or bad. On the one hand, I was happy to know there was nothing disturbing lurking in my son's computer; on the other, I was chewed up with frustration at still not knowing exactly what happened on Friday night.

'You may want to watch it in private, though,' Jo cautioned in a low voice, giving me a kind smile as she headed to the door. She glanced back at Nick's silent, immobile form, adding: 'I don't mean for his sake. I mean for yours.'

She was right. Desperate as I am to hear Nick's voice again, I know it's going to upset me. I glance at Craig. He's absorbed in a newspaper, reading the financial pages, sitting quietly in the corner of the small hospital room. For reasons of security, Nick is being cared for well away from the busy main ICU. Craig and I have hardly seen another soul, and neither of us have left Nick's bedside for more than a few minutes over the last night and day.

'I can call you, you know,' I say softly. 'If there's any news.'

'Sorry?' He looks up with a slightly dazed frown, as though lost in thought.

'Dr Lynch said Nick's finally stable. Now might be a good chance to catch up on some sleep. I know you've taken the week off work, Craig, but—'

'I'll go back when I go back.' His hand carves a dismissive wave.

'Likewise. Laura told me to take as much time off as I need.' I bite my lip. I don't want to come straight out and ask him to leave;

I know he's waiting with equal trepidation for Nick to show any sign of recovery. But I really want some time alone with Nick. And his diary. I try again. 'Time passes so slowly in hospital, doesn't it?'

'A watched pot never boils, so they say.' His attention returns to his newspaper.

'Exactly. Knowing my luck, I'll be in the bathroom or something when Nick wakes up.' I roll my eyes. 'At least there's no chance of me being asleep. Not on those things.' I nod at the low hospital beds where we've both been camping out for the last twenty-four hours.

'I've slept on concrete floors more comfortable,' he agrees, without looking up.

'I know. My back's agony. Yours must be too. In fact, there's no point both of us torturing ourselves, is there? We could take it in turns to suffer,' I suggest lightly, even though I have no intention of going anywhere. 'Why don't you go home for a bit?'

'*Our* home?' He finally puts down the paper, looking quizzically at me.

'Sorry?' Craig and I are getting on so much better, and it's good to have someone around who is praying for Nick as hard as I am. Only I'm pretty sure this new truce between us is mainly due to the relief of finding Nick, the worry of waiting to see if he'll recover and the tension of the ongoing police investigation.

'No, *I'm* sorry. It was a stupid thought. It's your house. I don't live there any more.' He watches my face for a moment then folds his newspaper and stands up, reaching out to lift his coat off the back of his chair. 'You're right. I'm exhausted. I should go and get some rest. At my own flat,' he clarifies with a wry smile. 'If you're sure you'll be OK here?'

Instantly I feel guilty at how I've manipulated him into leaving. 'I'm sure. You've seen the police officer outside. No one's getting past that guy.'

'Good. That's good. Because you and Nick . . .'

'I'll call you, I promise,' I jump in, rescuing us both from the awkward pause. 'If he . . . if there's any change. OK?'

'Sure.' Craig hesitates a moment longer then moves slowly towards the door. Eyes lingering on Nick, he gives me another small, lopsided smile. 'I guess neither of you are going anywhere.'

'Favourite colour. First pet. Darn it.' I tap yet more password attempts into Nick's laptop, wishing I'd thought to ask Jo what it is before she left. The police must have cracked it, or managed to bypass it somehow, but I'd wrongly assumed Nick wouldn't have set one up – as he didn't on his phone. 'Favourite film. Ballet . . .' His screensaver remains stubbornly in place, with a quote wiggling across the middle: *Art is a lie that makes us realise the truth.*

'Your dad used to say that. It was one of his favourite quotes,' I tell Nick, wishing he would sit up and ask me why I've never told him that. I should have; I should have told him *everything* about his dad – not just the happy stuff but the difficult bits too. Still thinking about Alex, I type his name with a sigh and press enter.

'What the . . . ?' My heart feels like it is pumping at a thousand beats per minute as the laptop's home page opens up, and even though Nick's middle name is also Alexander, I have a sudden intuition that he chose that as his password because of his dad, which makes me feel sad and happy all at the same time.

I open random files in his directory, not sure where to start looking, but all I find is homework assignments, book reviews and some playlists of music tracks for his dance classes. In frustration, I start clicking frantically on anything and everything, stabbing the keys with my fingers, wishing I'd never bought the damned laptop in the first place.

I'm about to give up and call Jo when the screen suddenly lights up. I must have accidentally clicked on the correct link, and my heart beats faster as a video uploads. I turn up the volume and press my hand against the screen as it starts playing, my eyes glued to the sight of Nick in his bedroom, sitting cross-legged on his bed, with Marzipan curled up next to him. From the angle of the film, the laptop is on his desk.

'Oh, sweetheart.' The contrast between the familiar sight of our messily comfortable home and the sterile room where Nick now lies trapped brings a lump to my throat. Nick is so rarely still; I'm aching to see him move, dance, smile again. I wait impatiently as the video suddenly buffers, leaning closer to the screen when it bursts into life once more.

Hey, people. This is me. And this is my diary. So if your name's not Nick Brookes, do one!

Nick is looking shyly away from the camera, just as he struggles to look people in the eye. After his plucky introduction, he stops talking and seems to clam up, experimenting instead with different poses, blue eyes half-hidden by his fringe. I press 'pause' for a moment, suddenly conscious that I'm invading his privacy. Jo said they found nothing relevant to the investigation; maybe I shouldn't watch. I swipe the cursor towards the 'close' button . . .

But I can't. I'm desperate to remember Nick as he was – as I am praying he will be again. 'Sorry, darling. You can tell me off later for snooping.' I blow him a kiss, then turn back to the laptop and, before I can change my mind, press 'play'.

Sorry, did I say Brookes? I meant Blake. Or is it Blake-Brookes? That would be kinda cool. Two dads are better than none, don't you think?

The video buffers again and I sit back in frustration, staring at the freeze-frame of Nick's image. There is more than a slight hint of American about his accent, I realise; I recognise it from the YouTube vloggers he seems to find hilarious. He's clearly trying to imitate their slick, cool patter, yet beneath the jaunty banter and constant hair-flicking I see the same little boy who used to dress up and put on shows for me in our living room.

I've never seen this side of my son, though: a young boy rehearsing his future teenage self. I'm guiltily fascinated to see more; I'm also struck by the reference to Craig. Curious to know if and how I will feature in Nick's vlog, I watch eagerly as the video restarts.

So much homework. Yawn. Don't these teachers know I've got a show to rehearse for? The boy with flying feet. *That's me. I'm famous. Huh. You can keep fame. I know Mum was proud I got my name in the papers. But it was just like one big, dumbass advert. 'Look at this guy, thinks he's legit. You should totally batter him!'*

Anyway, I guess secondary school is better. Well, the book group is. I've even got some mates. Hashtag miracle. Or maybe not. I'm not sure. It was easier when I trusted no one. If you know everyone is out to get you, you always know where you stand. I think I've figured out what to do about it now, though. It's showdown time. Bring on the sleepover . . .

THIRTY

'What are you watching?'

'Craig! You made me jump!' I close the laptop with a snap, suddenly reluctant for him to know about the diaries. It's not that I want to shut Craig out; it's more that I've worried so much about losing my connection with Nick, and I feel a jealous need to guard even these tiny secret snippets of insight into his thoughts. 'Nothing. Just . . . browsing. Passing time.'

'I meant on the TV.' He nods at the screen in the corner.

'Oh. I'd forgotten I left that on. I was hoping Nick might hear it, and . . . you know. Familiar theme tunes. Favourite programmes. I thought it might help. Anyway, how come you're back so soon?' I check the clock on the wall; he's only been gone half an hour. 'I thought you were going home. Is there a problem?'

'No problem. Only that I felt bad leaving you to cope alone. I made that mistake a year ago. I meant what I said, Isobel. I'm trying to put things right. Turn over the proverbial new leaf.' He shrugs and gives me a rueful smile.

'Sure. I can see that.' I try not to show my irritation at his bad timing. I appreciate his thoughtfulness, but I wanted to hear more of what's been going on in Nick's head. The police obviously didn't think his reference to the sleepover was a big deal, but it's been so long since Nick confided in me, I'm greedy to hear what else he has to say.

'Any word from DCI Maxwell on this Suspect A, as they're calling him?'

'Or her,' I point out. 'Though I grant you, somehow it feels more likely to be a man. We hear it all too often on the news, don't we? I've got a terrible image in my head already. Almost certain to be wildly inaccurate.'

'The bogey man. Yes. Everyone has their own idea of what a monster looks like. I guess murderers come in all shapes and sizes, though. And sex offenders.'

'Sex offenders. Oh God.' The term terrifies me. Both the detective and Dr Lynch assured me there's no evidence to suggest Nick has been assaulted in that way; I still can't shake the fear that it was the ultimate motive behind his attack – especially if someone had contacted him online, perhaps after seeing the photos Nick posted on Facebook.

'The police are looking again at everyone local on the register, yes?' Craig asks, moving to Nick's side and gently stroking his hair.

'So DCI Maxwell said.' I have no idea how many names are on that list, and I was reluctant to ask. The thought that I could be living next door to a known sex offender is horrifying. Part of me wants to know; the other part is too scared to find out. I shudder, remembering the intruder in my garden, the Range Rover I thought was tailing me to the press conference. I put both incidents down to the over-active imagination I seem to be plagued by, but to be on the safe side I should mention them to the police, I decide.

'Good. Let's hope they come up trumps. Sick bastard needs locking up before they do it again to some other poor kid.'

'Don't say that, Craig. I can't stand the thought of them still being *out there*.' I look anxiously beyond him towards the plain-clothes officer talking to someone in a low voice outside Nick's room. DCI Maxwell instructed 'no visitors'. I haven't seen anyone, which means either there haven't been any visitors or the officer is doing a great job of turning them away.

'I know, but ... Isobel, look.' Suddenly Craig grabs the TV remote from Nick's bedside table, pushing buttons until the room fills with the strident voice of a newsreader.

I swivel around, staring mutely at Nick's image on the screen. Underneath, the rolling headlines confirm that the 'missing child inquiry' has been upgraded to 'attempted murder'. It's the photo I chose for the press conference, I realise, rage and disgust roiling through me at the thought of someone having seen other pictures of my son – eating pizza and messing about with his friends at the sleepover – and deciding to target him. 'Switch it off. Please.'

'Sorry.' Craig quickly turns off the TV.

'It's OK. I just need to not hear it for a while, you know?'

'Yes. I do know. Sometimes it helps to bury our heads in the sand a little. Pretend life is normal. It will be again soon, I promise.' Craig gives me a small, slightly sad smile.

I sit quietly for a moment, reflecting on the change in our relationship. I'm almost starting to feel sorry for Craig, I realise. I know he's hoping things between us can go back to the way they were; I don't feel the same, but maybe we can be friends.

Two dads are better than none, Nick said in his diary. Until he wakes up and talks, I can't know how he really feels about his stepdad. They used to be close, but distance has definitely crept in between them over the last year. For now, I think the best policy is to stay on cordial terms with Craig: friendly but not intimate; close but not personal.

'You OK?' he asks, when the silence stretches into minutes.

'Yes. Sorry. Just thinking.'

'Ah, I thought I could hear the cogs turning,' Craig quips. 'It's funny. Nick's such a quiet boy, but I can't get used to him saying nothing at all.'

'I know. The silence without him at home was so . . . empty.'

'And uncanny, I bet. I remember feeling like we never had a moment to ourselves when I lived there. One of my biggest regrets is not making more time just for us. I realise I probably spent more time with Nick. I just wanted to be a good dad. *Stepdad.*'

'And you were,' I tell him truthfully.

'Was I?' He sighs. 'I tried. Maybe too hard. I think I wanted so badly to make everything perfect that I was too . . . ' He hesitates.

'Judgemental?' I finish for him. I won't lie about how Craig hurt me at the end of our marriage, but I am glad he at least has the good grace to admit his mistakes.

'Ouch.' He mimes a stab to the heart.

'But Nick's always been very fond of you.' I know that much to be true, even if I've seen little sign of it lately. After all, Nick has closed off from me in exactly the same way.

'Well, that's good to know. It feels like such a long time since we were a family. Look, I know this might be bad timing. But I just want to say—'

'Craig . . . '

'Please, hear me out. I so want to make things up to you. You *and* Nick. Actually, I've had an idea. It's looking a bit ahead, but assuming Nick gets the all-clear at some point' – he holds up crossed fingers – 'how about the two of you hang out for a few days at my cottage? It would be perfect for Nick to recuperate. Give you a change of scene, too.'

'Your place in Twickenham? I thought it was tenanted?' And I'm pretty sure Nick would rather go straight home. I've never been to Craig's rental property, I'm not even sure what creature comforts it

190

offers, and Nick is going to need as many as he can get if – *when*, I mentally correct myself – he wakes up.

'It was. But the last tenant left a while back. I needed them out so I could spruce the place up. It's been a while since I decorated it, but it's got a pretty view of the Thames. Nice private plot. No one will bother you. Not even me. I mean it,' he adds seriously, when I look surprised. 'I don't want to rush you, Isobel. The cottage would be all yours. I'll keep my distance. Leave you and Nick in peace until he – you – let me know if you want me around.'

'Right.' I'm still not sure. 'It's really kind of you, Craig. It's just … You know, I think Nick would actually prefer to go home. Once he—'

'Sure. Understood.' He holds up his hands. 'The offer's there if you change your mind, though. When the time comes, I mean. Just say the word.'

'Thank you. And I will think about it.'

'Excellent.' Craig's smile widens. 'I hope you do. You'd love it, Isobel. I've often thought we should have made more use of it. Maybe we will in the future. Who knows?'

I smile, not wanting to dash his hopes or provoke a return to discord between us. But all thoughts of my future are on hold – at least until I can be sure Nick will be part of it.

THIRTY-ONE

My voicemail is full of good-luck messages from the staff and pupils in Nick's dance class – and from some of his classmates at school, which is a heartening surprise. But the one voice I'm hoping to hear is absent: there is nothing yet from DCI Maxwell, not even one of the keeping-in-touch messages DS Clarke used to leave me.

I miss her quiet, steady presence, I realise, and it dawns on me that I've come to rely on her almost as a friend. I'm tempted to call her. I know she's busy with the investigation, though, and I don't want to cause any delay. I've had another long chat with Jo, in any case, and she confirmed that DS Clarke is 'in the throes of intensive inquiries'. I can tell how hard Jo is trying to take her place, so much so that I didn't like to shoot her down when she said it sounded like a 'brilliant idea' for Nick to recuperate at Craig's cottage – when he wakes up.

We're all talking so deliberately in terms of *when* rather than *if* – even Dr Lynch, who reiterated that she's a firm believer in the medical benefits of positive thinking, and that I should keep talking in those terms to Nick.

'He needs to know his mum believes in him,' she said.

'Always,' I told her, squeezing Nick's hand.

'What's his "happy place"? Have you ever talked to him about that?'

I remembered DS Clarke asking me that too, and I gave the doctor the same answer. 'On stage. Cuddled up with Marzipan. Daydreaming by the river.' I tried not to think of Jason, but that was another reason for my uncertainty about Craig's offer: Jason drowned outside Eel Pie Island boat yard; a cottage on the island is just too close for comfort.

'The river? Lovely. Your husband's cottage sounds perfect, then.'

'Ex-husband.'

'Sorry.' She pulled a grimace. 'I didn't mean to put my foot in it.'

'You didn't.' I knew she was really just trying to keep my spirits up. 'Craig and I are separated. As far as I'm concerned, that's the way it's going to stay.'

Something soft brushes against my face. 'Marzipan. Get *off*.' I turn over, frustrated at being woken up by Nick's cat. *I'm so tired . . .*

'Izzy? It's Dr—'

'What's happening? *Nick?*' I fight my way out of sleep, panicking when I see Nick's petite, dark-haired consultant standing over me.

'It's OK. You just nodded off. You're allowed.' She winks, helping me sit up.

Still half in a dream of home, it takes me a moment to realise that the softness I felt wasn't Marzipan but a blanket someone has laid over me. *Dr Lynch?* I feel like she's been looking after me as much as Nick over the last two days. Seeing two unfamiliar doctors at her side, however, I scrabble to my feet.

'Is he all right?' I stumble towards Nick, adrenalin kick-starting my brain.

'They're going to reverse his coma, Izzy.' Craig, standing sentry at Nick's bedside, looks as shocked as I feel.

'Your son's done brilliantly,' one of the other doctors tells me. 'The brain swelling has receded. He's breathing independently. We're confident he's strong enough now for us to stop the drugs. That will allow Nick to emerge naturally from his coma.'

'How long?' Joy fizzes through me; I beam at him, and then at Dr Lynch, wanting to launch myself around the bed to hug her. 'How soon until he wakes up?'

'Hard to predict.' Her tone is measured but her smile matches mine. 'Given he's been sedated less than forty-eight hours, we shouldn't have long to wait. Hopefully a few hours – maybe ten max. Depends how determined he is. Judging by how hard he's fought to stay alive, I'd say extremely. This is one very determined young man.'

'A few hours,' I echo, gazing down at Nick. He looks thinner, painfully fragile, but there is a little more colour in his cheeks now. I stroke the bandage on his forehead, jumping when his eyes flicker. 'I can't believe it. I can't believe he's actually going to be OK.'

'He'll be very weak to begin with,' Dr Lynch warns. 'We'll need to keep him under intensive care for at least another twenty-four hours. After that, all being well we can start to talk about a rehabilitation programme.'

'All being well.' Nervously, my thoughts leap ahead to school, dance classes. 'Can you tell yet? If he's going to be OK, I mean. Completely back to his normal self.'

'Well, as my colleague here said, Nick has done extremely well. I'm cautiously optimistic. But we'll only know for sure once he regains consciousness. Cognitive function. Motor skills. We'll need to assess them all. There's everything to be positive about, though.'

'Thank you. I can't thank you enough.' Impulsively, I give in to the urge to hug her.

'A rehabilitation programme.' Craig digs in his pocket for a handkerchief, takes off his glasses and slowly cleans them. 'That sounds pretty involved. Can it be home-based?'

'All depends on our initial tests. Nick might need specialised care. Physical therapy. *Emotional* therapy such as counselling. Or he might just need a period of quiet recovery at home. Being in familiar surroundings can certainly help,' Dr Lynch tells him. 'I can't give you a definitive care plan at this stage, I'm afraid. He's suffered a significant trauma, and there are too many variables. Our discharge planner Ben Holt will guide you through his patient journey. And I'm here. My whole team is here to support you. Whatever happens when Nick wakes up.'

'Memory loss?' Craig steps forward, gently touching the bandage on Nick's head.

'Too soon to say. In fact, let's not get ahead of ourselves. We'll talk more in due course. For now, though, I think we should all take a moment to appreciate a small miracle.'

'And wonderful care from his doctors,' I say, unable to stop smiling now.

'We aim to please.' Dr Lynch's dark eyes twinkle as she smiles back. 'Good work, team.' She nods at her colleagues, makes a few notes in Nick's file, then turns to leave.

Craig intercepts her. 'I want to extend my thanks too, Dr Lynch.' He settles his glasses back on his face then holds out his hand. 'And a donation to the hospital. If I may.'

'That's very kind of you,' she says, accepting both his handshake and his offer.

'Not at all. After everything you've done? It's the very least I can do.'

For the next few hours, I sit and wait, determined not to miss the moment Nick regains consciousness. My heart is bursting with hope; my mind is imploding with fear. Every time I start to feel excited about the prospect of Nick coming home, a voice in my head whispers that there's still a killer out there. The police can't tell me who that is, or why they targeted my son; nor can they guarantee they won't try again.

'Maybe we should just run away,' I whisper in Nick's ear, leaning close. 'Far, far away, where nothing and no one can ever find us.'

'Mum?'

A tingle feathers down my spine. *Did I just imagine that?* 'Nick? *Nick?*' I take hold of his hand, my eyes filling up as his fingers twitch; tears spill over as he squeezes back.

'My head hurts.' Blue eyes open briefly before blond lashes sweep down again.

'Oh, sweetheart.' *I thought I'd lost you.* I press his palm against my cheek, feeling the hairs on the back of my neck prickle, exactly as they did the very first time I held Nick, when the midwife laid his tiny body on my chest. I look up, sending a prayer of thanks into the universe. Everything around me suddenly looks brighter; the sterile white walls seem to glow. I feel like a solar eclipse has passed over, bathing the whole world in brilliant sunshine.

'My throat hurts too.'

'Don't try to speak, darling.' I can barely force out words myself. 'The doctor said you'll be sore all over for a little while. But they're taking good care of you. You're going to be just fine.' I sweep back his fringe, taking care not to touch the freshly changed bandage.

'What happened?' His body suddenly flinches, his eyes snapping open now as he tries to sit up. 'Where's—'

'Shh.' Gently, I urge him back against the pillows. 'It's OK. Just rest for now.'

'Your mum's right.' Dr Lynch smiles as she appears in the doorway, accompanied by a nurse, both of them moving swiftly to Nick's side. 'Hello, Nick. I'm very pleased to meet you. My name's Dr Lynch and you've been paying me a little visit in hospital. Do you remember? You had quite a bump to your head. But we've fixed you up good as new. All you need to do now is lie there and take things easy. You have my absolute permission to be lazy. OK?'

'I'd make the most of it while you can, mate,' the nurse at her side jokes. 'Doc's a slave driver. She'll have you making your own bed, if you're not careful.' He chuckles, using humour to distract Nick from a deft-handed assessment. 'Lungs are clear,' he says quietly to Dr Lynch.

'I'm so tired.' Nick closes his eyes again; a tear trickles out of one corner.

'Sleep,' I tell him, wiping my own eyes. 'I'm right here.'

After sitting with Nick for half an hour more, just gazing at him as he drifts in and out of exhausted but thankfully natural sleep, I leave the doctors to wheel him off for yet another CT scan and more tests, and hurry out of the room in the direction of the bathroom.

Locking myself in a cubicle, I lean back against the door, cover my face with my hands and cry until my throat is raw and my chest feels like I've been punched. I've been trying so hard to be strong, but now the avalanche of emotions I've fought to hold in check finally overpowers me. I've felt the storm coming; I just haven't wanted to show any sign of distress around Nick, even while he was unconscious.

I'm determined he'll see only a new, positive me from now on. My son has come back to me. The police *will* find their Suspect A. I'll take Nick home, start life afresh, and together we'll make new dreams to obliterate this nightmare. I feel like I've been given a second chance with him – a second chance to be a better mum – I'm not going to waste it.

THIRTY-TWO

'Here you go, Marzipan.' I give her extra tuna, feeling bad about leaving her alone while I stayed at Nick's bedside for a further twenty-four hours. Even after Dr Lynch encouraged me to take a break, it took Craig another hour to convince me to leave – to come home and have a proper bath, change into fresh jeans and jumper and get the house warmed up.

Nick can come home. I fly upstairs to make his bed, tidy his room and check there are no unsettling signs of the police search. I put his laptop back on his desk, then change my mind and hide it under my bed. I still want to talk to Nick about why he didn't tell me he was on Facebook; I need to understand who he's been in contact with online. But all that can wait.

For now, I want to keep him well away from the internet. I'm avoiding it too. Every time I turn on my own computer, or the TV or radio, I hear Nick's name and see his photo. DCI Maxwell was spot on about press speculation; the tabloids are having a field day with the breaking local story. If I see the headline 'SLEEPOVER SLASHER' one more time I'll go mad. Until Nick can tell me himself what happened on Friday night, I don't want sensationalist scaremongering to get into my head.

I know the detectives are as eager to question him as I am. DCI Maxwell tried, with little success. Nick stared blankly at him, looking even more confused when Jo asked if he could remember who was with him in the woods. It's obvious Nick remembers little, if anything, and Dr Lynch warned the police not to push him too hard too soon. I hope that once he's home, surrounded by his own things, his memories will start to filter through. In fact, it's the reason I've finally declined Craig's offer: Nick has never been to the cottage, and I'm worried it will confuse him to be taken to a strange place.

Propping Sleepy Bear on his pillow, I wonder if the button-eyed, patched-up golden bear Nick's had since he was a baby will be forgotten too – along with Marzipan, perhaps even the dance steps Nick has spent a lifetime learning. 'Memory is unpredictable,' Dr Lynch told me: many victims of violence remember only the big details; sometimes it's tiny, inconsequential things that come back to them; occasionally they recall nothing at all. Craig joked that it was usually bankers like him that had a selective memory. He's trying hard to stay upbeat, but I can tell he feels as power-less as I do.

We can't force Nick to remember, and with no new police leads, his testimony alone will hold the key. Somehow, I need to help him release it, and my decision to take Nick home was reinforced when Dr Lynch suggested that familiar smells and tastes can often trigger memories. Craig immediately offered to do a food shop for all Nick's favourites. I check my watch as the doorbell rings.

'That was quick!' I call out, sparing one last glance at Nick's room before heading along the landing and down the stairs. The doorbell rings again, insistently this time, swiftly followed by the sound of a car alarm. It's very close. *It's mine.*

'Oh, what?' I hope Craig isn't leaning on the doorbell because he's bumped my car trying to squeeze his behind it on the short drive. Hurrying through the hall, I have to put my fingers in my ears to block out the strident wail. 'Damn it. *Car keys.*' I dash into the living room, then the kitchen, hunting for my bag, before striding back to the front door. 'Coming!'

As I flick up the latch, a shadow moves in my peripheral vision. I hear footsteps, and suddenly I'm gripped by a shiver of intuition that something isn't right. Craig hasn't called out to me in reply, as he generally would, or rapped on the door with his usual jaunty knock. Opening it slowly, I peer out cautiously before stepping into the porch. There's no sign of Craig, nor any shopping bags. Only my car sits alone on the drive, headlights flashing.

I quickly deactivate the alarm, but I can't switch off the jangled sense of threat so easily. Déjà vu envelops me as I cross the front garden, remembering the broken plant pot outside my window, the heavy footfall in the alley. Feeling like I'm re-enacting a play I once watched, I walk slowly to the side of the house, tingling again with the panic that kept me cowering against the wall a week ago.

This time, there are no footsteps disappearing into the distance. Nobody is there. Maybe someone reversed on to my drive and bumped my car, I think rationally. Perhaps they rang the doorbell to let me know, then changed their mind. I walk around my already somewhat battered Mini, checking it for yet more scrapes, freezing in shock when I get a clear look at the rear window: it's completely caved in, demolished in a glittering spider's web of shattered glass. This was no minor bump; it wasn't an accident at all . . .

Turning sharply, I try to run back to the house. But fear has stiffened my body and my boots slip on the icy path. I fall flat on my face, the jolting impact knocking the breath from my chest, while the bang to my forehead sends pain splintering through my brain. For a second, I can't move. All I can do is lie on the frozen ground and stare up at the graffiti spray-painted across the walls of my home: *Liar! Bitch mother! Guilty!*

Unable to tear my eyes away, I pull myself slowly to my feet, groaning as I touch my fingers to my forehead and they come away wet with blood. Red, sticky blood. The same colour as the words emblazoned across my front door: *You're next, slag.*

'I was waiting for Craig. He went shopping for me. Why isn't he *here* yet?' I feel angry, *violated* by what's happened, and unfairly some of my agitation spills out towards Craig. 'He might have been able to stop them. Or seen who did it. Who would have *done* this?'

'We've got officers knocking door-to-door.' DS Clarke comes to sit next to me on the sofa, flannel in one hand, sticking plaster in the other. 'Let's hope your neighbours are more forthcoming this time. We spoke to most of them when Nick went missing. No one saw anything. Knew anything. That's cities for you. People keep themselves to themselves.'

'I'm pretty lucky with my neighbours, actually. Most will have been at work, though. Mr Thompson next door is retired and recently widowed. I don't see much of him. Sally the other side works away in the week. Ouch.' I flinch as she dabs my forehead. Thankfully the cut will be covered by my fringe. I don't want Nick worrying about me.

'Sorry. I'm trying to be gentle. I bet it hurts.'

'I'm fine. Couple of paracetamol and I'll be good to go.' The bump on my head is nothing compared to the wound on Nick's; the malicious graffiti only reminds me of the bullying taunts he has suffered. *Sticks and stones may break my bones*, I hear in my head.

'Here. Take these.' DS Clarke reaches over to the coffee table, then hands me a glass of water and two tablets. 'You'll have a nasty bruise. No lasting damage, though. Wish I could say the same for your car. It's going to be out of action for a bit, I'm afraid.'

'It's fine. Craig can drive me to the hospital.'

'Or Sergeant Rogers. He'll also take you and Nick to the cottage. The officer who's been standing guard outside Nick's room,' she reminds me when I look blankly at her. 'He's going to be providing you with on-going security. No arguments, Izzy.' She gives me a steady look. 'I meant what I said. You can't stay here now. You mentioned someone might have been hanging around in your garden. Maybe tailing your car. Whoever threw that brick—'

'I know but . . . *brick?*'

'From your own garden wall, by the looks of it,' she confirms.

'How ironic.' A slightly hysterical laugh bubbles up. 'I wonder if it's the same one I grabbed on Saturday night. This wasn't just kids messing about, though, was it?'

'I think we can safely say this wasn't a prank, Izzy. It's strictly personal.'

'Do you think it was one of those reporters?'

DS Clarke shakes her head. 'That would be a serious breach of professionalism. Highly unlikely. It is possible someone's been tail-gating the news, though. Following Nick's story. Seen your face on TV. Decided to express their own ignorant judgement.'

'Yes.' I close my eyes, trying to stop seeing the offensive scrawl. 'I've got to wash it off.' I make to stand up from the sofa, but DS Clarke stops me.

'I'm really sorry, Izzy. I'm afraid we need to leave it all there for now. I've taken a few snaps on my phone, but we'll need to photograph everything properly for evidence. Not just as an act of vandalism. We can't rule out a connection with what's happened to Nick.'

'*You're next.*' I look at her in horror. 'It's a warning, isn't it?'

'A threat,' DS Clarke corrects me. 'Whether it's a hollow one or not, we can't take that risk. You're not safe here now, Izzy. Nor is Nick.'

*

'The police are right. I know you're disappointed, but I can't take the risk of leaving you here either.' Craig's voice is muffled as he pulls two dusty backpacks down from the loft.

'I know. I *know*. I just ... I so wanted Nick to be back in his own space.'

'The cottage is ready. I can take all the food I bought there instead. I'm really sorry I took so long getting it. If I'd gone to the local shops, I might have been here in time to—'

'It's not your fault,' I say quickly, able to acknowledge that now I've calmed down. 'But I appreciate you want to look after Nick.'

'And you.'

'What, *bitch mother*?' I remember Sean Newton saying that's the worst thing about bullying: that even when it stops, it never leaves you. I should call him, I think. He texted me to say how happy he is that Nick's recovering; I owe him a proper thank-you for his support.

'Don't let it get in your head. DS Clarke was right. It's probably some crazy person. But though I hate to say *I told you so*, there's no chance of anything like this happening at the cottage. They won't be able to find you there.'

I give him a dubious look. 'Maybe.' *Two clicks on Google and you can find anyone these days*, I remember DS Clarke also saying.

'Definitely. The cottage isn't listed in your name, only mine. Unless someone physically follows you there ...' Craig sighs, then rests a hand on my shoulder. 'Come on. Throw a few things into these bags. I'll take you back to the hospital, we can collect Nick, then I'll drop you both off. I know you want some time alone with him. I won't hang around.' He pauses, pushing his glasses up his nose. 'Unless, of course, you want me to.'

I hesitate, tempted to give in. Then I think of Nick, the need to keep things as familiar as possible. When he went to the sleepover, Craig and I were separated – and Nick has no memory of anything since. I've yet to tell him about Jason's death; somehow, I need to break it to him that he's at the centre of an attempted-murder investigation. It's all too much.

'Actually, it would be great if you could take our things straight to the cottage,' I say slowly. 'But I won't need a lift to the hospital. DS Clarke said Sergeant Rogers will come and get me. He's going to be watching over us.'

'Perfect.' Craig smiles.

'Let's hope so.' I touch the plaster on my forehead. The pain is gone, and so has the graffiti now, documented and then scrubbed away by the police. But fear remains.

THIRTY-THREE

'All ready?' Craig hovers in the kitchen doorway half an hour later, watching me shove playing cards and a book into Nick's backpack.

'Almost.' I straighten up, contemplating the tins of cat food I've also bagged up. 'I was just wondering how you'd feel if I pack a slightly grumpy cat. I think Nick could do with the comfort. Maybe she'll help nudge his memory, too.'

'Good thinking. Is her travel box still in here?' He opens the kitchen utility cupboard. 'As soon as Sergeant Rogers arrives, Marzipan and I will make tracks. I'll drop everything at the cottage so it's ready and waiting for you. Then I'll head home and leave you to it.'

'He'll be here soon. Why don't you go now, Craig? No point hanging around.'

'If you're sure? Looks like I'll have my hands full anyway.' He nods at the backpacks I've propped against the kitchen dresser, next to where Nick's school bag still sits.

'Sorry. I tried to pack light.' Hopefully we'll be home in a couple of days, if the investigation continues with the intensity DS Clarke assured me it would.

'No problem. I guess that just leaves one last thing.' Craig's grey eyes fix intently on my face for a moment, then he reaches into his pocket and hands over a set of keys.

'Ah. Yes. Of course.' I smile, hiding my small sigh of relief. 'I'll call you,' I say, as he picks up the backpacks, his only reply a curt nod as he makes for the kitchen door.

Twenty minutes later I'm pacing the hall, starting to wonder if Sergeant Rogers has forgotten about me, when the doorbell rings. *At last.* I try to ignore the butterflies in my stomach. Surely whoever vandalised my house and car wouldn't be stupid enough to return to the scene of their crime so soon? Even so, my hand freezes halfway to the front door.

'Katie!' I stare at her in shock as I finally steel myself to open it.

'I hope you don't mind. I had to see you.' She looks anxious and exhausted. 'The police told me you thought that Jason . . . that he made Nick—'

'Oh, Katie. I'm so sorry. Please. Come in. Let's talk.'

'I can't stay long. Nathan and I are on our way to the coast. Just to get away from . . . everything. Christ, how long is it since I've been here?' she says, looking around as she follows me into the kitchen.

'A year,' I tell her over my shoulder, heading for the kettle and flicking it on. As I reach into the cupboard for mugs, I think back to that time. Nick was in hospital then, too – the only difference being the severity of his injuries, and the fact that it was school bullies rather than a would-be killer who put him there.

'Just a year. It feels like a lifetime. *Jason's* lifetime.' Katie slumps down on a chair.

'Why did he do it? Do you have *any* idea?' I gaze sadly at her as I carry our coffees to the table. Normally so chic, she looks fragile in jeans and a black jumper that hangs off her slender frame. Grief and bewilderment are etched in lines that weren't there a week ago.

'Who? Do what? Oh, you mean Jason.' For a second, she seems confused, and it occurs to me that she might have been prescribed antidepressants to help cope with the pain.

'I'm so sorry, Katie. *Your boy*. The police said he didn't leave a note?'

'Nothing. I've looked everywhere.' She downs her coffee in one go, as if she hasn't drunk for days, and I remember not being able to eat or drink after Nick went missing.

'That's so hard. You must be going out of your mind wondering.'

'Nathan said I'm driving him mad. He can talk. He won't leave me alone for a second. In fact, I should go.' She jerks out of her chair. 'Don't want to keep him waiting.'

'Have the army given him compassionate leave?' I stand up too, following her back into the hall.

'He lost his job, Izzy. A while back.' She rubs her hands tiredly over her face. 'He's been teaching fitness part-time at local schools, but he was fired from the army. That's why he was home on Friday. And why he had to fly back out to the Gulf late that night – to sort out whatever mess he'd left out there. God knows what he did, but the army booted him out.'

'What?' I stare at her in surprise until the penny drops. 'Ah. So that's why you were so frazzled when I came to see you. The night after Nick disappeared.'

'Yes. Nathan and I had just had a filthy row on the phone. I was in a terrible place. Drunk. Angry. But I shouldn't have taken it out on you. I didn't mean to. I genuinely thought Nick had just run off in a huff. I felt awful when I realised he wasn't coming back. I hope you got my text.'

'I did.' It was the reason I went to her house the following day, and found Nick's phone – *deepening my suspicions about Jason*, I reflect sadly.

'I wanted to say more. Ask you to come over. There were things I wanted to say to you in person. But the family liaison officer arrived, and . . .' She draws in a breath so deep it seems to make her whole body quiver. 'I heard you ringing the doorbell. I just couldn't—'

'I know. The police told me Matt Haynes was with you.' I pause, knowing we're both remembering that awful moment. 'What was it you wanted to talk about?'

'Oh, stuff. Guilt. Not just for being so awful to you last Saturday night.' She sinks down onto the bottom stair. 'I also wanted – I *want* – to say sorry about this last year. For always telling you I was fine when I wasn't. For not being your friend. For not supporting you when Nick got beaten up. I still feel awful about it. I mean, so Nick walked to school by himself. Big fucking deal! I gave Jason a key to the front door when he was nine.'

'Really?' I study her face in surprise. 'That's not what you said at the time.'

She screws up her nose. 'I guess I felt I owed it to Craig to agree with him. He's been so kind to me. He knows Nathan's jealous of him. I think he felt guilty about that. Maybe in a funny sort of way he wanted to make up for it. He was amazing with Jase, too.' Her eyes fill up again. 'Giving him lifts, taking him swimming. Pizza afterwards if I had to work late.'

'Craig did all that?' I remember him once offering to show Jason round his office; I had no idea his help went so much further. No wonder Jason texted him when Nick went missing. I sit down next to Katie, realising how much I've missed her.

'I really am sorry I haven't talked to you about this before, Iz.' She leans against my shoulder. 'I've had so much on my plate with Nathan. I've let the house go, my work slide. And I knew you hated me. I didn't blame you. I deserved it.'

I recall my surprise at the air of neglect in her house. I know Katie's marriage has been on shaky ground for years; it finally seems to be crumbling, and it must have been tough for her to accept. I realise, too, how hard she must have found it to contradict Craig when he blamed me for Nick getting beaten up. He clearly seems to have become something of a rock for her – and Jason, too. I guess it's to his credit; I just wish I'd known.

'I never hated you. But I was angry with Jason.' I won't lie to Katie; there have been too many misunderstandings between us already. 'I *did* think he'd done something bad. I'm so sorry I misjudged him. He had his whole life ahead of him. It's unfathomable.'

'Teenage boys are hard enough to figure out when they're alive.' She wraps her arms around herself. 'When they're dead . . .'

'Have the police told you any more? It was definitely . . . ? They're sure he took his own life?' I know the detectives were investigating the connection between Jason's death and Nick's attempted murder. It suddenly strikes me that the so-called *Suspect A* may have been guilty of both. 'Oh, God. I'm sorry.' I stare at Katie's stricken face. 'I shouldn't . . .'

'No. You're right. I've thought that too.' She turns to me, grabbing my arm. 'I can't believe Jason would take his own life, either. That's what's driving me mad. I keep searching through his stuff, looking for something, a clue . . . *anything.*'

I remember doing exactly the same in Nick's room. 'I just don't get why anyone would want to hurt Nick – *or* Jason.'

'Bullies don't need a reason to be cruel. You know that as well as I do. Nathan's a prime example. He's convinced I'm having an affair with Craig. I never have, Iz. Honestly. Oh, I know I flirt too much. But I'd never do that to you. Nor would Craig.'

I try to meet her pleading gaze, but I can't help my eyes going to the silver charm bracelet on her wrist, pulling my thoughts back to when Craig gave an identical one to me. It was the evening after our third wedding anniversary, and Katie had come round with a celebratory bottle of champagne. Craig was working late; Nick and Jason were playing upstairs. Nathan had been posted abroad again, and Katie wasn't happy about it . . .

'He's just never here, you know?' Katie kicked off her tan leather loafers and tucked her feet up on the chesterfield. Even with her long red hair falling loose round her shoulders, and dressed, for once, in casual chinos and a V-neck sweater, she still managed to look elegant.

'Craig works long hours too. But at least I know he's somewhere in London. It must be tough not even knowing what country Nathan's in.'

'His movements are "classified".' She rolled her eyes as she mimed speech marks. 'Sorry. It's your anniversary. Here's to husbands!' She raised her glass, but didn't take a sip. 'Sorry,' she apologised again, wiping her eyes. 'It's just . . .'

'Just?'

'Well, sometimes I wish he could be more like Craig, you know? I try so hard to keep the house nice. Nathan wouldn't care if we lived in a tent in the woods. He's never taken Jase to the theatre. He doesn't even own a suit, for God's sake. Sorry, here I go again. I didn't come here to moan. We should be celebrating. Is that your present from Craig?'

'Yes. The first part, anyway.' Still worrying about Katie, I fiddled with the bracelet. 'The second part is dinner and, um, tickets to the ballet. Tomorrow night. With Nick.'

'Wow. You see? I know dating ads are a lucky dip. But you really struck gold.'

'I think you can take some of the credit for that.' I smiled, knowing I'd never have met Craig in the first place if Katie hadn't encouraged me. I wouldn't lie to myself that I'd married him for entirely romantic reasons, and much as I, too, admired Craig's sophistication and mild-mannered charm, his inscrutability was sometimes frustrating, and he could be infuriatingly wedded to his own opinion. Still, he was also kind and generous; hidden behind a mask of companionship, love had crept up on me, and now I couldn't imagine life without him. Or Katie. I raised my glass to her. 'Forget about husbands. Here's to best friends!'

'Sorry. Do you mind that I bought one the same?' Katie's touch on my arm pulls me back to the present. 'I know that bracelet was a special gift to you from Craig. I just liked it so much, when I saw this one I ... You didn't think – you weren't worried that Craig and I ...?'

'No,' I lie. Katie has more than enough to deal with.

'Good.' She squeezes my hand then sighs. 'I'm glad. I know I haven't been the best of friends, but I'm not a cheat. Not that Nathan believes me. He thinks Jason killed himself because of *me*.' Her voice is raw. 'Because I was going to break up our family.'

'Oh Katie, *no*.' I turn to look at her in horror. I'm not really surprised that Nathan has accused her of being unfaithful, but I'm appalled he would use that to blame her for Jason giving up on life. Being a mother comes before being a wife; I know Katie believes that too.

'I never had any intention of leaving Nathan. Oh, I probably should have. He can be a bastard. But I married him. I'm not a quitter. Nor was Jason.'

'It's not quitting to walk away from unhappiness,' I say softly.

'Maybe. See, I always knew you were stronger than me.' She pulls a wry smile; it dissolves into tears a second later. 'Jase was too. Nathan knocked him down. He got right back up. The only thing that really got to him was seeing others hurt. I know that's hard to believe.' She sighs again. 'He was tough on the outside. But it was only skin deep.'

'He was your son,' I say, hugging her. 'You knew him better than anyone.'

'I think maybe . . .' She slumps, her body seeming to fold in on itself. 'It's possible he killed himself because he was ashamed. About Nick. He truly was devastated, Iz. And terrified. He literally hid under his duvet all Saturday, he was so scared.'

'Scared of the police?' I frown, remembering Jason squaring up to DCI Maxwell.

'More likely of Nathan. Of being punished for bringing disgrace on him. Oh, the irony. Nathan was the one dismissed under a cloud. I blame *him* for Jason coming up with the stupid dare in the first place. All his stories about *secret missions*. It was all crap. He had a desk job even before he was fired. In his head, he felt like a wimp. He overcompensated with his fists. And Jase saw way too much.'

'Are you saying you think Jason took his own life rather than face his dad?'

'I don't know. I won't *ever* know. That fucking sleepover. I only wanted a few hours off so I could speak to Nathan. I didn't mean for Jase to go away and never come back.'

THIRTY-FOUR

'I think there's a little ferry we could have taken. I'm not sure where to find it, though. I think it must be somewhere further along the river.' I look around curiously. 'At least most of the snow's gone. Although it's definitely still hot-chocolate weather, you'll be glad to hear. With squirty cream and extra marshmallows.' I smile at Nick. 'Dr Lynch's orders.'

I keep up a steady flow of chatter as I push his wheelchair across the arched footbridge leading to Eel Pie Island, trying to reassure Nick without expecting him to say anything in return. He still has a dressing on his forehead, and he's wrapped up like we're going on an arctic expedition, but physically he's making bigger strides than I can believe – even than Dr Lynch expected, I suspect. It's only mentally that he's taking baby steps.

'Sounds good to me,' Sergeant Rogers says, zipping up his leather jacket. 'I might cadge some of that myself. If it's not rude to invite myself to the party.'

'You're very welcome.' I smile up at him. 'I'm glad you're here.'

'Sorry I was a bit late. I had to check in with my colleague,

Sergeant Barnes. He's taking over my shift at eight thirty. You'll have twenty-four-hour cover here. Boss's orders.'

'Thank you,' I say gratefully, looking anxiously over my shoulder as we step off the bridge and on to the island, still feeling nervous despite the presence of the familiar plain-clothes officer. Everyone has been very reassuring: Dr Lynch about Nick's recovery; DCI Maxwell about the security rota he's put in place. But every time I close my eyes, I see the knife the police found in the woods . . . the red spray paint on my house: *You're next, slag.*

'I'm a champion Monopoly player, too,' Sergeant Rogers says, grinning. 'If you're up for a game, Nick?' He rests a hand on his shoulder. 'Bags I get to be the dog.'

'Ah, that reminds me. I've got a little surprise for you when we get to the cottage, Nick.' After stowing our backpacks in his car, Craig returned as promised for Marzipan. Hopefully, she'll be curled up on a sofa right now. I can't wait for Nick to see her.

He doesn't reply, and as I stoop to check his breathing, worried the cold air might set off his asthma, I see he's fallen asleep. I'm not surprised. It was tiring even for me watching Dr Lynch and the nurse complete their last checks, issuing a list of instructions about Nick resting, eating well, not getting over-excited – not rushing to talk about what's happened . . .

As DCI Maxwell introduced me formally to Sergeant Rogers, I caught a hint of his frustration that the consultant has advised no further police interviews for the time being. 'He needs peace and quiet. Proper rest. And lots of love,' she told me. '*As do you*,' she added, checking out the small wound on my forehead, even though I protested that I was fine.

'Wow. Nice place. I've never been here before,' Sergeant Rogers comments, looking around as we wander along the pretty tree-lined pathway that winds across the island.

'Me neither, funnily enough. I knew Craig had a rental cottage here. He bought it before we were married, though. More as an investment, really, I think.'

'Lucky guy.'

'Yes. I suppose he is.' I've never given it much thought. Craig might make self-deprecating jokes about being a typical banker, but he's right in one respect: he has extensive assets, probably other property. I always considered the cottage as part of his portfolio rather than a place for us to use. 'Oh, look! This must be it.'

Pushing Nick's wheelchair a little faster now, I hurry towards the 'Welcome' bunting strung across the veranda of a quaint, pink-painted timber house that looks like something out of a fairy tale. 'And I guess this is the welcome committee,' I add, chuckling as I point at an eclectic array of gnomes and goblins clustered around a swing bench. Coloured lights are woven through the trees, and a collection of comical gargoyles peep out from overgrown bushes. I smile up at Sergeant Rogers. 'I think we've just found Santa's secret grotto.'

'I hope he's got one of his little helpers to stick the kettle on. Temperature's dropped again. We might be in for another freeze overnight.'

'You think?' I pull the blanket tighter around Nick.

'Yeah. Fingers crossed Father Christmas has central heating.' He smiles, then snaps into professional mode. 'I'll just have a scout around out here, then we'll get you inside.'

I watch him stride off to check the perimeter of the plot, feeling a frisson of nerves at being alone. It's a beautiful place, but isolated. *Quiet*. No traffic is allowed on the island, and I can't even hear the usual planes roaring overhead as we can at home. I feel like hugging Sergeant Rogers when he returns, giving me a confident thumbs-up.

'No other houses close by,' he says. 'You're nice and private here. It's all good.'

'Hot chocolate, then?' I offer brightly, trying to reinstate a slightly festive mood as I notice Nick beginning to stir. I'm concerned how anxious he looks as his eyes fix on Sergeant Rogers; it reminds me that I still don't know how much he's remembered – if he has any idea that whoever tied him up and left him for dead is still out there . . . and might come back.

'All right if I take a rain check? I'll take a quick peek in the cottage before I help you guys in. Then I should really do a more thorough recce around the island. Here's my number, though. In case you're worried about anything. Or need extra marshmallows.' Sergeant Rogers winks at Nick as he hands me a card. 'And you have the boss's contact details already, of course. Failing that, just yell, OK?' He gives Nick's shoulder a quick squeeze. 'I'll be around.'

'Thank you.' *I'm counting on it*, I whisper in my head as the officer takes the door keys from me. 'Don't be long!' I call after him, looking around anxiously. The wind catches the trees, rustling ominously. Misshapen shadows dance around the quirky statues in the cottage garden, the rapidly descending winter dusk now turning the gnomes' comical grins into ghoulish sneers. Feeling spooked, I hurry up the steps. 'Sergeant Rogers? You there?'

'What's up?' He comes skidding to the door. 'Is everything—'

'Sorry, we're fine,' I say, feeling guilty at the worried expression on his usually open, smiley face. 'Just freaking myself out a bit. I'll be OK once we get Nick safely inside.'

'Sure. Let's do that, then. Sorry to make you wait.' He bumps Nick's wheelchair across the veranda, up the steps and into the hallway. 'Just you take care of this one,' he says kindly. 'Let me worry about everything else. At least until half eight. Like I said, Steve will take over then. He won't disturb you, but he's a good bloke. He'll be here. Probably bang on time, too.' He rolls his eyes, acknowledging again the slight delay in picking me and Nick up.

'Thank you,' I say again, realising as he finally takes his leave how much I'm going to miss the young officer's friendly, reassuring presence.

Locking the stable front door behind him, I tuck the keys in my handbag and look curiously around the square hallway, grateful that Sergeant Rogers thought to turn on all the lights in the cottage. 'This looks like a comfy place, hey?' I say to Nick, before realising that he's nodded off again. 'That's right, you sleep, my love.' I press a gentle kiss to his forehead, deciding to settle my jitters by exploring the cottage first, before helping Nick into bed.

It truly does have the feeling of a cosy cabin at the North Pole, I think, wandering into a living room that's simply furnished with white wicker furniture. Sliding glass doors at the rear frame the promised river view, now colour-washed in purple as the sun sets over the Thames, while a door on the left of the hallway leads to a kitchen that could best be described as retro: stripped-wood units are lavishly stencilled with wild flowers, with candy-pink wooden chairs set either side of a long refectory table.

The bathroom next door is an explosion of nautical design, with shells lining the sink and a mermaid mural covering the wall above a freestanding claw-foot tub. Staring at the kooky motif, I'm gripped by a slightly unsettling feeling of peering through a window into another part of my ex-husband's life – his personality, even. This whimsical, *softer* side of Craig is something I've never seen before, and as I stroll back into the chintzy living room I ponder again the kindness I didn't realise he had shown to Jason – or Katie.

I do trust her assurance that they've never had an affair, but I realise how much my friend's revelations have stayed with me. It feels like there is a whole other side to Craig's life that I never knew about, a feeling that intensifies the more I wander round his cottage. Craig said he decorated it himself, but this place is nothing like our old scruffy but traditional family home – or the ultra-modern, minimalist flat he moved into when he left me. I wonder if he used to come here when we were married; I wonder what else I don't know about my ex-husband.

Enough with the paranoia, I lecture myself in exasperation. I've already exhausted myself trying to be an amateur sleuth, and it got me precisely nowhere. Giving myself a mental shake, I stride purposefully into the smaller of the two bedrooms, accessed directly from the living room. There's no sign of Marzipan, I notice, looking around in concern, but I see Craig has left Nick's backpack by the wardrobe, and set out his toiletry bag and phone on the bedside table.

I'd forgotten the police had even returned the little Nokia, no longer needing it for their inquiries. It was kind of Craig to think of bringing it here, I reflect, especially as I left Nick's laptop at home. Although it wouldn't have been much use to him, in any case: the WiFi and phone reception are both terrible, I realise, tutting as I take out my own phone to check. I haven't spotted a landline, either. I said I'd call Craig and let him know when we're settled; it looks like I won't be able to, but maybe he'll pop by in the morning to check on us.

He's been so thoughtful, I remind myself, shaking off my prickle of unease about the unfamiliar cottage. Husbands and wives rarely know everything about each other; estranged couples even less so. Craig has always been private. Self-contained. A little old-fashioned and earnest, but a genuine family man. It was what most attracted me to him when we started dating . . .

'I'll get this.' Craig grabbed the bill before I could reach for it.

'You don't have to.' Pointedly, I picked up my handbag and took out my purse.

'I know. But I want to,' he insisted.

'I do have a job, you know? You've paid for every meal we've had so far.'

I looked around the restaurant, a far more glamorous and expensive place than I would usually choose, and admitted to myself that I could ill afford even half the cost of the fancy three-course dinner we had just eaten. But I wasn't going to let Craig act like a beneficiary: if we were to continue dating, I was determined to pay my way.

'And I'll *keep* paying.' He reached across the white-clothed table to squeeze the tips of my fingers. 'If you're kind enough to keep accepting my invitations.'

'Kind.' I laughed. 'You make it sound like I'm doing you a favour.'

'You are. But I hope to return it. With interest.' After handing his credit card to the waiter, he leaned towards me, flint-grey eyes unblinking behind his black-framed glasses.

'This is your serious face, isn't it?' Nerves rippled through me at his sudden intensity; I sensed he was building up to some kind of declaration ... *a proposal?* I reached for my wine glass, almost knocking it over, my hands clumsy and my mouth suddenly dry. I liked Craig; I wasn't in love with him. Not yet, anyway.

He was a nice guy, and I had enjoyed getting to know him over the last few months. As I suspected when I first read his letter, he was a tad on the staid side, but kind and gentle, with an old-fashioned chivalry that was charming. He bought me flowers, held doors open for me. I didn't need him to, but after managing by myself for so long, I appreciated the thoughtfulness.

And he *always* wanted to hang out with Nick: for our last few dates, he'd even invited him along, buying tickets to shows he knew Nick would love. It felt good to have the sense of being almost like a proper family, and I could see that Nick enjoyed it too. But I couldn't marry a man just because he was nice to my son . . .

'Serious face. Hmm. I was aiming more for *passionately devoted*.' One eyebrow arched. 'But you've let me in to your family, Isobel. Shared your son with me. There's no bigger favour, in my book. Nick likes me, doesn't he?'

'He likes the extra-large pizzas you bring over on Friday nights,' I joked, trying to steer the conversation in a less personal direction.

'I'll take that as a yes, then. I'm glad. He's a sweet boy. Such a shame he's been picked on so much. I bet he wouldn't if I turned up at the school gate. Showed the other kids who's boss. I've always wanted to be a dad. Anyway, here's to us.' He raised his glass and clinked it against mine. 'To happy families.'

THIRTY-FIVE

'Maybe you'll feel hungry in the morning. The fridge is fully stocked. Pancakes, waffles, strawberries. More waffles. All your favourites.'

I deliberately hold my smile as Nick looks up at me, trying to mask my worry as I notice how white his face looks against the pillow. He's barely said a word since we arrived, only looking vacantly at me when I asked if he's been here before. He certainly seemed to know where the bathroom was, making a beeline for it after I wheeled him into his bedroom.

I wanted to ask again whether Craig had ever brought him here, but when he emerged, having changed into his pyjamas, Nick looked so pale and exhausted that I let him climb straight into bed, rather than pressing him to talk. He sat staring at his phone for a while, then slumped down under the covers, pulling them up so high it looked like he was hiding.

'You'll feel better after a good sleep, sweetheart.' I bend to kiss his cheek. 'Doctor's orders, remember? You're here to get well. No school. No rehearsals. Just rest.'

'Night, Mum,' he murmurs, eyes already closing.

I hover a moment longer, reflecting that while Nick might be here in body, part of him is still in those woods; trauma has pushed him into the furthest corner of his mind – a place so dark, I can sense him cowering there; so deep, I'm not sure how to reach him. He's retreated somewhere he feels safe – somewhere I can't follow, no matter how badly I want to hold his hand and help him fight his way back to me.

'Nighty night, darling. I love you.' I kiss his cheek one last time, then quietly close the door behind me, drifting thoughtfully to the sofa. I stand up again almost immediately, then wander from room to room, unable to settle, alternately wondering about Nick, Craig, and the police investigation. Away from familiar surroundings, I feel edgy and paranoid.

'If only we could have stayed at home,' I complain to Marzipan, watching her prowl restlessly too. At least she's finally come out from wherever she was hiding; I was starting to worry that she'd somehow got out of the cottage and run off, getting lost on the unfamiliar island. There could be any number of dangers lurking in the lush evergreen shrubbery and quiet pathways, I think with a shiver.

'Stop spooking yourself already,' I say firmly, deciding that a glimpse of the river vista might help relax me. I pull open the chintz curtains, but night has turned the sliding glass doors into a mirror; all I can see is a reflection of myself. Determined to enjoy the view, I switch off the Tiffany lamps on either side of the sofa and like magic the garden appears.

'Oh my *God*!' I jump as I see a face pressed to the glass. A moment later, a dark figure pulls sharply away. Heart pounding, I scrabble for my phone, letting out a long, ragged sigh of relief when I notice the time that flashes up on the screen: *8.30 p.m.*

'Come on, Izzy. Get a grip!' Sergeant Rogers told me he'd be swapping shifts around now, and that his replacement – *Steve*, was it? – wouldn't disturb us. Clearly this is him, and he's just getting on with his job. Even so, I quickly dial DS Clarke's number, eager to double-check the identity of the second plain-clothes officer – and remind myself that while we might be alone here, we're not completely out of contact.

'Perfect. No signal.' I press redial twice more; the call fails both times. 'Dammit.' Peering outside, I can see no sign of the officer, only the moon staring at me from an indigo sky, and willow trees stooping low over the river, as if dabbling their fingertips in the water. I hear the tinkle of wind chimes, and as my eyes gradually adjust to the dark, I spot a wooden gazebo strewn with sun-catchers and beyond it a wharf.

'Wow. This place has its own mooring.' I listen to the calming splash of the river, imagining I can even smell its brackish tang. 'Oh, no *wonder*. Look, Marzipan!' As a draught prickles the hairs on my arms, I notice that the sliding door is open a tiny crack. I thought Sergeant Rogers checked all around the house; he must have missed this door, and I kick myself for having interrupted his checks by calling out to him.

It takes a little effort to jam the door shut, but after a quick glance around I spot a small wooden box on the bookshelf, inscribed 'keys'. There is only one inside; thankfully, it fits the lock, and after double-checking that the glass doors are secure, I head quickly into the bedroom, where I check behind the curtains and under the bed before lying down next to Nick. I keep my boots on.

'Mum? *Mum?*'

'I'm here, darling. Everything's OK. Are you thirsty?' I help Nick take a sip of water, then tuck him back in. He falls asleep again immediately, and I suspect he wasn't even awake when he called out. 'Once upon a time, there was a boy who loved to dance,' I say, stroking his hair. 'He had golden hair, wings on his feet, and his mummy loved him *so much*.'

223

I press my face into the pillow to stifle a sob. Nick stirs, then rolls over on to his side. I notice his thumb make its way towards his mouth. *He's almost a teenager but still a little boy*, I think. He truly is stuck in the middle, in every sense: caught somewhere between child and young adult; between vulnerability and independence; between wanting to impress new friends and becoming his own person. Between me and his stepdad?

Staring into the darkness, my thoughts plummet back to the time Craig left me. To that dreadful day a year ago. Closing my eyes, I relive the sense that something had happened between Craig and Nick before he ran out of the house. I remember Nick being so edgy, uncharacteristically defiant; I remember Craig being unusually angry . . .

'What the hell were you thinking?'

'Me? What was *I* thinking? How did this become *my* fault?' I glared at Craig as he slammed around the kitchen. 'Look, let's not take this out on each other. We're both tired. It's been a long day.' Thankfully, Nick was making a good recovery from the attack at the school gate: he had a nasty cut to the left side of his forehead, and he was being kept in hospital overnight for any signs of concussion to be monitored. But he was going to be OK.

'You don't think you're to blame? Our son's been picked on every day at that school. So what do you do? You let him walk there alone. What kind of mother does that?'

'I didn't *let* him. I meant to stop him. But we do need to think about this. I can't be walking Nick to school when he's thirteen. We're not doing him any favours babying him.' I bit my lip, regretting my choice of words. 'No, that's not what I meant. Of course he's still my baby.' I sat down at the kitchen table, the fight going out of me – and I wasn't even sure why we were fighting.

'*Your* baby. That's the truth of it, isn't it? He's your son. Not mine. And you always do what *you* think is right for him. Doesn't matter what *I* think. You're his parent, and who am I? Nothing. Nobody. Some bloke you met through a dating column. I have no rights here. You haven't even let him change his name, for God's sake.'

'Craig, that's *not* what I think. And Nick's the one who said changing his name would be confusing.'

'That's not what he said to me.'

'Really?' I frowned. 'Well, anyway, he does call himself Nick Brookes sometimes.'

Craig tutted. 'When you're not around, perhaps?'

'Is that what this is really about? Is that why you're so angry? Because you feel I'm not acknowledging your role in this family? Because I do, Craig. Very much so.' I sighed, conscious of how many times I had deliberately deferred to his decisions, not wanting him to feel he didn't have a say. He was being unfair, and his anger seemed out of all proportion.

'No, you don't. You're his mum. I'm just the guy who pays the mortgage. Well, news flash. You can pay it yourself from now on. I've had enough. You want to make all the decisions? Go ahead. You're an unfit mother, Isobel, and I want no part in it any more. You're on your own. Just the way you like it.'

I didn't think he was serious; I genuinely believed that once Nick was home, Craig would calm down, come to his senses and realise he had over-reacted. But he didn't; he kept his distance, only making contact to set up fortnightly visits to see Nick. I went along with them because it was hard enough Nick waking up one morning to find that his stepdad was gone; it rocked the stability I had worked so hard to create for him.

Part of me missed Craig, too. I'd thought we had a good marriage, and I was baffled when he returned to pack his bags; I was

225

distraught when I turned to Katie and she said Craig 'had a point'. And I was glad when he stood in my kitchen a week ago, saying he regretted his mistake and wanted to put it right.

Only that was then. I'd been desperate to know where Nick was, half blaming myself for driving him away. The last few days have been a torrent of stress and activity; now, all the commotion around me has come to an abrupt standstill, but perversely my mind has gone into overdrive. I can't stop wondering who hurt Nick – who tried to hurt *me* – and in truth I'm no longer completely sure who I can trust.

'Shall we ask the man in the moon?' I whisper to Nick, remembering how he always used to say that when it was just the two of us. *What shall we do, Nick?* I would say, tucking him up at bedtime. *Ask the man in the moon*, he'd reply. I always told him it might be a *mummy moon*, and Nick would sneak his hand into mine, give me his crooked smile, and tell me the moon wouldn't be there when he woke up. Nor would his daddy. But I was, always.

THIRTY-SIX

Branches scratch my face; footsteps pound behind me. I'm reaching out for Nick, grasping his cold hand to pull him with me. *We have to get away ...* I hear children laughing and turn around, panicking as giggles turns to screams. Nick's icy fingers slip through mine, and he's falling, falling ... I throw myself after him, trying to shout his name, only someone has their hand over my mouth, smothering me, whispering in my ear that *my son belongs to them.*

My head bangs against something hard, jolting my already tender forehead with such pain that I wake up. I claw at the blanket tangled around my face, fighting terror as I stare around the dark room, until I remember where I am. The cottage is so quiet. All I can hear is my own heartbeat – and the sound of a key turning in a lock.

Sidling through the cottage towards sudden clattering noises in the kitchen, my heart is in my mouth. 'Oh God. It's *you*.' My heart pounds painfully as adrenalin floods my body.

'Sorry, I hope I didn't scare you.' Craig turns to smile briefly at me, before continuing to unload groceries on to the kitchen work-top. 'I did send an email before I left my flat. Internet reception here isn't great, though. WiFi signal has a rather teenage tendency towards mood swings,' he quips, bending to stash bottles of clean-ing fluid under the sink.

'So I gathered.' I lean shakily against the doorjamb, holding on to it until the jelly-like feeling in my legs subsides, and the last unsettling wisps of my bad dream finally evaporate.

'I knocked a couple of times before I let myself in,' Craig adds, straightening up and watching me with a concerned frown. 'You OK?'

'Yes. I . . . You let yourself . . . Ah, spare keys.'

'Yes. For emergencies, really.' He holds up a bottle of red wine. 'This also comes in handy in a crisis.'

'Right.' I half-smile, unsure if he's joking. I'm not used to Craig being so relaxed. I'm not used to seeing him in jeans and a jumper, either. Or his usually clean-shaven face showing the beginnings of a beard. I have the slightly unnerving feeling that a stranger has just walked into the cottage – a secret bolthole I wasn't even aware he used.

'Are you sure you're OK, Izzy?' Craig says gently, pausing in the act of stowing yet more provisions in the cupboards. 'That was quite a tumble you took. Dr Lynch did say to let her know if you have any headaches or confusion.'

'I'm fine. Just a bit muzzy-headed. I think I crashed out,' I say, to excuse the edginess I don't quite understand myself. 'But I see you've been busy.' I nod at the grocery bags on the kitchen table. 'We've got enough food now to see us through a siege.'

'Ha. Well, you never know. Weather is set to turn. I've been snowed in here before.'

'Really? I was hoping to get Nick home. As soon as he's feeling better – and the police have caught whoever . . . Sorry. I'm feeling a bit over-emotional,' I admit, as tears unexpectedly well up. 'Relief, I suppose. Worry.' I draw in a breath. 'Fear.'

'You mean about the police investigation? Or . . . Are you still worrying about that graffiti?' Craig sighs. 'Look, whoever chucked that brick was a nutcase. They'll have seen you on the news, that's all. You know how fired up with self-righteous indignation some people get.'

'*You're next*. That's what they wrote, Craig. The police can't rule out that whoever did it is the same person who hurt Nick. They still have no idea who that is.'

'Nick remembered anything yet?'

'Nothing. At least, not that he's telling me.'

'Are you sure? He hasn't said anything at all? It's just you seem a bit edgy, and—'

'Well, we are rather like sitting ducks here,' I say, only realising as I speak the thought aloud that it's exactly how I feel.

'What? *No*, Isobel.' Craig moves swiftly towards me, resting his hands on my shoulders. 'I wouldn't have suggested you and Nick stay here if I didn't believe it was safe.'

'You can't guarantee that, though, can you?'

'There's a detective outside, isn't there?'

'Yes. Yes, you're right. Two, actually. Sergeant Rogers and another one. They're alternating shifts. I saw the second officer earlier.'

'I didn't see anyone.' Craig frowns. 'Although I did come by boat.'

'By boat? Oh, yes. I saw the mooring. Huh. A world away from the Jersey Road.'

'Don't get too excited. It's a lot less glamorous than it sounds.' He smiles. 'Little more than a dinghy, in fact. But with a small outboard motor. Useful for hopping back and forth across the river when I've got stuff to carry. That's the one disadvantage of having no road access here.' He gives a small bow. 'Your luggage arrived via the scenic route, m'lady.'

'Nice. I didn't know you were into boats.' I stare curiously at him, half expecting him to tell me he's got a Harley-Davidson parked outside; right now, nothing would surprise me.

'Well, I'm no Aristotle Onassis. But *Lady Luck* comes in pretty handy. Fortunately, I've just got her back from the boat yard.'

Jason's face flashes into my head, and for a moment I'm distracted, wondering if Jason ever visited here after his Sunday job, and how long it will be until the coroner returns a conclusive verdict on his cause of death. 'Oh? Was there a problem?' I say at last.

'No problem as such. Just needed a bit of TLC after the winter. Anyway, this officer you saw. What did he look like?'

'Dark hair. Slim. Average height. Wearing a leather jacket, I think. Sort of like the one Sergeant Rogers wears. I guess it's standard plain-clothes uniform.'

'Right.' Craig brushes past me, striding out of the kitchen towards the front door. Using his own keys, he unlocks and throws it open.

'Oh, Marzipan! Come back, sweetheart.' I reach for her as she slinks around my legs and darts out of the cottage, disappearing down the path. Apart from worrying about her safety on the unfamiliar island, I wanted her to be here when Nick wakes up, curled up on his bed in the morning, as he always finds her at home.

'Did he show you ID?' Craig persists, ignoring my efforts to summon Marzipan.

'What? No. Of course not. I didn't speak to him. But he arrived exactly when Sergeant Rogers said he would. Bang on eight thirty. I thought I should just let him get on with his patrol.'

'Wait here. I'll check it out.'

For a few moments, Craig's steady stare sifts the darkness, then he steps out to check all around the small front garden, finally leaning over the gate to look up and down the path. I picture it twisting into the distance, weaving between the other houses nestled behind tall hedges, with picket fences and wrought-iron gates creating a hundred hiding places. As Sergeant Rogers predicted, the temperature has plummeted. But it isn't the cold that makes me tremble as Craig finally comes back inside, locking the door behind him.

I can't stop worrying that someone is out there. Watching. Waiting ... The presence of police security offers some comfort, but I have no idea what kind of threat Sergeant Rogers and his colleague might have to face. DCI Maxwell talked about Suspect A playing *a game of mental cruelty*. I'm certainly going out of my mind waiting for their next move.

'I think we're good,' Craig says, snapping on lamps and settling down on the sofa, patting the cushion next to him. 'Come. Sit. I've got some time. Let's talk.'

'Sure.' I sit down but leave a gap between us, still a little uncomfortable being alone with him; somehow it feels different than when we were at the hospital. The police presence there was a distraction; now it's just the two of us – and the elephant in the room: our dead marriage. 'I hope the police are making progress,' I say, to break the awkward silence.

'I'll check in with Maxwell first thing tomorrow. Last time we spoke he was still focusing on the online grooming angle.' Craig's mouth twists. 'The glories of the internet age, hey?'

'Indeed. I guess that remains the most likely scenario. That someone was following the boys' posts about the sleepover. Don't you think?'

'Perhaps. That could be anyone, though.' Craig tuts. 'Those boys effectively advertised themselves to every pervert with an internet connection.'

I think about the images I saw on social media while I was looking for photos of the sleepover. Some of them were eye-wateringly personal; inappropriate for public view, even. 'I suppose, for some people, there's a fine line between taking an interest in other people's kids – and taking *too much* interest, if you know what I mean?'

Craig gives me a direct look. 'The rule is simple. You can look but don't ever touch. Whoever did this to our son has crossed way over that line.'

'But looking is OK?' I persist, frowning as I keep turning over images in my mind: Katie, Nathan and Jason in their swimsuits on holiday; friends of friends that I've never even met displaying intimate moments for all the world to see. Romantic clinches with their partners; their children at bath time, splashing naked in clouds of bubbles.

'Sorry?' Craig leans forward, frowning.

'Oh, I was just thinking about social media. Parents like to show off about their kids, don't they? And Instagram appears to have an epidemic of selfies. Kids posting videos of themselves doing silly things. Innocent stuff to their friends. Maybe not so to others.'

'There's a big difference between admiring someone's holiday snaps and perving over their kids in swimsuits. I should know. I've taken dozens of photos of Nick. And other kids, come to that.'

'Yes. I suppose you have.' I turn to look at Craig, startled by his sharp tone. He sounds angry. No, *defensive*. Hurt? I try to read the expression in his eyes, but lamp-light catches the lenses in his glasses; all I can see is my own reflection in duplicate: two pale, worried faces frozen in miniature, trapped in square black frames.

He leans closer. 'I hope you've never thought—'

'No! Never,' I say quickly, although suddenly I can't stop myself picturing the dozens of photos of Nick in our house. Craig has taken almost every one of them, but I've never suspected him of getting any kind of kick out of it beyond that of a proud stepfather.

'Good. Because anyone who takes advantage of children for their own gratification is sick.' He grips the arm of the sofa, his knuckles turning white. 'And if the police find out that the bastard who hurt Nick—'

'Craig, it's fine.' I rest a hand on his knee, surprised to see him getting so worked up. 'Both Dr Lynch and DCI Maxwell were clear. Nick wasn't sexually assaulted.' *Thank God.*

'No. But he was battered and bruised. Terrorised and abandoned.' Craig stands up from the sofa and paces across the room in agitation. 'And if I ever get my hands on whoever did that, I'll make them wish they'd never been born.'

THIRTY-SEVEN

I make us both coffee, then curl up on the armchair opposite Craig, watching him. Even though I feel just as much rage towards whoever hurt my son, it strikes me that Craig's uncharacteristic fury seems to be coming from a slightly different place. It feels almost *personal*, unconnected to Nick, and I have a sudden hunch about the man I was married to for three years yet am suddenly realising I don't know as well as I thought.

'Craig,' I begin hesitantly, as he sips his coffee, eyes fixed on the dark window behind me. '*Craig*,' I repeat, when he doesn't respond.

'Sorry, what?' He jerks out of his thoughts, setting his cup down on the rattan trunk and running his hands through his hair.

'I was just wondering ... Have I touched a nerve?' I dig my fingernails into my palms; it's too late to backtrack now. 'When you talked about kids being taken advantage of – you sounded like it might have reminded you of something. Or someone,' I say tentatively.

'You mean Jason.'

'Sorry?' I frown in confusion. 'No. I was thinking more of—'

'I've never laid a finger on him.'

'Of course you haven't!' I say, puzzled at the misunderstanding. Maybe I'm wide of the mark after all, and whatever secrets Craig may or may not be hiding have nothing to do with problems in his own childhood. 'Poor Jason,' I say with a sigh. 'His death must have hit you hard. Katie mentioned that you spent quite a bit of time with him after we separated.'

'Yeah. I felt sorry for him. His dad's a nut-job.'

'Well, Nathan's never been my favourite person. Although maybe spending so much time with his son wasn't the best idea. Nathan's always envied you. You know that.'

'The man's pathetic,' Craig spits. 'Always trying to compete with me. Bragging about his medals. I knew it was all idiotic bravado. He was taken off active service ages ago. He had a desk job in the army. Did you know that? And now he hasn't got a job at all.'

I look at him in surprise, a penny dropping. 'Is that what it was all about? Hanging out with Jason, I mean. You were using him to get at his dad?'

'What? Of course not! I'm a grown man, Isobel,' Craig says sternly. 'We're not in the playground. Christ, you have no idea what you're talking about.'

'Oh.' I sit back, stung by his sudden hostility, watching despondently as he stands up and starts pacing the living-room floor. I can almost see him pulling the shutters back down, hiding his feelings, as he always used to. 'Then why don't you tell me?' I invite softly.

'Helping Jason, spending time with him . . .' Craig stops pacing and turns to look at me. 'No, it was never about getting one over on Nathan. I did despise him, though. And I felt sorry for his son. I know what it's like to have a father who's hardly ever there. And who talks with his fists when he is.'

'Ah.' *So I was right.* 'You've never told me that.' I try not to sound accusing, but I feel a little resentful that while I've told Craig everything about my own family, and Alex, he kept something so enormous to himself the whole time we were married.

'Because it's in the past. Buried.'

'I'm not sure that's how it works, Craig. If you bury bad stuff, it only festers. You have to let it out, you know? Share it. Otherwise you end up just putting on a false front.'

'I prefer to think of it as choosing what kind of person I want to be.'

'Putting on a mask, you mean. Fine, go ahead,' I snip, exasperated that, once again, he's shutting me out. 'Act like the person you wish you were. But it is acting, isn't it? So how is anyone supposed to know the real *you*?'

Suddenly I think of Katie. I knew her marriage was struggling; I had no idea Nathan hit her – that he hit Jason. If she hadn't tried so hard to maintain her perfect image at all costs, sugar-coating the truth even to me, her best friend, I would never have misjudged her – and I might have understood sooner why Jason behaved as he did towards Nick.

'This is the real me, Isobel. It's not an act. But we all play different roles in life, don't we? I wanted to be a husband. A father. I was happiest being that Craig Brookes.'

'I get that there are different parts to your personality, Craig. I just feel like you've never trusted me enough to be completely yourself.'

'I don't trust *myself*. That's the point. The stuff I've buried. It's bad. You have no idea. I thought if I let it out ...'

He leans on the back of the sofa, fists clenched, seeming to battle his emotions for a moment, and sudden alarm prickles across my scalp as I remember Katie referring to Craig's *hidden depths*. I think of his angry declaration that he would make whoever hurt Nick wish they'd never been born, and it occurs to me that having experienced violence himself, Craig's own aggression might sit closer

236

to the surface than I've ever realised, ready to burst out with even greater force after being repressed for so long.

'That sounds so . . . exhausting.' I glance anxiously at Nick's bedroom door, wishing Craig would leave now, so I can shut myself in with my son – shut the world and my too-complicated ex-husband out, go to sleep and wake up when this whole nightmare is over.

'Tell me about it. This place . . . ' He looks around almost wistfully. 'It's been a haven of peace for me. I'm sorry I let you think it was just an investment. It's been so much more.'

'I wish you *had* told me. I wish you'd believed enough in our marriage to . . . Oh, I don't know. *Dance to your own tune*, as Nick's teacher would say.' I'm so proud of my son for holding true to the things he loves – and the things he doesn't. I wish Craig had been honest enough to paint mermaids in our bathroom at home. But it's too late now.

'I don't dance, Isobel. I leave that to Nick.' He straightens up, looking me in the eye now. 'It's what I've always loved about him – his lack of inhibition. The way he really is just completely . . . himself.'

'Is that why you asked me to marry you? Because of my son – being a dad to Nick?' I'm hurt, but I can't blame Craig for doing what I did myself: I agreed to marry him because I wanted a stepfather for Nick; it sounds very much like Craig proposed for a similar reason.

'I always told myself I'd never have a family,' he says after a long pause. 'I didn't want to end up like my father. I got to thirty-seven managing to avoid it all. Marriage. Kids. I threw myself into work, but I got lonely. I wanted children, only I wasn't sure I could handle fatherhood. And when I met you, I thought . . . I naively thought being a stepdad might be easier. No blood tie. Not quite the same paternal . . . pull.'

I remember pondering the same thing: if Craig was able to detach himself more easily, because Nick wasn't his own flesh and blood. 'And *is* that how it was?'

'Not a bit.' His laugh is a humourless bark. 'I loved – *love* – Nick like he's mine. I've only ever wanted to protect him. I was angry last year because I thought you were stopping me doing that. I didn't want him to walk to school by himself. I couldn't believe you let him. But that's not the reason I left. It just felt like you were determined to make the point that he was *your* son. Like not changing his name.'

'No.' I shake my head. 'That's absolutely *not* what I was doing. And you were the one who said you didn't want to legally adopt him,' I point out.

'Because I wanted him to make that decision for himself, when he was older. Whatever, this isn't about us. It's about Nick. What's right for *him*,' Craig cajoles. 'Isn't it?'

I look at his familiar handsome face, with its uncharacteristically plaintive expression, and I can't shake off the sudden thought that this really is all an act, after all, and that somehow, for some reason, I'm being played. Craig has an agenda; I feel sure of it. I just don't know what it is. But if it involves my son, I'm shutting it down right now.

'And you still think you know best, don't you?' I stand up too, eyeing Craig defiantly. 'That's why we're really here, isn't it? Your house. Your rules.'

He crosses the room in two strides. His face is tense but his hands are gentle as he rests them lightly on my shoulders. 'Please, Isobel. Please stop being so *angry* with me. I told you. I'm sorry. I still love you. I love *Nick*. And I'll do whatever it takes to be his dad again.'

THIRTY-EIGHT

'Houston, we have contact.' I leap on my phone as two precious bars on the screen indicate a faint but viable reception. My hands are shaking, and my body aches with exhaustion. I sink down on to an armchair to make the call I've been waiting all night to make.

I hardly slept a wink after Craig ended our almost-row by letting himself out of the cottage, promising he would return in the morning so we could talk some more. I don't want to talk to him again. I didn't even want to stay here, but Nick is too weak for me to move by myself, and with no landline, internet reception or mobile signal, I had no option but to spend a restless night replaying Craig's parting words, wondering exactly what he meant by them.

Whatever it takes to be Nick's dad again. I can't decide if it was a challenge to my parenthood, or a promise to woo me back. Neither option fills me with joy, and I've never been so happy to see the sun rise. I crept out of bed just as pale fingers of light began to steal through the bedroom curtains, letting Nick sleep on while I packed our things.

Now my phone is finally picking up a signal, I'm going to call

DCI Maxwell and ask him to send someone to collect us. I don't care where we go. A hotel. Or maybe Beth's house. Katie is away, and in any case, I don't want to put her to any trouble. Or see Nathan. I sympathise with his grief, but I don't like him and I can't fake it. Wherever Nick and I go, I just want to get away from here – where Craig clearly intends to come and go as he pleases.

I glance out of the window for the hundredth time, frowning as I still see no sign of Sergeant Rogers. Nor can I find the card he gave me. I was sure I put it on the rattan coffee table while Craig and I had our coffee, but it's not there now. At least I have DCI Maxwell's number stored in my phone. It pings repeatedly as I turn it on, and I wait impatiently as messages flood in: a quick one from Katie saying she was glad we talked, a panicky one I can't make head nor tail of from Beth, and a request from Jo Peters to call her.

There are no messages from Sean Newton returning the ones I left thanking him for his help, and when I listen to the final voicemail, from DCI Maxwell, I realise why. I need to call him back. And speak to Beth. Probably Ayesha, too. But first I have to talk to my best friend . . .

There's no answer from her mobile, so I call her landline instead, about to hang up when she finally answers with a breathless 'Hello?'

'Katie. It's me. Izzy.' I take slow, deep breaths, fighting to stay calm.

'Where are you? There's a dreadful echo on the line.'

'Sorry, the signal's awful. I'm . . . Never mind.' I can't bring myself to tell her that I'm a few hundred metres from where her son lost his life. 'Are you OK? Are you home?'

'Just this moment. Well, *I* am. Nathan's gone AWOL as usual. Anyway, what's up?'

I can tell that, typically, she's trying her best to act brave, appear strong, hide her grief. I can imagine her true feelings; I'm also certain she wouldn't be this calm if DCI Maxwell had already spoken to her. 'I'm guessing you haven't heard the news.'

'News?'

'DCI Maxwell didn't call you?'

'Hang on. Let me check.' Her voice drifts away, and I hear rustling noises. 'I left my mobile at home while we were away,' she says, returning after a moment. 'I needed some time out, you know? Just walking by the sea. Not thinking about anything. Or trying not to, at least. Why? Has something happened? Nick—'

'Is doing OK. It is about him, though. All the boys, in fact. But first I want to say sorry again, Katie. About Jason. Not realising exactly how upset he was last Saturday. You said he was terrified. You thought he was holding something back. You were right. I know what it was now. Adrian Atkins has made a statement to the police. I know DCI Maxwell wanted to tell you himself, though, so—'

'Oh, screw that. Tell me, Iz. You're worrying me. What is it?'

'It's about their teacher. Mr Newton.' I take a deep breath. 'He's been arrested.'

I lay out jeans and a sweatshirt for Nick on his bed, then unzip his toiletry bag to check he has everything he needs. As my fingers touch a small bottle of cologne, I feel sick. Rushing to the bathroom, I snap the cap off the aftershave and pour it down the sink.

'Bastard. Deceitful, sneaky bastard.' I watch the pungent liquid disappear down the plug hole. If only I could get his face out of my mind so easily, but I know I'll be seeing Sean Newton's bright blue eyes and floppy blond fringe in my nightmares until my dying day.

I remember the aftershave I smelled on him when he came to see me; it reminded me of Nick. *No wonder.* To think that his teacher sat in my living room, pleading how desperate he was to help. With every calculated word out of his mouth, he was setting up his alibi. And all the time he knew where Nick was, and that the longer everyone was chasing around looking in all the wrong places, the less chance there was of finding him alive.

'*No!*' I lean over the tub, feeling like I'm going to wretch.

'Mum? Are you all right?'

I turn to see Nick in the bathroom doorway. Still dressed in his pyjamas, he looks so young. Innocent. *Defenceless*. All the boys were, I think bitterly. And Sean took advantage of that. The so-called initiation trial was a total fabrication, but Nick believed every word. Only it wasn't real; there was no dare. That was just a ready-made excuse prepared in advance for the boys by their teacher. The truth was that he had instructed them to send my son into the woods as a cautionary punishment – because Nick had been threatening to blow the whistle on Sean, who had slowly but surely been grooming the boys through the book group.

'Nick, love, come and sit down.' I draw him into the living room, urging him on to the sofa and pulling a blanket over him. 'How are you feeling?'

'I've got a headache.'

'You need your medicine.' I stroke his hair. 'Can I get you something to eat too?'

'In a bit. Where are we?' He looks around curiously, eyes wide.

'Craig's cottage. Don't you remember?' I worry that he's not only struggling to recall the past, but that his capacity to hold on to new memories might have been damaged.

I need to take him back to see Dr Lynch, I decide – probably even before he speaks to the police. DCI Maxwell has been desperate to interview Nick since he woke up, and he made it clear in his message that, following Adrian's statement, he needs to do so as a priority. But now Sean Newton is in custody, the weight of fear has lifted: I know Nick needs to speak to the police, but his health comes first. As soon as we can get out of here, I'm taking him home – via the hospital.

'Cottage? Oh yeah. I remember.' Nick hunches his legs up, hugging them.

'Have you, um, remembered anything else yet?' I ask gently.

'Bits.'

'That's good. Do you want to talk about it?'

'Not now, Mum. I'm tired.' He closes his eyes, soft brows drawing into a frown.

'OK. I understand.' I swallow frustration, but I don't want to upset him by pushing too hard. 'I just want you to know that you're safe now, darling. Mr Newton has been arrested. Adrian told his mum everything. You were so brave to want to speak out. And to encourage your new friends to do the same.'

'Mr Newton has been arrested?' Nick's eyes snap open.

'Yes, love. I'm so sorry. I could tell you've had something on your mind these last few weeks. I should have asked what. I thought it was . . . ' Guilt floods through me once again at how I suspected Jason. 'It doesn't matter. I've let you down, that's all. And messed everything up. Again.' I rest my head against his.

'Mum. It's OK. It's not your fault.' He sits up straight, pushing the blanket off.

'It's my job to keep you safe.' *Not Craig's*, I decide, as my phone vibrates in my pocket and I see his name on the screen. I'm glad he's finally opened up about his past. It explains some things, but it doesn't change everything. I open his text: *I'm coming over.*

'It's not always easy knowing who to trust.' Nick tucks his head into my shoulder.

'You're absolutely right.' I stare at the text a moment longer, then press 'delete'. 'I remember you said as much in your—' I break off, not wanting to bring up his video diaries just yet. I'm desperate to understand everything Nick said in them; I want him to know that while diaries are private, there are some things it's better to tell. But all in good time. My biggest fear, however, can't wait. 'Mr Newton ... Did he ever ... touch you?'

Nick's eyes widen until the pupils shrink into pinpricks. 'Touch me? What?'

'It's OK, darling.' It's obvious he has no idea what I'm talking about, and I don't want to push him into remembering horrible things. Not until he's feeling a lot stronger.

'What do you mean, Mum?' His fingers dig into my arm.

'Don't worry,' I say quickly, concerned at the slight wheeze in his voice. 'Dr Lynch said your memory will be fuzzy for a while. But just so you know, Adrian has told the police everything. He's a very brave boy. And so are you.' I give him a hug, shocked to feel how much weight he's lost. He was always skinny; now he feels like if I squeeze too hard he might snap. 'But you're both safe now.'

I give Nick his medicine, then help him back to bed. It will be good for him to rest while I make final preparations for us to leave. Hopefully very soon. I would book a taxi to meet us on the other side of the bridge, except DS Clarke gave me strict instructions not to go anywhere without a police escort. I've left both her and DCI Maxwell two voicemails now, frustrated not to be able to get hold of them but realising they'll have their hands full interviewing Sean Newton.

The detective said in his message that they're also questioning the teacher about his movements at the time my house and car were vandalised. They haven't ruled out that he was responsible for that too – as a malicious postscript to his attack on Nick. I'm mightily glad the investigation finally seems to be coming to a satisfactory end, but I feel a little abandoned here on the island. *Like sitting ducks*, I recall saying to Craig. Except that Suspect A is now safely behind bars, I remind myself firmly.

I'm just settling down on the sofa, drifting off into a daydream of Nick getting better, maybe the two of us even moving house and starting life afresh somewhere, when I'm jolted out of my thoughts by a weird, almost unearthly yowl. Hurrying to the sliding glass doors, I peer out towards the river. I can't see anything, but as I hear the noise again, I realise it's coming from the front of the house. Making my way quickly through into the kitchen, I peer out of that window instead, seeing nothing but trees swaying in the wind.

'Darn it. I'm going to have to go and look.' I grab the keys from my bag and head into the hall, then find myself hesitating. Even though I know we're safe now, I'm not keen on venturing outside. Maybe I'll just open the front door and take a quick peek …

THIRTY-NINE

'Oh! Adrian! You gave me a fright.' His was the last face I expected to see as I finally unlocked the top half of the stable door. But no twelve-year-old boy made that weird sound; I look over his shoulder, waiting to see if it comes again. 'I thought I heard a strange noise. Did you . . . ? Never mind. I must have imagined it. What are you doing here?' I glance around to see if he's alone. 'How did you even find us?'

'Nick texted me. I wasn't sure I'd got the right house.' He pulls a face. 'This place is Creepsville. Can I see him?'

'Nick texted you? Right. I see. That's nice.' It's a small sign of Nick returning to some kind of normality, and I'm thankful for that, even though I don't want him to get sucked into texting again. All the messages have been wiped from his phone now, but I haven't forgotten the last one Jason sent; I still have no idea what it really meant. 'But to tell you the truth, Nick's wiped out. He's actually asleep right now.'

'I can wait,' Adrian persists. 'I'll be quiet. Honest.'

'Well . . . Hang on. Did you hear that?' I strain my ears, trying to identify another odd noise, slightly softer than last time, but I definitely didn't imagine it.

Adrian looks over his shoulder. 'Probably a fox. I saw one on my way here.'

'Oh, right. Of course.' I've obviously spent so long feeling scared that I'm now jumpy and suspicious of every little thing.

'I bet it's fighting another cat. I saw a dead one over there.' He nods at the front gate.

'A dead ... *Oh God.*' I quickly unlock the bottom half of the door and almost tumble down the steps as I push past Adrian, skidding cross the veranda and out on to the footpath, spotting Marzipan almost immediately.

'No! Oh *no.*' I crouch down, a sob tightening my chest as she strains to lift her head. 'Shh, it's OK.' I stroke the soft body that has always looked so plump and sturdy, but now feels flat and frail. She wouldn't have stood a chance against a fox, I think, fighting tears as she lets her head sink into the wet grass, her usually bright, knowing eyes turning glassy.

'Is it dead?' Adrian appears at my side.

'Her name's Marzipan. She's Nick's cat.' I lift her gently, cradling her against my chest. 'But yes. I'm afraid I think she is. I can't see any blood, though.' I gently feel around her body. 'Maybe it wasn't a fox.' I look around anxiously; the island is covered with all kinds of plants that, for all I know, could be toxic to animals.

'Let's have a look?' Adrian lifts her paw, bending to prod and examine her tummy.

'The vet will know. I'll take her there later.' I nudge his hand away, feeling protective of Marzipan even though I know she can no longer feel pain.

'We should bury her,' he suggests, stooping for a better look.

'No. I think I'll just ... '

I stand up abruptly and hurry back to the kitchen. Finding a basket under the sink, I lay Marzipan inside, trying to imagine I'm just settling her to sleep. But all of a sudden I can't fight the sob gathering force in my chest. Not wanting to distress Adrian, I carry the basket into the spare bedroom, hiding it under the dressing table where Nick hopefully won't find it. Then I sit down on the bed, grab a pillow, bury my face in it and let the tears come.

It's not just Marzipan; it's everything that's happened over the last few days – the last year, even. I so wanted life to be better. I thought the sleepover signalled the start of a new, happier phase. I couldn't have been more wrong, and for a few minutes I feel paralysed by the emotions flooding out of me. By the time I pull myself together enough to return to the kitchen, Adrian has found the cookie tin.

'I could take Nick a snack?' His face is a picture of innocence as he surreptitiously brushes crumbs off his chin.

'Sure.' I smile as I watch him grab a handful more, shoving them into his coat pockets. Maybe it will be good for Nick to see his best friend, I decide; I'm certainly missing mine. 'OK. I'll go check if he's woken up yet,' I tell him. 'You wait here.'

'Thanks, Mrs Brookes,' he says politely.

'You're welcome. Although I'm the one who should be thanking *you*.' I pause in the kitchen doorway, reflecting on the enormity of everything Adrian told DCI Maxwell. 'You were very brave to tell the police the truth. These last few days must have been horrible for you too,' I say gently.

'Yeah.' He nods, then grabs more cookies.

I laugh at his eagerness. 'Didn't you have breakfast this morning?'

'This *is* breakfast.' He shoves a whole cookie into his mouth, chewing rapidly. 'Mum sometimes makes me toast at the weekend. She never bothers on school days.'

'Oh!' I suddenly notice he's wearing his school uniform underneath his coat. I've lost track of days, time. I glance at the clock on the kitchen wall. 'Shouldn't you be in school now? Your mum does know you're here, right?'

Adrian shuffles his feet. 'It's Friday. I hate Fridays. It's book group day.' His eyes, so like Beth's, widen into green pools. 'And Jason won't be there.'

'Ah, yes. Of course.' I realise I've been so preoccupied by Katie's grief, I've overlooked how Jason's death will have impacted Adrian – and Samir too, no doubt. 'It's so sad what happened to him. I, um . . . I haven't talked to Nick about it yet. If you wouldn't mind not mentioning it? He's been through so much. I want to find the right moment to tell him. OK?' Adrian nods, looking so solemn that I feel compelled to add: 'Mr Newton can't hurt you any more, you know. He won't be allowed near any of you ever again.'

'Good riddance to bad rubbish. That's what my dad said.'

'Your dad. Is he . . . ? Never mind.' I stop myself asking whether Mike Atkins is finally home. I don't want to pry into other people's family business; after all the salacious speculation I've read about myself, Nick and Craig in the papers, I'm sick and tired of people poking their noses into mine.

'Can we have another sleepover soon?' Adrian cocks his head. 'It's Nick's turn.'

'Well, I . . . ' Every instinct inside me screams, *Never again*.

'We shouldn't have done it at my house.' He shoves his hands deep in his pockets, looking grumpy. 'Mum was useless. She's a lush.'

'She – sorry, what?'

'You know, an alcoholic. Whenever Dad's away she pours gin in her coffee. She thinks I don't see, but I do. Or maybe it's vodka. Whatever. It smells gross.'

'Are you sure about that, love?' I'm certain he's got the wrong end of the stick. Nick also hates the smell of alcohol, so much so

249

that I've occasionally worried someone has secretly forced him to try some. Or perhaps it's simply a child's need for their parent to be fully capable, *reliable*, I reflect now. With relations seemingly strained between his parents, maybe Adrian has started worrying about Beth drinking too much, even when she isn't.

'I'm just worried about Molly,' he says, his eyes turning watery. 'Sometimes Mum doesn't wake up when she cries. She didn't even blink when we went out on Friday night.'

I can feel my heart pumping. 'Let me get this straight. You're saying your mum didn't check on you at the sleepover? She didn't come upstairs and say goodnight? Make sure you were all OK? Turn out the lights ...?' I think through the evening as Beth described it.

He shakes his head. 'She crashed out on the sofa after the pizza guy left. I fed Molly and put her to bed. Mum only woke up the next morning because you rang the doorbell.'

'You've got a visitor, sweetheart. It's your friend. You remember Adrian?'

I poke my head around the bedroom door, keeping my voice soft in case Nick is still asleep. I find myself hoping he is. My mind is buzzing with everything Adrian has revealed about his mum, and I'm worried about Adrian skipping school. I have to call Beth.

'I need the bathroom, Mum. Can you give me a hand?' Nick is sitting up in bed, skinny legs dangling over the side. He has a little more colour in his cheeks but is clearly still not confident about walking without help so soon after waking up.

'Of course. Hang on just a sec.' I tap on Beth's number, tutting when I can't get a connection. I try texting her instead, but it won't send.

'Mum. Please?'

'Sorry, darling.' I slip my phone back into my jeans pocket; I'll have to try again in a minute. 'Let's get you dressed, shall we? We can skip showers today. Here we go.' I support Nick as he stands up, but after a few steps he seems to find his strength. Tentatively, I let go, holding my breath as he heads slowly towards the bathroom.

'Hurry up, dude. I've got something to show you.' Adrian flings himself on to Nick's wheelchair, bouncing up and down and then trying to make it do a wheelie.

'What are *you* doing here?' Nick spins around. 'Didn't you get my text yesterday?'

Adrian looks hurt. 'I didn't think you meant it.'

'I did. Anyway, read the sign.' Nick points to the hand-painted driftwood hanging by a ribbon on the bathroom door. 'It's *private*. Keep out, yeah?'

'Why don't you wait in the living room, Adrian?' I suggest, puzzled by Nick's tetchiness but knowing that, after years of taunts in school changing rooms, the need for privacy has become ingrained in him. Adrian huffs before leaping up from the wheelchair.

'I don't want him here, Mum,' Nick whispers as soon as Adrian has disappeared.

'Really? Oh! Sorry, darling. I thought you might like to see a friendly face. I thought it might help put a smile back on yours,' I add softly, reaching out to stroke his cheek. A moment later, I hear the tinkle of glass. 'Bang goes that delightful dolphin figurine on the book shelf.' I roll my eyes, which finally draws a reluctant smile from Nick.

'OK. I'll just get dressed.' He throws a last glance towards the living room, rolling his eyes now at the lively commentary we can both hear from Adrian as he explores the room.

Once Nick has disappeared into the bathroom, I seize the chance to try Beth again. The signal is still very weak, which probably explains why I've heard nothing from Craig since his text. He said he was coming over, but it's taking him a while; usually he would send a message if he's delayed for any reason. I'm waiting for his next move, I realise – still pondering his comment that he'll do whatever it takes to be Nick's dad again. It's making me feel tense and a little anxious.

Almost as agitated as Nick seems, I reflect, wondering if seeing Adrian has brought back bad memories. I don't want Nick upset; on the other hand, perhaps it's a good sign that he might be starting to recall bits and pieces. Chatting with his friend could even release the mental block that trauma has left in his mind. We're clearly stuck here for another little while; anything is worth a try to see if I can finally get Nick to remember . . .

FORTY

'How about I go make some hot chocolate? Leave you two to catch up,' I say as Nick emerges from the bathroom, looking more himself in his jeans and favourite red hoodie.

'No, Mum, don't go. I wanted to ask you something.' His fingers curl around my arm. 'You were saying before about Mr Newton. That he was arrested. What did you mean?'

'Why don't we all sit down and have a chat, hmm? I think Adrian's eaten all the cookies, but I'm sure I can rustle up another treat.' Nick looks doubtful, but I gently urge him into the living room, helping him get comfortable on the sofa.

Adrian skips over from the window. 'There's a boat out there. Can we go in it?'

'In this weather?' I smile, even as goose bumps chase up my spine at the possibility that it's Craig's boat, and he's back. He said he was coming right over; I wonder again what's taking him so long. 'Anyway, we should probably get you to school.'

'*No*,' Adrian yells, making me jump. 'I don't want to. You can't make me!'

'No, of course not. OK, don't worry. You're fine here,' I back-track quickly, seeing his cheeks turn pink. 'I'm just worried that your mum—'

'I can't go back there. Not *ever*. Jason's dad does military fitness in P.E. now.'

'So?'

'So he'll kill me if he sees me.'

'*No*, sweetheart,' I say gently. 'Why would he? Anyway, I really don't think he'll be there for a while.' Katie said he'd gone AWOL; my guess is that someone as tough as Nathan prefers to do his grieving in private. 'In any case, he isn't going to blame you. The dare wasn't even your idea. It was all down to Mr Newton. I know that. So will Jason's dad.'

'Dare?' Nick's eyes open wide as he sits bolt upright. 'What dare?'

'You really don't remember?' I squeeze his hand, looking anxiously at the mottled blush spreading across his pale cheeks now. 'Maybe Dr Lynch was right,' I say, more to myself. 'Perhaps talking to a counsellor might be the best thing.'

'She means a shrink, dude.' Adrian pulls a face as he slumps into the wicker armchair next to the sofa, putting his feet up on the rattan chest. 'A head-doctor who asks, like, a zillion trick questions. Then gets you to draw pictures about things you're scared of.'

'Ah, right.' I'm a little surprised Beth has been so quick to find a therapist for Adrian, but I'm forgetting that while time has stood still for me over the last week, life has gone on for everyone else.

'I think I freaked the doc out.' Adrian pulls a face. 'I drew some pretty weird stuff. My dad said Mr Newton deserves to be shot for what he did.'

'Mr Newton?' Nick leans forward, eyes wider still.

'You seriously don't remember?' Adrian stares at him then shakes his head. 'That whack on your head must have really mashed your brains.'

'What are you *talking* about?' Nick looks close to tears now.

'Why don't you take your coat off, Adrian?' I say, more to slow things down. He's coming on too strong, too fast, now. I'd hoped a friendly chat would help Nick; I don't want to open up painful wounds either for him *or* for Adrian.

'Nah. I'm OK.' Adrian wraps his coat even tighter around himself. 'And you know what I'm talking about.' He nods at Nick. 'Mr Newton and Jason. The Perve and Army Boy.'

'OK, that's enough.' I'm not surprised by Adrian's vitriol towards his teacher, but I'm shocked he can speak ill of his dead friend, who was in the same boat as all the boys – and if the post-mortem does indeed indicate suicide, took the most horrific way out of it.

'Squeezing up against us in the book club. Spying on us in the toilets.' Adrian's face is bright red now. 'Remember, Nick?'

'Oh my God. Did you tell all this to the police?' I liked Sean. I *trusted* him. How could I have been so wrong?

'Yeah. I told them about Jase, too. He was just as bad. Telling us we'd "better do what sir said, or else". Then he had the nerve to show up at *my* sleepover.' Adrian crumples completely now, hunching in on himself, his eyes filling with tears.

'I'm calling your mum.' I reach into my pocket for my phone.

'I wouldn't bother.' He shakes his head vigorously. 'She doesn't care. She didn't even let me stay off school. I had to get Dad to write a note. He's back now, anyway. I told him about Mum's drinking. And what happened at the sleepover. He said he'd sort everything.'

I feel a flash of concern for Beth, remembering the feeling I had on Saturday morning that I'd walked into the aftermath of a row. Beth was so flustered; I have no idea if that's because Adrian is telling the truth – that she had crashed out drunk the night before – or if her edginess was the after-effects of a row Mike Atkins has now turned up in person to finish.

'Well, I'd like to speak to her, all the same.' I scroll through my contacts, tutting at the weak signal. Maybe it's stronger outside ... I stand up, deciding to go and check, and I'm surprised when Nick grabs my arm. 'It's OK, love. I'm not going anywhere,' I reassure him.

'I don't get this.' He stares at me, then at his friend, his eyes huge in his pale face.

'What's not to get?' Adrian glares back. 'Jason gatecrashed my sleepover to shut us up, to stop us telling tales on him and Mr Newton. Especially *you*. You got his text, right?'

'What text?' Nick looks even more confused as he pulls his phone out of his jeans pocket and stares blankly at the screen. 'But Ade, I *asked* Jason to come to the sleepover,' he says after a moment. 'I told you all that I wanted to talk to you. About the website you showed me on your phone. *Dare or Die*. I wanted Jase to get rid of it. Remember?'

'*Dare or Die*. Yeah.' Adrian suddenly grins. 'Props to Jase for that. Never thought he'd have the brains to come up with it.'

'What do you mean? It's not a joke.' Nick's eyes widen. 'My dad ...'

'Nick, not now. We need to talk about this alone.' I cup his face with both hands, trying to contain the panic I can almost feel whirling around inside his mind. He resists, his body rigid, eyes fixed, as though he's picturing the terrible scene he didn't even witness.

'He hung himself.' Nick doesn't take his eyes off the living-room wall.

'Oh, love.' I wrap my arms around him, wishing I could take all the bad things away.

'I had nightmares about it. About someone else doing that. *Dare or Die*. I mean, you might really, actually die. I told Jason on Friday night to ditch the website. But he didn't have a clue what I was on about. He said his dad told him about guys getting legs and arms blown off. That was the real deal, he said. Not kids acting like they were in the SAS, or something.'

'Jason Baxter was a liar,' Adrian spits. 'He set up the website. He probably got Mr Newton to help him, too. He came up with the dare. He wasn't your friend, Nick. *I* am. And I'm glad he's dead. True friends don't tell. At least he had the bottle to stick to it.'

'What?' Nick's body spasms. 'Jason's *dead*?'

I watch his pupils dilate; I'm sure I can see the precise moment shock unlocks a door in his mind, allowing memory to flood through it. I reach for his hand. 'Sweetheart . . . '

'If you don't believe me about what Jason was like, look at this.' Adrian fumbles in his pocket for his phone. 'I'll show you *exactly* what he did.'

'You don't need to, Ade,' Nick says quietly, before turning to look at me with blue eyes that are clearer, brighter, than I have seen them for weeks. 'Mum, I remember.'

FORTY-ONE

'We watched this movie. There was a guy locked in a room. He couldn't move. Rope . . . no, he had *chains* round his ankles. There was only one way he could escape. By sawing his own leg off.' Nick stops talking, looking confused again. 'I don't know why I told you that.' He shakes his head, a bemused puppy that's tripped over its own feet and landed upside down.

'Just say it as it happened, sweetheart. Take your time.' I try not to show how shocked I am that the boys watched such an inappropriate film – that Beth *let* them. 'Pretend you're telling me the plot of a movie. Only not that horror one. Your *own* story. OK?'

'Adrian said he watched his dad cut up dead animals,' Nick continues after a moment, eyes once again fixed on the wall, a blank screen where he is clearly projecting memories as, very slowly, they begin to resurface. 'He said he hated the blood. That he could "never cut a real person's skin". Mrs Atkins turned off the film then. She put on a kids' movie and said she hoped we didn't all have nightmares, or our mums would get Social Services on her.'

I glance at Adrian, half expecting him to jump in with an opinion. For once, though, he's sitting completely still, almost as though he's transfixed: legs crossed in front of him on the armchair; eyes wide and trained firmly on Nick's face. I turn back to him, resting a hand on his arm. 'So you all watched TV together. Then what, love?' I prompt gently.

'Mrs Atkins ordered pizza. Samir ate most of it. I told him he'd be sick. He said, "Good job you're sharing Ade's bed not mine, then." Sammy doesn't say much, but he makes me laugh. He's totally into computers. He said he only joined the reading group because his mum said she wanted his head out of Minecraft and in a book. It was Jason who told me about it. *He* said he only went because it was on Friday lunchtimes. It was that or litter duty. He likes Mr Newton, though. He said he lets you do assignments how you want. Like, you can do a photo story. Or paint a picture, or write a poem.

'Anyway, I texted Jase about the sleepover. At first he said no. His dad was home. He didn't want to leave his mum. I don't know what changed his mind, but he looked gutted. I thought it was about the pizza. There was none left, and Jase had a go at Sammy for stuffing his face. It was a bit awkward then. Jase said sorry, he was in a grouch. He hated his dad, he said. Ade said, "Why? He's a hero. He's killed hundreds of baddies." Mrs Atkins said, "All parents have bad patches." I told her mine didn't. That our family's perfect. Or used to be.'

Nick pauses, and I reach out to him, ready to offer comfort, but he looks straight ahead, clearly locked into his thoughts as the memories keep coming, thick and fast now.

'I think Jase knew I didn't want to talk about it,' he says after a moment. 'He got me to show him where to put his stuff. We chilled upstairs for a bit then. He asked why my stepdad hung around his house so much. He and his mum just sit in the kitchen, talking, drinking wine, he said. He was worried his mum was turning into a lush. Adrian came in and asked what a lush was. Jase told him to "get lost and google it". Ade didn't like that.

'Everyone thinks Jason's a bully. He's actually pretty good to talk to. I guess he does boss people around. I think it's his way of feeling he's not the only one getting picked on. His dad hits him. I reckon Jase takes it out on other kids. Not me. Well, he did for a bit. When our mums fell out. He said that was dumb. That I was like a kid brother to him. He told me he's got a brother in heaven. I felt bad for him. I said, "I bet my dad's looking after him."

'Then Ade came back. He was filming us and saying we were being gay. Jase told him to "get his effing phone out of his face". Ade said, "Come outside for a snowball fight, then." But Sammy wanted to play video games. Jase said he was just gonna crash. But his feet hung off the end of the camp bed, so I offered to swap with him. Ade said he'd rather die than sleep with "Army Boy".

'Me and Jase went downstairs then. Molly was crying and crying, and Mrs Atkins was getting really stressed. She kept apologising, saying it was teething pain. Jase and I made up games to try and distract her. The house got proper messy, but Ade's mum said it was OK, and she wished Adrian played with his sister more.

'Then someone kept banging on the door. Ade's mum said it was "no one important", and to ignore it. So we all went upstairs. I got my book out. It's the one I was reading for Mr Newton. Jase was right, the guy's legit. I told him on Friday what happened at my old school. He didn't get all preachy about it. He just said, "Dance to your own tune, son." I told him that's what got me into trouble in the first place. That made him laugh.

'I really wanted to talk to the guys about the website. But I didn't want to get called a wuss or a snitch. I'm not. I was just worried kids would get hurt. Then Mum phoned and I felt bad cos I didn't want to chat. I just wanted to get it over – tell Jason to

260

ditch the website. Anyway, Ade kept messing about, taking selfies. I told him he'd better not post any photos of me. He laughed and said I was a "saddo" for not being on Facebook. He took my book off me and called me "teacher's pet". I was mad cos I wanted to know how it ended.

'He went off in a strop then. When he came back he was all dusty. I said I didn't want to fall out with him, and asked where he went. He said "the dungeon", and not to piss him off or I'd end up there. Jase threw a pillow at him, and Sammy said we should have a midnight feast. Ade said he'd roast *him*, if he didn't shut up about food. Then his mum came up to say goodnight, and we all pretended to be asleep.

'It took me ages to say about the website. I jabbered a bit. About the show. That I was worried it would be in the papers again. Ade said he thought it would be cool being famous. He said there's nothing special about him. I said yeah there is: "You're the gadget king." He said, "Big deal. Jase is rugby captain. You're a dancer. Sammy's school chess champion." He said no one's interested in him. His mum's busy with Molly. His dad's never there. He said the *Dare or Die* thing made people notice you. Like being a celeb. I said, "Who wants to be famous for getting your skull smashed when you fall off a roof?"

'Jase said it was all a load of crap, and went off to the bathroom. Ade followed, and I heard Jase shout at him to stop taking pictures, or he'd ram the "effing phone" down his throat. He went to get Mrs Atkins, but she was yelling at someone downstairs, so he went to sleep in the spare bedroom. Sammy was asleep now. I kind of wanted to go home, so I didn't bother with my PJs. I reckoned I'd get up early and leave. I knew I wouldn't sleep.

'I kept thinking about my dad. And the website. I kept thinking maybe the kids who battered me last year filmed it and put it on YouTube. I thought I could tough it out with them. I wanted to prove I could hack it. Walk to school by myself. But it all went wrong and I didn't want anyone else to get hurt, ever. I just wanted everything to be OK. To have friends. *Real* friends. Not just online. For things to be *normal*.

'I guess I fell asleep, because I woke up when something touched my face. It stank. Kind of soapy. My legs started to feel rubbery. I wanted to be sick, so I got up. Ade came out. He held on to me, said I just needed fresh air. He helped me put my trainers on and we went outside. It was so cold. I couldn't breathe. Ade said, "Here, take another sniff of this." But it made me even more dizzy. Like on a rollercoaster.

'I started seeing things, too. Like, there was a man standing right in the middle of the road. I thought it was Mr Newton. Then it looked like my stepdad. I couldn't see properly. I felt like it was snowing in my head. Then I realised it *was* snowing, and I started to run towards the man. I suddenly thought it was my dad, and I wanted to talk to him, to tell him to look after Jase's brother in heaven. But Ade said I needed to walk off the dizziness. We walked and walked. We climbed a bit, too – a wall, I think. I don't remember. I just remember trees. Rocks. Then everything went black.

'The cold woke me up. I had no top on. There was a Christmas tree smell, and I thought, *I'm dreaming*. I called out for Mum, but she didn't answer. It was so dark. I couldn't find my phone, and I needed my inhaler. I tried to stand up but my arms and legs wouldn't move. I was shaking so bad, and I thought: *Do you still shiver if you're paralysed?* Then I felt the ropes. I think I screamed, but no sound came out. I kind of freaked out then, bashing around. I felt something sharp, and I knew it was a knife.

'I started to cry. I remembered the film. I thought, *Someone wants me to kill myself.* I remembered a hand shoving my back. I tried to think who pushed me. But my head really hurt, and my chest felt like it was being crushed. I thought I could see Mum's face. She looked sad. I wanted to tell her I love her. She always says that to me. I haven't said it back for ages. I picked up the knife and hacked at the rope. Sawing and sawing.

'I couldn't believe it. I was free. But my legs felt numb, and I had to drag myself across the ground. I found a gap in the door. I pushed and pushed, but it didn't move. I poked my fingers through the gap, and pushed harder. Then I got the knife and stabbed at it. I managed to get my head through, but then I was stuck. I was so tired. I wanted to sleep. But it was freezing. I knew if I shut my eyes I would die.

'I heard noises in the trees when I got out. I thought someone was coming for me. I held up the knife to protect myself, but my hands were so stiff. I dropped it. I started crying again. I just sat there, rocking. I thought, *The bullies have come back*. I knew I couldn't fight them. I felt so weak. I kept thinking I saw faces in the trees. But nobody came.

'Then I saw lights. I wasn't sure they were real – like the man on the street. I was worried I was going crazy. I tried to run, but I kept falling over. I kept seeing the same weird tree stump. I thought, *If I still had the knife, I could carve symbols on the trees*. Like Hansel and Gretel. But I'd lost it. I tried to pile snow on the stump. Like a sign. But it melted away.

'I thought I saw Marzipan, her orange eyes in the trees. I thought of the poem Mr Newton showed me. *Tiger, tiger, burning bright, in the forests of the night*. I chased after her and tripped over a rock. It really hurt, and I was hopping around and slid down these rocks. I was flat on my back and there was this massive pain in my head. I looked up and saw the moon. I remembered Mum used to say: "Shall we ask the man in the moon?" I asked him where my mum was. The next thing I remember is waking up in hospital, and she was right there.'

FORTY-TWO

'You said your mum didn't blink when "we" left the house. You meant you and Nick. He didn't sneak off by himself. And you knew exactly where he went. You've known all this time. Where he was hiding. Where he'd been hidden. Because you put him there!'

The second Nick finally stops talking and slumps back against the sofa, I turn to glare at Adrian. He's still sitting as though mesmerised. *Gripped by hearing the tale of his own horrible endeavours*, I realise. I take hold of Nick's hand, rubbing it as though it's still frozen. I'll never forget how cold it was when I found him; I'm struggling to believe that his so-called new best friend was the one who led him into that hellhole.

'Maybe. Maybe not.' Adrian shrugs carelessly, but his eyes are bright with curiosity, as though he's gauging, almost savouring, my distress.

'You're evil. *Evil!*' Nick spits the word I'm trying to bite back, then hauls himself to his feet, lurching unsteadily towards the bedroom and slamming the door behind him.

I decide to let him stay there. Partly to give him a chance to recover from the stress of his memory returning so violently, but more to shield him from the conversation I now need to have with Adrian. 'You might not be evil,' I say, turning back to him, 'but it was a very stupid thing that you did. Or did someone put you up to it? You can tell me, you know.'

'I'm not stupid.' He doesn't seem offended – more . . . amused. 'Everyone goes on about Sammy. "Clever Sammy, he knows all about computers." Well, so do I. They're like toys. You just need to know what buttons to push.'

Suddenly he leaps off the armchair and begins strutting up and down the living room, head up and chest puffed out, as though he's enjoying holding centre stage. *Even* bad *attention is attention*, Beth had said about Molly. And Adrian's mum is always so busy with his sister. But her son craves the spotlight – and at last he's found it.

'I know you like computers. Gadgets.' I force myself to keep speaking calmly. I don't want to scare Adrian off before he's answered all the questions burning in my mind.

'My dad gets me whatever I want. All I need is an internet connection, and bingo! I can do *anything*.'

I have a sudden hunch. 'You mean the website, don't you? *Dare or Die*. I saw it. It was . . . ' Disturbing. Horrific. 'Was that you? Did you set it up?'

'You didn't seriously think Jason could have done it?' he sneers.

'Well, his name was all over it, so . . . yes, I assumed he did. I guess you had everyone fooled.' I rein in my anger, deliberately playing to Adrian's pride in an effort to coax more information out of him. Under normal circumstances, I would never try to manipulate a child, but I have an alarming feeling that Adrian is still playing some kind of game. He clearly came here not to check on his friend, but to gloat. But then what? He really *isn't* stupid, and he'll realise he's in big trouble. Now I know what he did, all I have to do is call the police.

I shift my position on the sofa, feeling in my jeans pocket for my phone, keeping a slightly nervous eye on Adrian. He's small for his age; I'm sure I could overpower him. In fact, I have to clasp my hands together to stop myself launching across the room to grab him, *shake* him. I thought he was different; I was sure Jason was the bully. I was completely fooled by appearances: one so small and sweet-faced; the other a cocky-looking hulk like his dad. I transferred my dislike of Nathan on to his son, I realise; I misjudged him. *He's nothing like the others*, Nick said. It's only now, too late, that I realise he meant Adrian.

'People are easily fooled.' He throws a smirk at me. 'If it's on the internet, they think it's real. None of it is. Facebook. Instagram. It's just crap people make up. Fake accounts are a cinch. No one uses their *real* names or ages anyway. You can hack anyone if you have ID. All you need is a couple of letters. Old bills. Anything like that.' He stops pacing now and throws himself back into the armchair, legs hooked over the arm.

'*The recycling spread over my front garden*. It wasn't a fox.' I glare at him.

'Well, it kinda was. Mr Fantastic Fox.' He laughs. 'I can see *that* as a headline.'

The childish reference to a book Nick loved when he was much younger is in stark, sickening contrast to Adrian's cynical actions. 'So that's what this was all about? Fame?'

'I think you mean *going viral*.' Adrian rolls his eyes.

'Nick might have died,' I say quietly. 'Is that really what you wanted?'

'But he didn't, did he?' he bites back, for the first time looking rattled.

'No, but Jason did.'

'He deserved to. He was always sneering at me. Telling me to "run along, little boy". I needed to do *something*. I had to have *my* claim to fame.'

I stand up from the sofa and stride across to the glass doors. It's dank and grey outside; thick fog hangs low over the river. I can't make out if Craig's boat is still there; I don't bother to check my phone to see if he has texted again. I wish I didn't even own one – that there were no mobile phones, no secret apps, websites or social media . . . that, as Nick said, he could just have real friends, in the real world.

I glance back at Adrian, still struggling to get my head around him being capable of such things. *He's just a kid*, I think, staring at his too-big parka, his scuffed trainers – suddenly recalling Beth complaining that he'd lost his new ones. DCI Maxwell said there was no way the boys could have been in the woods, because they couldn't have cleaned their shoes without Beth hearing. Only Adrian didn't have to: not if he ditched his before he came back into the house . . .

'What made you do it?' I study his face, searching for clues.

'Nick gave me the idea,' he says, too quickly, and again I sense how desperately he wants his day in court: to be the centre of attention; all eyes on him, for once.

'Nick did.' I raise my eyebrows, allowing him to see my scepticism.

'Yeah. It was *my* sleepover. I wanted to hang out. Eat pizza. Have snowball fights. And Sammy was hogging the computer. Jase was in a strop. Nick was *reading*.'

'Well, he likes books. That's how you became friends, isn't it?' I say pointedly.

'Duh. *No*,' he drawls. 'Mr Newton just sat us together in form room.'

I glance towards Nick's bedroom door, hoping he isn't listening. 'So you weren't happy about Nick reading. You decided to punish him.' I'm boiling with rage now, but seeing Adrian smirk, I force myself to sit calmly back down on the sofa. I don't want him seeing how badly he's getting to me; I get the horrible feeling he's enjoying it. 'Couldn't you have just asked him to put his book down?'

'I did. Well, I sort of made him.' His chin juts. 'Fine, I was gonna burn it. I took it down to the cellar. I had a look inside first, though. Just to see what was so gripping.' He swings his legs to the floor, sitting upright and alert now, as though he's reliving the excitement of the moment. 'This boy went looking for his dad. He got lost, and everyone was looking for him. I thought, *What if Nick goes missing?* After a bit, I could go and find him.'

'Then you'd be a hero, and everyone would finally pay attention to *you*.' I shake my head. 'You've done what you've done, Adrian. But now you're going to have to tell the truth. To the police. And to your mum.' Fleetingly, I think of Beth. I feel sure she'll blame herself, but at twelve years old, surely Adrian is old enough to know right from wrong?

'Why would I do that? So they can call me a headcase, like my shrink does?'

'They won't,' I say firmly, wondering whether his counsellor has perceived signs of mental disturbance in the boy. He's always fidgety, but now his movements are agitated, *erratic*, as he jumps up and strides to the sliding doors, pressing his face against the glass as though looking for an escape from the trouble he's got himself into.

'She says I've got *issues*,' he mutters. 'Stupid cow.'

'Then prove her wrong. Show everyone how brave you are and own up. Maybe that will be your headline,' I say, trying again to steer him towards capitulation.

'Nah. I've thought of a much easier way to get famous. You've always gotta have a Plan B, haven't you?' He pivots around to face me, his expression gloating again.

'Look, I know you're clever. You made it look like it was Jason's website. You got rid of it to cover your tracks. But nothing really disappears from the internet. You obviously know a lot about computers. You must know—'

'More than you,' he scorns. 'And the police. They won't find anything. My dad sells software. He got me a widget that nukes stuff. I tanked it all. Jason's text. The website, Nick's Facebook.'

'Actually, the police managed to reactivate that. But why set it up in the first place?' I want to scream as I remember how that mis-directed the detectives, convincing DS Clarke that Nick was holed up somewhere – not lying half-dead less than a mile from his home.

Adrian grins, clearly impressed by his own cunning. 'Nick always said you ban him from social media. I thought it would be funny to send you a friend-request from him.'

'I never got one,' I say dubiously.

'Yeah, well. I changed my mind, didn't I? People started liking his Facebook. I had to get rid of it.'

'You mean, you only wanted people to follow *you*. You didn't want them to like *Nick's* stuff. Even if he didn't actually post it.' I tut. 'Identity theft is illegal, you know.'

'What? I didn't steal anything, did I? I didn't hack your bank account. I could have,' he brags. 'People are so dumb about pass-words. Their kids' names. Favourite, uh, pet.'

'Oh my God. You killed Marzipan.'

'No, I didn't. She ate the poison,' he says cheekily. 'I never made her.'

'You really are proud of yourself, aren't you?'

'I am, as it goes. Jason had the nerve to call *me* dumb. He was the idiot. He didn't even know his name was on the website. Or that I sent the text from his phone. *True friends don't tell*. He went mental when I told him. But it was too late. Nick was gone. And Jase was stupid enough to hide his phone for me. I said, "Dude, if you don't hide it, they're gonna find that text and come knocking on your door."'

269

'Nick never even read it.' I can't hide my scorn now.

'Yeah, well, it didn't matter anyway. I knew Jase would never tell on me. I told him, "Shut the fuck up, man, or I'll show everyone what you look like with your kit off."'

'You took photos at the sleepover. You threatened him with those. You told him if he didn't keep his mouth shut, you'd humiliate him. Expose him.' As understanding dawns, my pity for Jason grows. Katie was right: his toughness was skin deep.

Adrian lifts his hands, shaping his fingers as though to frame me in a shot. '"One click and the world sees," I told him. I never thought he'd go and top himself.'

'How *could* you? Nick may have survived. No thanks to you,' I spit. 'But you'll have Jason's death on your conscience for ever.'

'I didn't mean for him to do it!' Hands back in his pockets, Adrian scowls petulantly. 'See, nobody gets me. It was all supposed to be a joke. Why can't anyone see that? Sammy freaked out too. I told him, "Nick's only in the woods. Jase didn't have to go and jump in the river!" It was just a game. I was gonna get Nick out of there.'

'But you didn't. You didn't tell anyone until it was almost too late.'

'Yeah, well. I had to stick to the plan.'

'Plan?' My heart leaps. 'And was it just *your* plan?' I press, again wondering if Adrian's childish spite provided an opportune platform for a very adult crime – if he was merely the go-between and the real villain is still out there.

'Course it was.' He gives me a dirty look. 'It was my sleepover. My game. I couldn't let Sammy blow it. He said he was gonna tell the police. I said, "Mate, no one's gonna believe you." He said, "Mr Newton will."'

'So you got in there first. You defamed an innocent man,' I say angrily, guessing what's coming next. 'Telling the police he'd abused you. And it was all just more lies. I suppose you lied to Mr Newton about Nick seeing a girl, too.' Bitterly, I remember the fleeting hope that unexpected news gave. 'Do you even *know* a Cass Parker?'

'I heard the name in assembly a couple of weeks ago.' He shrugs. 'Mr Newton was being such a slimeball. The others fell for it, but I didn't. "You can tell me, boys,"' he mimics. 'I just told him what he wanted to hear. Then I told the police exactly what he did to us in the book group.'

'But it wasn't true! Any of it. And Mr Newton has been arrested. Because of *you*.'

'He deserves it. He's a teacher. He's not supposed to have favourites. But he kept banging on all the time about Nick being "so talented", such a "poetic soul". Why does it always have to be about *Nick*?' he whines, jabbing a finger towards the bedroom door.

He's so wrong, I don't know how to begin to put him right. 'Your teacher could go to prison, Adrian. You said it was all a game, but . . . ' Words fail me. I reach for my phone.

'Go ahead,' he sneers. 'Who's gonna believe a teacher over a kid?'

I think I'm going to faint. *He's such a sweet boy.* That's what everyone thinks. It's what I've always thought. Then I remember him prodding Marzipan as she lay dying, and it reminds me of the cupboard under the stairs in his home – his dad's taxidermy collection.

He's seen his dad cut up dead animals. He's watched Mike Atkins pose disembowelled wildlife to look as though it's still alive. How confused, how desensitised Adrian must have become about the finality of death, growing up absorbing the idea of dying as some kind of game – or to win a paltry fifteen minutes of fame by posting shocking stunts on YouTube . . .

I think of the website he pretended Jason set up: it made celebrities of the kids who posted on it, he told Nick. And as Adrian reaches into his coat pocket, pulling out his own phone, I suddenly grasp what his Plan B is, and why he's come here: *to film one last video.*

FORTY-THREE

'Put that down!' The words are in my head, but they come out of Nick's mouth as the bedroom door swings open and he flies through it, bowling towards Adrian.

'Adrian. Put the phone down. *Now*,' I order, standing up too. 'My son is not your clickbait.' I leap forward, managing to intercept Nick and pull him against me, gently restraining his arms. Fumbling to grab my own phone, I pray I can get a signal this time.

'I don't think so, Mrs Brookes.' Adrian pitches forward, still filming. 'It's your turn now. This is your big moment. Don't spoil it.'

Taking me by surprise, he snatches the phone from my hand, and I watch in horror as he lets it drop to the floor. Then stamps on it. Glass splinters everywhere, tiny slivers embedding themselves into the oatmeal carpet. Still Adrian keeps filming, angling his phone as though trying to get the best shot.

'No!' I run at him, reaching for it.

'What is your *problem*?' Nick gets there first, but Adrian dances away.

'That's it, Nick. Keep it coming,' he encourages. 'How many likes d'you think I'll get for this one? Shame you look like a ghost. Never mind, I'll zap a filter on it.'

Nick shoves Adrian with the little strength he has, the tendons standing out on his neck telling me what the effort costs him. Over the years, he has always heeded my advice to *walk away*; he's learned to grit his teeth and save his tears for his pillow. He never, ever, fought back. Now, as I see his face contort with rage, I hate Adrian for spreading his poison, provoking my son into a battle he cannot win. Not against someone whose biggest goal in life is to be in the spotlight, by whatever means, good or bad.

'That's *enough*.' I push myself between the boys, trying to smack Adrian's phone out of Nick's face. Once again, he dodges out of the way.

'Screw you, Adrian Atkins. You want to be famous? You think some stupid video is going to make people like you?' Nick yells at his friend-turned-enemy.

Or was he ever truly his friend? I have a sudden flashback to Nick's video diary, how he spoke of the sleepover: *It's showdown time.* Maybe he planned to do more than appeal to the boys about the website; perhaps he knew even then that Adrian was a false friend and wanted the chance to confront him, with Jason and Samir there for moral support.

'I've got hundreds of followers,' Adrian brags. 'How many have *you* got, loser?'

'Give me the phone, Adrian. Give it to me!' I watch the rapid rise and fall of Nick's shoulders. I sense him summoning up energy to go for Adrian; I hear the beginnings of wheezing low in his chest. Fearing an asthma attack, I lay a hand on his arm. 'Nick. It's OK.'

'Jason's dead, Mum. *Dead*. He can't get away with it.'

'He won't,' I say firmly, bracing myself to grab Adrian.

Before I can take a step, a strident ringtone I'd recognise any-where blares out. I whirl around at the same time as Adrian lurches forward, hand outstretched to grab the small Nokia that Nick takes out of his jeans pocket. But this time, I move faster.

'Nick?' a familiar voice barks as soon as I connect the call. 'It's DCI Maxwell.'

'No. It's Izzy. I'm here with Nick. We need help. Can you—'

'Is Rogers there too?' the detective cuts in. 'He's not picking up. Is he with you? Izzy, listen to me very carefully. Jason didn't commit suicide. We know who killed him. We need to find Adrian. We've got Molly, but we can't find her brother anywhere.'

'He's here. He—'

'He's there? Right. We're on our way. But Izzy, you need to get out of the cottage. Immediately. I think—'

I don't hear what he says next. Just for a split second, my atten-tion is distracted as Adrian suddenly backs away towards the other end of the room. My eyes are on him; my head is stuck on the news that Jason was murdered. My whole body feels like it's gone into shock, and I don't see the impact until it's too late. The first I hear is a fizz, followed by a loud pop; the first I feel is a powerful draught, like a wall of wind pushing me backwards.

My arms flail and I scramble helplessly as Nick's phone slips from my hand; my back twists awkwardly as I sprawl on to the floor. Fighting pain, I look up in time to see the pretty view of the garden crack and fold in on itself. Tiny chips of grey sky and weep-ing willow explode, firing off in all directions like multicoloured shrapnel as the sliding doors splinter in a shimmering mass of flying shards. Then I feel heat. I smell smoke. I see flames . . .

'Nick!' I scrabble towards him, running my hands quickly over his head, back and arms, brushing away sharp crystals of glass. 'Are you hurt? Are you OK?'

'Mum. Mum, I can't breathe.'

I sit back on my heels, giving him space, hurriedly scanning our surroundings. The carpet where I was standing seconds ago is now covered by huge, jagged sheets of glass; dense smoke billows in front of me, rolling up to the ceiling, clogging the air and obscuring visibility. But beneath the heavy ash-coloured cloud I can see the unmistakeable lick of fire.

'Nick, we have to get out of here. *Now.* As fast as you can, OK? DCI Maxwell's on his way. We just have to get out of the cottage.' I stare at the carnage behind me, shivering with the recognition that I was within inches of losing my life. 'Can you walk?'

He manages to pull himself on to his knees, but remains bent double. 'The rock. It was coming right for you, Mum,' he gasps, pointing.

'But it didn't get me, sweetheart.' I grip his hand, trying to transmit a confidence I don't feel. Staring numbly towards the shattered doors, I have to squint to try to make out if anyone is there. Smoke writhes through the broken glass, and it suddenly dawns on me that the cold air rushing in will feed the fire. I haul Nick upright, shielding his body just as a sudden flare of heat confirms that the flames are gaining force.

'Let's go!' I haul Nick away from the small but vicious blaze beginning to eat up the carpet. He coughs, and I feel it gurgle all the way up through his back. Racking my brains to think where his inhaler might be, I realise it's in my handbag. In the kitchen . . .

'Where's Adrian?' Nick digs his heels in to the carpet. 'We can't go without him.'

I look into his bright blue eyes, watery from smoke but piercing with conviction, and I feel a momentary pang at the undeserved loyalty. But he's right: I can't leave without knowing Adrian is safe. 'Go – wait for me outside the cottage.' I give Nick a gentle push. 'Your inhaler's in my bag. In the kitchen. Grab it first. And shut this door behind you!'

As soon as the living-room door closes, I turn back to face the hot acrid cloud that is beginning to thin out slightly now, but still burns my eyes, ears and lungs. 'Adrian?' I call out, then bend over, coughing as smoke is sucked into my throat.

'Hello?' a voice yells back. 'Anyone there?'

'Adrian, is that you?' Still coughing, I head blindly in that direction, arms stretched ahead of me to feel my way. I only manage two steps before I hear the air-pistol crackle of flames grow stronger, and see fire leaping up a shelf unit like an acrobat up a rope.

'Step back!' the disembodied voice calls again.

I watch transfixed as a dark shadow charges through the smoke. It sweeps past me to grab a blanket from the sofa, twisting around to throw it over the hissing, yellow curl of flames, before stamping down on it and beating at what's left of the wicker shelves. The fire is extinguished in seconds; a lingering smell of lighter fluid betrays the cause, the pungent chemical stench reminding me incongruously of bonfires and autumn barbecues.

Briefly, I close my eyes, picturing Craig and Nick dragging a homemade Guy Fawkes to sit in triumphant doom on top of branches they'd gathered together in the woods. Instantly my mind's eye pans to the shed where Nick was tied up. The association makes me feel sick and I start to sway dizzily, before strong hands grasp my forearms.

'That was a close call. Come on. Let's get you out of here.'

The shadowy figure materialises into a slim, dark-haired man whose face is smudged with the sooty residue of smoke but nevertheless instantly recognisable. 'Oh! Thank God it's you!' The plain-clothes officer spooked the hell out of me last night, with his face pressed against the window, but I'm mighty glad to see him now. '*Thank* you.'

'No problem. Are you OK? You're not injured?'

'I don't think so. But ... Who did this? Did you see anyone?

DCI Maxwell just phoned to warn us. He told us to get out.' I burble anxiously, at the same time hunting for Nick's phone, seeing no sign of it. *Or Adrian*. 'There's another boy. Did you see him?'

Hyper with adrenalin, I don't wait for a reply but hurry into the hall to check on Nick, panicking when I see the front door shut. I yank at the handles, top and bottom; neither gives. *Of course they won't.* I've kept the stable door locked at all times, to stop intruders getting in. I never imagined someone would blast their way through the windows instead. I left the keys in the door, though. *So where is Nick?*

'Mum! I'm in here!'

'Nick! Are you all right?' I quickly follow his voice into the kitchen, relieved to see him sitting at the table, my handbag open in front of him, inhaler pressed to his mouth.

'Did you find Adrian?' His voice rasps as he takes another puff of medicine.

'I got him.' The officer appears behind me. 'Thankfully he had the sense to hide in the bathroom. Safest place in a fire. He's just splashing his face. Feeling a bit sick.'

'Thank God he wasn't hurt.' Despite what Adrian has done, I realise I mean it.

'Or you guys too,' the officer says, pulling out a chair and slumping down on it.

I cross to the sink, filling a jug with water and grabbing glasses from the drainer before setting it all down on the table. Then I sit down too, resting a hand on Nick's chest to check that the ominous gurgling sound has cleared from his lungs. Hearing his breathing slow and steady, I lay my cheek against his hair, fighting to control my own panicky breaths.

Craig was right: this place is so far off the radar that we could only have been found if someone was following us. I think of Adrian's comment that he was 'sticking to the plan', and terror trickles through me as I wonder again if the events of the sleepover were part of an even bigger bully's grand scheme: if punishing Nick was just the first step. Jason is dead, and DCI Maxwell said on the phone that it wasn't suicide. The sudden attack cut off the end of his warning, but I got the gist: someone wants me dead too. *You're next, slag.* And even though the fire may be out, whoever started it could still be outside ...

I watch the officer help himself to water. 'They might come back,' I say anxiously. 'Should you go and check? See if anyone's out there?'

'No point. I came in round the back. I saw someone making a dash for it as I came down the path. Kids, probably. Time on their hands. Looking to get into trouble.'

'Oh. You think?' I frown, not convinced. 'Even so. Shouldn't you—'

'Really, I'd never catch them. They'll be long gone. I'll call 999 if you want, though? You'll need to report this for the insurance. I can help you take photos, too, if you like?'

I think about Craig, wondering again where he is, knowing how upset he'll be when he arrives to find such devastation in his *haven of peace*. No doubt he'll have the place insured up to the nines, but that's the least of my worries. 'It's not my cottage. I don't care about the insurance,' I say impatiently. 'I just want to know who did this. I want them *caught*.' I want the officer to interrogate them about what other crimes they've committed ...

I wish Adrian would hurry up. I haven't forgotten how he scampered away from the doors at the critical moment – or the way he was peering out of the window only seconds before. I want to ask him if and how he knew the attack was imminent. What Adrian did to Nick is horrendous, but if he *was* under someone else's influence, he might have one last chance to redeem himself – if he confesses and leads us to that person ...

'You should install CCTV,' the officer advises. 'Isolated place like this, you can't be too careful. I'd be happy to recommend the best systems. I'm a bit of a tech geek, you could say.' He takes a black iPhone out of his leather jacket pocket and waggles it. 'This beauty hasn't even gone on general release yet,' he says proudly. 'Always got an eye on the latest gadgets, me. Security doesn't have to be expensive. Or obtrusive. Cameras these days are pretty neat.'

'Cameras?' I say impatiently. 'I didn't think we'd need them. Not with a police guard outside.'

'Police?' He sits back, frowning as he puts his phone away. 'Really? I didn't see any.'

'Sorry, what?' I stare at him in confusion for a moment, then my heart starts to hammer against my chest as I take in his casual demeanour, his unwillingness to give chase to whoever attacked the cottage.

Craig asked whether I saw the officer's ID last night. I didn't, nor did I get to speak to DS Clarke to confirm he was Sergeant Rogers' replacement. I wonder where he is, and why neither officer has returned for the morning shift. I wonder if the stranger sitting in front of me knows full well there's no point chasing any assailant: *because it was him.*

Reaching for Nick's hand, I try to think fast and assess our options, glancing up in panic as Adrian skids into the kitchen. I open my mouth to call out a warning for him to stay away; the words dry in my mouth when he bounces up to the man and tugs on his arm.

'Can we go home now, Dad?' he whines. 'I'm hungry.'

'Wait. No. Are you . . . ?' I look between the two of them, and something about their eyes, the round shape of both their faces, triggers a mental slideshow of the family photos in Beth's house. She told me her husband was working away, and I believed her. But I saw his boots in the hall – muddy Timberlands – the same ones he's wearing now . . .

FORTY-FOUR

'You're Mike Atkins. You're not a policeman at all.' My voice is a croak. My throat has closed up, not just from smoke but from a sudden raft of fear that squeezes as tight as the asthma in Nick's lungs. Did Beth's husband throw that rock – did he try to set fire to the cottage? Is *he* Suspect A?

'Policeman? Me?' Mike's eyes widen in surprise. 'Not likely. Who said I was?'

'I saw you. Last night. You were outside the cottage. You were *watching* us.'

'Oh, right. Yeah, sorry. That was me. I hope I didn't scare you. I just came over to—'

'There's a real police officer out there,' I interrupt him. 'And more on the way.'

'Good. I hope they get a move on. See if they can catch whoever did *that*.' He nods towards the hallway, the drift of smoke still meandering through the cottage.

'It wasn't you, then?' I stare at his boyish face, confusion mingling with fear now.

'Sorry? No way! Like I said, it was probably kids. Why on earth would you think it was *me*?' He turns to Adrian, who has climbed on to the worktop to hunt in the cupboards for food. 'You were right, son. They really do seem to have it in for our family.' He turns back to me with an accusing scowl. 'Why is that? What's my boy ever done to you?'

'You've got to be kidding me.' I turn to look at Nick, wondering if he's as baffled as I am. His cheeks are blotchy and mottled. He's used a lot of his inhaler, I realise; a panic attack now could be fatal. I reach for his hand. 'Come on, sweetheart. We're leaving.'

'Stay.' Mike reaches out and grabs my arm. 'Please,' he adds with belated politeness. 'There's clearly been a misunderstanding. We need to talk.'

'Let go of me.' I pull my arm away. 'I told you, the police are on their way. You can't keep us trapped here. You've played that trick once already.' I remember the cellar full of taxidermy equipment, the drugs … and the knife found in the woods. *It must have been his.*

'What? Look, I'm sorry I didn't introduce myself properly. I didn't exactly arrive in the best of circumstances.' Mike huffs and rolls his eyes. 'But I thought you recognised me. Your Beth's friend, aren't you? Mrs Brookes. Izzy.'

'New friend,' I qualify. 'And no, I didn't recognise you. I've never met you before.'

'Sorry,' he says again, his manner disingenuously meek now. 'Of course. You're right. Well, in any case, I came here in good faith. To talk to you about your son.'

I glance at Adrian. 'Don't you think we should talk about yours first?'

'My son isn't a bully.' Mike's voice hardens again, his eyes narrowing. 'You tell her, son. Tell her what you told me.' He nods at Adrian.

'He's a bully.' Adrian's finger shoots out like an arrow towards Nick. 'He was going for me just now, Dad. I only came to see he was OK. I wanted to ask if we could make up.'

'Make up?' I can't believe what I'm hearing. 'You were the one who tricked him into those woods!'

'Nick *wanted* to do it,' Adrian says tearfully. 'He said he wanted to show everyone he wasn't a wimp. How was I to know he'd change his mind?'

'You're lying!' Nick yells, hammering the kitchen table with a fist.

'I'm not. Honest.' Adrian shakes his head, his pink cheeks and wide eyes reminding me of his baffled innocence on Saturday morning. 'I knew you'd say this. You're always trying to make me look dumb. Like forcing me to buy that dirty magazine.'

'*You* got that magazine,' Nick shouts at Adrian. 'You said it was your dad's. You said your mum would be upset if I didn't hide it for you.'

'My son doesn't tell lies.' Mike leans forward, eyes fixed on Nick. 'You were taunting him, weren't you? At his own sleepover. Come on, admit it.'

'That's rubbish,' I snap. Resting my hand reassuringly on Nick's back, I glance at the window, watching for the police. Frustratingly, all I see is trees. The closest properties are some distance away; not even the home-made explosive has alerted anyone's attention.

'You did the right thing texting me, son. Last Friday *and* last night.' Mike nods at Adrian. 'I know your mum means well. She's just too trusting. She shouldn't even have invited this boy into our house. But don't worry. I put her straight. And *you*, my lad—'

'Honestly, there's been a mistake,' I say quickly, as I see Mike's fists clench. 'Nick has never bullied *anyone*. He's been picked on his whole life.' I'm annoyed to hear my voice crack, long-time pain and a baffled sense of injustice leaking out.

'I'm not stupid. I know my own child.'

'I'm sure you do.' I deliberately aim for a conciliatory tone now. 'But they're growing up so fast, aren't they? We don't always know everything they get up to. Look at how Adrian bunked off school to come here today. And he obviously looks up to you. I guess it's understandable that he lied about Friday night – so you won't think badly of him.'

'I don't.'

'But he almost killed my *son*.'

'She's making it up, Dad!' Adrian leaps down from the worktop. 'Nick wanted to go into the woods. He wasn't scared. I haven't a clue who tied him up. I just went with him to the shed. I didn't lock it. It was meant to be for a laugh. A *game*. You saw us. You know.'

'It was *you*. In the street.' Nick's eyes are wide as he turns to look at me. 'It was *him*!'

I glare at Mike. 'Did you take my son into the woods? Did you lock him up?'

'Of course not!' He looks genuinely affronted. 'Listen, I'm not the bad guy here.' He holds up his hands, as though in surrender. 'Honestly. I got a load of texts from Adrian last Friday night. He said he was being picked on. I went to check he was OK. That's it.'

'That's *it*?' I stare at him in disbelief.

'He was horrible to me,' Adrian chips in. 'It was my sleepover. He ruined it.'

'He only went with Nick into the park to try to sort things out between them,' Mike says pleadingly. 'Like all good friends should.'

'That's really what Adrian told you?' I give his son a sharp look; he might have fooled his dad, but he's not fooling me.

'Yeah. I was worried, obviously. But kids need space to fight their own battles, don't they? Like I said, though, I checked they were OK. I went to the house to talk to Beth – fine, to give her a piece of my mind,' he admits.

'You were inside the house. On the night of the sleepover.' I glance at Nick, suddenly recalling him saying that he'd heard hammering on the front door that night, and Adrian's mum arguing with someone downstairs. It must have been Mike.

'Yeah. But I left my boots in the hall, you see. They were muddy, so I changed into some old ones. Things got a bit heated with Beth, though, and I forgot to pick up my boots on the way out. When I went back to get them ... well, that's when I saw the boys in the street. I watched them head over to the park, then I decided to head straight off and get my boots another time. They seemed fine when I left. Boys need adventures, after all.'

'Adventures.' My head swims at the understatement.

'Absolutely. God knows, life's dull enough when you're a grown-up. Schlepping up and down the motorway. Flogging software to companies that don't want it. Beth calls *me* useless. She's the one who wanted another kid just so she could stay home and play house. I told her, "Get off your backside and do something!"'

'Charming.' No wonder Beth pretended her husband was working away. She was obviously too embarrassed to admit the true state of their marriage, and by the time the lie was out of her mouth, it probably felt too late to come clean about Mike having been there.

'Yeah, well. She didn't like that, either. Told me to get the hell out – of the house I'm still paying for, for Christ's sake. Look, all I mean to say is, kids need to have fun. I checked they were OK, then I went back to my hotel. Ask the police if you don't believe me. They've already confirmed all this with the night manager. He knows me. I've been living there, pretty much out of a suitcase, for six months. Seriously. I'm telling you the truth. I swear it on my son's life.'

I stare at his hunched shoulders and weary expression and think of the list of jobs Beth said she had waiting for him. Mike Atkins doesn't look like a murderer. Then again: what does a would-be child-killer look like? I suspected Jason; I fully believed it could have been Sean Newton. And I have no idea if this pent-up but ordinary-looking man is anything more sinister than a frustrated, rejected husband with a severe case of parental denial.

My thoughts spiral deeper, but one keeps floating to the top: if Mike truly isn't DCI Maxwell's Suspect A . . . *Who is?*

'Let me get this straight,' I say, staring at him. 'You saw Adrian and Nick going off together in the dark, in the middle of the night, and you didn't stop them?'

Even if he *is* telling the truth, I'm furious as I recognise what a missed opportunity that was. Nick may well have insisted he was all right. He was delirious, hallucinating. He ran towards this man who could have helped him. I don't care if Mike believed my son was a bully; he should have put that to one side to help a child in obvious danger, just as I fought through the smoke to look for Adrian.

'I should have. I realise that now. Of course I do. And I'm so sorry.'

'It's a bit late for apologies.' I'm all out of sympathy.

'Sure. But you've got to understand, I was *angry*. Your son was picking on mine.' He jabs the air with a finger in childish emphasis.

'Adrian's the bully,' I say firmly. 'Not Nick.'

'Well, it seems to me it's his word against Adrian's. And I know who I believe. I was worried about your son, though. I hung around your house a couple of times. Just to see if he came home. I even called you. Then I got cold feet and hung up.' He shrugs and sighs. 'I followed you to the press conference instead, but they wouldn't let me inside.'

'You came to my house. You followed me to the TV studio. The black Range Rover trailing me . . .' I think back to all the little incidents I put down to paranoia. 'That was *you*?'

Mike shifts awkwardly. 'I just wanted to know what was going on, OK? The police wouldn't tell me anything. Oh, they checked me out. Poked around in my business. Then that was it. I have no "parental responsibility" any more, you see. Beth made sure of that. So I had to find out for myself what was going on.'

'By spying on me.'

'It seemed like a good idea at the time.' His hands rasp over his face. 'I went to the hospital. I even asked the doctors about Nick. Not one single person asked me about Adrian – how *he* was coping. The nightmares. Whispers at school. Ade told me what the kids were saying about him last week. Calling him a murderer.'

'Really?' I wonder if that's a lie, too. Another example of Adrian courting his dad's sympathy. 'Well, he almost was,' I point out tersely.

'When are you going to get it? Nick *wanted* to go into the woods. He was trying to prove himself. Show off, I don't know. Get attention.'

The irony of it takes my breath away. 'Your son was *filming* Nick. At your house. Then here. Filming us. *Me.* He—'

'I'm sorry you can't accept the truth about your child. But I won't have mine suffer as a result. I went to the hospital to ask after Nick. Then, sure, after he got better, I thought I'd make sure he knew I wouldn't let him get away with intimidating my son again.'

I think of his face at the window. 'You came here last night to warn him. Nick texted Adrian yesterday that we weren't at home. That we were *here*. He was trying to put Adrian off visiting him, but Adrian wouldn't let it go. He texted you. Asked you to sort it out.' I feel sick as I piece it all together. 'So you came here last night to scare Nick off once and for all.'

'Well, "scare him off" is a bit harsh.' Mike screws up his face, looking embarrassed now. 'I didn't want to frighten him. Just have a quiet word, you know? I realised I'd spooked you, though. Looking through the window like that. I'm really sorry.'

'You could have just come to the door! Introduced yourself. Why didn't you?'

'I was going to. But there were these two blokes chatting round the front of the house. I thought they must be friends of yours. Didn't fancy explaining myself to them.' He grimaces. 'One of them was built like a tank.'

'He's a police officer,' I say pointedly, realising that I was right: Mike appeared at the back of the cottage exactly at the point Sergeant Rogers was switching shifts with his colleague. It was an easy mistake to make, I console myself.

'Right. Anyway, I managed to leg it before they spotted me. I realised it was best to come back in daylight. Only when I got here someone had literally dropped a bomb on you. And here we are.' Mike sits back, arms folded but expression a little sheepish now.

I think it all through, trying to see it from his point of view, realising that, furious as I am, I do – finally – believe him. But while I accept that Mike didn't come here intending violence, it doesn't lessen my fear. If he wasn't complicit with his son, or using him as a puppet to carry out his own agenda, I'm still certain that someone else was – and that they're outside right now.

'Yes. Here we are.' I look around the kitchen, spotting a set of knives on the worktop, wondering if I should grab one.

Mike follows my gaze. 'Look, please don't do anything rash. I got a bit carried away trying to be clever, sure. Sneaking around. But I didn't lob a rock through any window. Or try to burn this place down. Or hurt you. Or Nick. Truly. I just wanted to make sure he knew not to mess with Adrian again.'

'But you've got the wrong boy!' A voice in my head reminds me how badly I misjudged Jason. Only I'd witnessed his bossiness many times, with my own eyes; Mike condemned Nick entirely on the word of his *own* son. And there is no one so blind as a guilt-ridden parent, I have come to realise ... But I know he won't believe me until he hears the truth from Adrian's mouth. 'Tell him, Adrian. Please. Be brave now, and tell the truth.'

I spin around to appeal to him one last time. The kitchen is empty. Adrian is gone, and so is Nick. A second later, I hear the front door slam shut.

FORTY-FIVE

My lungs are on fire. They drag in icy air and blow out raw, exhausted sobs. My feet pound the footpath twisting between sleepy island homes, now curtained behind afternoon shadows. Disoriented in the fog, I run chaotically, first one way then the other, finally retracing my steps towards the bridge, suddenly fearful that the boys have headed to the river.

Jason died down there, by the boat yard. DCI Maxwell said it wasn't suicide, and if the person who killed him isn't Mike Atkins, and it wasn't Sean Newton, who does that leave? Who else knows my son – knew he was going for a sleepover – knows where I live, and how to find this isolated cottage? Whoever Suspect A is, they have managed to stalk me and elude the police for seven days and nights with almost military stealth . . .

Suddenly I think of Nathan Baxter – the father Jason feared; the man Adrian said would kill him if he saw him. He's always been jealous of Craig. Possessive of his wife; violently controlling of his son. Looking fearfully around me as I run, I imagine his eyes glowering behind every tree. I picture again the knife the police found in the woods – *an army knife?* And while Katie returned from the coast, she said Nathan had gone AWOL . . .

'Nick! *NICK!*' I scream at the top of my voice, straining my ears to catch any reply. Behind me, I can hear the erratic tattoo of Mike's boots; I can't tell which direction he is running in, until I hear him shout out to his son too.

'MUM!'

It's my son who finally answers, Nick's terrified shriek cutting through every nerve ending. I run even harder, faster, looking all around to find something, anything – a stone, a piece of wood – that I can use as a weapon. But I see nothing other than occasional lumps of dirty, melting ice pockmarking the grassy verge along the path.

The snow is all but gone now, the air turned damp and fetid by the murky haze rolling off the river. It catches in my throat; it will be filling Nick's lungs, already clogged by smoke. I listen for the sound of his cough, but all I hear is the low rumble of a boat's engine, the steady slap of water nearby.

As I near the corner where the path bends towards the river, I notice a large, round mirror positioned at the junction of the two paths, giving visibility to cyclists or pedestrians approaching from either direction. My eyes are drawn to the reflection of a dark-red shape that fills the rust-speckled glass. I squint, trying to understand why it looks familiar, but fog drifts between the hedgerows, clouding my eyes, swallowing everything along the winding path. I hurry around the corner, jumping as a storm light snaps on, its beam stretching out to halo the mystery shape . . . the prone body lying across the path.

His head rests on a cushion of meadowsweet; his feet are hidden beneath a bank of stinging nettles. Outstretched hands tangle in the feathery stems of a rambling hemlock plant, as if he was trying to drag himself away. Blood pools around his body, seeping into the long, wet grass. I open my mouth to scream, and a bright-white flash behind my eyes is the last thing I remember as blinding pain in my head turns daylight to darkness.

FORTY-SIX

Two weeks later

'Here you go, Izzy.' Jo sets down a mug of hot tea in front of me. 'How's your head?'

'Fine. Just needed a few stitches,' I dismiss, taking short, quick sips of tea to avoid saying more. There's no point mentioning the headaches, night terrors and constant flashbacks, but I can feel DS Clarke's gentle brown gaze linger on me as she slips into her seat at the table between Jo and DCI Maxwell. The young detective visited me in hospital; she knows exactly how I am: heart, body and soul.

'Sorry to bring you in to the station to do this,' she says. 'We wanted to avoid more painful associations at your house. Though Matt said your friend Katie is selling it for you?'

'Yes. I . . . ' I take another sip, my throat suddenly dry. 'I can't live there any more.'

'I'm so sorry, Izzy.' DS Clarke leans across the round table to squeeze my hand. 'I know there are happy memories there too.

But I understand how you feel.' She opens a file like the one that held Samir's statement three weeks ago, only a lot thicker. 'Are you ready?'

'No. Never.' I take a deep breath, then nod at the file, silently asking her to begin.

I look around me as she talks, realising we're in the same impersonal, stuffy interview room where DCI Maxwell brought me when they first found out that Nick was in the woods. But while I was overflowing with questions then, now it's all I can do to sit and listen.

I listen without really taking anything in as DS Clarke quietly relays a stream of technical details: about the angle of the knife, the internal organs penetrated, the extent of blood loss. Only when her calm falters, her mouth wobbling as she concludes by stating that the injury caused almost unavoidable cardiac arrest, does meaning at last begin to penetrate.

Almost unavoidable. The phrase leaps out at me, tormenting me with the finest thread of possibility that things could have ended differently. If only I'd never gone to stay at the cottage; if only I hadn't said yes to the sleepover ... How far back would I need to rewind time to make a difference? In the end, maybe the outcome was always going to be the same; maybe he would always have found a way to get to my son. I can never know.

'Thank you for taking so much care with the investigation,' I say, as DS Clarke finally closes her file. 'Thank you all.' I look at each of the three detectives in turn.

'We got him in the end, Izzy.' DCI Maxwell leans forward to smack the file with the flat of his hand. 'At least justice will finally be done. You can count on that.'

'Justice. I suppose I've been more concerned with finding the *truth*,' I tell him. Briefly, I shut my eyes and remember every theory I've concocted since I first stood at the bottom of Beth's stairs and heard her tell me that Nick had 'vanished into thin air'.

'That too. Justice. Truth. And, most importantly, *evidence*. Sarah here made sure of that.' He nods at DS Clarke. 'Do you want to run Izzy through how you finally nailed him?'

'It was a lucky break, I guess,' she says with typical modesty.

'It was thorough, methodical police work,' her boss corrects her.

'Sure. Well, it all came together pretty fast in the end. I was talking to the guys down at the boat yard. Something about Jason's death was bugging me, so I asked to review their CCTV. Really just to see if Jason had been caught on camera. But there he was. Our Suspect A.' She sits back, brown eyes wide, as if she still can't quite believe it. 'Standing on the boat yard wharf next to Jason, bold as brass. Knife in one hand, phone in the other.'

'He threatened him with the knife.' I grip the china mug in front of me to stop my hands shaking. 'He forced him into the water. Just like he forced Nick into the wood shed.'

'So we thought at first,' DCI Maxwell says, mouth twisting wryly.

'Sorry?' I frown at him in confusion. 'When you phoned me at the cottage . . . you told me that Jason had been *killed*?'

'Yes. And at that point, that's exactly what I believed. It certainly appeared that way on the raw CCTV footage Sarah showed me. The images were very grainy.' He coughs self-consciously. 'On closer examination, however . . .'

'It was an easy mistake to make, Chris.' DS Clarke rests a hand on his shoulder. 'The boys were arguing about the phone, Izzy. Violently. It fell into the water. The first time we reviewed the security tapes, it *did* look like Jason was pushed. The footage skipped around all over the place, you see. The tech guys managed to enhance it for me, though. When I played it back a second time later that day, I found a bit with Jason taking off his coat. He put it on a bench with his own phone.' She pauses, waiting for me to catch her meaning. 'It was Jason's decision to go into the water, in other words.'

'It was an accident, Izzy.' DCI Maxwell shakes his head. 'A terrible, freak accident.'

'Jason waded in pretty deep,' DS Clarke continues, 'to get the phone. *Adrian's* phone. Tragically, he got snagged on some kind of boat winch. It dragged him under the water.'

'He should have just left it,' I say. 'Knowing Adrian, the photos were probably already in the cloud. If not, they'd have been lost with the phone.'

'I'm afraid it wasn't the right one anyway,' DS Clarke says. 'After I'd viewed the CCTV footage, I went to see Beth. She told me Adrian has dozens of phones. His dad gets them for him. Adrian took a fake phone to the boat yard to taunt Jason. He kept hold of the real one with the sleepover photos on it.' She nods at the black iPhone next to her file.

'But Jason wouldn't have known that,' I surmise. 'The threat of exposure had already stopped him telling on Adrian. The shame of humiliating images being texted around. Posted online. He knew Adrian would do it.' *One click and the world sees*, I remember Adrian saying. 'Yes, he'd have been distraught. Not thinking straight. Poor Jason.' I bite my lip, hating the tragic pointlessness of his death.

'By the time we realised his death *wasn't* murder, I'd already phoned you at the cottage,' DCI Maxwell explains, 'to warn you that Adrian was dangerous. The school had called Beth to say he hadn't shown up for registration. I guessed immediately where he'd gone.'

'To finish what he'd started at the sleepover,' I say bitterly. 'Did you find the knife?'

'Both of them,' DS Clarke confirms. 'The one he used to intimidate Jason was stashed under tarpaulin at the boat yard. The other, of course, he dropped on the footpath when Sergeant Rogers arrested him. I recognised the blades immediately. They're out of the same set as the one we found in the woods. All three are from his dad's taxidermy tool kit.'

'Adrian wore gloves when he took Nick into the woods,' DCI Maxwell elaborates. 'Those have been located now. Along with the muddy trainers he dumped in a recycling bin near his house. But his fingerprints were on both the other knives. His alone. Conclusive, incontrovertible proof. We might also pick up DNA from the rock he struck you with. In any event, Sergeant Rogers witnessed that. He's devastated he didn't get to you in time.'

'I kept looking and looking for him,' I recall. 'I thought there must have been some kind of slip-up with the security rota.'

'Rogers did pull a double shift,' DCI Maxwell says. 'By his own choice. He'd grown very attached to Nick. When Steve Barnes showed up for his stint, Rogers sent him home.'

'Yes. Mike Atkins saw them talking outside the cottage.' I sigh again at that mix-up. 'I don't blame Sergeant Rogers. Please let him know that.'

'Rogers patrolled the island all night, Izzy,' DS Clarke adds. 'Frustratingly, he spoke briefly to Jeremy Kane. The guy who attacked the cottage. He was all kitted out like he'd just enjoyed a day's fishing. Waders, waterproofs. He had a bunch of angling equipment in his bag, too, which concealed the incendiary device, naturally.'

'And his can of red spray paint,' DCI Maxwell adds meaningfully.

'Why did he do it?' I'm baffled that a complete stranger would deface my home, attack the cottage – that he would want to hurt either me or my son. 'I don't even know him.'

'Jeremy Kane knew you, though. Or thought he did,' DS Clarke says. 'He'd been following your story on the news. I guess you could call it a case of transference. His wife ran off with his best friend, you see. And she took their son. It all got tangled up in

Kane's head with what he'd read about you. He wanted to punish his wife. He punished you instead.'

'We found newspaper cuttings at his house. And internet searches about Craig in his browsing history,' DCI Maxwell adds. 'He knew where you lived. He knew about the cottage on Eel Pie Island. It's listed in Craig's name with various letting agents.'

'As soon as he approached the cottage, Sergeant Rogers intercepted him,' DS Clarke says, eager to defend her colleague. 'But Kane was prepared. Rogers never even saw what hit him. It was a fishing reel, incidentally.' She winces. 'He was out cold long enough for Kane to carry out his attack. Came round just in time to see Adrian launch himself at you on the footpath. Unfortunately, by then it was too late to grab the knife off him.'

'That's when we arrived.' DCI Maxwell shakes his head as if remembering the scene. 'Luckily, with back-up. Two officers were required to assist Rogers in subduing Adrian. Another three to apprehend Kane. Mike Atkins came with us of his own volition.'

'He's devastated, Izzy,' Jo interjects. 'And ashamed of what he's done. Or, rather, didn't do. Step in when he saw the boys in the street and realised the sleepover had turned nasty. Call the police when Nick didn't come home.' She shakes her head too.

'He'll have time enough to ponder his mistakes behind bars,' DCI Maxwell says. 'Perverting the course of justice warrants a custodial sentence. Ignorance is no defence.'

'He believed he was protecting his child.' I'm shocked to hear myself defending Mike. Yes, he did the wrong thing, but in his mind it was for the right reasons. He's a scorned husband, a frustrated absent father, and in his desperation to gain favour with his son, he lost all common sense, even his moral compass. Mike believed every devious word Adrian said to him, and he realised his mistake far too late. Adrian, after all, is an extremely plausible liar.

I didn't need the police psychologist's report to tell me that;

I've witnessed it for myself. It did come as a shock, however, to discover that he's been seeing a psychotherapist for months – the 'head-doctor' he'd scathingly referred to. Beth called her son a 'good boy'; I realise now she was burying her head in the sand. And when I remember her nervousness about fibres and DNA being found at her house, and recall the lost brand-new trainers she neglected to mention to the police, I wonder if she guessed at Adrian's guilt all along.

According to DS Clarke, his therapist had already flagged up concerns about a paranoid personality disorder, citing in her report that it was 'both illustrated and exacerbated by Adrian's extreme social media fixation'. In her opinion, that addiction not only fed his narcissism and fuelled his need for affirmation, it had also compromised his sense of identity.

Nick called Adrian 'evil'; I think it's closer to the truth to say that he's a lost soul. Disassociated from reality, disconnected from his family and resentful of his seemingly more talented friends, he created his own avatar: a clever, popular daredevil. And he believed it so much, he became it. The sleepover might have been Nick's idea, but it gave Adrian the stage he craved. There was no accomplice hiding in the wings, helping him carry out some *grand scheme*; there was only ever one star in his show: Adrian Atkins.

FORTY-SEVEN

'He won't bother you again, Izzy.' Jo rests a hand on my arm. 'His defence will put forward extenuating circumstances, of course. His troubled family background. The possibility of a personality disorder. But DS Clarke is prepared. She won't let you down.'

'Adrian's twelve,' DCI Maxwell adds. 'Two years above the age of criminal responsibility. He'll be in secure detention for a long time. The youth court will see to that.'

'He needs help as much as punishment,' I acknowledge, and we all sit quietly for a moment, reflecting on Adrian's crimes and his fate. 'I guess that just leaves one last thing,' I say finally, staring at his phone. It sits like a ticking bomb next to DS Clarke's file; I marvel at the devastation such a small, shiny device can wreak.

'Are you sure you want to do this?' She looks concerned. 'You don't have to, Izzy. We've reviewed everything on it. It's all been documented for the court case.'

'Maybe it's better to see than to imagine,' DCI Maxwell says knowingly.

I wonder if he's thinking about his own children. I was impatient with the senior detective at first, convinced he wasn't taking Nick's disappearance seriously. Now I realise he was trying to save me from my worst fears. He's a family man, after all, and as he said himself: delivering bad news about a child is the worst part of any police officer's job. I know he still only wants to protect me, but I came here determined to find out everything that happened to my son, and truth has no half measures; reality should need no filter.

'Yes. I need to see ... everything,' I tell him.

'I understand. And there's plenty to see.' He shakes his head. 'It would be easier to list what Adrian *didn't* photograph or film.'

'We were all bit parts in the drama of his life. Don't you think?' I say sadly.

At some point in the future, maybe I'll feel more sympathy for the young boy who has changed my life for ever. But that day is a long way off. Right now, all I can think of is what he did to *my* boy. Nick was so brave; he fought so hard for life. I owe it to him to walk through that tragic night in his shoes one last time. I hold out my hand.

Pizza crusts. Pyjamas on the pillow. Molly's half-empty milk bottle. Snow piling high on the window sill, condensation rolling in fat drops down the glass. The opening shots to Adrian's sleepover movie are strikingly banal. They give no hint of the horror that follows ...

A pillow fight that turns nasty when Adrian yanks down Jason's jeans. Jason again, half-naked in the bathroom, swearing as his privacy is invaded. Samir in his pyjamas, bingeing on nachos, eyes glued to the computer as electronic missiles blast across the screen. Scenes deliberately filmed with blackmail in mind – the threat of humiliating public exposure enough to silence Jason and Samir, to keep them from revealing Adrian's guilt.

I scroll forward to see Nick curled up in the wood shed, arms wrapped around his trembling body. He's rocking, and I catch a faint whisper: 'Mummy, help me.' His terror rips through me. I can't bear it and I press 'fast-forward': to grinning gnomes outside Craig's cottage, Marzipan innocently devouring a dish of poisoned food, Nick's clenched fists as he defends himself against Adrian in the living room. The footage shakes as Adrian chases Nick along the footpath, his red hoodie disappearing into the distance. Once again I hear the scream I will never be able to unhear. Then the screen goes black.

He really believed he was directing a movie. I'm certain Adrian was planning to compile each clip into a full-length film; I can't bear to think how many have already found their way online. DS Clarke promised she will remove everything she finds. I hope she can, before the world gets to see the worst night of my son's life – of his friends' lives – *of mine.*

Mr Newton assured me that he's stamping down on school gossip. He's a good teacher; I know that. I've always known it, which is what made the allegations against him so shocking. Adrian, of course, continues to maintain his story about abuse in the book group; the transcript of his statement read like a soap opera, DS Clarke said. Whatever questions I still have about why he did what he did, I feel certain I won't find the answers from him.

I slide the phone back across the table. 'It's over. I want to let it go.'

'I think it's the right decision, Izzy.' DCI Maxwell picks it up, tucking it into his pocket. 'It's enough that you're both alive. Leave the rest to us. You and Nick need to move on now. Get well. Live your lives. Adrian has stolen a big enough slice already.'

'Of Craig's life, too.' I'm gripped again by the horrible image of his big body lying prone across the footpath on the island, blood pooling around him. Shock had transfixed me, blinding me to the rock Adrian impulsively wielded towards my head. My last two thoughts as I lost consciousness were: *Thank God Nick is alive . . .* and *I can't believe Craig is dead.*

He'd only meant to calm Adrian down; he had no idea that the mixed-up young boy had gone way beyond listening to reason, or that underneath the coat he'd refused to take off was another of his dad's taxidermy knives. Like a cornered animal, Adrian had lashed out; the knife wound he inflicted was so severe, Craig will be in hospital for some considerable time.

Maybe when he recovers we'll talk – if only to prevent Craig feeling he has to fight to be Nick's dad again. That's never going to happen, but I loved Craig once, and I'll never forget that he almost lost his life trying to protect my son. He's always been meticulous, fastidiously punctual; it's a bitter irony that this, the one time he's been late for anything, could have been his last. He arrived back at the island just as Adrian was chasing Nick across it. It breaks my heart a little that, after texting to say he was 'coming over', Craig was only delayed because he'd stopped to buy Nick's favourite pizza, as a peace offering to us both.

Craig isn't a bad man, but he wasn't the right husband for me – and he's the wrong stepfather for Nick. He left us a year ago, and no matter how many times he tries to justify that decision, it doesn't change the fact that he walked away when the going got tough. I married him to give stability to my son; I can no longer trust Craig to provide that. From now on, I will do things my way. I'll keep listening to my heart. *And my son.*

I was over-protective of Nick when he was born: I had lost his dad, I was alone. I was determined my precious child would never know pain. When he survived to school age, I foolishly breathed a sigh of relief. I still cannot fathom the wickedness that made other kids torment him; the growing-up years feel fraught with more peril than the childhood illnesses I used to drive myself mad worrying about. Playground cliques, dark temptations and unseen monsters on the internet, the lure of teenage freedom he craves but is too young to handle . . .

I still want to protect Nick, but I have to accept that he's not my little boy any more. He's far stronger than I knew, and we're closer than I feared. But whether I like it or not, he's growing up in a world very different to the one of my childhood. *We have to know the world our kids live in.* That's what his favourite teacher said, and I realise that even though I almost lost Nick, what I've found is greater understanding of what's going on in his head – and hopefully stronger trust between us: the confidence for both of us to hide less and share more.

For the time being, he has retreated into his thoughts, but I hope that with counselling, and the support of true friends, he will gradually re-emerge. I've left him with Katie, Ayesha and Samir right now; they're helping him make a memorial for Marzipan, in her favourite spot at the end of the garden. Tomorrow, Nick and I will lay flowers on Jason's grave. I'm thankful for his friendship to my son; I'm grateful I haven't lost his mum's.

Afterwards, I'll take Nick to see the small memorial plaque that was all I could afford for his dad twelve years ago. I'll tell him the truth about Alex, and that he is like his father in so many wonderful ways, but that he is his own person too. As Sean Newton also said: *Nick dances to his own tune.* He's always been a little different, but that's what I love most about him. My boy with the flying feet. I hope one day he'll dance again, both on stage and in life. If he does, I know he will soar. *My little sunbeam.*

EPILOGUE

The curtain rises in a scarlet swish; the spotlight is a gold circle, centre stage. I turn in my seat to see three sets of eyes staring anxiously ahead; I catch the whispers from row upon row of close to a thousand people behind us.

Filming is not permitted: no cameras, no phones. There will be no clips on YouTube, no Facebook photos. This tale begins and ends here, a one-time electric connection between cast and audience. Three hours of drama; a lifetime of memories for me. Beginning with the first moment, as exhilarating as Nick's very first step, yet infinitely more nerve-racking.

A bell rings somewhere backstage; I slide my palms down my jeans.

'Cookie?' Ayesha offers. 'Pass them along, sweetheart. Chocolate chip. Homemade.'

'I *love* these.' Sammy takes three.

'You put us to shame, Ayesha.' Katie smiles. 'Senior accountant *and* master chef. How are we supposed to compete with that? G&T, anyone?' Surreptitiously she opens her bag to reveal three slim cans of ready-mixed spirit.

'Thanks, Katie.' *I'm not talking about the gin.* I reach between us to squeeze her hand, knowing what it cost her to come here tonight: to sit surrounded by excited children and proud parents; to be without her son.

'Jase would have wanted me to be here.' She squeezes my hand back.

My eyes blur with tears as I turn back to stare at the stage. I blink them away, not wanting to miss that first intake of breath, the first public step for a whole year. My darling son reborn on the stage where he has lived the happiest moments of his twelve years.

Shadows flit in the wings, music soars into the gilt domed ceiling, and suddenly he leaps on to the stage, his body launching into a furious, dizzying spin. I hear a collective gasp from the audience as he controls the feverish whirling motion into a dead stop, face miraculously forward to gaze steadily – *defiantly* – out into the auditorium.

He seems to be searching, and I can tell the exact moment he finds what he's looking for. Head held high, Nick's eyes are so blue they dazzle as they fix on me. I hold my breath, waiting for him to launch into his next move, nervously wondering if he's forgotten it.

I needn't have worried. Brave, uncompromising, unapologetic, my son claims his right to be who he wants to be, no matter what anyone else thinks, on the most public stage he could find. The crooked smile I adore crinkles his lips, and then, so clearly it's as though he's shouted them out loud, he mouths the words he hasn't said to me in so long.

'I love you, Mum.'

ACKNOWLEDGEMENTS

A personal word of public thanks to all the people who have helped keep my bookish dreams alive ... Enormous gratitude to the hardworking, clever and extremely talented people at Piatkus and Little, Brown, especially the brilliant Emma Beswetherick and Hannah Wann, and to Alison Tulett for superb copy editing once again. Huge appreciation to all the publishers around the world who have shown such faith in my writing, and warmest thanks to every reader (you know who you are!) who urged me on to write 'Book 2'. And to Eugenie Furniss, my fabulous agent, the most heartfelt *thank you* for all your support.

A big shout-out also goes to George and Thomas Kirton, for letting me eavesdrop banter on all those Avithos games nights! I'm so thankful for the kindness and enthusiasm of good friends, lovely neighbours and the generous championing of my family, near and far. In particular, this book would never have been written without the love, patience and epic cheerleading of my amazing husband and children.

Paul, Hani and Rafi: thank you for believing in me, and for encouraging me to believe in myself. However proud you are of me, I'm a million times more so of you. Keep dancing to your own tune; I cherish every beat of it.

AUTHOR Q&A

The premise of *The Sleepover* is a terrifying thought for any parent. What inspired the novel?

The seed of this story was planted the morning my husband walked our then ten-year-old daughter to school and, an hour later, I found a message on our home phone asking why she was absent that day. By the time we uncovered that there had been a simple administrative mix-up, my husband had sprinted to the school – and my mind had raced between dozens of horrific scenarios. Had our daughter been snatched? Had she run away? *What was the last thing I said to her?*

The terror of that morning stayed with me and, as our children are both of an age when sleepovers are a common request, it also fed into my anxiety about leaving them at other people's houses. *What do I really know about their friends' families?* I wondered. How many questions is it polite to ask before I entrust my child to someone I may only have chatted to in passing at the school gate?

As I pondered these dilemmas, the fear from the day our

daughter *almost* went missing returned in force. I relived the bewilderment and terror of leaving my child somewhere I believed they were safe, only for them to mysteriously disappear. I tormented myself wondering who I would suspect if it happened for real, where I would look for answers – and what those could possibly be ... And in one anxiously palpitating heartbeat, the idea for *The Sleepover* was born.

Why did you decide to make Nick twelve years old in the story?

I made Nick twelve because it's an in-between age: he's neither a young child nor quite a teenager. I wanted to take a snapshot of this complex pre-teen stage and invite the reader to ponder how tightly we should try to control our children's lives, and at what age we should give them more of the freedom and independence they crave. How do we protect without smothering? This is Izzy's dilemma in the story, and it plays out in her clash of parental authority with Craig.

I also wanted to explore the themes of moral responsibility and parental denial. The age of criminal responsibility in England, where the story is set, is ten years old. Adrian is old enough to know right from wrong, but is he mature enough to fully understand the consequences of his actions? As parents, we all want to believe our children are good people who will make the right choices; it's tough to accept that this may not always be the case. Beth and Mike Atkins are blind to Adrian's shortcomings, and they fail to question how their own parenting may or may not have played a part in them. Izzy *does* question herself about her parenting, and her greatest fear is that in trying so hard to give Nick space to grow up, she has lost the closeness she once had with him.

The Sleepover is about a mother's quest to find her son again: not just physically, but emotionally too. Nick will always be Izzy's 'little sunbeam', but she knows the day will soon come when he considers himself too big for cuddles – and questions! – from his mum. Intuitively, Nick recognises this, which is why the story ends with him choosing to make a very public declaration that he loves her.

How do you think Nick's bullying shapes his relationships in the novel?

Bullying is an attack on a person's sense of identity and self-worth. It can make life miserable on a daily basis, but it also goes deeper to potentially undermine the development of personality, behaviour and relationships. One of the central themes in the novel revolves around our capacity and willingness to truly be ourselves – to 'dance to our own tune' – and because Nick is a young boy who has never seemed to fit in, Izzy worries about the impact this has had on him. At her darkest moment, she agonises about the possibility of his suicide; at the very least, she wonders if he has felt the need to change himself in order to be accepted by others: friends, bullies, teachers and even his parents.

When Nick starts secondary school, it does seem that he might have taken the opportunity to reinvent himself. He begins to dress like the teacher he admires; he also becomes more withdrawn, and Izzy fears that bullying has taught him to be secretive and submissive in his relationships, easily dominated by stronger characters, even abused by them. She worries about his relationship with his stepdad; she is cautious about Nick's friendship with a bossy older boy, Jason. But as the story progresses, Izzy is forced to reflect on the false assumptions she has made. Jason had the appearance of a bully, but he was in fact Nick's truest friend. Adrian seemed like a confident, popular and kind boy, but he was the opposite. And in spite of (or because of?) the bullying Nick has endured, he has developed an inner resilience and integrity in all his relationships that Izzy never fully appreciated.

What issues around social media and the internet did you want to explore in the novel?

We all know that the internet is a double-edged sword: it's the place we go to for information and answers – as Izzy instinctively does when her son goes missing – yet it's also a conduit for hidden dangers: cyber-bullying, grooming, stalking, secret apps and chat rooms, along with websites (such as 'Dare or Die' in the story) that have been known to incite risk-taking or self-harm. Rather than feeling more connected with the world, the impact of social media can be isolating, with young people especially feeling excluded by cliques. I wanted to highlight all these issues and, in particular, explore the theme of reality versus fantasy: the fakery of social media.

For instance, Izzy's friend Katie hides behind happy photos on Facebook to conceal the truth about her marriage, and Adrian uses the internet to create a fictional persona for himself. The pictures of the sleepover posted online also give a false impression of what really happened that night. I invite the reader to reflect on the pressure social media inflicts on us all to 'keep up appearances' or compete with our peers – and, especially in the case of young people, to give the impression that they're something they're not. I wanted to explore the mental health implications of this, and how parents can find their phone-fixated children disappearing down a rabbit hole where they are unable to follow.

Beyond these obvious dangers, I wanted to explore the significance of social media in terms of *identity*, which is a core theme in the novel. Izzy worries that Nick has used the internet to create a false image of himself in order to fit in and appease bullies. She catches a glimpse of him rehearsing different sides to his personality in his video diaries, and his dilemma as to which surname to use also underlines this. Nick is at an age when he is grappling with how to be himself yet avoid being cruelly singled out by others as 'the odd one out'.

If there is one overarching message I try to give my own children, it is the Shakespearean adage: 'To thine own self be true'. Nick's form tutor Mr Newton is a drama teacher, and he tries to encourage his pupils to 'dance to their own tune'. Adrian hasn't yet figured out what that means for him; he's a lost soul who has become disassociated from real life through his internet fixation. While Nick has been bullied, ultimately, he is the strongest character in the story. He is bravely, truly, unashamedly himself.

Your first novel, *The Choice*, is about a mother and the impossible choice she must make between her two children. What compels you to write about motherhood in your books?

As a writer, I always want to create stories that resonate emotionally with me and which arise from the psychological issues that fascinate me as a qualified psychotherapist. At this stage of my life, family challenges are at the forefront of my personal experience: without doubt, the choices I make regarding our children are the hardest, and my fears about their safety and wellbeing are the darkest. Parenting is an emotional minefield and a part of life that right now seems to generate more drama – more potential for triumph and tragedy – than any other. Fertile ground for story ideas!

I also want to portray empowered women conquering challenges, rather than waiting to be rescued. Too often I've read news stories in which the mother bears the brunt of criticism either for her life choices or how she has cared for her family. I touch on this at the start of the story, with Izzy feeling that everyone is pointing the finger at her; I wanted to show her determination to *do* something, not just sit back and wait for her son to be found. As a mum, I know I would do the same. Motherhood, for me, equates to strength as well as kindness: no lioness is fiercer than when her cub is attacked, and – with apologies to all dads – the true hero in my stories is usually the mum!

Why do you think parents and the relationships they have with their children are such a big focus in thrillers at the moment?

These days, the pressures faced by parents seem to be more intense than ever, not only because of the issues arising from pervasive technology, but also as a result of challenging social and economic times and volatile political situations. I've often heard it said that children seem to grow up faster these days. I'm not sure if it's true, or if their dexterity with gadgets merely creates that illusion! I do know that the world has never felt more unpredictable, yet instantly accessible: children can see anything, at any time, and speak to anyone online, without ever leaving their bedroom. 'Stranger danger' has new, unchartered meaning at a time when physical presence is no longer a prerequisite to influencing impressionable, vulnerable minds. A parent's power over this sprawling, secret underworld feels infinitesimal; keeping our children safe feels like a daily challenge. For any thriller fan, there are endless nightmares to keep us up – writing, reading and worrying – at night!

The Sleepover **is located in a similar part of London to** *The Choice.* **Was this a conscious decision?**

Yes, because I wanted the story to feel very real, as though it could happen on any street, in any town or city in the world. By setting the novel in an area where I have lived for many years, I hope I was able to create a sense that my characters are so familiar with their environment that they find it hard to believe bad things could happen there. The backdrop is ordinary, unremarkable: there is nothing exceptional about the quiet suburban streets where Izzy lives and works, or the local parks and schools where Nick hangs out. Izzy comments that the area is as familiar to her 'as the back of her hand'. The last thing she expects is that the place she feels safest will harbour threat – and tragedy – beyond anything she can imagine. After all, what could be more commonplace than a sleepover? They take place all over the world, every day of the week, on streets just like mine – and yours . . .

How did you find the process of writing your second novel different to the first?

By the time I sat down to write *The Sleepover*, I had read all the reviews for *The Choice* and celebrated its publication in numerous other countries. I had a head full of 'dos and don'ts', along with a massive dose of self-expectation! Everything readers had said they liked about my debut novel, I wanted to give them more of; anything I'd picked up that they hadn't enjoyed, I wanted to avoid. As a result, the process of writing my second novel became more self-conscious than when I was writing my first. It took me a while to tune into that quiet writing voice in the shadowy corners of my head, where characters really come alive and emotions run unfettered. Once I was able to stop worrying about what I *should* be writing and focus on what I *wanted* to write, the story – thankfully – flowed more easily!

Were there any challenges along the way?

When I first set out to write *The Sleepover*, I planned to write about a mother whose daughter goes missing. I quickly realised that I felt pulled more to tell the story of a mother and son. Nick's character formed in my head very fast; he broke my heart as I began to imagine his life, the trials he'd faced and how he dealt with them. I wanted to write about a group of young boys – their friendship, squabbles, worries and growing-up pains. I can well remember the foibles of pre-teen girls, having been one myself and also having a daughter. But our son is younger than Nick, and while there are many similarities between boys and girls at that age, there are also differences. In order to ensure that Nick's characterisation was authentic, I had to do a lot of eavesdropping on friends' pre-teen sons!

Similarly, I only dabble in the world of social media, whereas children of Nick's age are steeped in it. Apps change constantly, which is why, for the purposes of this novel, I restricted the presence of social media to Facebook, because of its popularity and the fact that both adults and teenagers use it. Even so, I researched many different platforms and apps, most of which I found baffling. I witnessed both the fun and the dark side of social media, and some of the things I read and saw were deeply upsetting and will stay with me for a long time.

Are you working on anything new at the moment?

Yes! As with my first two books, one small incident has sparked one enormous fear, and I'm currently immersed in creating a new family whose ordinary life is devastated when, with five little words, a shocking secret is uncovered that reveals a deadly threat in their midst . . .

Don't miss Samantha King's bestselling debut novel, *The Choice*

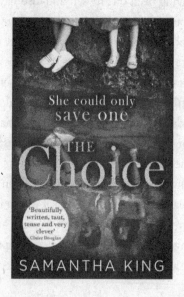

Madeleine lived for her children. She'd always believed
she'd die for them too.

But on the morning of her twins' tenth birthday her love
is put to the test when a killer knocks on their door and forces
her to make a devastating choice: which child should live, and
which should die – her son, or her daughter?

**'Beautifully written, taut, tense and very clever'
Claire Douglas**